HE SAW HER.

She was *swimming.* Long and sleek and elegant, like a dolphin. Something glowed around her belly.

Fence forgot himself and nearly choked as he started to inhale a shocked breath. Then, realizing what he'd nearly done, he blew the air out and a cough threatened. It rose in his lungs, and he was too far below to reach the surface in time, and he had no air left . . .

His mind went blank with terror and the water rushed into him, and he flailed and rocked into something hard and rough that scraped his forearm and temple. Sharp, stinging pain sliced beneath his arms, around his ribs. Cold water flushed inside, and Fence became aware of falling, sinking, of coughing and trying to breathe.

Suddenly, she was there, appearing like a pale angel, her hair spreading in a gentle ruffle around her. He lunged for her, knowing he'd drown her, too, but he was already breathing the water, dragging it in, and his body would soften and slow and sink . . .

Romances by Joss Ware

NIGHT FORBIDDEN
NIGHT BETRAYED
ABANDON THE NIGHT
EMBRACE THE NIGHT ETERNAL
BEYOND THE NIGHT

NIGHT FORBIDDEN

JOSS WARE

AVON

An Imprint of HarperCollinsPublishers

This is a work of fiction. Names, characters, places, and incidents are products of the author's imagination or are used fictitiously and are not to be construed as real. Any resemblance to actual events, locales, organizations, or persons, living or dead, is entirely coincidental.

AVON BOOKS
An Imprint of HarperCollins*Publishers*
10 East 53rd Street
New York, New York 10022-5299

Copyright © 2012 by Joss Ware
ISBN 978-0-06-201864-9
www.avonromance.com

First Avon Books mass market printing: August 2012

Avon Trademark Reg. U.S. Pat. Off. and in Other Countries, Marca Registrada, Hecho en U.S.A.
HarperCollins® is a registered trademark of HarperCollins Publishers.

Printed in the U.S.A.

10 9 8 7 6 5 4 3 2 1

To Erika Tsang,
for always making it happen

NIGHT FORBIDDEN

PROLOGUE

"There's nothing more I can do for him, Fence," said Elliott. "The septic infection . . . it's too strong, too deep."

Fence could see that even in the flickering light of the fire, safely contained in an old sink, Elliott's face was as strained as his voice. Nevertheless, the doctor's elegant hands continued to move over Lenny's limbs and torso as if searching for some other option.

He blinked away a sudden stinging. An EMT himself, Fence had already suspected the truth even before Elliott spoke. He'd been watching what started as a simple cut on his friend's arm, which had then gotten infected, for a week now. He opened his eyes and tightened his grip around the warm, clammy hand of his best friend and business partner. Lenny: the marketing brains behind Fence's adventurous brawn, the rear-end guard to his bold lead. He'd been the Michael Scott to Fence's Jim Halpert, the Harold to his Kumar.

"If only I had even some penicillin," Elliott, who'd been an emergency surgeon, muttered in frustration. "Or . . . something. *Anything*."

But there was no help—nothing in this new and horrible world of 2060 they'd somehow found themselves in.

Nothing even remotely like hospitals or pharmaceuticals or even cell phones to call for help. Not even roads or vehicles or even—son of a bitch—not even very many people. Few had survived the catastrophic events of half a century ago.

Fence still didn't understand how it had happened. He couldn't explain it, and he sure as hell couldn't accept it.

On June 10, 2010, he and Lenny had taken three men on an expedition into the cave he called the Ball-busting Bitch—more commonly known as Ferrester's Pocket.

Elliott and his two friends were on a weekend get-away, and they'd hired Fence and Lenny to take them deep into the most dangerous and unpredictable cave—hence the nickname—in Sedona, Arizona. Fence and Lenny had been enjoying the hell out of being with a crew that actually knew what the hell they were doing in the ink-black, twisting, close caverns. Elliott and his friends were well-prepared and well-equipped . . . but nothing could have prepared any of them for what happened that day.

While they were inside, all hell broke loose: earthquakes, storms, and cave-ins, and they were knocked unconscious in the depths of one of the tunnels. A sixth man named Simon was also caught inside the cavern with them. When they woke back up—or whatever they did, because it was looking more and more like they hadn't just been doing a Sleeping Beauty—and came out of the cave, they found themselves in a completely fucked-up world.

Fifty years later.

Which explained the vast expanse of stars skirting the sky through the hole in the tattered ceiling of the building they were staying in—stars that were no longer smogged out by the remnants of man's love for machines.

And now, instead of the constant rumble and whoosh of cars, planes, and other technology, there were the vivid howls of wolves and lions, and the cries of owls and other nocturnal creatures.

And there was the deep, awful groaning *"Ruuu-uuuthhh"* that came from horrible, orange-eyed, staggering monsters with flesh falling from their bones. Zombies.

The devastated towns, cities, neighborhoods, highways . . . everything that had been normal in 2010 was now overgrown, broken, and lush—like the 'hood being plopped into the middle of a jungle and left to live or die on its own.

One thing was sure: Mother Nature was going to win the arm-wrestling match over man's bricks, mortar, and metal.

Fence hoped like deep hell that his mama and dad had gone quickly. And his brothers and sisters and the rest of his family and friends and everyone else he'd ever known.

Everyone else. Gone. Erased like a motherfucking line in the sand.

It was simply . . . inconceivable.

But it was real.

It had been three months since he and his five companions, who now included the quiet man named Simon, left Sedona behind them. They traveled in a small band, searching for answers that were supposedly to be found in someplace called Envy. The few people they encountered had been born long after the Change, as they called it, and only had stories about the apocalyptic events told to them by survivors and their children.

But if they could get to Envy without getting torn apart by zombies, they'd find a few people who had actually lived through the earthquakes and tsunamis and the raging storms that went on for days.

They had to have answers. They had to have answers about what happened, and how they'd traveled fifty years into the future—or been suspended in time, or whatever—to find that everything was gone.

Lenny groaned and his eyes fluttered. His lips moved.

"What is it, bro?" Fence asked as he adjusted the pillow beneath Lenny's head, which was nothing more than a folded-up blanket he'd scavenged from an old JCPenney.

Still wrapped in plastic fifty years after being put on the shelf, the quilt was pristine and as fresh as new. Mother Nature might be able to beat back the concrete, metal, and glass of the twenty-first century, but the man-made plastic was giving her hell.

They'd been here in this overgrown apartment building for two days. While Elliott did what he could to help Lenny, who'd become too weak to walk, the others scavenged for tools, clothing, and other necessities during the day. A plastic-wrapped pair of briefs was just as much cause for celebration as an unbroken bottle of whiskey. And rolls of duct tape . . . Fence salivated at the prospect.

At night they were forced to hole up above ground

level in order to avoid the zombies. Now, Quent, Simon, and their sixth companion, Wyatt, were sitting in the corner, talking quietly as they prepared for sleep.

Fence forced his lips into a smile, made himself chuckle deeply. It sounded rough. "Whatcha need, Lenny? Wish I had a cold one to offer you—I bet that'd get you back on your feet." He gave his friend a gentle nudge. "A beer, and maybe a thick, rare steak to go with it? Remember that time we seared that fresh venison, up in Montana, after we gave our last rations to those kids who lost their packs?" They'd helped the group of Boy Scouts find their way back to the Scout meeting point, then continued on the second day of their three-day hike without any food, knowing they could live off the land. "That steak was so damn bloody, I thought it was gonna bound right off the plates. Man, I've never had anything so good in my life."

Lenny stirred, and in the flickering light of the small fire, Fence was sure he saw his lips twitch in something like a smile.

"Yeah, you remember that . . . and the time we had those two old ladies who wanted to go down Lutchner's Canyon? They had to be at least sixty apiece." Now he chuckled for real. "I'da been willing to pay *them* for the experience—it was one helluva weekend, wasn't it, bro? The sassy one who nailed the rattler with a stone from ten feet away—dude, if she'd been thirty years younger, I'da wanted to nail *her*. She was mad crazy. Remember how her friend roasted the snake meat on a spit over the fire, putting her own damned seasoning on it? Who the hell brings shit like that on an extreme camping trip? And it was hot as hell—musta been ancho chilis or something. I swear, I started sweating the minute she slapped it on my plate. I'm still wondering why they bothered to pay us to guide them out."

Fence forced another chuckle—they'd reminisced over that, and other scenes, many a time with a cold brew in hand. He knew just what Lenny would be saying, if he could speak. If he could even hear him. "Yeah, I know . . . they just wanted a coupla big, ripped mo-fos in the pictures with 'em so they could show their friends back at the retirement community."

Lenny gave a little shiver that could have been an attempt at a chuckle . . . or maybe just a wave of pain. Fence swallowed hard and got serious. "You know, bro . . . I couldn't've done it without you. I mean, you were the one who got the whole business off the ground. Hell, I'd've just been happy to go on weekend trips, take a few people now and then, drive the ambulance during the week . . . but you were so fucking determined to get it up and running, and smart about the whole marketing thing. Extreme Adventures on Tap. What dude could resist that?"

Lenny closed his eyes and his face slackened.

For a moment Fence thought he was gone, but then he felt the shallow, rough movement of his chest. Resting. Just resting. The twinge in his belly eased.

Not yet. He wasn't ready yet to lose the last connection to his old life.

Suddenly needing fresh air, Fence pulled himself to his feet, ducking so his six-foot-five frame could pass beneath the low ceiling without collecting cobwebs or bat guano on his head. He avoided the random piles of rubble and rodent shit as he walked in bare feet to the window. This one actually had a partially intact pane of glass covered with mildew, layers of dirt, and even a wayward branch of vine. A large pyramid-shaped piece had fallen away from this living room window in a sixty-year-old building, and he was able to look down and survey the outside without difficulty.

As he looked out over what he was fairly certain had once been part of Nevada, Fence smoothed a hand over his bald head—which for some reason hadn't sprouted the least bit of stubble in the last six months since they came out of that cave. Nor had he or the others grown any beards. Beyond weird.

Below and beyond there weren't any glowing orange eyes announcing the presence of the zombies. That was good, but since the motherfuckers couldn't climb up stairs or ladders, he and his companions were safe up here on the second floor anyway. All around, the ragged, bushy outlines of caved-in, overgrown buildings were bathed in moonlight. He could make out the once-familiar yellow M on a McDonald's sign, outlined in the distance by starlight.

There were no other lights: no streetlights, no headlights, no lamps burning in homes. It was dark and unnervingly silent without human noise.

The others had gone to sleep. Fence heard Elliott murmuring to Lenny, and the soft rustle of blankets, the quiet slop of cleansing, nourishing water.

There's nothing I can do.

He hardened his heart against the pain.

More pain. Uncountable losses. Beyond any grief he'd ever experienced—beyond even when he couldn't save Brian.

Fence nodded to himself, straightened his spine, drew in a deep breath, and turned back to continue his vigil.

He'd get through it, find something on the other side, as he used to say to his dad. "I'll see ya on the other

side," he'd promise when he had a test or a game or was
going on a trip or whatever.

The problem was, he was living in a world nothing
like his old one—a world where daily survival was as
uncertain as a roll of the dice, where, without Lenny,
he was with a bunch of guys he didn't really know but
who expected him to guide them safely through this
postmodern wilderness, and where he had a liability as
wide as a Mack truck.

A world where there was no fucking "other side."

Just this hell.

CHAPTER 1

The City of Envy
Eight months later

Fence took a healthy gulp of beer. That was, at least, one thing that hadn't disappeared since the Change. Man hadn't forgotten the important things in life.

As beer went, this was pretty damn good too. Ice cold, solid and dark like he was, bold and strong—like his sense of humor. Fence grinned to himself and took another drink. *Damn, I'm a fucking comedian.*

It had been a year. An entire year since he and Lenny led a bewildered group of men from deep in the caves into a world straight out of *I Am Legend.*

A world complete with zombies, and Fence playing an even more ripped, and bald, Will Smith. No shit. And if the glances from that table of fine-looking women on the other side of the pub were any indication, they'd appreciate it if he'd do a few pull-ups. Shirtless. Just like his man Will had done in the movie.

"What can I get you?" asked the waitress, leaning in close so she could make eye contact and provide what he called a glimpse of Happy Valley: a good, solid view right down her shirt. To be fair, Cindy also had to get close to be heard over the live music coming from the stage next to them, but her girls looked as if they were dying to pop out and say hi.

"Depends what's available, sugar," Fence told her, giving her his long, slow grin. An old girlfriend had told him it was like sliding into a steaming hot tub. Cindy giggled and ogled back at him.

"Oh, just get her number and be done with it," Elliott said with a roll of the eyes and the twitch of a smile.

Easy for him to say. Elliott'd been shacked up with Jade, the smoking hot redhead currently singing an old Bonnie Raitt song, within two weeks of their arrival here in Envy.

Which, as Fence had learned, was actually N.V. Or New Vegas. Because they were currently sitting in what had once been a little Irish pub in the New York–New York casino, one of the random buildings that survived the Change.

And by "number," Elliott meant room number. No one had phones anymore, or even email, and definitely not Facebook. They didn't drive cars. Even here in Envy, the largest settlement of humanity, there was limited electricity, with only an occasional DVD player and flat-screen TV that had survived for half a century. The disks of movies, music, and other shows were hoarded and protected like a national fucking treasure.

As it turned out, the casino/hotel had become sort of a commune for what was left of a good portion of the human race, at least here in New Vegas. Everyone lived in their own rooms, but most people ate (and took their turns working at or otherwise contributing to) the communal restaurants. It was sort of like *Cheers* on steroids: literally, everyone knew everyone's name, because they saw each other every day.

That didn't include the pub, however. The establishment was like pretty much every other sports bar Fence had been in, except there were no televised live-action sports. Once all the hell that broke loose during the Change had settled into something resembling normalcy, the guy who cleaned up and scavenged the space had learned to brew beer after the kegs that survived were emptied. (Fence figured, what with the world going to shit and everyone thinking it was the Apocalypse, that had probably happened within a few hours.) His kids and their spouses still ran the place. They were paid in casino chips, which were the only currency available, or through barter.

According to Lou Waxnicki, one of the guys who lived through the Change, Jody Stearns's first few attempts at brewing ale had tasted worse than horse piss . . . but apparently he'd gotten better at it. Or at least his kids had, because, here they were, fifty years later, drinking a dark, nutty beer that rivaled Guinness.

Fence settled back in his chair and gave the waitress a sidewise look, but he didn't ask for her room number. Not yet. They had all night to get to that point . . . and there was that table of women in the corner. He had his eye on one of them, if she'd ever look his way.

"Yo, Vaughn, do you know those ladies over there?" he said, shifting closer to the mayor of Envy, who was nursing his own beer.

In this world, Fence figured being the mayor of the largest settlement of mankind was akin to being the President of the United States back when it still existed. Vaughn Rogan, who looked like a cross between the Marlboro Man and David Beckham—not Fence's words—was a guy who took his position seriously. He was also one of the few people in Envy who knew the truth about the guys from the Sedona cave: that they'd somehow time-traveled or slept through fifty years without aging.

Vaughn also knew that some of the men had acquired an array of odd, superhuman abilities—and some of them hadn't. Fence was one of the ones who hadn't, and he figured he was one of the lucky ones.

Not long after Lenny died, Elliott realized he'd somehow obtained a healing touch—except that every time he healed someone, it came back to kick him in the balls and created even bigger problems. He'd confessed to Fence that because he hadn't understood—or even realized the existence of—his new ability, he might have accidentally contributed to Lenny's death. Poor son of a bitch, Fence thought, to have that guilt on his conscience along with everything else they had to accept.

And Quent, the British guy who'd been the one who hired him in the first place, could touch something and tell its history. That wasn't so bad as long as he didn't get sucked into a comalike state of memories that made him not only vulnerable, but also threatened to keep him in that infinite vortex . . . which had almost gotten him killed once or twice.

Then there was Simon, who somehow learned to become invisible—now that was something Fence figured he could use. He chuckled deeply to himself at the thought, then shook his head. Probably the reason the good Lord hadn't seen fit to bestow that particular skill on him. He knew him well enough.

And, hell, with Happy Valley Cindy trying to hypnotize him with her girls, he guessed it was a moot point.

The other member of their strange group, Wyatt, seemed to also have been overlooked when they passed out superhero abilities. So although he and Fence had finally begun to grow stubble again in the last few months, just like the rest of their companions—which, along with Lenny's unfortunate death, at least proved that they hadn't become immortal or remained frozen in time—they hadn't been altered in any other way.

"Three of those women are from around here," Vaughn said, glancing over at the table. "I don't recognize the other two." He slid his gaze to Fence, a smile lurking in his rugged face. "You want me to introduce you?"

Fence snorted. The day he needed to be introduced to a woman was the day hell froze over. And since, even though the world had ended, hell obviously hadn't frozen because there were still assholes and evil in the world, he didn't need the help. "Naw. Just wondered."

Speaking of assholes and evil in the world . . . Fence's jovial mood faltered. He turned to include Elliott in the conversation. "I just got back an hour ago and haven't been down to the computer lab yet," he said, referring to his two-day trip helping move some Envyites to a new settlement. His guide and survival skills were in great demand since he'd arrived in Envy, for people rarely traveled more than a few miles beyond the city's protective walls. There weren't many navigable roads, nor were there convenient methods of transportation, hotels, or even that many settlements. "Any updates from Theo or Lou?"

Theo and Lou Waxnicki were computer geek twins who'd lived through the Change and over the last fifty years had used their knowledge of 2010 technology to try and piece together what had happened to the world, and how. They had long suspected the Strangers—an elite group of men and women who wore crystals that made them immortal—either had something to do with the devastating events or at least had prior knowledge of them. Either way, through Theo's expert hacking into their communications network they knew that the Strangers had used the destruction of the world for their own benefit—obtaining immortality while keeping their fellow humans controlled and relatively helpless.

Meanwhile, the Waxnicki brothers had secretly begun to build their own post-Change version of the Internet in order to have an underground network for their silent, insurgent group called the Resistance, and to harvest and organize whatever data could be culled from the caches of surviving computers and mainframes. In fact, Elliott's main squeeze, Jade, traveled from settlement to settlement as an itinerant singer in order to secretly collect computer components. Theo and Lou were currently in a settlement called Yellow Mountain, more than a hundred miles away, where they'd found a well-preserved collection of electronics from one of the members of the Strangers' inner circle. Nevertheless, they were still in communication with the Resistance members in Envy via their network.

Elliott's face looked grim, and he exchanged a quick look with Vaughn before replying. "Theo's getting some information from the Strangers' communications network, but there doesn't seem to be as much chatter since Quent stole that crystal from them. The bastards are obviously aware that someone is a threat to them now, though, so Theo thinks that might be part of the reason they've quieted down. They don't know what we know and what we don't."

"Hell, *we* hardly know what we know and what we don't," Fence said grimly. "Except that those motherfuckers are into some evil shit, trying to sell kids into slavery and turning people into zombies and God knows what the hell else."

"Not to mention what they did to Jade those years they had her imprisoned," Elliott added with a glance up at the sexy redhead onstage. Her eyes met his over the microphone, and even from where he sat, Fence could feel the sharp, hot sizzle between them. No doubt about it . . . Elliott Drake was one *fortunate* dude. Jade wasn't just a pretty face and a curvy body—she was smart and brave too. Fence wondered what it was like to have a woman with the whole package.

"I don't like it," Vaughn put in, his face sober. "It's too quiet . . . I keep waiting for them to storm the walls or attack us here or something. It's as if we're waiting for the other shoe to drop. But none of the patrol have seen anything suspicious, even though I've increased their numbers and sent out a few scouting parties. You didn't run into anything suspicious?" This last was directed to Fence.

He shook his head. "And I was looking. It's almost . . . eerie." He couldn't explain how he did it, but he'd also paid close attention to the natural world—the birds and other animals, watching for signs in their behavior as well as tire tracks and campsite locations. Nothing seemed out of place or off.

"Even when I got the Mullinses to their new place and tried talking to the others in the village, no one had anything unusual to share. They hadn't seen a Stranger in months. Zombies, yes, but the Strangers and their Humvees . . . no."

"But they've got to be looking for that crystal Quent

took—hell, they saw him escape with it—and they've got to know he's here in Envy," said Elliott, grim frustration in his voice.

Fence nodded, but there was no need to speak. They all understood the threat, and they all knew it was only a matter of time until something happened. If only they had an idea what to expect. The only thing they could do was wait, watch, and be prepared. All of which they were already doing.

Ready for a distraction, he glanced over at the group of women again, trying to catch the eye of the one who'd snagged his attention. She sat at the side of the table, so he had a good view of her profile except when she looked toward the stage. Then he got to see her face full-on—but she still wouldn't look at him.

She couldn't be more than twenty-seven or so, and the fact that he was technically . . . oh, seventy-nine; no, eighty, hell, he'd had a birthday back in February . . . didn't bother him a bit. For all intents and purposes, he was still twenty-ni— No, thirty.

The woman looked as if she lived outdoors. Even in the low light of the pub, he could see the rich golden color of her skin and long brown hair streaked different shades of blond by the sun. She had a long, oval face and a long slender nose; wide, full lips; and from what he could tell, a killer body. Another guy might imagine her lying on a beach, tanning on the sand as the waves splashed up next to her—but that was not a fantasy Fence enjoyed. He had her soft and mussed in a bed of white sheets, the sun spilling over her body in its golden glory.

If she'd just look his way, he could catch her eye and hopefully start something.

"I thought you and Marley were . . . uh . . ." Vaughn

said, setting his beer glass down, watching Jade on-stage but talking to Fence.

"Marley and me? Nah," he said, holding back on making the obvious joke. Vaughn might not get the movie reference, being a guy living after a good portion of the world was destroyed, and Fence didn't like it when his jokes fell flat—it felt like his shield had been shattered.

Although he wasn't strictly speaking the truth. He and Marley *had* . . . but it had been a temporary thing for both of them. That was the only way Fence wanted it anyway. At least until he figured out what the hell he was doing in this world and how to live here. Aside from that, there were other things he'd jump off a tall mountain before he told anyone about. Only Lenny had known, and understood—as much as he could.

And that, Fence thought wryly, was why he'd never found—or looked for—a woman with the whole package: looks, brains, humor, strength. Because a woman like that wouldn't understand.

He looked at Vaughn, who was still watching Jade, but whose attention was clearly on Fence's explanation. "Marley and I hung out for a while, but we're just friends."

It had been Marley, in fact, who described the mayor as a cross between the Marlboro Man and David Beckham, with a little bit of Barack Obama's serious political persona tossed in when he was doing mayoral things. Fence was pretty sure it had been a compliment, and he wondered why the two of them, who clearly noticed each other, hadn't hooked up.

Where there was smoke, there could be a whole blazing fire if you didn't waste time beating around the bush. He grinned to himself.

Jade finished her set, took a bow, then left the stage, Elliott following her. In her wake came recorded music, bar music. Some things never changed.

Vaughn lifted a finger, and Cindy reappeared with three more beers for the table as Fence shifted in his seat to look over again at the sun goddess. And lo and behold, she was laughing at something one of her companions said, and she looked even more glorious and enticing.

And then, as her laughter subsided and she settled back in her seat, humor still lighting her features, her gaze scanned the room and she looked right at him.

She almost caught him by surprise, but he was good at this. He met her eyes purposely and gave a little nod of hello, followed by a smile. To his satisfaction, she tipped her head in that way women did, lifting her chin as she held his gaze for just long enough to acknowledge the interest. And then she looked away.

He wasn't certain if that was a little smile playing about the corners of her mouth or was just a trick of the low light. Either way, he liked it.

"She's not from around here," Vaughn said, obviously noticing the exchange. "I think she comes from up the coast, a ways on the northeast curve."

"Wonder what she's doing here. And for how long," Fence said, considering his next move. Send a drink, or take himself over and strike up a conversation? If she was leaving soon, he didn't have time to waste.

"I could go on over and do my duty as a good public servant and welcome them to our town," Vaughn said. "And you could go with me."

Got your eye on one of them yourself? Or do you just want to keep me away from Marley? Either way, he'd play. "Sure."

His fingers curled around the cool glass, and he and Vaughn wove their way through the heavy round tables and the assortment of mismatched chairs that clustered between them. Whether it was a sign or not, "California Girls" was the tune of choice blaring through the speakers—the Beach Boys' version. An oldie but a goodie . . . but every single track on whatever CD or iPod that had been found was an oldie to the people here. To them, it was all the same: ancient history.

Fence swallowed the lump in his throat along with a big swig of beer and focused on the here and now as they approached the table.

"Mayor Rogan," said one of the ladies, who seemed more than a little thrilled about their visitor. "And you're the one named Fence, right?" She had to shout to be heard over the music.

Before Fence could reply, she was leaning over to her friends to explain, "He's one of that group who saved Sam Pinglett's kid from the gangas when those teenagers got lost. It was a few months back, remember? They're practically heroes here in Envy," she added with a big, welcoming smile. "All five of them."

Fence took that as an invitation to sit, and since time was a-wasting, he snagged a chair from a nearby table and straddled it backward, resting his hands on the back. Since there wasn't a seat directly next to the sun goddess, he sat so he was across from her. "Well, I wouldn't say heroes," he said, a little niggle of discomfort trickling down his spine. "We just did what anyone would have done." *Some of us, anyway.*

He took another drink of his beer and pushed away the sour thoughts that threatened to ruin his evening. Yeah, he'd nearly fucked up . . . but he hadn't, and he'd gotten Benji back from her zombie abductor in the end.

The sun goddess was looking at him from behind the rim of her glass, and he was itching to talk her up. But his mama had taught him manners, so instead Fence smiled at the woman sitting to his left, who was one of the teachers in Envy's hundred-pupil school. "How's it going, Donna? You working on trinomials yet? Or still only on those boring binomials?"

She laughed and patted his arm, leaning closer. "What, you have a strong preference?"

"The way I look at it, anything with three is always better than something with two, you know, sugar." He grinned. He'd always been really good in math, and found that ability helpful in his navigation with the sky charts, as well as plotting with geographic maps— particularly now, in this horribly altered world.

The devastation had not only shifted the Earth's axes, but it also changed the climate of the Nevadan desert, and somehow a landmass the size of Texas had appeared in the Pacific Ocean not too far off the coast of where California once was. Any compasses or maps he'd had or could find, as well as his knowledge of astronomy and the geography of the western United States, had become frighteningly fallible.

"Well, we'd love you to come back and do that talk about constellations and how to recognize and navigate using the stars again. The students really enjoyed it, and the ones who missed it have been begging us to have you back. When you started arranging them in the position of the Big Dipper, and made Andrew the North Star, they thought that was the funniest thing." She was shaking her head in amused affection.

"No problem," he told her, noticing with delight that

the sun goddess seemed to be listening to their conversation. "Just let me know when."

"All right. And I heard you got up there and sang with Jade one night," Donna said, quickly changing the subject, as if to keep his attention on her. "Too bad I missed it. I heard you were really good."

"I can carry a tune," he said with a smile, thinking about Lenny's mournful harmonica accompaniment over many a campfire. "As long as it's the right one."

To his relief, the waitress came over with a tray of drinks and stepped between their chairs, giving him an opportunity to shift his attention to the sun goddess.

"So you're not from around here, Vaughn tells me," he said, noticing the very faint sprinkling of freckles over her high cheekbones, and the blond tips of her dark eyelashes. She had green-brown eyes and long, slender hands, but her nails were bitten down short. She'd probably be almost as tall as he was when she stood. Tall and lithe, but not skin and bones, judging from the peek of collarbone from behind her scoop neck shirt.

"No, just visiting for a few days," she replied. "I'm going home tomorrow." She settled back a little bit in her chair and gave him a bold, speculative look. "So you're a hero, are you? And a math whiz? *And* an astronomer. Oh, and you can sing." A little smile tugged at the corners of her mouth. "Is there anything else?"

"What can I say . . . I'm multitalented. And that's not even the half of it." He smiled, long and slow, the way the ladies liked it.

"So how'd you get a name like Fence?"

He shrugged and leaned a bit closer. *Mmm.* She smelled good too. Sunny, like lemons. Warm, like something else. "I never tell that story on a first date," he said. "But maybe I could make an exception."

"Oh, I wouldn't want you to make an exception for me," she replied, giving him back a lethal smile of her own. One that sent a surprise little twinge darting deep in his belly. "But how about if I guess how you got the nickname, and if I get it right, I win?"

"Well, now, sugar, it would depend what the prize is. But I'm certain," he said, dropping his voice into its lowest range of bass, "we could agree on something."

She continued to contemplate him, and Donna was left to gape, her attention ping-ponging between them.

"I could really use a new saddle for my horse," the sun goddess said, and he swore she gave him a *look*.

Fence almost swallowed his tongue. "So you do a lot of . . . *riding*?" he asked. He couldn't help it. It just slipped out. But he stopped himself from making any further comments about horses and being hung like one.

"Okay then . . . well, let me think," she said, interrupting the runaway train of his thoughts. Probably a good thing. "The first thing that comes to mind regarding a nickname like Fence is that you're *really* good with a sword," she said, her voice smooth with dusk, her eyes meeting his.

It was all he could do to keep his expression cool.

"But," she continued before he could speak, "that's sort of obvious. And you don't seem like an obvious sort of guy, Fence, so . . ."

Was that a compliment or a little parry and thrust of her own? Fence couldn't hold back a smile this time, and he felt his eyelids go a bit droopy with an edge of seduction.

" . . . maybe you can't ever make up your mind about things? That you sit on the fence all the time?"

Ouch. That was definitely another parry and thrust,

but instead of being offended, he still found her wit amusing. A smart woman with a killer body, who held her own. "I don't know . . . there are certain things I'm pretty sure about," he replied, holding her gaze. "No fence-sitting here."

Her eyes danced. "All right, then, am I getting warm?"

"Smokin', baby," he said, and liked the way her eyes widened briefly.

"A guy with a name like Fence," she said, mulling, her fingers drumming on the table as she copped a speculative look. "Could it be because you build a lot of fences around you? Close people off, keep them away?"

Okay, that was a direct hit. Di-*rect*. He felt a little breathless at her accuracy, and at the same time stimulated in all the best ways. "What, are you psychic?" he replied, allowing a bit of seriousness into his joke. "But who doesn't have secrets, walls of protection built around them?" he asked, sinking into a more sympathetic tone, making certain he didn't sound defensive. "Don't you?"

Her eyes flared again, and he felt her withdraw a bit. *Hmmm.* A direct hit of his own.

"Maybe," she said, recovering. Her eyes narrowed and he could almost see the wheels turning. "Could be you weren't watching where you were going and you ran into a fence?"

He shook his head, chuckling a little. *Closer*, but still way off. "Can we go back to the sword part?" he asked, reaching out with one of his large, brown fingers to caress her slender, golden ones. "I kinda liked the direction you were going there."

She chuckled and left her fingers beneath his feather-light stroking. "Somehow I'm not surprised."

Before he could respond, an unusual sound caught his attention and Fence turned as Vaughn rose to his feet. A man and woman were hurrying across the tavern with an air of urgency, and Vaughn moved to meet them.

Immediately, Fence shifted from flirtation to high alert. Almost everyone stopped what they were doing, watching and listening from their tables. With a quickly murmured, "Excuse me," he got to his feet and wended his way toward Vaughn, catching bits of whispered conversation as he went:

" . . . zombies?"

" . . . better check on the kids, Maddy . . ."

" . . . tiger attack last week . . ."

" . . . at the gate? Don't they have guards . . ."

Fence wasn't surprised that no one seemed concerned enough to mention the Strangers. But that was because most of the people in the room—hell, most of the people everywhere, both in Envy and outside of its walls—had no idea what sort of threat the Strangers were.

Most of them had no idea that the teens Fence, Elliott, and the others had rescued from the zombies were about to be sold into slavery to the Strangers—for everything from breeding purposes to hard labor. And that Jade had spent five years in captivity with one of the three leaders of the Strangers, and seen and experienced a variety of horrors at their hands. Most important of all, other than the members of the Resistance, no one realized that this group of immortals had somehow been involved with the Change fifty years ago, and would do anything necessary to keep their mortal counterparts from banding together and becoming strong again.

Even now, decades after the beginning of the twenty-first century, people still lived in blissful ignorance of the evils that went on around them. They still believed lies that were told to them over and over until somehow they became truths. *What you don't know will, yes, indeed, hurt you.*

Fence shivered. There were times when he wished he *didn't* know the truth himself. Knowing that the very same people who'd caused widespread devastation still lived, still walked on this soil and pretended to be like everyone else, was almost too much to bear. These people had destroyed his family, his friends, and everyone and everything he had ever known.

It killed him that he hadn't been able to do anything about it yet. None of them had. The Resistance was still young, and out of necessity a carefully kept secret. Although, now that Quent had stolen the crystal right from under the inner circle of the Elite, Fence wasn't certain how much longer they would remain secret.

As he approached, Vaughn was saying, "You found something on the beach?"

The woman replied, "Yes, washed up there. We thought you should know. It's really odd-looking."

"We'd better take a look."

Fence turned as he saw the sun goddess out of the corner of his eye. She'd stood, along with her friends, and, like everyone else in the room, seemed to be listening intently.

"Looks like something strange washed up on the shore," Vaughn said to him. "You coming?"

"Damn straight." Despite the fact that the very word "shore" sent a little ripple of awareness through him, Fence was game. As long as he didn't have to get *into* the ocean, it'd be cool.

The mayor's words seemed to be an invitation for several other people to rise from their chairs and start to filter from the pub. Obviously, entertainment was cheap here in Envy.

Fence turned to see the sun goddess inching her way awkwardly around the table, squeezing between chairs and the wall, and he waited for her to come around.

"How about we check out whatever this is, then we do a little dancing under the moonlight?" he said with his slow smile. "I could teach you how to fence, and maybe you'll figure out my nickname."

The words had just come out of his mouth, and they were still hanging there between them when he noticed the funny way she was moving, even now that she'd emerged from behind the table. Then he saw her leg, bared by the cargo shorts she wore.

Oh my God.

Mangled was an understatement, for that implied fresh wounds. But whatever had happened to make her thigh and calf look like that, twisted and deformed, her foot curled at an awkward angle and clearly impossible to dance on—let alone to fence—had happened a long time ago.

Fence swallowed, words suddenly disappearing from his mind. He felt like a damn fool. "I—uh," he began. "Here, let me help you," he said, offering her his arm.

As soon as the words came out, he realized it was exactly the wrong thing to say.

Ana couldn't help the flare of annoyance, and she knew it showed on her face. "I'm fine, I don't need your help," she said, knowing, too, that the words came out sounding sharper than they should have.

The guy—Fence—had a stricken expression on his handsome face, and she felt a twinge of sympathy that his easy, flirtatious mood had disintegrated into shock and embarrassment. But not too much. He was clearly an expert at this game, and much as she'd enjoyed the interlude, she had more important concerns than this guy's ego.

On the shore. Washed up on the shore.

Worry propelled her to navigate past him, inelegant as she always was when on two feet, and she brushed against his arm. Further annoyance that he hadn't given her enough space, and that her own shortcomings made her less than graceful, made her movements even sharper and more labored.

For pity's sake. She rarely noticed the awkwardness of her own body anymore; after all, she'd lived with her injury for more than twelve years. She didn't even try to hide it under jeans or pants; she wore whatever was comfortable—even if it showed all of the puckered mess. Over the years, she'd gotten used to men who wouldn't come near her once they saw the scars, or others who treated her like an ailing child, and even those who thought she was desperate and would be easily intimidated once they got her in a dark corner. As if she would settle for assholes like them.

Now, all of a sudden, this big hulk of a man with his wide, white smile had teased her into a warm flirtation, and then with a mere offer of assistance plunged her into a sea of ineptitude.

"Excuse me," she said, pushing on with her uneven gait. She could move quickly when and if she needed to, and although it wasn't a pretty sight, her mobility was efficient.

She felt Fence behind her, which made her feel even more awkward, *damn him*. As if she either needed to rush—although she was moving at a good pace—or that he was there, hovering behind, as if waiting for her to fall so he could catch her.

Ana ignored him. She'd made an excuse to her friends that she needed to go to the restroom, hoping they wouldn't follow her outside to the beach.

Washed up on the shore.

It could be anything. It was probably nothing out of the ordinary. Nothing to be concerned about.

But if it had to do with the sea, she'd recognize it. And . . . things had been odd out there lately. There was something unsettled about the ocean, deep in its cold, dark depths. She knew her, the Sea, the way she knew her own body. And if something was wrong, if She'd spewed something out that was cause enough for concern from the people here in Envy, then Ana needed to know about it.

Once outside, Ana didn't need directions to find her way to the water: of course she could smell the salt and sense the tug of its briny depths. The sun had just begun to set, to her left, and the big orange ball sat, bisected, on the edge of the world.

Straight ahead and to her right would be the moon when it rose; tonight it would be almost full and magnetic. She could almost feel the fat tugging of its pull on her and on the ground beneath her feet. The sensation of the waxing moon was even stronger when she was in the water . . . and then when it began to wane, the pull ebbed and relaxed.

"This all used to be a desert," came a deep voice in her ear. Fence was ambling alongside her now. He was tall. Much taller than she was. "Did you know that?

Before the Change, this was a huge, loud, exciting city surrounded by arid land and rugged mountains. And now . . . it's practically the Caribbean."

Ana spared him a nod. While she didn't know what the Caribbean was—although she'd seen those pirate DVDs—she'd heard vague stories about the place called Las Vegas, and how the main street that divided it, called the Strip, had fairly separated during the Change. According to legend, one side of the Strip had been dumped into the ocean, along with places called California and Washington. She believed that part, having seen vast examples of submerged cities and towns when she dove and scavenged beneath the surface where no one else could hope to go.

That was how she made her living: dragging things up from the deep, like an ancient Greek pearl diver.

"It's pretty crazy, the way this environment has changed," Fence was saying, and she got the impression he was speaking more to himself than to her. "Now it's green and lush, with lots of rain and water. And the frigging ocean right here in the middle of the desert. And Vegas . . . half of it underwater. The Venetian, the Bellagio, North Vegas . . . gone."

She glanced at him, pausing in her rushed trek. "You sound as if *you're* missing it."

He'd stopped, too, and now he looked down at her, as if recalling that he wasn't alone. "Yeah," he said vaguely. "It's just . . . impossible to believe."

Ana looked up at him for a moment and felt a little ping in her belly. He was so good-looking, she just wanted to stare at his strong, chiseled features: his broad nose, square chin, almond-shaped eyes. And he had such beautiful skin, so dark and smooth: the color of strong tea. He was bald, with a perfectly shaped skull, and thick, full lips that looked as if they'd be amazing to kiss.

The ping inside turned into full-blown regret. Grief, for what she couldn't imagine ever having. A superficial flirtation and bit of bantering was one thing, but anything more would be an incredible risk.

The briny smell on an uptick of breeze reminded her of more pressing matters than her self-pity, and she murmured, "Must have been terrible, the way it all happened."

She'd heard the stories, of course, about what occurred. About how the Atlanteans and a group of men called the Elite had worked together to create a new Evolution. Yes, that was the word they used. Evolution.

Her belly twisted and she blocked her mind from traveling down that familiar path, even as she felt sick at the knowledge of what her ancestors had done. Tightening her lips, she continued walking down a street that she knew had once been lined with tall, gaudy buildings flashing bright lights of every color.

Ana had seen pictures of Las Vegas, but surely those static images weren't an accurate portrayal of this brightly lit city Fence had spoken of. A limited number of neon lights still glowed weakly. The red and blue illumination was a beacon of welcome to any travelers who might stumble upon the town, which was enclosed by a twenty-foot wall to protect its inhabitants from the zombies and the lions, tigers, and wolves that roamed beyond.

A small crowd of people stood in front of Ana, at the spot where the thoroughfare ended, just beyond the protective wall, right at the sea. She inhaled the welcoming scent of salt and tried to edge her way through the crowd to see what they'd found.

The wall that enclosed Envy was built of old cars and massive signs called billboards, huge segments of rubble or roofs, and many other remnants from years ago that had been dragged into place. However, along the oceanfront, the wall had several gates to allow access to the fishermen and anyone else who wanted to walk along the beach. Because Ana came from the northeast on the very rare occasion when she visited Envy, she normally entered the city through one of those gates. They were left open during the day, for the walls were meant to offer protection to the inhabitants—not to keep people out or in.

As she approached, it was an automatic thing for her to slip off her shoes and allow her feet to sink into the sand. The uneven yet forgiving molding of the grains helped stabilize her bad foot and hip, and she moved even more readily through the crowd.

Ana was considerably taller than most women, just over six feet, and even before she got through to the center of the group, she could see the dark spot on the sand. A little uneasy flutter prickled when she saw the faint sparkling.

A pleasant rush of waves licked her bare feet as she made her way around the group on the sea side, and she curled the toes on her left foot into the damp sand. Her right foot, the twisted and deformed one, didn't have that sort of dexterity anymore, although she could feel the sensation of the sand.

Ana saw Fence's large, dark figure following in her path around the group. He, too, stood taller than most people, but instead of coming all the way around to the water where she stood, he turned and cut through the crowd. They parted for him, and she watched from a distance as he approached the mayor and his companions.

"What is it?" asked someone in the group.

Even Ana couldn't answer that question, whether she wanted to or not. The substance on the shore looked like a rubbery, oozing mass of melted plastic. It was gray-blue and it glittered and gleamed. About six feet in diameter, it sat on top of the sand without sinking into it, and when she sniffed, she could smell more than just the salt and vegetation of the sea. Something unpleasantly murky and old.

She hovered in the shadows, her gut tightening and an uncomfortable trickle of sweat suddenly rolling down her spine. She didn't know exactly what it was, but she knew one thing: it didn't naturally occur in the sea.

It had to be from Atlantis.

CHAPTER 2

The odd, sticky substance looked like something from a kid's joke shop—glittering boogers or fake magical slime.

"I don't see how it can have any connection to the Strangers," Quent said after looking at it, swirling a pencil through it and then sniffing the oozing blob. He'd already tried touching it with his bare hand to see if he could "read" its history, but for the first time ever, his mind came up blank. "But I sure as hell want it to."

"It doesn't look very threatening," Fence said, sliding his own finger through it. Remnants of glitter clung to his skin.

They'd already tested it for flammability, and no one seemed to have had any odd reactions from touching or smelling it. It didn't burn or sting or adhere like glue. Not even Fence, however, had volunteered to taste it.

Vaughn's rugged face was sober. "We've never seen anything like it here before."

"It did come from the ocean," Elliott reminded them.

The four men nodded, and Fence was sure they were all thinking the same thing: Had it come from Atlantis?

The very thought would have been crazy if they and the Waxnickis hadn't been putting the pieces of the puzzle together for months. They'd learned that a small group of the richest, most powerful people in the world before the Change had been part of a secret society called the Cult of Atlantis. These people, one of whom had been Quent's father, were now the Strangers—or the Elite, as they called themselves—and had not only lived through the catastrophe, but had the crystals to keep them forever young. Crystals, as Quent had reminded them, were the source of energy in many an Atlantean legend. That, along with the new landmass in the Pacific Ocean, had created the unnerving suspicion that somehow, Atlantis really did exist . . . and that it had somehow erupted from the bottom of the ocean.

Impossible. Fence knew it was scientifically impossible. He knew the Earth, and she didn't move like that.

But somehow . . . the pieces fit, and there seemed to be no other explanation for it.

"I'll increase the patrol along the shore side of the wall," Vaughn said, looking tense. "We don't go into the sea very often on the north side of Envy, or very far out when we do. Too many people have gone, and never come back."

Fence wasn't one bit surprised.

A week after the gray glop appeared on the beach, Fence was a little more than fifteen miles north of the city. He'd guided a group of travelers to a small settlement a bit farther east, and on his way back, he was stopping in a little seaside town to obtain some supplies for Elliott.

He was not only alone with the song he was humming

and the pack on his back, but he was at last moving at his own speed—without having to make constant pit stops. Every shift in the leaves, every new smell in the breeze, every sound of an animal, gave him information. He absorbed it like a starving man.

This was his world, his life: in the bosom—*heh*—of Mother Nature. Fence grinned. *I crack myself up.*

The salt of the sea tinged the air, and when he came to the top of a rise and was able to look down to see the rolling waves with their foam surging onto rocks and remnants of 2010, he paused and watched. The prickling of his skin and the nauseating flip of his belly warred with his admiration of the infinite expanse of the sea.

The town he was looking for lay to the right of his peak, and he saw about ten neat little houses near the edge of the water. New construction, built after the Change, which was fairly unusual; for most people simply maintained or scavenged old buildings. Small boats lined up along one side of a dock parallel to the beach. Trees, ruined houses, cracked roads, and even a rusted-out car with branches thrusting from its windows were scattered along the shore.

He wondered oh so idly if this happened to be the little town "up along the coast" where the sun goddess lived. Fence had learned that she—her name was Ana—came from a seaside village northeast of Envy. In the excitement over the gloppy gray stuff onshore, she had disappeared.

He wasn't sure if it bugged him because they'd left things so awkwardly, with his inept reaction to her handicap and her sharp words . . . or because she'd taken off without so much as giving him her name. And with all the other stuff going on, he hadn't felt compelled to go after the woman or even to hunt her down . . . but he *had* taken on the task of traveling up the coast knowing he could possibly see her again. Just because.

A shout from below and to the east caught his attention, and Fence turned to listen.

"Tanya! Tanya, where are you?"

Because the voice sounded urgent and a little panicked, he began to scramble down the hill, surefooted, with his backpack clunking rhythmically against him.

"Tanya?" came another voice, from a different direction. "Tanya!"

And then a male voice, from the original location: "Tanyaaaa!"

Fence followed the first voice, and as he came closer heard others calling the girl's name. When he emerged from between two overgrown houses, one whose roof had been flattened by a massive tree trunk some years earlier, he was conscious of his large size and the fact that his entrance was the sudden appearance of a stranger, so he slowed to an efficient amble.

"Hello," he called as the man and woman spun to look at him. Hope died from their faces. "Can I help you?" He smiled and stepped across a cracked driveway, its asphalt puzzle pieces outlined by tall grass and a few wild orchids.

"Who are you?" asked the man, but he seemed less nervous about Fence's unexpected presence than concerned about Tanya.

"My name is Fence, I'm from Envy. If you're from Glenway, then I'm in the right place. I'm looking for a guy named George."

"Yeah, he's here, back there," said the man, gesturing vaguely in the direction of the town. "Have you seen a little girl? About so tall"—he showed a hip-high height—"dark hair?"

Fence shook his head. "I heard you calling her and figured I'd come and help. I'm pretty good at tracking, following trails and stuff." It wasn't lost on him that despite the fact that a very large man, a stranger, had suddenly appeared in the woods where a young girl was missing, neither seemed to regard him with any suspicion or unease. He relaxed a bit. "If you can tell me where you last saw her, I'll be happy to help."

"This way," said the man, who introduced himself as Pete.

"We're her mom and dad," said the woman, whose name was Yvonne. "You're a friend of George?" she asked, her eyes wide and hopeful, her words falling on top of each other without logic. "*Tanya!*" she shouted, then turned back to him. "You'll help us? The last we saw her was about two hours ago. At first, we didn't worry . . . she knows to stay here in the play area. But . . ."

"I haven't met George yet," Fence explained, following Pete. "But he knows a friend of mine, and—"

"Here," said Pete. "This is where she was the last we saw."

A playground of sorts, a clearing beneath about half a dozen tall pines, with their lowest branches well above Fence's head. Their rust-colored needles made a soft, soundless cushion beneath tire swings and a few ropes strung between them for climbing and hand over hand swinging. Someone had taken more old tires and pieces of plastic and built an intricate play structure around three of the trees.

Fence nodded and started to look. "What color hair? How much does she weigh? What was she wearing on her feet, and how was her hair done—in pigtails or long or what?"

He needed to get a mental image of her so that he knew what to look for—how high she might brush against something, what color thread or fuzz she might leave behind, whether her hair was loose—to lose a strand more easily than if it were confined—how deep an imprint her feet would make and what the prints would look like. There were plenty of hours of daylight left. He didn't allow himself the distraction of worrying about a little girl lost in the woods or, worse, climbing into and through rickety old buildings. Or coming upon a cougar—the only wild cat that hunted during the day.

Not yet anyway.

Absorbed, Fence looked around and found an obvious trail leading from the playground, wishing that Dantès, the big wolf dog that Wyatt, his buddy from the cave, had sort of adopted, was here. But Wyatt was over in Yellow Mountain with Theo and Lou, and Dantès's owner, Remington Truth.

A quick glance at the sky told Fence that it was past noon, and the sun would remain high for another eight or nine hours. This whole shifting of the Earth's axes deal was a pain in the ass when it came to estimating sunrise and sunset, as well as location, but he was getting better at adjusting for the change.

As he followed the trail, looking for shoe prints and the threads of a pink shirt, the voices calling for Tanya faded into the background. Pete and Yvonne had gone off on another trail, everyone spreading out in a wide radius around the village and playground.

Reading the little girl's trail was nearly as simple as reading a book for Fence: he found broken sticks, rumpled bushes, scattered leaves, and footprints that led him farther from the playground. He jumped over a four-foot tree trunk and then skirted a rusted mailbox, its official royal blue paint and USPS logo long since peeled away, and called for Tanya, figuring he'd already gone more than three miles. An eight-year-old girl ought to be getting tired by now, and wanting to sit down and rest.

When he smelled damp in the air and heard the unmistakable sound of lapping waves, he began to get uneasy. Tanya's trail had led around a battered strip mall, with every one of the ground-to-roof shop windows broken, allowing trees and bushes to grow inside a hair salon, a café, a video store, and maybe a drugstore. But behind the strip mall he could see a pretty good dip in the ground.

"Tanya!" he shouted, the sound of water filling his consciousness so that it almost drowned out the small voice calling back. "Tanya!" he shouted again, listening intently as he started down.

"It's me!" He heard the little voice. "I'm here!" It didn't sound distressed, and he felt a little bump of relief in the vicinity of his chest.

But trees and a few old cars crowded the space around him, and he couldn't get a good view as he hurried down into the small ravine. At the bottom, a large pool of water looked as if it might have been a quarry, and as Fence peered around the trees, he saw the flash of pink from the girl's shirt. It seemed higher than it should have been, and then it was gone. Was she in a tree?

"Tanya!" he called, "your mama and daddy are looking for you! They've been really worried."

"I'm here! I'm okay," she shouted back, and then he came through the brush and saw her.

Oh crap.

She was walking on a tree trunk that had split and fallen into the pond—no, correction: she was *dancing* on a tree trunk above the water. His heart stopped, his body freezing. He slid the pack from his back and dropped it on the ground.

"Tanya, sugarbear, you need to get down from there right now," Fence said, fighting off the panic. *If she falls, if she falls . . . oh God if she falls . . .*

"I'm not a bear. I'm a tree fairy," she said, and did a little spin on her toes atop the broad trunk, and then a little jump as if to emphasize her words. His heart surged into his throat. The tree branch was about three feet above the water, and extended to the middle of an acre-sized pool.

"You're going to fall off there," Fence said, his voice more strident as he made his way around the edge of the pool to the fallen tree. "Please come down before you fall."

"No I'm not!" she shouted back. "I never fall!"

As she said that, her foot slipped on the bark and she did exactly what Fence had feared.

A little scream left her lips and she slid right off the tree and splashed into the water below, quick as a blink. Until her entire body went under, Fence wasn't certain how deep the pool was—but when she disappeared and didn't immediately reappear, he knew it was deeper than he could handle.

His heart in his throat, Fence ran to the tree trunk, cursing and swearing like a motherfucker. *No, no, no, not this, not this, not me, not here, not now.*

A sturdy branch in hand, he was out on the tree limb with quick agility, forcing himself to ignore the fact that there was water below. He was still dry and out of it, he was good. She was going to come back up in a minute, and he would hand her the end of the branch and she would grab it and he'd pull her out of the water. *Right? Right, God?*

A little splash caught his attention, and Fence saw her hand come up, then a shoulder and the top of her head, a little mouth, gasping for air . . . but she was too far away for him to reach even with the branch. She slid back under with hardly a sound.

No, dammit, come back here.

His stomach heaving and lurching, Fence reached as far as he could with the branch, calling Tanya's name, his heart pounding in his chest. His fingers clutched the branch as if he were about to fall. Her face emerged again and for a moment he thought she'd heard him, but her arms flailed helplessly, reminding him of Brian all those years ago, and she eased back under the water.

No. Not Brian again. No.

Everything was so eerily silent; there were no splashes, no cries for help . . . yet dark terror crushed down on him. *I can't. I can't, I can't . . .*

"Help!" he shouted, bellowing with every bit of air in his lungs, even as he stared at the water, willing her to reappear. "Help!"

Christ. How could he be calling for help? What the hell sort of pussy was he?

Just dive in.

I can't. I can't. Cold sweat broke out over his forehead, trickling down from beneath his arms. *Brian.*

The hands flailed again above the water, and she was even further from the tree branch, and Fence's whole body was turning cold and numb.

It can't be that deep. You'll probably be able to stand up.

His breath was coming faster now, shallow, making his head light and his lungs ache. He spun and ran off the tree trunk, back to shore, dashing through brush and over trees along the edge of the water, trying to get closer to Tanya. But she was in the center of the pool, drifting away from the branch.

"Help!" he shouted again, standing there, looking out over the pool of water—which seemed to have grown wider and larger since his arrival. "Help! Here!"

A hand appeared . . . a little white hand, the fingers curled . . . and then went back down into the cold, dark, heavy water. Fence stood at the edge, his belly churning, his body trembling. More sweat streaked down his spine. His mouth was dry, his limbs cold.

You have to do this, you mother-fucking idiot. You can't let her drown. You can't stand by and let her drown.

He took off his shoes, socks . . . quickly, without allowing himself to think about what would come next.

Just close your eyes and do it . . . or she'll drown. She'll drown.

His shirt—he stripped it off and flung it away, the air cold, chilling his body despite the sun beating down.

You know what she's feeling right now . . . the water coming into her nose and mouth, choking her. You can't let her die.

Fence realized tears had begun to leak from his eyes: tears of terror and shame as he fought his own weaknesses, staying safely on shore while a little girl drowned. His fingers shook and his stomach heaved violently. He stepped into the water, literally forcing his legs to move, focusing on the other side of the pool. Not on the water.

She's just a bitty thing. Weak. Tiny. Small.

The cool sensation made his teeth chatter, the terrible water, rising to his knees, and he stopped, gasping for air, his head pounding. *I can't. I can't. I can't,* he screamed inside.

The water was still; the only ripple was from his own movement. Tanya was falling to the bottom . . . down into the deep, dark, heavy water.

God help me, help me . . . And then, somehow, he made himself move out of the paralysis. Or something pushed him, but the next thing he knew, he was in the water.

The horrible weight covered him, just as dark and cold and heavy as he'd remembered, and he immediately began to panic. His limbs wanted to thrash and flail, his chest felt constricted, his heart pounded. He wanted to gasp air in, desperate and needy, but forced his eyes open, praying for strength, and somehow made himself move.

The water was surprisingly clear, and he saw Tanya's shadowy figure, suspended midway between the bottom and surface. Her long hair floated eerily in the pool, her arms loose and one of her legs half bent at the knee. Around her were other random shapes, or perhaps tricks of the light: snakelike and undulating, perhaps a submerged tree or some twisted metal remnant of life before the Change.

Fence's brain screamed, his body rebelled in terror as his limbs moved awkwardly and then more smoothly as he found his rhythm and forced his way to her.

She was slender and light, nothing like Brian, who'd desperately fought and kicked, and Tanya hardly moved as he wrapped his arm around her waist, tugging her as he kicked up, up, up . . . seeming to take forever. He felt it when her head broke the surface, and then the cool air on his uncovered head, and he gasped a draft of oxygen-laden air. *I did it. I did it.*

He focused on those thoughts, kicking toward the shore, praying he hadn't been too late, that he could get her there, push the water from her lungs . . . for she hadn't moved since he touched her.

Then something caught at his leg, scratching it, curling around it, and Fence lost his tenuous hold on sanity. Blind with panic, he thrashed wildly, lost his grip on Tanya, began to descend into the darkness of terror. The tug on his leg seemed to grow stronger and he felt his eyes bulging wide in the water. Something sharp cut into the sides of his torso, beneath his arms, and he kicked, crazed and desperate, the water growing darker and his lungs full and hard, painful, as he tried to free himself.

He needed oxygen, he needed to breathe . . . he kicked, but now his other leg was captured, and he felt himself being pulled down, deeper, deeper . . .

And then he gave up. He just . . . gave up.

I guess this is the way You want me to go, huh, God? You've tried twice already . . . so the third time's the charm.

He gave up, let the last bit of air out of his lungs, and knew that when he could no longer hold off, the next breath would be water, rushing into him.

I'm sorry I couldn't save Tanya. I tried.

He felt oddly free now, oddly relaxed . . . and then he saw a shadow out of the corner of his eye, above, near the surface.

And suddenly, Tanya's legs, which had been floating near him, were gone. Someone was there! They'd pulled her free!

The panic rushed back, the terror, and the desperation—*save me, save me!*—and Fence gulped in a relieved breath of air a split second before he realized he couldn't.

But it came in, deep and filling, and he didn't choke.

He didn't cough as the water rushed into his lungs, the cuts on the sides of his torso stinging a bit. This is what it's like to die, he thought . . . and breathed out, and in again. *Painless. Numbing. It's like breathing in the womb.*

His panic had receded, and with it, he began to move, dreamlike, in the water. He saw now what had caught on his leg . . . what had caused him to tumble into such panic: some vinelike plant that wasn't pulling him under but simply made him feel that way as he panicked; and the more he'd struggled, the tighter it seemed to get.

His leg freed, for an instant he lingered between life and death, almost enjoying this protected, womblike state, suspended there in the water.

Was this how it had been for Brian?

And then the shadow appeared above him again, and Fence looked up, a sudden desperate desire to *live* rushing through him. He kicked, hard, and then, with an absurd lack of effort after all of his struggles, he broke through the surface.

Fresh air—oxygen—filled his body, and he realized where he was and what had happened. The terror barreled through him again—almost as if now that he'd lived, the panic that had eased during those comalike moments came rushing back in full force.

His arms flailed awkwardly, his legs tried to kick, and the black paralysis once again overtook his consciousness as he battled the water and his fears. He might have connected with or struck someone—he felt as if he touched human skin—but his terror was complete. Panic ruled him, and he could only focus on getting out. Getting out. Getting safe. Desperate, desperate . . .

When his foot struck ground, Fence had a surge of hope. The deep, black terror, the blind desperation, fell away as he found purchase with his other foot, and he lunged through the water, toward shore, blindly rushing to safety, his body shaking and weak, his belly surging. There were pangs from the wounds on his body as he stumbled onto shore, and then his stomach rebelled.

Fence collapsed on the ground, puking violently into the rubble-filled grass. His body shook like a leaf in strong wind, and he couldn't even lift his head. Tears—he wasn't certain if they were of gratitude, fear, or shame—streamed down his face, which he kept buried in the ground. His fingers curled desperately into the grass and stones and he couldn't stop shaking. It was as if he were having a seizure, completely uncontrollable and violent.

A hand touched his bare shoulder, a voice asked, "Are you all right?"

"Leave me *alone*," he snarled in a broken voice, mortified and furious with himself, with his display of weakness and cowardice. "Go away."

He tried to get himself under control, to sit up and breathe normally, but his body would not cooperate. He felt as if he'd been pummeled and thrashed on the football field without any gear . . . and the terror, the dark nightmare, still lingered, still made his belly ache and churn.

"Go away," he said again between clenched teeth as he half rolled and propped up on a shaky elbow. And then, as he looked at the new arrival, his stomach surged violently again and a renewed wave of disgust flooded him.

It was Ana, the sun goddess, who crouched next to him.

CHAPTER 3

At his furious command, Ana eased away from Fence. A little stung, a little shocked, and very concerned, she pulled herself gracelessly to her feet and limped a step away. She had no idea what this man was doing here, so far from Envy, yet she'd recognized him even from a distance by his sheer size.

But the sight of him now, collapsed on the ground and fighting some sort of internal demon, chilled her. At first she'd thought he was drowning, but then he came staggering out of the water, and now . . . he was reacting so oddly.

He vomited, but not water from his lungs as one who nearly drowned would have done; it was the full contents of his belly that came up. And the violent trembling and shuddering of such a massive, powerful body . . . it was almost as if he'd had some terrible reaction to something.

A low cough from Tanya caused Ana to turn, checking on the girl. She'd spewed up a good lungful or two of water, and her eyes were red from the effort—but she seemed fine now. "Hi, honey," she said, gathering her best friend's daughter back into her arms again, giving her a tight squeeze. "How are you doing?"

She rested her cheek on top of Tanya's cool, damp head and closed her eyes for a minute, holding the precious little body close against hers and trying not to think about what had almost happened. Tanya was the closest thing to a daughter Ana had—and would ever have. The memory of her small white hand slowly sinking under the water still made her cold and sick. If Fence hadn't gotten here first . . .

She glanced over. His hand was over his face, his thumb and forefinger rubbing his eyes. Even from where she stood she could see his fingers trembling.

The little body squirmed in her embrace, and Ana gave a soft laugh as she released the slippery, twisting girl. Obviously, she was feeling better. "Are you okay now?" she asked.

"I fell off that log," Tanya said, pointing to a large tree trunk over the water. "It was really scary."

"I'm sure it was. But that man tried to save you," Ana said, glancing from Fence to the girl and declining to mention that he hadn't done a very good job of it. If she hadn't arrived, Tanya wouldn't have made it out, and it was unclear whether he would have either.

Maybe Fence couldn't swim and he'd jumped in anyway. She'd heard his shouts for help, which was how she came to be there. Her horse stood placidly, his reins looped around a sapling, as he nibbled on a bit of grass. If it weren't for Bruiser, she would never have made it down that steep incline.

"He 'stracted me and made me fall in," Tanya told her, folding her arms mutinously over her little chest.

"How did he do that?" Ana asked as Fence dragged himself to his feet with the help of a tree. She watched him stumble to his shirt and shoes, taking care not to look in her direction. Whatever.

"He told me I was going to fall, and I *did*!" she said with all the logic of an eight-year-old.

Just then, they heard the shouts of Tanya's parents at the top of the ridge. Ana watched the tearful reunion of the little girl with Pete and Yvonne, all the while trying to keep her own emotions at bay.

The sight was heartbreaking and heartwarming at the same time. The emptiness billowing inside her mingled with affection and love for Yvonne, and the quiet knowledge that she'd always be an observer rather than a member of a close-knit family. She'd always be a surrogate mother instead of one herself. She'd always have to be on her guard about letting anyone too close to her.

She'd always have to remain a little . . . apart from the people who lived on land.

By the time the family left together and Ana went over to get Bruiser, she realized Fence had disappeared.

With a mental shrug, she used a tree trunk to climb onto the horse—something she preferred to do without an audience because it was as difficult as it looked—and started back home. Today or tomorrow, Dad was expecting someone to arrive from Envy to take a load of—

Oh.

Ana gave a little *tsk* of understanding. It could be no coincidence that Fence, a man from Envy, had appeared around here on the very day someone from Envy was expected to take some of Dad's medicine back to the doctor there. She could picture George in his bright little laboratory, peering into plastic and glass containers. He grew medicines like penicillin from moldy bread and was working on growing other possible curatives from sea algae.

At least, he did when he wasn't lecturing her with those big, sober eyes about all the time she spent in the ocean.

Ana took her time riding back through the woods toward the house she shared with her father, unsure whether she wanted to see Fence again—and certainly wondering whether he'd want to see her. The fact that he'd disappeared without a word spoke volumes.

So when she felt the beckoning of the sea and tasted salt on the wind, it wasn't a difficult decision to blow off meeting up with Fence in favor of a dive, or at least sticking her feet in the water.

Sure, the guy was rock hard and solid—those *shoulders*!—and he was so good-looking with those luscious lips and square jaw it made her mouth want to water, but she could already tell he'd be too much trouble. He had an ego, that was one thing. You had to be on your toes when sparring with him, not to mention he seemed more than a bit prickly. She didn't have time for anything that complicated . . . and she couldn't let it get into anything past a flirtation anyway.

Ana's heart squeezed and she felt that familiar dull, empty feeling. Yvonne was so lucky to have Peter and Tanya. A normal life. A family, a child. Someone to share her deepest self with.

A partner.

She'd thought at one time that she, too, might be able to have a normal life—especially when she met Darian. He, at least, was someone from whom she hadn't had to hide her past. Too bad he'd had other plans.

That was an unpleasant memory, to say the least, and Ana put all thoughts of Darian and Fence out of her mind as she tied Bruiser to a tree. Fortunately, she had an apple and a pear tucked into her pockets—both of which he liked, even though they were dried and brown—and she offered them to him before kicking off her shoes.

Despite her off-balance hips and curled foot, she shimmied easily out of her shorts and let them fall to the ground in a wad. Around her waist she wore a small belt that held her knife, and she checked automatically to make certain it was there, in its slot. Then, dressed only in her panties, a tank top, and bra, she waded into the water.

Ana would have been more than happy to swim naked, or even in her underwear, but if someone should see her, they'd surely notice the crystals. Even now, as she smelled the tangy brine and felt the familiar surge of water around her calves, those very gems began to grow warm in her skin. They vibrated with energy as they always did in or near water; a soft, tactile buzz that told her they were alive.

The eight small blue crystals, four in the front and four in back, studded the left side of her torso between the bones of her ribs. Their placement was random, and each was no larger than a child's fingernail, but because of them she could spend hours underwater, and at the greatest of depths.

And it was because of these tiny crystals that the ocean called to her, that her heritage must be kept secret—and it was because of them that her leg had been destroyed.

Ana dove into the surf and was immediately immersed in a world of wonder and comfort. The crystals helped her breathe, using their ancient energy to enable her left lung to pull the oxygen from water while her other lung worked like that of a normal human being. She didn't fully understand how the Atlanteans had managed it, and her father had never tried very hard to explain it—but after all, those living in the depths of the ocean had thousands of years to figure out the powers of the deep-sea crystals.

Thanks to her mother's heritage and her ability to spend hours beneath the surface, Ana knew every ripple of sand beneath the water, every rock formation, every spire, chimney, or rooftop from every ancient and waterlogged building near her home. She even followed long-submerged roads and streets, using them for direction just as she did on land. Now, she was twenty feet below the surface. The sun's rays still filtered down and the plants and animals were still in full, vibrant hues.

As she swam along the edge of a deep, dark crevice, she could make out a group of automobiles another twenty feet below. When the road had cracked and split, they tumbled into the depths. She knew from past dives that coral and sea grass had begun to grow tenaciously in the dirt and sand caught in the edges and dents in the metal. It gave the vehicles a scruffy, overgrown look.

Her hair streamed behind her as she darted about, her injured leg as smooth and agile in the water as her other one. This was the place where she felt whole and uninhibited, and fully at home. Was it any wonder it was the sea that had brought her and Darian together?

They'd swum together, sleek and cool, their bodies entwined, lips and mouths fused . . . Ana felt a rush of longing, of loneliness.

She hadn't had to hide her crystals from Darian, of course, because he had his own . . . but he'd wanted more than she was willing to give. And now she was alone.

Being alone is better than going back.

At least, that was what she told herself. She could never be part of that world, accept that race. So she put the impossible out of her mind and enjoyed the beautiful, comforting embrace of the sea.

As she slipped and ducked and dove above and through the remnants of a world left behind, she absorbed the essence of the sea into her consciousness: its scent, its sounds, the pattern of its movement, the changes in the sand and grit and positions of regular landmarks—even the taste of the briny water. And, again, as she'd known for weeks now, there was something different. Something was changing.

It was a subtle difference—not as noticeable as the pull of the moon as it changed the tides. Not as if a storm were brewing, ready to lash out into the sea and stir up towering waves. Just . . . an uneasiness, as if She—the Sea—knew something was about to change.

Ana would have dismissed this sense of wrongness weeks ago if not for the sparkling gray gloppiness that washed ashore in Envy. She managed to sneak a little sample of it, which was the reason she'd rushed back here to Dad, hoping he could help her identify it. After all, she was only thirteen when they escaped from Atlantis, and her memory was understandably faulty.

Now, she paused near an algae-covered column of brick she suspected had once been a chimney and smacked her palm against the top of her fist three times in rapid succession. The sharp sound carried through the water. She followed it with a clicking sound deep in her throat. It echoed through the water just as other occasional clicks and whistles did.

But other than those occasional noises, the world was silent.

Ana skirted the brick column and swam through the glassless window of another building, where furniture rotted and strands of sea hair swayed with every ripple of movement. A school of red and black fish appeared and swarmed like large flies around her head. When she shooed them away, they darted into the next room of the house.

She noticed the sand-strewn concrete driveway with the mailbox that still stood at the end. Cracked and uneven, the drive sported a few bunches of seaweed springing up from the dirt, swaying in a water breeze. The door on the mailbox was long gone, but out of habit—more compulsive than anything—Ana couldn't resist a peek inside. Of course there was nothing there, other than a lot of sand and grit, and a disgruntled crab, but it was compulsive: she always had to check, even though it reminded her of Darian. They used to leave little gifts for one another in old mailboxes, as Ana imagined other lovers might have done long ago on land.

If it was empty, that meant he hadn't found her, and she could relax

Just then, a long, dark shadow eased through the water above her. Ana made the clicking sound in her throat again and shot up from the rusty, waterlogged mailbox with a powerful thrust.

The long shadow was joined by another, and she made a slightly different clicking sound of greeting as she slipped between them, sliding her hand along the smooth, warm skin of a dolphin. Jag, the female, turned her sleek body belly-side toward Ana in greeting as they swam together.

The other dolphin, one of the two males who visited Ana regularly, was on her other side. Marco was a bit less subtle than Jag, and he bumped insistently against Ana until she patted him on the dorsal fin in what he considered an appropriate greeting. She grinned in the water at his maleness, for he reminded her of Fence with his need to be recognized by a member of the opposite sex. As she smiled, Ana felt the cool ocean against her teeth and in her mouth, and she used the energy of the crystals to push out from her working lung and spew the water from her mouth and nose.

The flush created a wake of bubbles in front of them, and the dolphins opened their own mouths in an attempt to capture the luminescence. They each had neat rows of small, sharp teeth that had long ago ceased to concern Ana. She'd had those teeth around her arms and legs more than once. Her mammalian companions seemed to simply like to run them over her skin, as if they wanted to learn the texture of her outer covering, just as she'd wanted to learn theirs. It was a dolphin thing, she decided.

And so was the distraction of a school of fish.

Jag and Marco, the latter of whom had spotted a group of fish, darted off after them.

Ana made the slapping sound of hand on fist in farewell and swam off on her own. Despite her own niggling worry that something was wrong in the water, Jag and Marco didn't seem to be acting any differently, and that comforted her.

When the sea had rushed in during the Change, covering cities and villages for hundreds of square miles over what had been California, Nevada, and parts of Washington and Oregon, many of the buildings were intact, and remained so, despite being waterlogged and algae-laden a half century later. But there were also tsunamis and earthquakes and storms that destroyed some of twenty-first century western America, sending houses, stores, and highways toppling into each other or down into deep valleys before the Sea had Her way.

Despite the hours and days Ana spent in the ocean, it was so vast and there was simply so much that had been swamped that she had only diligently explored a small part of the remains of the pre-Change world within five miles of where she now made her home. Today she wanted to return to what seemed to be a whole cache of fascinating things.

Because no normal human could dive as deeply, or for as long as Ana could, there were treasures that had lain untouched for decades, often still wrapped in plastic that even the salt and strength of the sea couldn't destroy. She'd recovered DVDs and clothing, along with tools and utensils and numerous other items. Today, she wanted to return to a big brown truck that had been filled with boxes and packages when it tumbled into the water. She'd only had the chance to peek inside before.

Of course, most of the cardboard packaging would have long rotted away, but not in every case. And whatever had been inside those boxes, often wrapped in plastic, now lay strewn in and around the vehicle.

Ana slipped just inside the angled crack of the truck's door and found herself in too much darkness. She stripped off her tank top and tied it around her waist, thankful for the other benefit of her crystals. The soft glow they gave off helped to illuminate the darkness here, and in the depths where the sun couldn't reach.

A pleasant blue glow cast around the space, which was the size of her bedroom and filled with odd-looking shapes, and as she hovered near the entrance, watching, one of the shapes rose from a far corner. It was as tall as a man, but half the size.

She reached for her knife and saw the glow of its eyes in the instant before it shot toward her, yellowish-green and blue sparks lighting the space from its anger at being disturbed.

Ana swore and ducked out of the door just as the eel crashed into the space behind where she'd been floating. The sound of its furious launch slamming against the metal wall echoed through the water in a dull clang, but she didn't waste any more time. Over six feet long, mad as a hornet, and exuding electrical sparks, the eel was not her friend. He would come after her if she invaded his den. Her knife would hardly be enough to defend herself against the shocking pulses of energy.

Damn, damn, damn. Her heart pounded from the close call as she surged through the water away from the truck. *That was too close.*

Yes, she'd been cautious—but not cautious enough. Usually, she tossed something into a dark space like that before even going in, but—

Ana felt the change in the current behind her and turned just in time to dodge the sparking eel again. She felt the tingle of electricity jolt through the water as he shot past her. *Shit, he's not giving up.* Her eyes wide, her heart slamming harder, her crystals warm and burning with effort, she whipped around a bicycle fused into a rocky reef and swam off into a different direction.

But still he came after her, violent and angry, and she had to duck and dive through windows and around houses and vehicles as she fled from him. Her only advantage was her agility, for though the eel was snake-like and slithered through the water, when attacking he launched himself straight and hard like a javelin. But then he was too quick and sleek for her to get a good slice with her blade.

He shot past her again, surprising her when she thought she'd lost him, and she cried out soundlessly from the sting and burn on the right side of her body even as she stabbed at him. The electricity made her nerves shudder, and she suddenly felt heavy.

Oh no you don't, she thought, gritting her teeth. The eel's modus operandi was to numb and paralyze with its electrical surge, and then to attack its helpless victim. She was not about to fall prey to that trick. Though her body's movements had become clumsy, she was able to manipulate herself toward a heavy concrete and rock formation. There, she waited, plastering her body against it as she readied her weapon, waiting for her muscles to start to work again.

Sure enough, the eel came stealing around the corner, its blue and green sparks preceding him as warning.

Ana held her breath as he shot toward her, his eyes glowing like ugly green-yellow marbles. *Three, two, one, move!*

She dodged at the very last moment, clumsier than usual but effective enough so the creature crashed into the stone at full force just as she slammed the knife down. He was close enough that she got another surge of electrical power, flashing over the front and side of her torso again. But while she was only slightly numb and slow, he was stunned and disoriented—although not yet dead. His blood would attract other creatures.

Ana didn't waste any time. She replaced her knife in the belt and stumble-swam away, paddling awkwardly with her hands like a dog. Her legs tried to frog-kick, but instead fumbled all over, knocking into things. But the wounded eel wasn't following her now—she kept looking back to see—and she made her way back to where she'd left Bruiser.

Her heart was still pounding when she staggered from the water, the waves lapping over her breasts and arms as she found footing and walked up toward shore, feeling the change in her body as one lung took over the process of breathing from the other one. She realized she'd lost her tank top during the chase, but no one would be around to see her—

Oh, Nemo's busted sword, what were the chances?

Fence was standing on the shore near Bruiser, watching her emerge from the water.

Of course. It would be him. Were the Fates conspiring? Or was it just bad luck? *Crap.*

Ana paused in the water and eased back a bit so the waves splashed up against her torso. It wasn't the fact that she was in her underwear that stopped her—she didn't have that sort of modesty, not after the things she and Darian had done. It was her crystals she was desperate to hide. They were bare beneath the band of her bra, and Fence couldn't help but notice them. *Now what?*

She realized she was trembling; not from the sudden breeze or change in temperature, but from the eel's assault on her body. Now that she was on foot, upright, the remnants of those electrical charges seemed to skitter even more powerfully through her. Something ached on her torso, and she looked down to see mottled red and purple marks along her right arm and waist, rising from beneath the water. Based on the pain, she guessed it went all the way along her leg as well.

A sudden thought struck her: What if the eel had shocked the left side, where her crystals were. Would that have disabled their energy?

"Yo!" shouted Fence. He'd walked toward the water. "You okay?"

Considering the last words he'd said to her were *Don't touch me* and *Get away*, Ana found that rather . . . mundane.

Despite her battered body, her brain was still sharp. "I dropped something," she said, and went back under the water. Scooping up a bit of mud, she wiped it over her left side as she came back up, hopefully obscuring her crystals from notice until she could find a shirt.

"Are you sure you're okay?" he asked as she walked out, quickly, keeping her left arm curved in front of her ribs.

She noticed that his big dark feet were bare, sunken into the wet sand as if he'd curled his toes into it. And then her attention traveled up along solid ankles and muscular calves, past his shorts and a T-shirt that stretched to far boundaries over his shoulders. She had to swallow hard and take a deep breath. As Yvonne would say, he was sweltering.

Don't get sucked in.

But it would be so easy, she argued back with herself. *And he's—*

He'd have your clothes off in two seconds flat . . . then you'd be in the deep sea.

"You're shivering," Fence said, "and you're filthy. And—what's that?" He was, fortunately, looking at the burns on her skin rather than the mud-covered crystals.

Again Ana thought quickly. "I'm freezing," she said, hugging herself and making her teeth chatter audibly—which wasn't difficult, as she was frighteningly trembly and weak.

"Here," he said, as she'd hoped he would, and yanked off his shirt. "What's that on your side?" he asked again.

The T-shirt was warm and soft, and it smelled fresh

and piney and like man, and Ana pulled it on gratefully. "Oh that? I scraped myself on a rock."

"Didn't look like a scrape to me," he said. "Let me
take a look. I know first aid. You might get infected."

"I'm fine," she replied, then turned it back onto him.
"What are you doing here?"

"Your father—uh, I didn't realize he was your father
. . . George. I'm here to pick some of his medicine and
take it back to Envy. Anyway, he told me you'd probably be here. He offered me something to eat, then realized you weren't there to—uh—make it. He seemed
surprised that you weren't." He gave her a sidewise grin
that made her stomach go soft. "So he said I should go
fetch you."

"Sounds like my dad," she said with exasperated affection. But she couldn't really complain—Dad was a
terrible cook. She limped over to Bruiser with even less
grace than usual. Her legs, dammit, were still weak.

"You shouldn't be swimming alone," Fence said,
coming up behind her as she picked up her shorts and
tried to put them on without falling onto her face.

"Yeah?" she said innocently, turning to look at him
over her shoulder once the shorts were up in place.

"Yeah. Anything could happen—you could get lost
or injured or even attacked by a shark."

She could have sworn he gave a little shudder as
he looked out over the infinite expanse of sea. "Well
maybe next time you'll come with me," she told him,
partly because she was wondering about his reaction to
saving Tanya.

"Yeah, well, I don't like to get my hair wet," he said,
smoothing his hand over a very bald head. "Oh, wait
. . . heh," he added with a deep laugh. But the chuckle
sounded strained and forced.

Ana looked at him again and saw a flash of something else behind the humor in his face. Then it was gone. And then she realized she was looking *up* into his face—unusual for her in light of her six-foot height. Fence was at least three or four inches taller than her. But despite his size and confidence, there was that something uncertain lurking in his dark eyes, and because it seemed like such an anomaly in a big and flamboyant guy like him, her curiosity was aroused.

"I can teach you to swim," she said, putting on her shoes. She had to take her time, for her muscles were still weak and trembly. She'd never been stung by an eel before. How long would this last? And how the heck was she going to hide it from her dad?

"Oh, I can swim," he replied flatly. "I told you," he continued with an odd smile, "I don't like getting my hair wet." Then his eyes, which were almond-shaped and framed with ultra long, curly lashes, narrowed. "Don't think I haven't noticed you trying to change the subject."

"What subject?" she asked. "You were lecturing me about swimming alone."

He huffed in annoyance, but she saw a glint of humor in his eyes. "Yes, but before that I was demanding that you let me take a look at whatever happened to your skin there."

"Yes, demanding is the word. I'm glad you recognized that," she replied, lining Bruiser up next to the tall rock she always used to mount him. It had little natural indents she used for steps.

"Hey, I call 'em like I see 'em," he said, and she felt him watching her carefully as she arranged the reins so she could climb up onto the boulder.

The hair on the back of her neck prickled. If he suggested that she needed help, she was going to cream him. Of course, if he did that, it would give her a reason not to find him attractive. Which she kind of needed about now.

"And that isn't a damned scrape from a rock. Why are you trying to be so heroic? I've seen enough people—including my best friend Lenny—die from something that starts off being nothing, but then turns septic or into something that ends up killing them."

"Maybe," she said, using a sapling tree branch to help herself up onto the rock, all the while feeling him watch her. She was certain his body was tense and ready to jump to her aid if she slipped on her unreliable leg. So she took extra care. "Or maybe you're just trying to get under my shirt. Your shirt," she corrected herself, facing him on top of the rock. Now she was taller than he was, and he had to look up at her. And, dang, he was even better looking from this angle. She suppressed a little shiver of attraction. "I know how guys like you work."

Oh, did she. Darian notwithstanding. Greg Luck had been trying to get her undressed for six months now, and he was only the most persistent. But Ana was adept at keeping them all at arm's length—out of necessity as well as disinterest.

A smile lurked in Fence's eyes now and twitched his full lips. "Well, since it's my shirt, if that's what I wanted, I—you know, 'a guy like me'—just wouldn't have given it to you. You looked pretty damn good coming out of the water like that." He frowned and looked around. "Where's *your* shirt, anyway?"

"Thank you," she said, not about to tell him she'd lost her tank top in a skirmish with an eel, and turned to launch herself onto Bruiser. Unlike most people, because of her leg, she didn't mount on the left side. But this time, when she fit her right foot into the stirrup and lifted her other leg up and over, her weakened muscles didn't cooperate and her knee buckled.

She tipped backward, and the next thing she knew, she was tumbling off Bruiser . . . and, of course, into Fence's arms.

"You were just waiting for that to happen, weren't you," she said, testy and a little out of breath. Mortification heated her cheeks as she worked her foot out of the stirrup, where it had twisted and caught.

"Not at all," he said seriously, then added, "but I'm a little suspicious you might've planned it that way. Otherwise, how else were you going to get into my arms? Not that you even had to ask, or anything . . . after all, you already got me to take my shirt off."

Ana snorted a laugh that was more humor than she wanted to admit. Her heart was slamming in her chest, surely hard enough to be felt all the way from behind her ribs through her skin into his really warm, really solid and broad and chiseled *bare* chest. It was like stone . . . but smooth and *warm* and alive. She swallowed away the quivering in her belly . . . and lower. "Okay, well—"

"Before I put you down, though," he said, somehow holding her against him with one arm and using his free hand to push a strand of hair from her cheek, "I'm thinking I'm gonna have to kiss you."

"Really?" she managed to say, horrified at how breathless she sounded. Her lame foot dangled freely, but somehow her right leg had curved a bit around him. For stability, she told herself—even though he was holding her around the waist, against him, and from the feel of it, she wasn't going anywhere. She was practically straddling the man's hip. *Oh my God.*

"Really," he said, then waited for a fraction of a second . . . as if to give her a chance to decline . . . before moving his face toward hers. His other hand went around her, between her shoulder blades.

Because of the way he was holding her, she didn't have to worry about him easily feeling her crystals. Their faces were right there, and so, therefore, were their mouths. His full lips were tender and soft, and she felt her own ease in response as they fit together. Sweet and gentle. Pleasure sizzled through her as he shifted, parting his lips and nibbling on hers as if he had all the time in the world to explore her texture and the way they meshed.

The sensuality of his full, soft mouth, the quick, sleek swipe of tongue between her lips, had her closing her eyes and stifling a sigh of pleasure. Ana was no stranger to kissing handsome men, but it had been a while, and this was an exceptional kiss. She rested her hands on top of those immense shoulders, feeling the fluid shift of muscle there as he eased her feet back to the ground.

Their kiss broke gently then, as she steadied herself on her feet, his arms still comfortably around her. His eyes were dark with heat and pleasure, and his lips were even more full, glistening a bit from tasting hers.

"Well," he said. His voice, which was always very deep, seemed even deeper now. "You've gotten me to take off my shirt, and now you've got my knees fixing to give way. I don't know if that's what you had in mind, but it worked."

"I didn't have anything of the sort in mind," she said, and deftly extricated herself from his arms. Her own freaking knees were weak, and the eel burns on her torso ached from his grip. But she hadn't noticed that discomfort until now. She'd been distracted by the kiss.

"How about if I help you this time," he said as she prepared to mount up on Bruiser again.

"No, I don't—" but her words were cut off in a whoosh as he lifted her as if she were as light as Tanya, and plopped her right onto the saddle.

"It's not because of your leg, Ana," he said. His dark, velvety eyes were serious, but there was the underlying warmth of levity in his voice. "It's because I know your knees are shaking just as much as mine are."

"You don't know that," she said primly, gathering up the reins. But a smile twitched at the corners of her mouth. He was obnoxious, yet she couldn't resist his charm. It was okay to banter, wasn't it?

Just so long as he didn't get his hands up her shirt.

"Baby, I know women. And I can tell—that kiss pretty much knocked you off your feet."

Her appreciation of his charm evaporated and she drew in an outraged breath to tell him off, but he continued with a smooth sidewise wink and a long, slow drawl, "But that's okay. I'm not gonna make it any worse for you, sugar. At least, not right now. A gal can only take so much of Fence at a time when she ain't used to him."

CHAPTER 4

Ana was a prickly one, all right, with her long, sleek, golden body and sun-streaked hair. Prickly and crazy sexy: a great combination. Keep him on his toes while he was trying to get her on her back.

Fence wasn't ashamed to admit—at least to himself—that his knees were still shaky. He'd been the one making the moves, but she was the one whose kiss had thrown him so hard for a loop that he started talking about himself in third person, and with a hint of his grandma's southern.

Lordy, the last time he'd done that it had been with a Victoria's Secret model who'd wanted to go on one of On Tap's wilderness tours until she found out there might be snakes. Losing that gig had been the biggest disappointment of his career, and he and Lenny had moaned about it for a week.

But, hot damn, Ana'd looked *fine* walking out of the ocean like the chicks from those James Bond movies. Less like Halle Berry—though she was his personal favorite—and more like the other one, who also wore a knife around her waist. Ursula Andress. No, Ursula *Un*dress.

He chuckled aloud at that one, even though the joke was older than he was. Good thing Ana was on horseback, and just ahead of him on the way back to her house, or she probably would have wanted to know what was so funny.

If he could come up with an excuse to stay in Glenway for another day or two, see what other sort of heat he could stir up with the sun goddess, he might just hang around a bit longer.

But he couldn't take the risk. He needed to get back to Envy—just in case something went down. And aside from that, George had grown some penicillin that had to be delivered to Elliott before it rotted or went bad or something—which Fence wasn't quite clear on, because wasn't it mold anyway? And hadn't it grown from something old and rotted in the first place?

Although he loved math, chemistry was not his strong suit—except between a man and a woman, then he did just fine—so Fence figured he'd eat whatever Ana was going to cook for him and George . . . then he'd have to be on his way before night fell. At least on the trip back he'd have the memory of her sweet body with all those mad, hot curves sliding all along him to the ground.

And now he knew where to find her. How long did penicillin last, anyway? Surely Elliott would need more at some time in the near future.

By now Ana was climbing off her horse outside the little cottage she and her father shared, and Fence was walking up the low incline to the house. On the back of the weathered gray building was the laboratory, which once had been a semi-truck trailer. He'd seen the inside, and it was pretty amazing for a post-Apocalyptic world.

The house itself was one room, with a kitchen and living room taking up the lower level, along with a bathroom and, he presumed, two bedrooms on the upper level. His impression of the living space was of cluttered comfort, while the attached laboratory was pristine and neat. Nearly cold in its organization, with a great number of lights running on wind and solar power, the lab was nearly as large as the house.

Something else interesting, and a bit disturbing, he'd noticed while visiting with George—if you could call being the person carrying on a conversation with a guy whose nose was in a petri dish or his eyes clamped to a microscope the whole time "visiting." In one of the dishes there was some of that sparkly gray stuff they'd found on the shore in Envy, that first night he'd seen Ana.

The question was: Had George and/or Ana found their own sample of the stuff from somewhere else . . . or had Ana stolen some of it for her scientist father? And if it was the former, where had they found it? And had George figured out what it was? Or did they already know?

Now, watching Ana lead the horse into a third structure, which seemed to be a barn or stable, Fence saw no reason to hurry into the house when he could be admiring her tall, golden figure. Especially now that she'd changed into a different shirt—a close-fitting one—while in the stable, and was now carrying his T-shirt. Much more interesting than an absentminded, mildly socially confused professor-type guy.

She had to be at least six feet tall, which still put her four inches shorter than him, but not small enough that he'd feel like a damned gorgon next to her. Certainly not flimsy either—she had some good definition to her arms, and other than her messed-up leg, the rest of her was firm and toned. She looked like a girl who could hold her own anywhere from the wilderness to the kitchen to the bedroom.

"Coming?" Ana asked now, limping over to where he waited for her, near a patch of daisies and a tangle of wild grapes.

"Right behind you," he said, trying not to leer. Ogling wasn't good manners, his mama always said. But Ana did have a fine ass, and it *was* good manners to let the woman go first.

She gave him a withering glance, as if she knew exactly why he'd offered to follow, and he felt his eyes tighten at the corners as he smiled, meeting her gaze without shame. The woman should be flattered she had his attention magneted to her like that, he thought.

Then Anna went inside, and at her scream, his smile evaporated.

"What?" He bolted into the cottage and saw her kneeling by George, who was on the kitchen floor in an unmoving heap.

"Dad," she was saying, touching his face, patting it gently, giving his shoulders a shake. "Dad, wake up. *Dad!*"

Fence, who was not merely trained in first aid, but had also been licensed as an EMT as part of his guide services, eased down next to her and looked at the older man. George was breathing, albeit roughly, and his skin looked and felt clammy and tight, and it had a faint bluish cast beneath the gray. His pulse seemed normal, if a little fast, and his hands were cold. He had the beginning of a bump on the side of his head, probably from where he'd landed on the floor. Damn good thing it was hardwood and not stone.

Then George's eyes fluttered open and he looked up at them with a groggy expression. "Anastancie," he mumbled, and tried to sit. "What are you—"

"No you don't," she said firmly, sliding her arm beneath his shoulders to keep him off the hard floor. "Give it a minute, Dad." She looked up at Fence, and he saw fear settling in her eyes. "This is the third time in the last two weeks he's done this."

"I haven't *done* anything," George argued, but even Fence heard the weakness there. "Just got a little dizzy."

"So dizzy you took a swan dive onto your face? Again?"

"What happened?" asked Fence, gently palpating the older man's skull. A goose egg was forming, but it was a normal bump from a fall like this. "Before I get you somewhere more comfortable, I need to know: Do you hurt anywhere?"

"No," muttered George. "Not hurt, except my pride—"

Fence didn't wait any longer. He easily scooped up the older man, and before George could protest, deposited him carefully on the sofa. "Don't need to stay on the hard floor," he said as the man gave him a grimace.

Ana was at his side then, wedging a pillow under her father's head. "What happened, Dad?"

"I was just a little dizzy—that's all. Then the next thing I knew, I felt badly enough to try and sit down. I just didn't make it to a chair."

"How often have you been feeling this way?" asked Fence, closing his fingers around George's wrist to check for his pulse. Not too rapid, but definitely faster than normal. He didn't have a watch, and didn't see a clock anywhere, so he had to estimate timing and pulse count. He wished he had a blood pressure cuff.

"I feel a little faint maybe couple times a week. I don't pass out every time," he added defensively to Ana . . . then seemed to realize that wasn't necessarily a comforting statement.

She looked at Fence, who'd settled back on his haunches next to the couch so he didn't loom over his patient. "I don't know what to do about it," she said. "What if I didn't come back for a while, and there he was, on the floor all day or night?" Her face was lined with fear and indecision. "What if one time, he doesn't wake up? Or hits his head on something really hard or sharp?"

"I'm *fine*," George said. "I should have sat down, and I didn't. My mistake. I won't do it again." He pulled up to a sitting position and the pillow fell away. Ana patted the back of his hand, and Fence noticed that her skin was much darker than her father's—likely from the hours spent in the sun.

Yet, father and daughter shared quite a bit of resemblance: their body shapes—on him, tall and lanky; on her sleek and slender—the same light brown eyes with amber and green flecks, the same thick, wavy hair. On George it was a full head of brown turning to gray, and on Ana it was long and rippling.

"Gotta tell you," Fence said in the calm voice he used in everything from talking down a woman—or man—who'd found a black widow in his or her tent, to coaxing a suddenly claustrophobic client through the very tight channels of the Bitch, to explaining that, yes, there was a chance of getting seriously injured on a climb up Havasu. "You know, I think you should have the situation checked out. I've got some medical training," he continued—and realized that was probably a foreign concept to these post-Change people—"but my friend Elliott, who I'm taking your penicillin to, would be able to tell you exactly what's causing the problem. So you know whether it's something serious," he said, glancing at Ana, "or something like you just aren't getting enough iron in your diet. Or your blood pressure's down or something."

"Your friend Elliott? Back in Envy?" Ana said.

Fence nodded. "Fainting spells like this could mean anything from low blood pressure to heart problems to a bunch of other things—both minor and serious. I don't have the expertise or the tools to diagnose it further, but Dred will."

"Dred?"

He grinned. "Yeah. Elliott's nickname is as ridiculous as mine. It stands for Dr. E. Drake. D-R-E-D."

"I don't have time to go to Envy," grumbled George. "I've got things growing back there in the lab and—"

"We're going to Envy, Dad," Ana said firmly. "We've got to find out what's wrong with you. And besides," she added with a gleam in her eye, "I'm sure you and Elliott would have a lot to talk about regarding your experiments."

Fence winked at Ana. *Good play, sugar.* "We can leave first thing in the morning. Shouldn't be more than a couple days. Now . . . did you say something about dinner?"

"I might have," she replied, giving him a smile. He sensed her relief as they both stood, but before she could say anything else, there was a knock at the door.

"Ana?" came a cheery voice, and the door cracked open to reveal Yvonne's face poking around in a nimbus of golden hair. "I hope you haven't started dinner—"

She must have caught sight of George on the sofa, for her smile wavered. "Is everything all right?"

"Come on in," Ana said. "Dad just did another of his face-plants on the floor. We're taking him to Envy tomorrow to have him looked at." Despite her light words, Fence heard a faint strain of worry in her tone.

"*He's* here, Mommy," came a stage whisper. Tanya peeked around the edge of the door. Her hair, now that it was dry, was just as full and sunny as her mother's.

"I haven't started dinner yet, but was just thinking about it," Ana replied with a glance toward the kitchen.

"Well, don't. Pete and I decided we need a little celebration tonight, since everything turned out all right today. You and George, and of course you have to come too," she added, looking at Fence with an embarrassed smile. "And—oh heavens, I just realized I never thanked you for helping to track down Tanya," she added, clearly mortified. She stepped into the room, moving directly toward him. "And I don't even know your name! Ana told me if it weren't for you following her trail, we might not have found Tanya . . . in time—" Her voice choked, but she was still smiling.

"He *made* me fall in!" Tanya said, stamping her foot for emphasis. "He said I was gonna fall—and then I *did*." She'd come to stand half in, half out, with the doorjamb bisecting her right down the middle . . . except for her face. Both of her big brown eyes were visible and fixed on him.

Fence gave a soft, deep laugh, but inside his middle churned. He did not want to think about what had almost happened out there in that quarry today and how close he'd been to another tragedy. Instead, he focused on the little girl, who was about as cute as could be with her wild blond hair, hands on hips, and tapping foot. He'd always suspected females learned that stance at a very young age.

"That wasn't very nice of me, was it?" he asked Tanya, crouching so he was closer to her level. "Will you accept my apology if I make it an awesomely crazy mushy one?"

"What's a awesomely crazy mushy 'pology like?" she asked, moving into the doorway to stand fully visible, hands on hips.

"We-ell . . . it starts with a few pushes on that swing out there . . . and then it goes to a little bit of Mother, May I—and you'd be the mother . . . and then I'm fixing to show you how I followed your trail, so you can track things yourself."

"Ten pushes—no, *twenty* pushes on the swing. Super high. Without stopping to rest or fold clothes or cook dinner like Mommy always does. And you have to push my friend Carter too. I don't know what Mother, May I is, but if it's good, I'll do it. Carter can be the dad. You can be the child. If not, you have to think of another game. And it has to have running and jumping in it. And then you have to show me how to track a horse. And how are you going to fix showing me something?"

"Whoa . . . you're letting me off too easy," Fence said, swallowing a chuckle at her last question. "That's a deal!"

"I'll go get Carter!" And Tanya was gone in a flash.

Aware that Ana and Yvonne had been watching the whole interplay, he stood and turned back to them as he noticed that George had disappeared. "I'm Fence, by the way," he said to Yvonne. "I don't think I told you my name earlier—but you were a little distracted. Understandably so," he added with a smile when she started to speak, still obviously embarrassed at what she felt was a breach of manners.

"Thank you again," Yvonne said. "And I do hope you'll join us—I was thinking of a barbecue in front of our house and we could watch the sun go down on the beach with a little fire." She turned to Ana. "I was thinking of asking the Lucks and Davises too."

"Sounds great. I'll rummage around and bring over something to share," Ana said. "See you in a few."

After Yvonne left, Fence watched as Ana got busy in the kitchen, poking through cupboards and opening a refrigerator that had seen better days.

That was the thing about post-Change appliances: they existed, but they needed to be well-cared-for and maintained. He could tell that the door of this fridge wasn't its original one.

"Can I give you a hand?" he asked, looking around the cozy, cluttered space. "I'm good at chopping things up."

A few drawings decorated the walls: the little cottage surrounded by sprays of bright flowers, a group of young girls playing jump rope—one of them looked like Tanya—and a cozy still life of a table set for three with fat red apples, a wedge of cheese, and a bowl of grapes. On a long side table in the dining room, a wooden bowl held a starfish and the delicate white fan of coral. Someone obviously liked the sea, for there were also a few shells, some driftwood, and a small framed picture of a dark-haired woman with Ana's smile.

"That would be great, thanks," Ana said, and moments later gave him the tools to cut up a small pile of vegetables.

As he began to work, Fence realized with a sharp

pang that he hadn't been in such a comfortably domestic environment since coming out of the Sedona cave. He felt a wave of nostalgia and grief for times past, for sitting in his mama's or sisters' kitchens as they bustled about preparing or cleaning up a meal, often nagging him into helping. Or even in his own kitchen, in the little bungalow he rented at the foot of a small hill, as he slapped together a burger and salad for him and Lenny and whichever other friends happened to be around. He wished for a glass of water to ease his suddenly dry throat, and opted for a few strawberries instead.

"So who did the drawings?" he asked as he began on a cucumber.

"On the wall? I did," Ana replied, her back to him as she washed something at the sink. He didn't mind, because he had a great view.

"I like them. You have talent," he added, slipping a cool slice of cuke into his mouth too. He hadn't realized how hungry he was, and he could already smell something cooking outside. "Is that your mom?"

"Yes."

"I can see where you get your looks," Fence said, pausing to admire the drawing. The face gazing back at him gave off an impression of both serenity and strength. "Where is she now?"

"She died. About twelve years ago."

It struck him sharply then, that photographs were now a thing of the past—something people of his time had taken for granted, snapping pictures and videos on everything from their cell phones to computers to digital cameras. It had been so easy to capture an image, save a memory or a moment, that he'd taken it for granted. He'd hardly ever even uploaded the photos from his phone to computer, and never printed them off, knowing they'd always be there. But in this age, that wasn't an option. And he bemoaned the fact that his phone had been smashed during the earthquakes—and along with it, all of the pictures of his loved ones.

"You drew that twelve years ago? Or from memory?" Realizing that, he was even more impressed with her talent.

Ana was washing some dishes, and she turned as she dried a plate. She looked over at the image, her features softening. "I did it shortly after she died. So a little of both."

"Like I said, you're very talented." He picked up a tomato and began to slice it. "What happened to her?"

"Mamya got sick, and she never got better. She knew she was going to die, and I was fortunate in the sense that we had a few months to . . . to say goodbye. We talked a lot, spent as much time together as we could. I still miss her." Her voice had gone low, and she turned back to the sink as if to cut off her memories.

"You were fortunate you had time to spend with her before she passed," he said as a little ache settled over his heart. He blinked hard, then was rescued when the front door flew open.

"We're here!" Tanya announced, bursting into the room. She was followed by a boy about her age, a bit taller than she was, with skin almost as dark as Fence's and an Afro the likes of which he hadn't seen since *That '70s Show.* "Time for you to fix our awesomely crazy 'pology. Remember, you said twenty pushes *each* without stopping."

Fence looked up at Ana, who'd turned from the sink with a bemused smile. "Sorry about that," he said, bringing the knife and vegetables back to her. He could smell her sunny, fresh scent over the tang of garlic and onion. Both smelled delicious, but it was Ana for whom he had a sudden, sharp craving. He was suddenly horribly thankful that George had had a fainting spell. "Gotta run. Duty calls."

"By all means, you'd better go," Ana told him with a smile. "You have to pay your dues."

Fence grinned back and followed his little charges out the door, particularly pleased that the sun goddess's smile seemed to have grown even warmer.

"He's the one, isn't he?" Yvonne said, leaning closer so she could hiss in Ana's ear.

Not that anyone could hear what she was saying anyway—the small celebration had grown quite enthusiastic now that a few bottles of mead had been opened and the sun was beginning to set. No one worried about zombies here because this little settlement was surrounded by ocean on two sides, and the ravines on the other two sides were deep enough so zombies couldn't climb them, but easy enough for a man to traverse, using wooden stairs. Tanya had gone beyond the ravines earlier today, for the stairs weren't closed off except at night.

"He's the guy you told me about, you met in Envy?" Yvonne persisted.

"What exactly did I say?" Ana asked. She didn't remember telling Yvonne any such thing.

"Maybe it was Susie who mentioned it—that some sweltering guy had been hitting on you while you were there with her last week. Is this the guy?"

"Well, we did meet, and talk a little bit," Ana admitted. She sipped from her glass of mead, enjoying the sweet taste. It was Pete's specialty, the fermented honey, and everyone in Glenway looked forward to sampling each new batch. He'd added blackberries to this one, and that made it not quite as heavily cloying as the honey drink could be. It had been going down very smoothly, and she felt loose and warm.

"You talked a little bit? That's it?" Yvonne was saying. "Ana, really. Envy's not that far away—only a day and a half. Maybe two. You've got to give it a chance. I know things didn't work out with Darian, but that doesn't mean that every guy's a gorm. I mean, look at Pete."

Ana nodded absently. Although Yvonne was her closest friend, even she didn't know the whole story about Ana's past, or about Darian. Nor did she know why Ana could never fully trust anyone, let alone settle into the domestic life she so envied Yvonne.

Trying not to be obvious, Ana looked around, wondering where Fence had gone off to. He'd been over there a little while ago, sitting with Pete, John Luck, John's brother Greg, and Randall Davis. They'd been deep in conversation about something—but Ana hadn't been able to hear more than a few phrases about "halfbacks" and "quarterbacks" and "first downs."

"He's completely sweltering," Yvonne said. "And he's *tall*, Ana. Way taller than you—I was noticing it back in your house. His head nearly brushed the ceiling. Look how great he was with Tanya. And Pete thinks he's really funny too," she added, as if that were the deciding factor. "Plus Greg Luck's been giving him the evil eye all evening. I told you, you could do so much better than Greg."

Ana nearly spewed out a mouthful of mead, and she spun a horrified look at Yvonne. Half choking on her drink, she coughed and swallowed and managed to say, "Greg? You know damn well I have no—" Then she saw that Yvonne was laughing, and she rolled her eyes and nudged her friend with a sharp elbow as they both dissolved into mead-induced giggles.

"Hey, will you look at that?" Yvonne said suddenly, ending on a little girlish snort.

Ana looked over and saw Tanya, Carter, and two of the other kids crawling along the ground. They were in the area where the clearing met the wilderness, and they seemed to be searching for something in the tall grass.

"What are you doing, Tanya?" called Yvonne.

"Tracking a bear," her daughter replied absently. And then she squealed and pointed. "There!" All three of her companions dove to the ground, putting their noses right where she indicated. "A track! A bear track! I found it!"

"A *bear*?" Yvonne said, her voice squeaking with shock and concern.

"An' there's a broken stick, right where he stepped," said Carter, leaping onto something a bit farther into the tall grass. "He musta gone this way."

"Come on," said Tanya, disappearing behind a clump of bushes. "Let's find him! This way!"

Ana and Yvonne looked at each other and got to their feet. Yvonne was frowning as she headed toward the thin wooded area where the kids had disappeared. Their voices were still intelligible as they announced new finds and tracks, and then all of a sudden, the air was filled with a roar . . . followed by squeals and screams.

It took Ana only a moment to recognize that the roar was human and obviously fake, and then that the children were giggling and laughing—that their screams were of delight and surprise, not fear.

She started laughing. "It's Fence. He's the bear," she told Yvonne. "They were tracking him!"

And sure enough, moments later the four laughing and shouting children came tearing back into the clearing with a big, growling man lumbering bearlike behind them.

"We found you! We found you!" Tanya chanted, dancing around in jubilation.

"That you did," Fence said, and as he crouched down to talk to the kids, he happened to glance over at Ana.

Their eyes met, he smiled, and she felt her insides tumble into something soft.

Oh shit. I think I might be in trouble.

She didn't even dare look at Yvonne.

CHAPTER 5

The water rushed over his face, filling his mouth and nose, coming and coming and *coming*. He twisted and fought, desperate . . . choking . . . but it surged, fast and cold, rushing relentlessly, stronger and harder.

He couldn't breathe.

Water filled him, pummeled and beat into him as the world darkened.

At last, with a desperate gasp, Fence dragged himself free, bursting from the dream into wakefulness. Relief.

He lay there for a moment, shaking, his breathing rough and too quick, his heart ramming in his chest.

It took him a minute to remember where he was . . . and then the moonlit sight of a pencil drawing of three girls playing jump rope reminded him. On the too-short sofa in Ana's little cottage.

His fingers curled into the quilt, his eyes gaping wide, and he swore softly. *Fuck.* Hoped he hadn't been too loud. He should have slept out under the stars on a pallet like he'd planned to, instead of taking Ana up on the offer of her sofa. The last thing he wanted to do was explain his nightmares to her or her father.

Sonofabitch.

Even now that he was awake, his eyes open and his heart slamming, he had to fight to stay out of the dream. It still tugged at him, trying to drag him back under like the same rush that had nearly drowned him twice.

No. Make that three times now.

Fence knew he'd be unable to fall back asleep tonight . . . and he didn't want to, even if he could. Today's episode in the water—the first time he'd been in water for years—was too fresh and raw. He knew the nightmares would return as soon as he eased back into sleep.

Silently, he slid from the sofa, tossing the quilt on it, and padded on catlike feet to the window. The moon was waxing, just about to half size, and the stars were amazing—like a swath of glittering lace.

He never got tired of seeing the beauty of the night sky—so much cleaner and clearer than what he'd known before. There was Mars, not in the place he should have been for November, but in his new position now that the Earth had changed her tilt. And the North Star . . . not quite as north as she used to be, but cocked a bit more to the east.

Down and just beyond the cottage walkway, Fence saw the sea, heard its churning as it surged onto the shore; inky black and murderous except for a shimmering path lit by the moon. The familiar tightening began in his chest, followed by the ripple of panic in his belly, and he swore violently in his head, furious with himself. Mortified.

The very sight of water turned him into a mess. Even from this distance. The smell of the sea, the sound of the rush of waves on the shore of a lake or even the tumbling of water over rapids . . . all of it brought back the terror, paralyzing him.

Hell, when he was in the shower, with the water hitting him in the face, he got a little freaked out sometimes. His jaw tightened.

What the fuck kind of woman would understand *that*?

How a guy like him could be such a goddamn pussy?

The first time had been when he was seventeen. He and a buddy, Brian, were swimming in the lake. Both of them excellent swimmers, with no fear of the water at all. To this day he couldn't understand how it happened, but Brian got in trouble. Caught up in something or got a cramp or whatever . . . and so of course he had gone to save his friend's ass.

But Brian, like most drowning people, was beyond panic. Big and strong—bigger than even Fence—he grabbed onto him and they got tangled up, Brian's hands digging into Fence's head as he desperately tried to climb up over him to get out of the water. That pushed Fence down, down, where he couldn't move or breathe. It was dark and cold and Brian was on top of him, grabbing blindly, clinging, climbing, kicking, scratching . . . and Fence couldn't hold his breath any longer, he couldn't pull free . . .

The memory, like its accompanying dream, overwhelmed him now, and all at once, he was back in the center of that deep, dark lake, feeling his lungs ready to burst and the water pressing in on him, twisting and fighting with his friend. Fence had finally been released, finally dragged free and onto shore by someone who knew life-guarding techniques.

Brian had died, and Fence nearly did too. And so began his nightmares.

If he could have done it differently, if he'd been stronger, smarter, faster . . . But no.

Brian was gone.

The second time was six years later. After Brian drowned, Fence never got over his terror of swimming, the sense of helplessness. But he reluctantly agreed to join a group from his old Boy Scout troop on a white-water rafting trip. It would be fine, he told himself. He'd wear a life jacket, they'd be in kayaks, and there was a guide. He was going to prove once and for all that he was over his phobia. For God's sake, a big strong guy like him? Even his four-year-old niece didn't hesitate to jump into the lake in water over her head.

Plus he wouldn't even have to get into the water except to wash his hands or portage. It was time he got over this ridiculous fear.

Wrong.

God or the devil surely had it in for him, because halfway through the trip, Fence's kayak hit a bad spot in the rapids and he flipped out of the boat. The water was deep enough so he didn't slam into rocks beneath, but it also tumbled him downstream a mile or two. Even that might not have turned him into the basket case he now was, except that as he went over one of the rushing falls, his life jacket caught on a submerged branch and he got suspended there, twisted and caught on his back and unable to get free.

And all the while, the water rushed over his face, over his nose and mouth in great, violent surges as he struggled to right himself or pull up on the slippery rocks. It was like being waterboarded, he told Lenny later. *No wonder they call it torture.*

He was only trapped that way for five minutes, or so he was told, but that was all it took. Five minutes of struggling to breathe through a rush of water, ebbing and flowing with a chance for air, all the while pummeling him into sharp rocks beneath his back and thighs, and he was done.

Stick a motherfucking fork into him.

He was never going in or near water again.

And he hadn't . . . until today.

And even then, he'd been as incompetent and cowardly as possible. Nearly had another tragedy on his hands.

Fence swore again, acid rising in the back of his throat. *What the hell is wrong with me?*

Lenny had understood, though. He'd been with him on the kayak trip and saw what Fence had gone through. They'd even talked about it, about the irrationality of his fears, about Fence's guilt for being unable to save Brian . . . and Lenny didn't even look at him funny. But Fence felt as if he were half a man. As if he wore the big-ass flaw on his forehead like a brand.

"We've all got something," Lenny had said, wisdom burning in his eyes as he clasped Fence's wrist with a heartfelt squeeze. "We've all got something."

And now, here he was: a damned survivalist in an overgrown world . . . who couldn't wade up to his knees without turning into an infant.

And, fuck it all . . . he felt himself flush as he stood at the window, the gentle sea breeze cool against his bare chest. Ana had seen him afterward . . . what the hell she must think of him, puking his guts out after staggering out from a little pool like that. Unable to pull an eight-year-old girl to safety. He squeezed his eyes shut and shook his head. *So much for the sun goddess.*

Sure, she let him kiss her on the beach afterward—and what a crazy kiss that had been!—but that was just him seizing the convenience of the moment. That was the sort of thing he *did*.

And, true, they'd had that cozy domestic moment in her kitchen . . . and there was the way their eyes met when he was playing Track the Bear with the kids, the sizzle and warmth that came with it, but . . . *fuck*.

A smart, beautiful woman like Ana would want the whole package from a guy . . . and he didn't have it to give to her.

After their sassy exchange and that sweltering kiss on the beach in Glenway, Ana couldn't help but be surprised that Fence had taken her offer of the sofa that night without making any overtures—serious or joking—toward anything else. Not even a hint at a good-night kiss after several glasses of mead.

Not that she would have accepted the offer . . . but still. He could have *made* it. Or at least hinted around or joked about it.

Was it possible he'd . . . not liked kissing her? Or that her messed-up leg grossed him out?

Not that it mattered, except to her pride. It was a matter of self-preservation to keep him at arm's length and herself fully clothed.

As they started off for Envy, Fence seemed serious and almost remote.

He hardly spoke directly to her at all as he guided them along the long, wide expanse of an old highway. There was little left of the original concrete other than random islands of cement with a river of grass, brush, debris, and trees flowing around it. A few old signs indicated that it was either Highway 309 or 809.

She rode Bruiser, of course, for she could never have made the trip on foot. And Dad had his own mount, which she insisted he ride—despite his arguments to the contrary.

"There isn't any sense in making whatever is going on with you worse," she argued back. "If Elliott says there isn't anything wrong with you, then you can walk back to Glenway if it makes you feel better."

Dad had griped and complained, but he swung his lanky frame up onto the saddle and argued no further on that topic. Instead, he focused his compulsive attention on the safety and stability of the vials and bottles and little dishes he was transporting to Envy—a sampling of his experiments that he didn't want to leave unattended during his absence. Ana was glad to leave him to it.

She tried not to worry about what was wrong with her father, and whether this Elliott person would be able to help him. He'd have to do an examination of her father, of course, but there was nothing for him to find, like the energizing gems that were embedded in her own body. When they all lived with the Atlanteans, he'd hardly ventured from their protective island and into the sea, and therefore didn't need crystals to breathe . . . at least until they made their escape. Then his deficit turned out to be almost fatal, and had cost her the use of her leg as well as much of his memory of their life in Atlantis.

That happened more than twelve years ago, but she had no illusions that her mother's family had stopped searching for them. Ana shivered, remembering that terrible, whirlwind of a night so soon on the tail of her mother's death . . . and brought her attention back to the present.

Only Fence traveled on foot, but he moved along at a steady pace, seemingly tireless. She and Dad kept their horses at a comfortable walk, and whenever they stopped to rest—which, in secret deference to her parent, was often—Fence would go on ahead and scout out the way.

Even as they traveled, he often stopped to listen, to sniff the air, to climb up onto an old car or pile of debris and look into the distance. He pointed out where an elephant mother and her kid had crashed through the brush, and a spot beneath a low, wide tree where a small pack of wild dogs had slept. He identified black raspberries, wild corn, tangled cucumber vines, and edible mushrooms. Even a patch of potatoes in one unlikely spot near an old house. He held up a hand once, lifting a shushing finger to his lips, and pointed to a wild peacock wooing his nondescript female.

Ana knew she would never have seen or recognized any of those things had she been traveling with anyone else. It gave her a new appreciation for a part of the world she took for granted in favor of her beloved Sea . . . and a greater appreciation for the man with them.

When they left the remains of the highway and began to traverse rougher terrain, Fence led them across a long, open area with a big white pole at one end. Behind the pole was an old electronic sign, long corroded and weathered. Off to one side was a massive, twisted metal object.

"This used to be a football field," Fence told them, pausing for a moment. "That white post at the end is the goal—the top's broken off. It used to look like a wide, flat Y. Over there used to be the bleachers, where everyone sat." He pointed to the rusty, rickety framework of metal that resembled a tall, wide set of steps.

Ana could see it now that he filled in the missing images, remembering scenes from DVDs that featured football games. She recognized a note of sadness in Fence's voice and looked at him curiously. He stood there, looking up and down the field, which now sported grassy moguls and low-rising shrubs.

Then, as if shaking himself from some nostalgic spin, Fence started walking again. "We'll stop for the night in about an hour," he said, but his voice seemed unusually low and rough. "There's a place up yonder that's in good shape, with a place for the horses."

Sometime later, when they'd settled for the evening in a dilapidated house, he said, "I'm fixing to keep watch tonight." He glanced at the small fire she'd started in an old sink. Smoke wafted out the broken window above it, and beyond, the sun had set and the world was cast in shadows. "The both of you can sleep."

"What are you keeping watch for?" Ana asked, unpacking the satchel of food she'd prepared. "The zombies can't climb the stairs to get up here."

"Could be anything. Wildcats or coyotes. Or feral dogs. Other intruders."

"Oh," she replied, reminding herself that the cries and howls she heard while safely in Glenway could just as easily be from lurking cougars or wolves. And then she shivered—for when she and her friend had made their recent trip to Envy, they hadn't had anyone in their party of six keep watch at night.

Then she realized what he'd said: *other intruders.* Like . . . other people?

"That looks good," Fence said, wandering over to the package of flaky, grilled tuna she'd just unwrapped. "Do you need some help?"

Ana shook her head. "No, I've got it."

She thought he might sit down on the dusty chair whose upholstery had long been chewed or rotted away—but he didn't. Instead, he took the tuna, wrapped in a pieced of flat, floppy bread she offered, and wandered around the space, checking out each window. What was he looking for?

Or who?

They were just finishing up the meal when Fence made an urgent sound and turned from the window. "Put the fire out. Now."

Before she could react, he was hurrying across the room to put down the rickety ladderlike steps they'd climbed then pulled up after them. "Stay here," he said. "And out of sight of the window. I've got to hide the horses."

Ana had already thrown a blanket over the small fire, and now she gaped at him. "What—"

But he was gone, smooth and silent and quick—leaving her prickly and nervous. She exchanged glances with George, who'd looked up from his ever-present notebook.

"Probably a wolf or something," her father muttered, then returned to his notes.

But she didn't think so. She eased to the side of the window where Fence had stood and peered into the darkness.

At first she saw nothing out of the ordinary. But then she heard an unfamiliar rumbling in the distance, and at the same moment noticed a pair of lights, low to the ground, just beyond a low rising hill.

At first she didn't believe her eyes . . . but as it continued to roll along, and she heard the sound of a motor coming closer, she agreed with her first assessment.

It was a vehicle.

Fence slipped out onto the grass and edged along the ivy-covered brick wall. There wasn't much he could do to keep the horses from whuffling and snorting, but leading them deep inside an old storage room in what had been a small office building was the best he could do to muffle any noise they might make.

There was no reason to think that the Strangers or their bounty hunters—for no one else had access to motorized vehicles—would stop at this particular building out of all of the overgrown ones in this former suburban town, but Fence was of the mind that a guy couldn't ever be too careful. Ana had reacted quickly to douse the flames, and it was unlikely that the golden flicker or smoke had been seen by whoever was driving the car.

Fence took off in the direction he'd seen the headlights, cat-footed and quick through bristling trees, over rises and down falls and around lumps of debris. His senses were attuned not only to the brief flashes of light in the distance, but also to the environment: for everything from approaching predatory animals to zombies . . . to the scent or sounds of water. The last thing he was about to do was take a dive into some sort of pool or river.

He knew it was a long shot that he might catch up to the vehicle, or even that it would continue in the direction it had been going, but he figured he'd take the chance. He wasn't about to miss the opportunity to eavesdrop or spy on them.

It was difficult enough to drive on rough terrain and over nonexistent roads during the daylight, but nearly impossible to do so without breaking an axle or blowing out a tire in the dark. Therefore, he reasoned, they'd likely have to stop soon.

The low rumble of what was most likely a Humvee broke the silence of the night, and from the revving sounds and the ebb and flow of the noise, Fence could tell which direction it was going. He adjusted and his heart began to thump as he realized the truck was slowing . . . perhaps stopping.

That could be good, if he could get close enough to hear what was going on.

Fence picked up his pace and then halted, pressing up against the prickling bark of a tree when he saw a sleek feline shadow sauntering through the overgrowth. Among other things, he always carried a knife—but never liked to use it . . . and when the panther didn't do more than skim over him with its yellow-green eyes and then go on her way, he breathed a sigh of relief. He'd tangled with a wolf once, handheld blade to teeth and claw, and walked away the winner . . . but he hadn't enjoyed the victory in the least. He was a lover, not a fighter.

He grinned to himself in the dark.

Fence heard the rumbling louder now, and then a little creak, and then silence. The sound of a door slamming, then another. Low voices.

Yes.

Fence cast a quick glance to make sure the panther hadn't circled back around, then eased forward, moving like a shadow himself from tree to collapsed house to overgrown car.

The sound of water streaming onto the ground made him halt for a moment, and turning clammy, until he realized one of the men was taking a piss . . . about twenty feet away, on the other side of a fallen tree. From the sounds of it, dude had either been drinking heavily or it had been a long time since they'd made a pit stop. A really long time.

"Ready?" came a distant voice.

"Just a minute," the one closest to Fence called back, still in the throes of his evacuation.

Crashing in the bushes heralded the approach of the one farther away, and Fence crouched deeper in the shadows when he saw a silhouette shift in the distance.

Meanwhile, the first guy was *still* pissing.

"You almost done?" said the new arrival.

"Yeah," he replied.

"Christ on a crutch, what's taking you so damn long, Graves?"

"Takin' a piss," Graves replied, and the sounds of streaming water trailed off . . . only to start up again. Fence couldn't help chuckle silently. Dude could water the world if he kept going like that.

"Roofey's gonna *be* pissed if we ain't at the meeting place on time. He's all whacked out about finding this Quent guy before he figures things out. My bet's on him being in Envy."

"What're we gonna do—just walk in there and ask for him?"

"I told you—we don't even need to see him, Graves. Just make sure he's there—ask around, whatever, and then let nature take its course. That'll make things a lot more convenient—take care of both at the same time."

At last the streaming trailed off, gave a few spurts, then there was the rustling of clothing and the metal clink of a belt being rebuckled. "What if he's not there?"

"We'll keep looking. We'll find him," the second guy said. "But it really doesn't matter." His voice was lower, as if he'd turned around, and there was a whole lot of crashing in the brush as they walked away.

Fence strained to hear over the noise, easing out after them slowly and oh-so-silently.

"Why not?" Graves said, his words muffled a bit.

"Roofey told me that Kaddick said in a few weeks there won't be an Envy for that Quent bastard to hide inside anyway."

CHAPTER 6

Seventy miles away...

Remington Truth looked down at her bright-eyed, hundred-pound German shepherd dog and said, "Sit, Dantès."

His butt plopped to the ground, of course, and he looked up at her as if she were a goddess—which, Remy supposed, she was, at least in his eyes—and she bent down to hug him.

He was her best friend. Her only friend. Her guardian and savior and the only creature on this mangled earth that she could trust.

They were safely behind the walls of what had been the large estate of a computer and electronics genius before the Change, and deep in the privacy of small clusters of trees and bushes that littered the ten-acre grounds. Remy had taken Dantès far from the house, where too many people (four) lived for her own safety and comfort—although Selena and Theo and the others had been nothing but kind to her.

Perhaps even more than kind, particularly since she

wasn't being completely honest or forthcoming with them. Things had been more than a little complicated since she'd come to Yellow Mountain, a settlement about three miles from the old estate that was Selena's home, and the place she used as a hospice. Selena was known as the Death Lady, for she had a gift for assisting people through their last days of pain and into the afterlife, and she had met Theo Waxnicki when he showed up, nearly dead himself.

Now, what began as a brief show of approval for Dantès's perfect obedience became a longer, more desperate embrace as she crouched in the grass. Remy's eyes stung a bit at the corners and she tried to thrust away the memories.

But they came, fast and hard and dark, as they often did: the strong hands, the sneer of Seattle's mouth, his lips flat and curled back in a feral show of power, the harsh jolting of her body as her clothing was torn away. Cool air on her bare skin.

And the pain.

She squeezed her eyes shut, swallowed back the burning nausea. Dantès seemed to sense that his mistress was in distress, for he gave a soft, sad whine and twisted his head away to lick her nose and chin. Then he found the salty trail down her cheek and kissed it thoroughly away.

"Thank you, good boy," she whispered into his comforting fur. "Thank you for finding me."

She could hardly imagine what she would be doing now, what would be happening to her, if Dantès hadn't found her scent and come after her.

She'd been chained to the front axle of Seattle's vehicle, bruised, bloody, stunned and aching from his most recent assault. Her captor had been about to drive off with her beneath, dragging her over the rough terrain, when Dantès burst into the clearing. The dog had gone through the open truck window, grabbed Seattle by the throat with his lethal fangs, and ripped.

The bounty hunter named Seattle was no longer a threat to Remy . . . or to anyone.

If only it had just been Dantès who'd found her.

But, no. He'd had to bring those men from Envy. The ones who'd discovered her identity after Remy had successfully hidden for almost twenty years.

Now she was in a predicament.

Still recovering from the assault and beatings from Seattle, Remy wasn't quite ready to take her leave from this small settlement. She might be stubborn, but she wasn't stupid: she knew she had to heal, to get her bearings, and then to figure out what she was going to do and how she would survive on her own again.

And now that Ian—the bounty hunter who'd been her reluctant partner and sometimes lover—was presumably dead, no one other than the men from Envy knew that she was the granddaughter of the infamous Remington Truth.

The man whom the Strangers had been seeking since the Change.

The man who'd given her the small crystal she wore at her navel to keep it hidden and safe, who told her to guard it with her life.

Thank God neither Ian nor Seattle had recognized it for what it was.

Not that Remy herself had any idea what it was. She just knew her grandfather had told her it was important, and to keep it safe. *You'll know what to do with it when the time comes.*

Yeah, right.

"Dantès!"

The masculine voice had the dog's ears snapping up into full triangular attention, and to her annoyance, and—let's face it—hurt feelings, Dantès pulled to his feet even as Remy's arms remained around his neck.

She could feel him battling inside: wanting to stay with his adored mistress, with whom he'd lived and traveled for more than five years, and desiring to answer the siren call of another master.

"Dantès!" the voice called again, much closer now.

Remy tightened her grip in a brief, last bid to keep her only comfort to herself, then let him go. She'd decided it was a better balm to her hurt if she released him before he actually broke free.

Dantès nearly trampled her in his haste to go, and just then the man appeared from behind a cluster of bushes.

"Oh, Remy," Wyatt said. He stopped short, as if he'd slammed into a wall.

Why would he be surprised to see her, *with her own dog?*

Whatever else he might have said, or meant to say, was lost as he crouched down to receive his personal greeting from the fickle canine, who wriggled and whined and kiss-licked the new arrival.

Crouched there on the ground, they were all about eye-level with each other: man, woman, and dog.

The man, Remy had noticed more than once, was tall, well-built, and sturdy. He had dark hair in dire need of a cut, for it dipped and waved around his face and neck, nearly in his eyes and well past his collar. His dark brown eyes were most always flat and cold. The only time she'd ever seen them soften was when he was with Dantès, and, very occasionally, when he and the Waxnicki brothers were laughing about something.

He was good-looking enough in a rugged sort of way, though not nearly as handsome as Ian or Elliott. He might be more attractive if he smiled once in awhile, instead of always looking as if he were coldly disappointed with the world.

But, hell. She probably appeared the same way.

Smiles were inviting.

Remy pulled to her feet, standing over her traitorous companion and the man he was worshiping. She supposed she shouldn't begrudge Dantès his affection for Wyatt, nor the man's never-ending attention to her dog.

Because, after all, if they hadn't bonded so closely when she fled after being discovered by Wyatt and his friends, Dantès wouldn't have been around to scent and save her from Seattle.

Even though she'd had to throw a snake at the man when he was trying to keep her from running away from Envy, the fact was, he'd taken good care of Dantès during her absence.

By now Wyatt had located a fat stick and was showing it to the eager dog. Dantès looked so beautiful, standing there, his fur practically quivering with excitement, his eyes steady and his tongue completely contained as he waited for his favorite activity to begin. Remy was suddenly overwhelmed with love for him, and annoyed anew that his affection seemed divided.

The stick whipped through the air and the dog was off, leaving the two humans alone.

"Nice night," he said.

Remy looked around and realized it was, indeed, heading toward night. The sun had dipped below the walls of the estate. "It is," she agreed.

"How are you doing?" Wyatt asked. He'd stood to throw the stick and now looked down at her.

"I'm fine," she replied. As she always did when he asked.

"Any bad dreams lately?"

Remy's shoulders stiffened. "Not any more than usual," she replied, just as Dantès crashed back through the brush.

He dropped the stick and his tail wagged furiously as he waited for someone to throw it.

Remy and Wyatt both crouched at the same time, and narrowly missed clunking heads as they reached for it in tandem. He snatched his hand back immediately, allowing her the honor of picking up the stick. Dantès went rigid with expectancy.

"Theo and Lou got a message from Quent over the computer network," Wyatt said. "Elliott made it back to Envy all right."

Why you didn't go with him, I wish I knew. She winged the stick into the sparse woods with far less velocity and distance than Wyatt had.

"Thanks for letting me know." She was, nevertheless, sincere.

Since this whole debacle had started almost six months ago when her calm, simple life in RedLo had been disrupted by the arrival of Wyatt, Theo Waxnicki, and another man named Quent, she'd found herself most appreciative of Elliott's kind and easy demeanor.

Of course, she had needed his doctoring more than once. And he'd been so gentle and caring after Wyatt pulled her out from under Seattle's truck.

Dantès returned and Remy allowed Wyatt to toss the stick this time. The dog took off like a shot.

"You never did say what you were doing with Ian Marck," Wyatt said abruptly. His eyes settled on her, and he didn't even try to hide his suspicion.

"No, I never did." Remy was aware of her heart thumping madly. She wished she had another reptile—or something worse—to throw at him.

"So."

"So what?"

"What were you doing with a guy like him? A bounty hunter?"

Because being in the center of the snake pit was safer than being hunted by the snakes. Remy's fingers settled over the crystal beneath her shirt before she realized it, and she forced herself to ease them casually away.

"I was fully aware of his reputation," she said. "He and his father were so ruthless, the other bounty hunters would have been happy to have them out of the way. That's how I ended up with Seattle: he ambushed us and tossed Ian over a mountain to die."

"You've already told us how you ended up with Seattle. But what I don't understand is the allegiance to Ian Marck. Why were you acting as his bounty hunting partner, going around with him and terrorizing innocent people in settlements?" Wyatt hadn't moved, but something in his demeanor had become almost intimidating, and suddenly Remy felt uneasy.

Dantès bounded back into the clearing at that moment and dropped the stick at her feet. Apparently he'd figured out the pattern and knew it was his mistress's turn.

She flung it away with less skill than she had previously. Damn it. He was making her jittery. "That's what bounty hunters do."

"But you aren't a bounty hunter."

Remy shrugged. "You don't know anything about me." Then she turned away. "I'm going inside," she said over her shoulder as she strode into the tall grass.

"I know a few things. I know you throw a stick a lot better than you do a snake."

He didn't sound as if he was joking.

"**W**ell at least now we have something to go on," Vaughn said grimly. "They're going to destroy Envy, but before they do, those two assholes are going to come here looking for Quent. They won't find him," he added. "I've already taken precautions there—given your descriptions of Graves and the other guy to the patrols. But . . . Christ. What exactly are they going to do?"

"You're quite certain that's what he said?" Quent interrupted. " 'There won't be an Envy for him to hide inside anyway?' "

They were sitting, as members of the Resistance often did, in their subterranean computer stronghold two stories below New York-New York. Only members of the group even knew of its existence—let alone how to use an old elevator shaft and the right code to access the space.

Fence nodded grimly. "By the time the words sank in, the bastards were already back in the Humvee and driving away. But I'm sure that's what he said—I was close enough to make out their entire conversation."

"So what are they going to do? Bomb the city?" Vaughn said, rubbing his temples with a widespread hand. "Jesus. We won't let anyone within a five mile radius of the wall until they're screened."

Fence shook his head, reminded of the pre-Change world and its exhaustive security measures post-9/11. Despite this being a much wilder and woolier environment, he never would have thought such precautions would be necessary.

"What do you think?" he asked, turning to look at Marley. "Any ideas from what you know about them?"

Marley Huvane had been a friend of Quent's from before the Change. She'd not only lived through the disaster but was assured of immortality due to the crystal her billionaire father embedded in her skin—without telling her what it was. Now, she was an Elite who'd escaped from their stronghold of Mecca, living secretly among the mortals in Envy. If anyone had an inside perspective on the Strangers, it was her.

She was hot in a high society sort of way, without being brittle and overdone, and Fence was pretty sure Quent had tapped that more than once—at least before the Change. Now, of course, Quent only had eyes for Zoë, and had rebuffed Marley's recent overtures at hooking up—or so she'd confessed to Fence.

Marley shook her head. "They've got to be beside themselves knowing that you"—she looked at Quent—"got away with that crystal they use to communicate with Atlantis. So now they either have no way to communicate with them or they're afraid you're going to figure out how to do it yourself—or both."

The four of them glanced toward the old metal file cabinet where the crystal had been wrapped in cloth and hidden away. So far, Quent hadn't had a lot of luck with the fist-sized translucent-blue stone, for he couldn't hold it long without getting sucked into a comalike vortex of memories and images. While he could easily read the history of everyday objects merely by touching them, he was less able to control the immense flood of power behind the Atlantis crystal.

"But," Marley continued, "I don't remember hearing anything that could be construed as a threat to Envy. Not that I was in the Inner Circle or anything. In fact, they knew I wasn't happy about being there, being one of them, and that I'd been trying to escape. But as far as Envy goes . . . certainly, the Elite are aware of the size of the city, and they monitor it to make sure nothing they disapprove of is happening there—"

"Yeah. Like the use of computers," Fence added with a wry glance around the chamber. The space was lined with tables and desks, and each one held any number of computers, monitors, printers, and a variety of electronics—all of which had been either scavenged or rebuilt by the Waxnicki brothers. Here was the heart of the new communications infrastructure they were trying to build—all out of sight of the Strangers. "Or any sort of mass communication, or infrastructure. The way things are now, every settlement—large or small—is isolated from the next. It's like the motherfucking Wild West."

Marley nodded. "If they had any idea this place down here existed, it'd be gone. We'd be dead. I'm not sure what would worry them more: the possibility of a communication infrastructure that ties us together, or all the information and data that Theo and Lou and Sage have collected from the hard drives and main-frames they've found."

"Maybe the Strangers have somehow found out," Vaughn said, his face even more strained.

"We've been damned careful," Fence said. "No one knows about this but us, and none of us is fixing to tell."

He could almost imagine what the guy was think-ing: how so many lives were his responsibility, here in Envy. And how, if he weren't offering—or allowing—a haven for the Resistance, there likely wouldn't be a threat. The Strangers would let them live in peace—albeit a repressed peace that could be shattered by the disappearance of anyone at any time.

Fence studied Vaughn closely and wondered if the mayor of Envy would sell them all out in order to keep his people safe.

Or if he'd support them in their efforts to break the Strangers, despite the danger to so many lives.

Marley was speaking again. "If I had to guess . . . I'd think it would be logical to assume that any threat to Envy would come from the ocean."

Vaughn swore softly. "That sparkling gray stuff. We still haven't figured out what it was. But no one's ever seen it before."

But someone else had. Fence's eyes wandered toward the ceiling, where, two floors above them, Ana and her father were in Elliott's infirmary.

He hadn't told her what he'd overheard from the bounty hunters, but it was time to have a talk with the sun goddess anyway.

Ana streaked through the sea, leaving a trail of bubbles sparkling silently behind her. This area of the ocean, on the northern side of Envy, was a place she'd never explored. And now that she and her father had received good news from Elliott Drake, she felt free as her dolphin friends to swim and dart about in the place she thought of as her second home.

Once they arrived in Envy, Fence took a few minutes to get them to the doctor, and then to help her arrange for a place to sleep—and all without one teasing, sly comment about joining him. Then he took off somewhere else, and she hadn't seen him since.

To her great relief. It was a lot easier to ignore her attraction to him when he wasn't around.

In the infirmary, Elliott had scanned his hands over

her dad's body from head to toe. It took him all of five minutes to pronounce George severely anemic—which he then explained would be easily cured by changing his diet to include more iron. It was ironic that with Ana so tied to the sea, and having partaken of everything from seaweed and algae to fish and shellfish, that George would have such a deficiency—but then again, he often forgot to eat unless Ana forced him to do so.

Which she would be doing more stridently in the future.

And that was one of the reasons she was flitting through the blue-green waters right now: looking for the species of sea plant that contained a good amount of iron and protein . . . not to mention taking the opportunity to explore and see if she could learn any more about that odd silvery substance that had washed up on Envy's shore.

Unlike the ocean near her home in Glenway, the waters here were darker and murkier, even near the surface. Part of the reason was because they weren't quite as deep, and much of what had been Las Vegas was, in places, only fifty feet below the surface. Tall buildings, some still intact and others crumbled remains—just as on land—created an unusual waterscape.

But here, too, Ana felt that unusual, unfamiliar sensation in the sea. The subtle change she'd noticed back home was even stronger here—either because of the geographic location or the passage of time. Either way, it made her even more concerned about whatever was stirring the waters. Whatever the Sea was waiting for, preparing for.

With her shirt pulled up and tucked in place to expose her torso, Ana's crystals glowed brightly, illuminating the dim alleys between rooftops and towers.

She dove deep . . . down, down, down . . . along the side of some massive structure, as if she were tumbling off the top floor to the ground below.

It was black and close, and the water pressed down on her, but she wasn't frightened. This was her world. Red, pink, and yellow glowing fish and tiny anemones lit the darkness, and they scattered at her sudden downward rush. She darted through broken windows, the glass long gone, and out of rooms, through sagging doors, and along long corridors that in places were now hardly more than furry metal skeletons.

She turned a corner, spiraling up, up . . . and halted when she saw a flash of light at the corner of a dark building.

It was there for a moment, and then it was gone. Her heart lurched and she whipped herself behind an algae-covered column, startling a pair of sea crabs from their hiding place.

She hardly paid the creatures any mind . . . she was looking out from a shadow as she quickly pulled her shirt down to cover the glowing crystals.

The light given off by energy crystals was different from that of fishes and plants: it was sharper, more clear and steady, and cut more deeply through the murky deep. She knew what she'd seen.

A glow like that could only have come from an Atlantean.

She didn't see any more sign of the crystalline lights, so Ana slipped from behind her hiding place and darted to another shadowy spot in the direction the light had gone.

And watched and waited, her heart pounding madly, her belly in a twist. She reached blindly to make certain her knife was in place.

Something long and dark moved above Ana, patrolling for prey in slow, easy ripples. But like most wild animals—excluding those massive electric eels—sharks were little danger as long as they didn't feel threatened, so she set aside her concerns and listened to the sea.

She let her fingers float away from her body, spread delicately so as to sense the slightest ripple of change in the water. Ana concentrated, breathed through her crystals, and focused on the push of the ocean around her . . . and as she waited, breathing, feeling . . . something shifted, and she noticed the faintest alteration in the hum of the sea.

Moments later a human silhouette swam by, just above her head.

Ana tamped her shirt down closer to her torso and made certain the crystaled side of her body was toward the wall as she looked up at the figure sliding through the watery space. The sprinkling light of crystals around his torso was greater than her own, confirming her suspicion.

He was an Atlantean.

Raw fear and nausea gathered in her stomach and she squeezed tighter into the darkness. She slipped her knife from its belt just in case.

He was too far away for her to see any details other than the basic shape of a figure that reflected familiarly in her memory. Of course, she knew several Atlanteans. It could be any of them, she told herself firmly.

They weren't necessarily looking for her—or would even recognize her. Especially if she kept her crystals hidden.

If she had a better view, the little dots of light might identify him—for the crystal color and pattern on each Atlantean's torso was as unique as a fingerprint.

What was more important was that he was swimming unusually near the shore, much too close to the mortal world . . .

Ana's belly twitched nervously when a second figure came into view behind him. Again, high above her. More crystals, patterned like constellations, glowed like stars in the sea-sky. Another man.

Something was wrong about the way they were caravanning along. Curiosity propelled Ana to move silently behind and below the second figure, following his pattern of stopping and starting, ducking and hiding. And then she realized that *he* was following the *other* swimmer.

Two Atlanteans. One stealthily following the other . . .

Now that was curious.

She swam faster, silently, using an overhanging roof as a cover for her to catch up to the second man.

But then when she stopped and peeked out and up at the place one or both of them should have been, she saw nothing but darkness and shadows. A school of angelfish, then a trio of lizardfish and the coral-covered sagging door of a car.

And not a sign of glowing crystals shafting through the darkness anywhere.

Ana moved around in expanding concentric circles, careful to remain in the shadows, careful to cause hardly a ripple of a wave, watching for creatures that her sudden movements might startle and thus draw attention to herself.

But she saw nothing.

Where had they gone?

And what were they doing here?

After a long while she finally gave up and replaced her knife in its sheath. She began to make her way back toward shore, jetting sleekly through the water. She'd been out here for more than three hours, and even though George was used to her spending half a day or more in the sea, he had been ill and was in a strange place. She felt a little guilty about—

She stopped suddenly, her body jolting into a vertical position as she stared at the soft pink glow emanating from a dark cubbyhole. She cast a quick look around, heart in her throat.

There was no one about. Nothing moved.

She used the slightest flutter of her hands to propel herself closer. She hadn't been mistaken: there was a small pink crystal—no larger than her pinky fingernail—settled in the center of a pink and orange seaflower. Its flowing, petal-like spindles danced gently with the rhythm of the water.

Ana's heart did a little odd flip, and her palms suddenly felt dry and tight.

The flower had been placed inside an open mailbox—or some metal object from days gone by that resembled one. It had been arranged there purposely, as a message . . . just as Darian used to do when he wanted her to meet him.

It *was* Darian she'd seen.

Ana darted away, suddenly fearful that he lurked about—or that *someone* did—and was watching her. Her fingers curling around a rusted metal beam, she stopped to think, drawing long, cool drafts of water in through her crystals . . . and acknowledged the reality she'd tried to dismiss earlier. The familiar figure, the first Atlantean she'd seen swimming above her today: it had to be Darian.

Her eyes went back to the flower, bathed in its pink crystal glow. He was looking for her again. Did he know she was in the area? Or was there someone else with whom he might be exchanging mementos? It wasn't jealousy that touched her at the thought . . . it was confusion and apprehension.

The last time she'd seen him had been five years ago—when she learned exactly why he'd been so attached to her. She'd been beyond hurt and furious, and even now, a bolt of anger surged through her in a sharp reminder that she could never trust him. Or any Atlantean. But Darian . . . he'd spent all those months wooing and loving her just to trick her into going back with him.

And all along, she'd thought he really loved her. That she'd found someone she could be herself with, who already knew all of her secrets. She thought she'd actually found someone of her people who was honest, selfless, and kind.

But in the end she realized they were all the same: selfish and evil.

Because of that, immediately after her confrontation with Darian she and George moved to a different settlement. They moved far from the northern shore where they'd lived before—a hundred shoreline miles away from her lover and the memories of his betrayal and manipulation.

Ana turned and swam off. She left the flower there with its crystal, untouched, instead of leaving what would have been her own normal response: a gift or token of her own to let him know she got the message.

This was one message she didn't want to get . . .

Or did she?

Ana stopped again, this time pausing next to a large outcropping of anemone-covered rock. A spindly blue and green sea beetle darted across the back of her hand, but she hardly noticed it. If there was something happening in the sea, Darian might know about it.

Her insides swirled and she thought about the risk of responding to his message, of divulging her whereabouts after working so hard to keep them secret for years. About what it would be like to see him again.

Darian had, after all, been her first real love. The first man she didn't have to hide her crystals from. Heck, he'd been the *only* man she didn't have to hide her crystals from.

Fence and his hot, dark eyes flashed into her mind. She remembered the skepticism in his expression and voice when he looked at her muddied and scraped torso as she walked out of the sea. He'd be just as difficult to sidetrack as Darian had been—maybe even worse, because she couldn't just dart away into the water from him. On land, she was a lot less agile, and he was so graceful and—

Why was she thinking about Fence right now? He was nothing more than a flirt and a tease who relied on his charm to make his way in the world. Although he was one hell of a guide.

And look at the way he'd been with Tanya and the other kids.

And he was a sweltering kisser.

Ana frowned at herself and shoved away the disruptive thoughts as a cold spot in the water sifted over her. *What should I do?*

Did she dare respond to Darian and try to find out what he knew?

Why was he being followed?

And what in the deep dark depths was going on with her lovely Sea?

CHAPTER 7

Fence sat on the beach.

Beach was a misleading term, he thought ruefully as he adjusted his palms from the rough debris and rubble poking them, for the word "beach" implied a long expanse of warm sand . . . usually dotted with sunbathing beauties in string bikinis.

Or not.

He grinned, remembering a visit to his mother's homeland of Brazil and the topless beaches in Rio. That had been crazy.

But this shoreline, while there was some sand, was also strewn with rubble and pieces of metal. Trees and bushes clumped on it, and he was actually sitting on an old road that had broken off and now angled into the ocean.

Now, he sat here, relieved that the area was deserted. He'd looked inside—in the infirmary, the pub, all the common areas—for Ana, and then knocked on her door. Fence had finally ended up here, where he suspected he'd find her, though he'd been avoiding it. He'd walked along the shore for thirty minutes, from one end of the protective wall that rose behind him to the other end of this small cove, and saw no sign of anyone swimming. No boats. Nothing.

The area was as ghostly as some of the overgrown towns he'd traveled through.

Although Envy was situated on the sea, its residents had little interest in fishing as an industry. There were a few brave souls who took boats out on the southeast side, where the shoreline was more enclosed in a small, protected bay that was separated from this area by a long, slender piece of land, but here on this northwest corner, it was always devoid of people.

Part of the reason was due to the stories about people leaving, setting out from the north and heading to where Washington and Oregon used to be, and never returning.

It wasn't surprising, for the sea here seemed dark and angry—at least to Fence, and especially today. Perhaps it was because half of Las Vegas was very near below its surface, and the debris and ruins colored the water. Last week, when the tide was out and a violent storm tossed the waves, Vaughn had pointed out to him the glimpses one could get of the tops of the buildings. Eerie.

To the southwest, just inside the main wall, was the tall building in a deserted part of Envy. Called the Beretta, it resembled the weapon of the same name, and had been a brand-new condo building in 2010. It was in that still intact tower that Simon and Sage found an old computer flash drive that had belonged to the infamous Remington Truth, one of the instrumental members of the Elite.

The tower had been a storehouse, protected by the zombie-like gangas and the wild dogs that were their prey, until Vaughn led a brigade of men and women to clean the area out. It was too dangerous to have such a place so close to their settlement, where children played and others lived comfortably.

But here, a mile away from the Beretta, the waves lapped gently against the cracked edge of highway and a belt of sand and pebbles. Other than that rhythmic sound and the occasional call of a gull, the world was silent.

Fence was completely alone.

And that was why he took off his shoes and rolled up his cargo pants and inched a little closer to the water.

His heart was thudding like a blues bass line as he settled, knees up against his chest and arms wrapped around his legs. The waves licked his toes and he closed his eyes, trying to still the panic that threatened to overtake his mind when he thought about what lay beyond.

It severely pissed him off, how part of him wanted to slide into the cool, buoyant depths—to feel that freedom again of floating, flying through the water . . . and how the other part—the biggest, strongest, pussiest part of him—wanted only to turn tail and run. To *get away*.

His breathing had changed, becoming quicker and more shallow, and he felt the familiar nausea crawling up from the deepest part of his belly, tightening his lungs, burning the back of his throat. His forehead felt clammy and his skin hot.

Why can't I get over this? What the fuck is wrong with me?

He swallowed hard and sharply, and without opening his eyes, scooted closer to the water. Something stung his eyes, and he wouldn't even allow himself to consider whether it was tears gathering behind his lids or merely the burn from saltwater drops. It had to be the latter.

He smelled the salt, the tang of algae and the fishy scent of other creatures of the depths, tasted the damp. The water surged around him, soaking the seat of his pants, covering his feet and toes. Those appendages curled down into the gritty surface beneath and Fence forced himself to open his eyes.

The ocean was *right there*. Around him.

All he could see was rolling, tossing waves, waiting to pull him down into their dark abyss. The pressure, the weight, the ebbing and flowing. He couldn't banish the memories . . . nor could he ignore an incessant tug deep in his belly, as if the sea was teasing him, luring him in like a damn femme fatale.

No.

He closed his eyes again, the wave of panic rushing through him like a whistling train, leaving him shuddering and rattled in its wake. His chin dug down into the tops of his knees as he kept his face toward the waft of sea breeze, eyes squeezed shut.

You have to fight this, asshole. You have to get over this.

What happened the next time someone was in danger? This world was filled with threats and danger. People counted on him, relied on him to guide them, protect them . . . but here he was, with a deathly liability.

Sure, I'll keep you safe . . . unless you fall in the water. Then you're on your own.

Fuck.

Something damp rolled down his cheek, and it was not, *was no fucking way*, a tear. But his breath caught suddenly, shockingly, in his lungs and he fought the deep, dragging lurch of a sob, tightening his fingers into the arms he clutched around his thighs. *No. Stop. It. Stop—*

"Are you all right?"

The sudden voice and presence shocked Fence like a dousing of ice water. His eyes flew open and he looked up at her—Ana; he'd recognized her voice before he saw her—then bolted to his feet. Shame and anger swamped him and he said, "What the hell do you want?" before he could stop himself.

His fingers were shaking and his insides rolled, but through the momentary tunnel vision of mortification, anger, and weakness, he saw her jerk back as if slapped.

"Nothing," she said, stepping away quickly and awkwardly.

Her foot landed on a loose stone, and he had just enough time to note that her hair and clothing were wet as she lost her balance and started to fall.

Fence reached for her automatically, but Ana managed to catch herself before she landed on the rough ground. His fingers brushed against her damp arm just as she moved back.

"Forget it," she said, now that she'd recovered. Annoyance and embarrassment gave her a cold, closed expression. "Sorry I startled you." She turned completely around this time before she started away.

Fence swallowed hard, struggling to contain his confusion, shame, and fury—all of which was pointed inward—and tried to think of something to say. But she was already stalking as well as she could stalk on a bad leg over uneven ground, away from him.

Goddammit.

Frustration blazed silently through him, but he made no attempt to go after her. He was too out of sorts right now . . . and she was clearly displeased with every-thing, from his reaction to her own clumsiness.

And then he remembered that *he'd* been looking for *her*.

Dammit.

Ana fumed all the way back inside the big old build-ing where, it seemed, almost everyone in Envy lived and ate. She wasn't certain which emotion gave her the speed and unusual agility to get away from him: anger at the big jerkwad or mortification that she'd once again nearly fallen on her ass in front of said big jerkwad.

I can go for months without stumbling or tripping, but the two times I do, I have *to be in front of that man. Grrr.*

How the heck was she supposed to know he didn't want to be bothered? She'd surfaced from her swim and seen him sitting there on the other end of the beach. He looked like he was enjoying the gentle breeze, watch-ing the slow, easy rise and fall of the waves.

And, despite an internal warning bell, she had ap-proached, drawn to the solitary, solid figure swamped by the salty water as it lunged and eased around him. She admired the rich warm color of his skin baking in the sun—imagining how it would feel to touch it—the breadth of his shoulders and, as she drew closer, even the wide, angular feet, digging into the sand.

But when she padded silently in front of him and saw his expression—the eyes squeezed closed, the anguish furrowing his brow and crumpling his face . . . and even a damp streak down one cheek—she knew some-thing was wrong.

She should have just left. Instinct told her to do so,

for she remembered the last time she'd found him in distress. But she couldn't just leave him there.

And now she wished she would have.

Just as she'd left Darian's seaflower with its crystal still sitting in its cubbyhole in the ocean.

She could always go back tomorrow, she'd reasoned, and leave a response. But before she did, Ana wanted to think about the risk and whether she dared make contact with Darian again. And how she would protect herself if he tried something.

Should she tell George too? He'd been married to her mother, he'd lived with the Atlanteans longer than Ana had. Even if his memory of those times had been clouded after their escape, he could still offer advice.

Never one to rush into a decision, she went back to the room Fence had arranged for her to stay in while she and her father were here in Envy. She supposed she had to give the guy credit for getting them here safely and quickly, and for providing a place for her to sleep. But beyond that hospitality, and a quick, melting smile, and—oh, all right, that kiss on the beach had been amazing—there wasn't any other reason to hang around Fence anymore.

In fact, if he was in his funny, flirtatious, sensual mood, it would be darn dangerous to hang around him.

She frowned. It was as if he were two different people. Just like she was.

She didn't like *that* thought, so she pushed it away and dressed in dry clothes. She toweled her hair to damp and let it hang over her shoulders, then went to visit George . . . all the while considering what, if anything, she should tell him.

Her dad looked pink and healthy when she came into the infirmary. He was sitting up in bed talking to El-

liott and an older woman with strawberry blond hair
that had a wide white streak in front; a nurse, she assumed.

"And so I've been working on separating that strain
of penicillin to see if I can make a stronger medicine,"
George was saying. From the flush in his face and the
light in his eyes, Ana could tell he'd been talking for
quite some time. Lecturing, most likely. "If I could just
find some old resources from one of the medicine fac-
tories they had, I might be able to reproduce some of
the other treatments."

The woman, who seemed as comfortable as a plump
pillow, looked remarkably fascinated by George's
explanations—more so than Ana could comprehend.
Either she was a scientist herself or was simply a good
listener.

"I might be able to help you with that," Elliott was
saying. He flashed a guarded look at the woman, then
looked back at George. "We have some old books and
information that have been saved from libraries and old
bookstores over the years. I would find it immensely
helpful to have not only an alternative to penicillin, but
also some efficacious painkillers."

"I'll be happy to help look through some books for
you," said the nurse eagerly. "If you'll show me what
to look for."

"Well, it looks like you're feeling much better, Dad,"
Ana said, drawing everyone's attention to her. "You've
got some color in your face now."

"I told you, I was feeling just fine," George said.
"Really was no need for me to come here. Elliott says
I've just got to watch what I eat."

"Someone's got to make sure he eats enough red
meat and spinach," put in the nurse with a measured

glance at Ana—as if to blame her for her father's dietary deficiencies. The plump pillow had turned into a stern guardian.

"Now, Flo—" Elliott started, but before he could continue, they heard a loud, urgent voice.

"Now who's raising a ruckus?" Flo glared at the wall. "Heaven help me—it's not time for Zoë's next appointment is it?" She shook her head, pursing her lips. "She was just here last week, raising a fuss when you started laying down the law—"

But Elliott had risen and Ana turned toward the door. She'd heard it too: someone calling urgently for the doctor.

"I'd better go see what that is," Elliott said.

Ana didn't know why, but she started to follow him out into the hallway. Maybe she thought they might need help, maybe she was just curious. Or maybe she somehow *knew*.

And when she heard the voices, urgent and excited, and fragments of sentences—"washed up" . . . "from the ocean" . . . "think he's dead"—her heart began to race.

"I'll be right back, Dad," she said, poking her head back into the small room, causing his and Flo's to turn toward her from some intense conversation.

But she didn't have time to think about the implications now. She hurried down the hall toward the voices. When she reached the small room, the door was still, thankfully, open, and she was able to look inside.

Several people clustered around a bed. There was Elliott, of course, along with a man and woman Ana didn't recognize, and Fence. Ana was aware of a little jolt of relief that the body found on the shore hadn't been Fence, but she didn't examine that odd reaction . . .

especially now that her other fear seemed more possible. Instead, she tried to peer through the small crowd without drawing attention to herself.

Those in the room happened to be standing so it blocked her view of everything except two pale, bare feet that were large enough to be a man's. She needed a better look, for anything that came from the sea—whether someone had been killed or injured by some aquatic creature, or any unusual substance like the gray sparkling glop—was important to her and could give clues toward what was happening.

Suddenly, Elliott looked up and saw her. Ana flushed and started, and began to duck back out of the room, but he said, "You can come in. I might need your help. Shut the door so we don't have a whole crowd in here."

Wondering what sort of help she could provide that the others couldn't—or wouldn't—she nevertheless accepted his offer and did as he requested as Elliott turned back to the bed.

Fence had looked up at his friend's words, along with the other man and woman. His eyes met hers, and there was neither apology nor humor in them. It was almost . . . suspicion?

Ana straightened her shoulders and turned away from Fence's penetrating look, focusing on the figure for the first time. It was all she could do to hold back a gasp.

No, it wasn't Darian, as she'd feared.

But she knew him anyway, despite the damage to his face and the mud and blood streaking it. His name was Kaddick, and, like her former lover, he was from Atlantis.

From the amount of blood and the deep slashes across his torso and abdomen, she knew he was dead—

and likely so before he even came out of the ocean. Fear and unpleasantness gripped her belly. If he'd been following Darian, had he been discovered and a fight ensued? Or had he attacked Darian first?

Was Darian injured or dead too?

Or had some slashing stingray or whip-tail fish sliced into Kaddick and killed him?

The latter was the least likely, for there weren't many dangerous sea creatures that attacked without cause.

Ana moved closer to the bed as thoughts and questions raced through her mind. As soon as Elliott examined Kaddick, or even removed his clothing—which already was different than anything seen on land—he'd know the victim was not merely a man.

"Do you know him?" Elliott asked, and Ana realized with a start that he was looking at her.

Why would he think *she* knew him?

Her heart lodged in her throat as she tried to decide how to respond.

"There's a lot of blood," Fence said. "Are you all right, Ana?" He was watching her closely.

She latched onto that excuse and clapped a hand over her mouth as if about to be sick, turning her face away and trying to look pale and wan. Evading an answer was her best option right now.

"She needs air," Elliott said, and the other woman moved quickly to open the door. Ana gratefully walked out as she heard Elliott continue, "He's not from Envy. I thought she might recognize him if he happened to be from Glenway."

"What the hell is he wearing? What's that made out of?" asked the third man. "We could tell right away that he wasn't from around here. But I've never seen anything like it."

Ana leaned against the corridor wall as the door closed behind her. She could have told him that the fabric was made from the white seaworm's threads woven with a milkweed-type plant that grew in Atlantis. Together, they created cloth that was lightweight, shiny, and warm, as well as one that didn't swell and absorb water. It also carried a scent that repelled electric eels—most of the time—and the little sea scorpions that could kill with one small sting.

She knew all about the clothing, and more. But what should she tell them? Anything or nothing?

Nothing.

George had always cautioned her—needlessly—not to tell anyone about her parentage, but also not to even acknowledge the existence of Atlantis and her mother's people. Although all humans had descended from the same race more than two millennia ago, the Atlanteans were very different from those who'd continued to build their civilization on land. Her father was afraid that Ana would be ostracized, blamed, or even hurt and killed if the truth about the Atlanteans became known to those who lived on the land.

His words were unnecessary anyway, because Ana, no matter how much she'd loved her mother, had neither respect or affection for her mother's race. She knew who they were and what they'd done, and she wanted no part of them. She was ashamed to have the blood of Atlantis running in her veins.

If anyone learned she was Atlantean, and word got back to them . . . if they found her, they'd take her back there. Make her stay. Make her live with them.

She drew in deep, slow breaths. She wasn't going back there. No one was going to take her back. She and Dad had risked their lives to escape.

But if there was something happening, something threatening Envy—or anywhere else on land—because of what was occurring beneath the sea, didn't she have a responsibility to tell someone what she knew?

In case they could prevent it?

Of course she did. But she didn't have to tell them who she was. Or how she knew.

Ana turned resolutely from the small room and realized that at least one decision had been made for her: she was going to have to respond to Darian's message.

"**W**ill you look at this?" Fence said, helping Elliott tear away the rest of the smooth, shiny fabric of the dead man's clothing. "Dude's got more piercings than the guy from *Hellraiser*."

Even through the ribbons of flesh and the shine of white rib bones, he could see that a dozen or more pea-sized crystals had been embedded in the man's skin. Fence hadn't ever seen one of the Strangers and their crystals up close, but he knew Elliott had—and that the Strangers only had one or at most two glowing stones. And instead of being in the torso, between and around the ribs as they were in this guy, the immortalizing crystals the Strangers wore were always set into the soft flesh just south of the collarbone.

Dude looks like a fucking disco dancer. Saturday Night Sea-ver.

Damn, he cracked himself up.

Fence looked up at his companion, keeping the joke to himself this time. "Damn good thing you sent Wendy and Herb out of here before they saw this," he added.

Elliott nodded briefly. "I had a feeling . . . and we don't need stories being passed around until we figure

out what's going on and just who—or what—this man
is." He wasn't scanning the man yet, using his hands
like a full-color human MRI machine. Instead, he just
looked down at the body, wearing a pensive expression.

Other than the crystals, the man appeared completely normal—at least from outward appearances—
once he was fully stripped.

Fence was acutely aware of the irony that he had no
problem digging in and taking care of a body fairly
shredded into ribbons, but that the very whisper of an
ocean wave against his feet was enough to send him
into a full-blown panic attack. He merely dismissed the
knowledge, because it pissed him the hell off, and tried
to conjure up a joke about the guy's junk . . . but even
Fence couldn't find any more humor in the situation.
The guy just looked pitiful and pathetic.

Probably just how he would look after he drowned:
all floppy and wet and gray.

Not a happy thought, bro, for God's sake.

So he said, "Why did you really invite Ana to come
in here? There's no damn way you thought she'd recognize this guy."

Even though she had.

Elliott looked up at him, and Fence saw that his friend
had noticed Ana's reaction as well. "She was too curious. And there's something odd about her father. When
I scanned him, I found some weird markings in his
lungs . . . as if they'd been altered or something. They
seem to work fine, but there's something different . . ."

"She practically lives in the ocean," Fence told him.
"And I've been wanting to tell you and Vaughn that
when I was at their place, I got a look at George's lab.
Dude's got some of that gray sparkly stuff there. I don't
know where he got it from, but I'm fixing to find out."

Just then, there was a knock at the door. Fence opened it to admit Quent and Zoë, as well as Vaughn Rogan.

"Jade went to find Marley," Vaughn said as he closed the door behind him.

Fence nodded. That was good. If anyone knew what these types and placement of crystals meant, it would be Marley.

"He looks like fucking Elvis in that white suit," said Zoë, who must have seen the iconic photo once upon a time. "What the hell's with all those damned crystals? He afraid of losing his way in the dark?"

"Maybe he's like my father," Quent replied. "He kept adding crystals because he thought they'd keep him alive."

"Those are much smaller than the ones the Elites wear," Zoë reminded him.

"I'm going to scan him now," Elliott said, positioning his hands over the man's head.

As they watched, he slid them down over the inert body, from head to toe and up and down each limb, his eyes closed in concentration.

When he opened them, he drew in a deep breath. A little furrow between his brows disappeared as the door opened to Jade and Marley.

"Everything all right?" Jade asked, moving to stand right next to Elliott. Her face was tight with concern, and Fence knew it had to do with worry about the doctor more than anything. She was always trying to make certain he didn't injure himself while caring for others—something that had happened more than once. He'd almost died saving Vaughn's life when Elliott, Fence, and the others first arrived in Envy.

"He's already dead," Elliott told her, and Jade's expression eased as she slid her hand around his arm. Fence noticed their easy affection, the silent support and connection between them, and was reminded sharply, sadly, of his parents. "But not for very long. Maybe an hour or so, but not much longer."

"It looks like a horrible way to go," said Jade, transferring her attention to the bloody body.

"He's not an Elite," Marley said, her voice low and tight.

Fence saw that she'd turned pale and was gripping the edge of a nearby table. "Hey, sugar, better sit down. Now's really not the time to be fallin' to your knees around me," he said, giving her a grin. "We've got an audience." He pulled a chair around and helped her ease into it.

"How do you know he isn't an Elite?" asked Vaughn, his voice cool. "He's got crystals all over him."

"Too many, too small, and in the wrong place," Marley said in a rush, confirming Fence and Elliott's previous conversation. Her gaze was averted and her knuckles white.

"She's right," Elliott said, and all eyes turned to him. "These crystals are different—aside from all the other reasons Marley gave, they're also set into the body differently. In the Elites, the crystals have little fiber-optic-like threads that burrow through the whole body like the roots of a plant . . . or like the circulatory system, but originating from the crystal instead of a heart. But these crystals are like tiny cones fixed in the lungs, and there are—or were—at least a dozen of them. They do have small roots, but they're much shorter than the other type. And these merge with the bronchioles in the lungs. It's as if they're part of the organ itself, as if they've taken over their function. Perhaps even changing the lungs' functionality."

Everyone was silent, looking at him. Fence could almost feel the massive churning in the room as everyone's brains chewed on this new information.

"My guess," Elliott continued, "is that these crystals help his lungs to convert water to oxygen."

"So what in the hell are you saying? That the guy is a fucking fish? Or was," Zoë added, her voice going mildly softer as she looked down at the corpse.

"He's from Atlantis," Quent said quietly.

Fence saw that he was holding a piece of the man's clothing. "Atlantis? Can you see it?" he asked, his pulse bumping up. "What it looks like?"

Zoë edged closer to Quent, and Fence saw her link fingers with him. She was his lifeline, holding him in the present or bringing him back when the blur of memories threatened to drag him into unconsciousness.

"I just saw impressions of the place," Quent replied. He'd dropped the fabric and his face was pale under its tan. "It's wavery and bright, and contained. I'll get more later."

"You're hot damn right it'll be later, genius," Zoë said firmly. "Not fucking now. I'm not gonna be dragging your sorry ass—or arse—or what-the-fuck-ever you call it all the way the hell back up to our damned room when your knees give out and you conk your hard-ass head on the floor."

"And here we have the softer side of Zoë," Fence said with a grin, relieved to shove away his dark thoughts. And weren't pregnant women supposed to be more . . . fluffy and motherly and—what did you call it? Burrowing? No, nesting?

Zoë whipped her face around to give him a glare that would have shaved his head if he wasn't already bald. Her brows furrowed in a shut-your-fucking-trap look, and Fence realized he might have somehow stepped squarely in something. And he did *not* want to be on Zoë's bad side.

Especially if she was all hormonal. Uneasiness crawled up his spine when he remembered his sister and her pregnancy. *Ugly.*

From the expression on Zoë's face, and the suddenly pop-eyed warning look Elliott was giving him as well, Fence realized that Quent didn't yet know he was going to be a father. *Oops.*

How the hell had that happened? Everyone else knew except for Quent? Fence glanced at Elliott, who shrugged and gave a brief eye roll toward Zoë. Apparently she didn't want him to know. Fence had learned the news from Lou Waxnicki, who'd found out from Zoë herself before he left Envy to visit Theo. She'd been bitching about how Quent wasn't going to let her hunt zombies anymore as soon as he found out she had a bun in the oven.

That *was* going to be interesting: Quent trying to keep the type-A, athletic, stubborn as the day was long Zoë from riding around shooting at zombies all the time. Not that Fence would blame the guy . . . he'd want his own wife to be careful with his baby.

If he ever had one.

Fence's light mood dampened and he turned his attention back to the matter at hand . . . including his own women problems.

Now that they'd come to the conclusion that Mr. Disco here was indeed from Atlantis, the next thing to find out was just how Ana had known it—or known him.

"I'm outta here," Fence said, slipping behind Jade to get to the door. "Got some stuff to take care of."

He wasted no time getting out of the infirmary and back out to the beach. The tracks from Herb and Wendy's—and his—footprints were still there, but the spot where Mr. Disco had been found wedged between a rock and an old car was washed over by the waves.

Fence walked up and along the shore until he found Ana's tracks. There were marks going into the water but none going out. And he found a shirt and a pair of shoes tucked up in the branch of a sapling, so he knew she had to be coming back this way.

But as he stood there, shielding his eyes from the fully visible but lowering sun off to his right, he saw no sign of her. No bobbing head, nothing floating. The waves were relatively mild, so it wasn't as if she'd be hidden by them.

He watched and waited for more than ten minutes, his apprehension and concern heightening. Where could she be?

And then, all at once, he saw a head surge up from the water about a hundred feet out. A swath of long hair whipped up and fanned over, sending a spray of droplets glittering in the sun. Long, slender arms and sleek shoulders emerged, glistening and glowing in the golden sun. She was far enough away that he couldn't see her face or much detail, but he recognized the sun goddess.

Not sure how he'd missed spotting her all this time, Fence chalked it up to the glare of the sun and the waves. But now that he'd spotted Ana, he could keep an eye on her as she made her way toward him.

No sooner had he thought that than she arced up and down into the water like a freaking dolphin. She went up so high that he actually saw a half circle between her body and the horizon.

Crazy. Amazing.

He was going to have to eat a mighty big helping of humble pie if he ever wanted another chance to get their freak on together. And he did. The deep shiver of desire startled him with its intensity.

Shielding his eyes, Fence watched for her to re-emerge from the water. And watched.

And *watched*.

Nothing. Nothing broke the water. Nothing shot up through the waves. No golden head. Not even a disruption in the pattern of the waves from her strokes or kicks.

Fence frowned, his heart starting to pound harder. She'd been under for at least three minutes.

Then four minutes.

Jesus, God, no. Not again. Don't fucking do this to me again.

His mouth had gone bone dry and he was aware of a sickening feeling rising in his middle. The image of the dead guy, waterlogged, limp and naked, lodged in his mind.

Five minutes. No way.

He felt light-headed and ill and couldn't help but rage at the heavens. *What in the hell are you doing to me? Why don't you just take me, God, instead of playing around like this?*

His heart slammed in his chest and his breathing had gone shallow.

Six minutes?

She had to be in trouble. No one could hold their breath for six minutes underwater.

No one.

Aw, God. Why? He blinked hard and swallowed.

It was no easier this time, so soon after the last, for him to walk toward those crashing, rolling, furious waves. Toward the dark, hungry waters.

Fence flipped off his shoes without acknowledging the reason for doing so. Pulled off his shirt. Sweat rolled down his back, and his skin had gone clammy. He thought he was going to hork right here, or his knees were going to give away . . . but he couldn't leave Ana.

He closed his eyes, then opened them again, straining to see something, *anything*, out there . . . then when he saw nothing, squeezed them shut and ran.

As soon as the water hit his knees, he dove blindly. He knew if he did it any other way, any slower or more deliberately, he wouldn't make it.

As the dark, cold water closed around him, his mind went blank with panic. At first his arms and legs wouldn't move. For a hysterical moment he almost breathed, almost dragged in a lungful of water and let himself go right then and there.

But he thought: *Ana.*

And he pictured her lithe, golden body.

He forced his limbs into the rhythm he still knew, tried to ignore the weight of the sea, its heavy cloak. Fence opened his eyes, raised his head above the water and looked for Ana, for any sign of her.

Nothing.

His lungs and torso seized, tightening as if there were a band around his ribs. He allowed himself to slip under the water, hoping to see a sign of her beneath.

Shadows rose in dark, jagged spires everywhere, making the situation even more terrifying. He was aware of little bubbles coming from his nose, and for a moment the panic surged and overwhelmed him as he

imagined the bubbles that would erupt in a long stream
. . . and then end . . . when he drowned.

Oh God, oh God.

He forced himself to move, and then all at once, as
he floundered around a rusty metal bar, he saw a glow.

He saw her.

She was *swimming.* Long and sleek and elegant, like
a dolphin. Something glowed around her belly.

Fence forgot himself and nearly choked as he started
to inhale a shocked breath. Then realizing what he'd
nearly done, he blew the air out and the back of his
throat began to tickle and a cough threatened. It rose in
his lungs, that need to violently inhale and expel, and
he was too far below to reach the surface in time, and
he had no air left . . .

OhmyGod, ohChrist, ohJesus. . .

His mind went blank with terror and hysteria and
the water rushed into him, and he flailed and rocked
into something hard and rough that scraped his forearm and temple. Sharp, stinging pain sliced beneath
his arms around his ribs. Cold water flushed inside and
Fence became aware of falling, sinking, of coughing
and trying to breathe.

Suddenly, she was there, appearing like a pale angel,
her hair spreading in a gentle ruffle around her. He
lunged for her, knowing he'd drown her, too, but he
was already breathing the water, dragging it in, and his
body would soften and slow and sink . . .

CHAPTER 8

Even through the water, Ana saw the wild panic in Fence's eyes and instinctively ducked as he reached for her.

She looped around behind him with a powerful frog kick that sent bubbles spiraling and the water churning. He spun awkwardly, following her, his arms and legs flailing as if he didn't know how to swim . . . but he *had* been swimming. What was wrong with him now?

Somehow—she wasn't certain how—she managed to drag and swim him back to shore. As soon as his feet hit ground, he loosened the death grip he had on her arm and staggered out of the water, pulling her with him. He was gasping and coughing, and she felt his muscular body trembling as if he were freezing . . . or in some sort of shock.

Despite all this, he was solid and strong, and Ana not very stable on her own feet, so when Fence collapsed on the beach, she tumbled down with him. For a moment she lay there, the wind knocked out of her, half pinned to gritty, pebbly sand by a heavy, masculine body, confused and yet strangely satisfied. Her wet hair slicked over their skin, strands of it trapped beneath his arm and against his torso.

Ana didn't even attempt to move away from where they'd landed, for she was out of sorts and exhausted after swimming fast and hard to Darian's message place and back, and then she'd had to contend with fighting Fence back to shore. Plus, jeez . . . she sort of liked the feel of him next to her.

Suddenly, she realized that he wasn't moving. Had he blacked out?

"Fence?" she said, giving him a little jolt. "Fence?" She patted the side of his face to try and get his attention, still sprawled next to him on the sand.

He shifted with a soft, rousing sound. His breathing changed as his eyes fluttered open. "Mmm . . ." he muttered, a little smile curving his lips, as if he'd just awakened.

His hand moved . . . slid. Curved.

Settled over her bottom . . . and cupped her close.

"Well, since you're right here, and we're both still alive," he murmured.

He shifted. The next thing she knew, his body was not merely next to hers, but lining up along her torso, smooth and solid, as his arms gathered her close. His mouth found hers as one large hand slid up between her shoulders, settling over her hair, fingers curling through the heavy, wet strands.

Ana's initial surprise at this mercurial change evaporated as she tasted him again—this time salty and damp and warm from the sea. His mouth was delicious: a sweet combination of sensuality, softness, and lurid, bold coaxing. Along with the deep kiss came the slide of his big, powerful body against hers—his knee easing between her legs, the arch of his foot brushing against her ankle, the shifting of solid, muscular planes beneath her hands.

Ahhh.

She closed her eyes and eased into the moment, long harbored desire unfurling in her belly as their kiss deepened. His hands were everywhere, as if they needed to memorize her from head to toe, pulling her tight so every soft curve burned into his skin. In the midst of the deep sensuality, she still had the presence of mind, barely, to keep her crystal side toward the ground and her tank top in place . . . even when he slipped a strap from her shoulder and began to nuzzle along her throat and neck.

The tickle of his ridiculous lashes over her cheek, followed by soft, gentle nibbles along the curve of her neck, sent sharp tingles of desire through her. Ana couldn't hold back a soft sigh of pleasure as she rolled her head to the side, shivering when he circled his tongue gently in and around her ear. His hand found one of her breasts through her wet shirt and he closed a large palm over it, the heat of him seeping through the fabric as he molded and caressed, finding the hard nipple poking through her shirt and teasing it.

She was hardly aware of the gritty sand beneath her, and the little rush of waves surging up and around their toes. She tasted Fence—warm, dark, and so tender for one of such bulk—smelled the fresh, now salty scent from his skin, and wanted *more*.

She needed to stroke the broad expanse of his back, to slide her hands flat over his pectorals and up beyond the square of muscular shoulders . . . she wanted to nibble on his ear and slide down along the ridges of his torso. When she shifted, brushing lower against his belly and hips, he made a soft, surprised sound of pleasure in her ear and grabbed her closer. The kiss went deeper and hotter, his tongue sliding and slickly dancing with hers.

Ana wasn't certain what happened next . . . they'd shifted and moved during their furious tangling there on the beach—and perhaps the wind kicked up too—but all at once, a surge of water crashed over them.

It was more than refreshing, and sudden, and Fence yanked his face away. It was as if a bucket of cold water had been tossed on a yowling cat, and he released her with such immediacy that she had to catch herself.

She blinked, and came thudding back to reality. *Crap!* What the hell had she been thinking? She'd been about ready to let him take off her shirt . . . a mistake she'd never made with anyone before, except Darian. His hands had been on her breasts, her butt, her everywhere. And she hadn't cared. Her lips throbbed, and she couldn't deny the damp ache of desire that still teased her, but at the same time she was filled with regret and fear.

Yet when she looked at him, he didn't seem to be staring at her with accusation or comprehension. He was looking out at the sea, which had become darker and rougher in the last few moments. "'S'cool," he muttered to himself. "I'm good."

At last he turned to her, his face no longer soft with passion and seduction, although those gorgeous lips of his were even more full and sensual now. "What in the hell were you doing out there?" he demanded, doing that quick-change thing again. As he spoke, he pulled his warm, smooth body away from hers, and Ana felt a brush of cool air over her skin.

"What are you talking about?" She'd expected him to ask her about the crystals. This didn't make sense.

Maybe he hadn't noticed them after all. Maybe she hadn't messed things up.

But he wasn't looking at her. He'd sat up and was staring out at the water again, as if he'd never seen an ocean before. His chest heaved like he'd been running, and droplets of water glistened all over those dark, broad shoulders and curving biceps.

Despite myriad emotions battling for her attention—confusion, annoyance, apprehension—Ana couldn't deny the renewed flare of lust that stabbed her in the pit of her stomach.

"What in the hell happened out there?" he said, but once again he didn't seem to be talking to her. He sort of whispered it. Staring out into the distance, he settled a large hand over his breastbone as if to feel the rhythm of breathing.

"Fence?" she said after a moment, and couldn't help but remember when he'd raged at her earlier today. This man was . . . odd. Sweltering and sexy, but maybe a little crazy.

"I thought I was drowning," he whispered. "I *was* drowning. I was . . ."

Ana watched him, bewilderment sliding into disbelief and reluctant comprehension. If he'd been drowning, inhaling water, he would have been coughing it up, vomiting. She would have had to pull him onshore and pummel him to get him to spew it out of his lungs. He wouldn't have been conscious after all that time under the water.

But none of that happened. Instead, he'd practically seduced her, right here in the middle of Envy, without spewing up a thing.

Just as when he rescued Tanya, she recalled. He hadn't coughed up any water at all.

She was right. He *had* been breathing underwater. Her brows knit together. That didn't make any sense at all, for so many reasons she couldn't begin to count them. *He* wasn't an Atlantean. She knew that for a fact.

"I . . ." His voice trailed off, and he drew in a deep, shuddering breath as he skimmed a hand over the top of his smooth head. Then all at once he was focused on her again. His eyes were clear and held more than a hint of accusation. "What in the hell were you doing out there? You scared the bad-ass out of me!"

"I don't know what you mean." She was truly confused.

"I came to look for you and I didn't see you," he said, his voice steadier now, as if whatever had been bothering him had gone away. "And then you appeared, and then you went underwater. For a long damn time, Ana. No one can be underwater that long."

Busted.

His eyes caught hers and she couldn't pull her gaze away. *Not good. Not good at all.*

Ana shoved herself awkwardly to her feet, unashamed that she leveraged her hands onto his amazing, rock-hard shoulder to help her stand up. Hey, it was there.

She smoothed her hands over the tank top to make sure it still lay down and flat over her crystals. At least they wouldn't be glowing through her shirt right now. "I'm glad you're okay now," she said, starting to walk away.

"Not so fast," he said, suddenly upright with startling speed. He wasn't just taller than she was, he towered over her. Damn him. "I came after you, and you were swimming. And I saw a glow around you. Like from crystals."

She could see the pieces clicking into place in his brain, aided, of course, by the discovery of Kaddick's body only hours ago. *Just my bad luck.*

"I always swim," she said, trying to summon a flirtatious smile. Maybe she could distract him again. "I like the feel of the water licking against my skin." She dropped her voice to a low hum. No, wait, that wasn't a good idea. He might get her to take off her shirt . . .

The slightest flare of warmth in his eyes told her he hadn't forgotten what happened a few minutes ago. But then it was gone as his gaze turned from hot to pointed. "Lift up your shirt."

Ana didn't have to fake her outrage. "Like hell I will!" She stepped back, careful this time where she put her foot, and managed to do so without stumbling. "I don't know who you think you are—"

Even though he'd just had his hand *up* her shirt a minute ago. Dang.

"Ana," he said, and his hand snaked out to close around her wrist. He wasn't rough and it wasn't a tight grip, but she knew she was in trouble now.

"Take your hand off me," she demanded, trying to jerk away. She wasn't frightened. She was mad. Furious.

And scared—not of him, but of what he might discover.

To her surprise, he released her, and to her great relief, she didn't stumble at the sudden lack of resistance. She backed away, watching where she stepped, yet keeping an eye on him as well as she could, with the sun right in her eyes.

"I've figured it out, Ana," he said. "You don't have to hide it."

Her mouth was so dry she could hardly form the response. "What are you talking about?" She should just turn and walk away.

She should get Dad and get the heck out of Envy and never come back. She had to protect herself, and her father too.

But she also had to help Envy, if she could. Her resolve wavered, turned confused.

Fence hadn't moved, but the sun had, and his shadow now fell long and dark over the ground. She couldn't see his face, for the light came from behind him.

And then all at once she realized the weapon she had, and tossed it right back at him. "I know about you too," she said boldly . . . even though that wasn't strictly true.

Her bold taunt had a better effect than she'd expected, for he actually straightened and stilled. "You don't know anything about me." But his words sounded faintly terrified, and she could see his fingers curling up into a fist against his thigh.

"You and the water," she said, feeling her way blindly—for she could hardly make out his features. But the pieces of the puzzle of Fence were starting to settle into place in her mind. There was something about him and the ocean. He seemed almost . . . frightened.

So odd, for such a big, confident man who loved the wilderness. She had to be missing something.

"Ana . . ." he said. His voice sounded pained, and she edged to one side, hoping he'd turn so he wouldn't be shaded so much.

"I'm going inside now. Dad and I will leave in the morning, and you won't need to take us back," she said, starting off as quickly as she could limp.

She couldn't ignore the danger to Envy. She just had to figure out a way to keep her own secret safe.

"Ana, are you from Atlantis?" he asked, and she stopped dead in her tracks. Her heart seemed to explode, its pounding filling her ears.

"No," she said over her shoulder. And then she limped off, hideously aware that though she hadn't lied, neither had she been strictly honest.

CHAPTER 9

Fence didn't try to stop Ana from leaving. Not this time.

Instead, he sank back down onto the coarse sand and rubble and watched the sea grow dark with twilight.

His shoes were still off to the side, along with his shirt, where he'd flung them. Ana hadn't bothered to pick up the remains of her own clothing, she'd been in such a hurry to get away from him.

The indentations in the sand where they'd rolled and writhed together had only been partially obliterated by the wave that yanked him out of the dark, hot passion and reminded him where he was . . . who he was.

What he was.

But what the *hell* had happened?

He remembered little about those moments in the water but sheer panic, blind terror. He remembered sinking, the cold sea rushing into him, into his lungs . . . the sharp stinging pain beneath his arms.

Frowning, he felt around his ribs to see what had cut him, for unlike the other scrapes and bumps on his skin, he didn't feel any residual pain.

He found nothing there but a little ridge, very slender and hardly more noticeable than a scratch—in fact, he'd felt it some time ago, but paid it no attention. But then he realized there was one on each side, just beneath his arms, along the space between the two top rib bones. A delicate little cut. Two of them. Strange.

They weren't bleeding, nor were they red or even pink. But they were identical in placement and length. He had no idea how long they'd been there—there weren't a lot of mirrors after the Apocalypse.

He shrugged, smoothing his fingertips over the little ridge one last time, then turned to examining the scrape on his forearm. He concluded it wasn't serious, but that a good washing and maybe a bandage might be in order. As he'd warned Ana that first time after she came out of the sea, scraped in a similar fashion, the simplest cut could turn into a septic infection.

But even as his attention turned to practical matters, he couldn't dismiss the niggling thought that continued to prickle his mind. He'd been underwater. He'd sucked water in, he *knew* he'd sucked water in during those panic-stricken moments . . . he'd felt it shoot through him. Cold and unfamiliar. Stinging.

His heart pounded like a riot in Motown and he felt that clammy-skinned, light-headed feeling sweep over him again. He'd been under the water, he'd *breathed*, and he *hadn't drowned*.

Fence shook his head hard enough to make himself dizzy. Impossible. Simply impossible.

Ana had saved him; that was all there was to it. She'd gotten to him in time and saved him. Dragged him onshore.

And he'd been so damned happy to be alive, to have fucked over whatever grim reaper had tried to drown him once more *and* to end up with a handful of crazy hot woman at the same time that he'd slipped right into that.

In spite of all the horror, Fence grinned in the twilight. Hot damn. That had been the highlight of an otherwise sucky day: his hands and mouth sampling soft, sweet, salty-fresh Ana.

A particularly strong wave tumbled onto the shore in front of him, rushing around his feet and drawing his attention from the pleasant memory to one he'd much rather avoid. As the water receded, he trailed his fingers in the wet sand and allowed his mind to go back to the impossible. His grin faded.

No fucking way.

But . . . if Simon could turn invisible without the use of a cloak, and Elliott could read the inside of a human body and heal with his hands . . . was it so unbelievable to consider the possibility that he could breathe underwater?

He couldn't take his eyes away from the rolling, foaming sea. The very idea of putting his face in the water and inhaling, trying to breathe, was beyond terrifying. His palms went slicker than a used car salesman, and he put the thought out of his mind. He couldn't do it.

Even if it had happened before—if he'd breathed underwater—there was no fucking way in hell he'd ever do it again. He simply *couldn't.*

He wasn't a doctor, he didn't have any deep understanding of the physiological workings of the human body other than his EMT training. But he knew that he was breathing air just as well as he always had. He had to have imagined it all.

He didn't have crystals like that guy lying on Elliott's table . . .

Oh. Wait.

Ana.

She'd helped him. And he'd seen that glow around her in the water too.

He'd had his hands almost everywhere over that long, golden body . . . wouldn't he have felt the crystals?

Or maybe he'd been a bit distracted.

Fence's eyes half closed for a moment, his mind easily rerouted from the unpleasantness of facing reality to the delicious memory of Ana plastered all over him like frosting on a wedding cake—all those sleek curves and nonstop legs and generous handfuls of breast and hip and booty. Even now he felt that sharp, twitching response, that renewal of desire, rising inside him.

And rising outside him as well. He grinned again and lifted his hand to smooth it over his skull. Yeah, he wasn't finished with the sun goddess yet.

But he paused when he saw his fingers. Recently sliding through the last bit of wave, they glittered with drops of thick, gray glop.

Fence stared at the substance, then saw that it had clung to his bare feet as well. He didn't know what it was or why it was suddenly showing up on Envy's shore, but he knew it was time to get some answers from someone who did.

This time he'd do it somewhere *away* from the water.

Fence couldn't find Ana anywhere. She wasn't with her father, she wasn't in the pub or the common eating area, she wasn't in the hotel room that he had arranged for her.

She wouldn't be crazy enough to start back to Glenway on her own, tonight, would she? No—he talked himself down from that sudden worry—she wouldn't leave George.

In fact, Fence would have stayed with George and demanded some answers from him if Flo hadn't been lurking about, fussing with her patient's bedcoverings and giving him "get out of here" glares.

Never one to cross a woman with that sort of "I'll slice off your nuts" look, he left the room eagerly. A pissed-off or annoyed female was too messy, too dangerous, and too freaking much work. He preferred them soft, smiling, and teasing. Even tears he could handle—all you had to do in that situation was hold the woman, rub her shoulders, dry her eyes while listening to whatever was making her bawl, and then, when things settled, crack a few jokes. And, quite often, his being so "sensitive" led to other pleasant advantages.

The fierce and angry females, however, he avoided like a wild pitch. If he couldn't talk her down with his melting grin, he was out of there.

He'd given up on finding Ana—who, unfortunately, seemed like she was going to fall into the latter category of women, which wouldn't make his evening any better—and, with a rising sense of urgency, headed down away from the inhabited areas of the old casino and hotel.

Elliott had mentioned they were going to move the body of the presumed Atlantean to the secret computer chamber, and Fence figured he'd better head down that way to let everyone know what he thought he'd figured out—about Ana, at least.

He sure as shit wasn't going to mention what had happened to him.

He walked quickly down the dark, dim corridor that was purposely left unmaintained. Despite the cunningly hidden lights that gave a faint, seemingly natural illumination to the area, the hall appeared deserted. Just like every other abandoned structure, it was littered with rubble, rodent nests, and other random junk. The fewer people in this part of the building, the fewer who'd have the chance to discover the working elevator shaft that led to the computer lab below.

The Waxnicki brothers—who were not only computer whizzes but also sci-fi and comic book geeks— had created what they called their Bat Cave, accessible only if one knew the secret code for the elevator. Fence had memorized it: up-down-down-up-up, and when the doors opened, you had to push in another code using the floor numbers. The back doors of the stationary elevator would open then, revealing the secret staircase. The current code for the back doors—it changed every week—was the birthday of someone named Linus Torvalds. *Lee*-nus, Theo had told him—not *Lie*-nus.

Whatever.

Just as Fence came around the corner to approach the elevator shaft, he saw a shadowy figure at the door. A woman. He halted in surprise . . . it wasn't Jade or Sage, definitely not Zoë.

She was bent over, pushing buttons . . .

He shot forward. Her height and the hitch in her step when she spotted him confirmed that it was Ana, and he caught her upper arm before she ducked away.

She tried to jerk free, but he had the advantage of surprise and strength. His stomach had gone a little queasy with fear and regret, wondering how she'd discovered the secret hideaway of the Resistance. There was no other reason for her to be here, in this remote, empty, old area of the hotel, unless she'd somehow found out about it—perhaps she'd followed Elliott when he brought the body here. Sneaking around like this meant she had to be on the other side—whatever side that was, except that it was the opposite of his.

"What are you doing here?" he asked, backing her toward the wall, mindful of her lame leg, but firm nevertheless, using the leverage of his grip on her arm.

"I got lost," she told him. And the next thing he knew, she had that little knife in her hand, its blade glinting right beneath his chin in the dim light. Even in the poor illumination he could see the determination in her eyes. And maybe a little fear.

He knew how he appeared: tall and dark and freaking massive. Fearsome, for sure, especially here, in what passed for the proverbial dark alley. Normally, he was very aware of this, particularly around a woman, and he adjusted his approach accordingly. After all, life wasn't a football field. And hadn't they just been rolling around in the sand? But now he used this ferocity to his advantage and moved in sideways so his thigh wedged her in place. Jesus, she smelled good. "You got lost? All the way over here?"

"What are *you* doing here?" she shot back. Her knife wavered, but he hardly noticed, for that little thing wasn't any more of a threat to him than a tattoo artist's needle.

"Maybe I followed you," he said, and gripped her hand to move the knife aside.

"I doubt that." Her voice, though steady, was a little breathless, but she didn't cower from his gaze. "You were a wasted ball of nerves back on the beach. I don't think you were in any condition to follow me anywhere," she sneered.

He tried to ignore the insult, but a wisp of anger and humiliation rippled through him. So much for getting his freak on with her. "What the hell are you up to, Ana?"

"I have no idea what you're talking about," she said, and he felt her knife hand go limp in his grip . . . but he didn't release her. "And you can stop following me. Here, on the beach, everywhere. Leave me alone."

Fence considered his options. She wasn't going anywhere, and even though she happened to be a hot bundle of woman, he couldn't allow himself to soften. If, as he'd come to suspect, she was an Atlantean—or at least aligned with them—he couldn't trust her. None of them could trust her, but at least they could try to find out what she knew . . . without letting her in on *their* secrets.

He could lift up her tight little button-down shirt right here and see if those crystals that he was certain existed were in fact there in her torso . . . but his mama's pretty but stern face rose in his memory, along with her wagging finger and fierce, snapping eyes. *You treat all women with respect, all the time, Bruno Paolo Washington, or you're going to have me to answer to— either now or at the Pearly Gates.*

And somehow, he had always suspected that even his mama could take precedence over Saint Peter when it came to the afterlife and which direction he went.

So he couldn't just reach out and yank up Ana's shirt. As angry and concerned as he was, as nasty as she'd just been, it just wouldn't be right. Damn his conscience.

"Here's the deal, Ana," he said, leaning in closer— and not only to intimidate her.

She must have showered and washed off the sea salt,

because she smelled crazy, like flowers and delicious female. Her hair was almost completely dry, in long, loose waves that looked as if she'd just been tumbled into—or out of—bed. And in contrast to the soft, after-sex look, her shirt was buttoned up practically to her chin, her sleeves rolled up just below the elbows. All suited up and inside her cotton shield.

Despite the precarious situation, heat flared inside him at the thought of what lay beneath. "You can either lift up your shirt and show me that you don't have any crystals in your skin, or I'll do it for you. With pleasure."

He could feel her jagged pulse pounding against him, and the tension vibrating beneath her skin. Too damn bad it wasn't because of his good looks and charm.

Or what he could do with his mouth.

"You're disgusting," she said. "You'll try anything to get a woman undressed."

He avoided the obvious mental detour. "I'm going to count to five. If you don't, I will." He tried to keep his eyes hard instead of melting into the heat that thought generated. Button by button by button—

Yo, brother. Focus.

"One . . . two . . ."

Her chest rose and fell as she glared up at him. He thought he read indecision in her eyes, and that alone was almost all the answer he needed. If she didn't have anything to hide, she'd show him some skin.

He almost forgot to count, distracted once again. "Uh . . . three—"

Her arm moved suddenly—the one with the knife—but he stopped her in mid-strike.

"Jesus, Ana," he said, more offended than angry. It was a pansy knife, but she was wielding it like she meant it. "Now you're trying to kill me?"

"I was aiming for your upper arm," she said defensively. "That wouldn't kill a big guy like you. It would hardly ni—"

"Four," he said, because he couldn't argue with that logic.

She tensed, then relaxed in his grip. "Okay. But back away. I'll show you."

"Don't trust me to do the job, huh?" he asked, flashing a slow grin. "I'm real good with buttons."

"I don't trust you to do anything but piss me off," she said. "Now back off."

He stepped away far enough so he was no longer holding her pinned to the wall with his thigh but close enough to snatch her back if she tried to make a run for it. Not that she could run anyway.

A pang of guilt stabbed him at the reminder of his great advantage over her. He wasn't even going to get to see his mama at the Pearly Gates—he was going straight to hell.

He couldn't help but glance down at Ana's legs. They were encased in dark jeans, so all he could see was the imperfect curl of her bare foot next to a slender, normal one. But, jeez, she had long legs.

"Okay, start unbuttoning," he said, forcing command into his voice, reminding himself that sympathy would only weaken him.

She glanced up, then with her knifeless hand started to unbutton her shirt from the bottom. Slowly.

His breathing shifted and caught as she undid one button, then another. He'd seen his fair share of women undress, but this was the hottest striptease he could remember. His palm felt a little damp and he rubbed it inconspicuously against the side of his shorts as she undid another button.

Now he could see a triangle of skin, and he swallowed hard, his heart pounding. *Mmm*-hmm. Her jeans rode low, and her belly was smooth and pale like a moonbeam here in the dim light. He admired the dark crescent of her navel as she unfastened a fourth button, and he realized his knees were quivering.

Thank you, God, for not letting me drown today.

Another button revealed the gentle indentation of the hollow just below her breastbone, and Fence found himself mesmerized by that little spot. He needed to rest his lips there, to press a little kiss . . . and then a gentle swipe from the tip of his tongue.

A breath above that would be the bottom edge of her bra. If she was wearing one. If not . . . a spear of lust caught him in his belly. If not, there'd be nothing but that sexy, private undercurve of her breasts. Soft, warm, and scented deeply of Ana.

She paused, then flipped the edge of her loosened shirt away on one side in a big triangle, revealing the sweet curve of her hip and absolutely nothing else. *Hoo-weee.* He actually felt light-headed.

"There," she said. "Satisfied?"

Was it his imagination or was there a definite layer of huskiness in her voice?

"Not even close," he said, moving a little nearer. His fingers itched to slide over that smooth expanse of bare midriff, to see the contrast of his dark skin against her golden belly and feel the silky warmth of her, the little shudders in the wake of his touch . . . and then to slide down behind the bulky buttons on her jeans and into the delicious heat of the sun goddess.

"Fence," she said, her voice sharp . . . yet cracking, deeper.

Even through the sudden, powerful haze of lust, he

remembered what he was after . . . and the limitations
of what she'd revealed.

"The other side," he said, gently taking her knife
hand. "Show me the other side."

He felt the tension in her wrist. Her chest moved with
a sudden little jerk and she said, "Okay. Let go of me."

"Let me," he murmured, holding her wrist high,
pinning it firmly to the wall at her shoulder. *Let me.*
His fingers curled into themselves, his mouth dry. His
whole body was tight and throbbing.

"No," she said. Her voice cracked out like a whip.

No. He had no choice. The word was like an ice-cold
shower, a stone wall, a gun barrel pointed at him. He
eased back.

"Ana," he said. "We both know what you're hiding."
He focused on her, capturing her gaze and delving
steadily into it.

Her eyelids fluttered and he felt the change in her
breathing yet again. But she made no move to argue,
nor to reveal the left side of her torso.

"Why don't you tell me what you're up to," he said.
"What that gray stuff is—I saw it in your father's lab,"
he added when she drew in a breath to speak.

Not that he minded, for it brought her breasts up and
out, closer to his chest. He was suddenly, delightedly,
certain she wasn't wearing a bra. His knees weakened.

What happened to his dislike of angry, difficult
women? Even her knife wielding didn't send him running.

"I'm not up to anything," she said, her eyelids droop-
ing in a seductive way that totally worked for him.

"I'm going to have to look, sugar. I warned you . . ."
He moved one of his big hands to settle on her shoulder, holding her in place. Gently, but firmly. "Believe

me, I'd rather have a different reason for taking your clothes off."

With a quick, deft movement he flipped the loose shirt away from the left side of her midriff. Ana shied back as he did, then suddenly stilled and stopped trying to hide . . . because by then it was all over.

Holy Jesus.

Fence saw the four dark spots studding the spaces between her ribs. At quick glance they might have been mistaken for large freckles or beauty marks, but he had a bit longer than a glance to notice them, which gave the faulty light an opportunity to catch the facets of the crystals.

Dull glints came from the pea-sized stones, displaying a subtle hint of blue. He'd seen gems or piercings settled in a woman's navel, even Marley's Elite crystal, which was set below her collarbone . . . but this was different. Unexpected and exotic.

And at the same time, terrifying.

Anna had caught her breath, went as still as a statue as he stared down at the crystals embedded in her flesh.

"Do they hurt?" he asked, still holding her in place with one hand, as the other eased toward her skin. He had to touch her . . . to feel them. His heart thudded with anticipation.

Her belly danced in a quick shudder as his fingers skimmed over it and then brushed each of the four small rises of her gems. They were cooler than her skin, hard where she was soft, but each facet just as smooth as the rest of her.

"No," she said, and it took him a moment to remember what he'd asked her.

"What about when you got them. Did it hurt?" He touched one with the pad of his thumb, gently yet firmly to see if it moved. Her skin shifted slightly, then settled back into place. Fence realized he'd been holding his breath, and released it slowly.

His body hummed and pounded, and he fought away the urge to close his hands around her bare waist and pull her up against him, flush, from torso to hips to long, long legs . . .

"I don't know," she told him. "I've had them . . . for as long as I can remember. Let me go. You've seen what you want to see." Her voice trembled a bit, and for the first time he recognized fear in her eyes.

But he wasn't finished with her.

"Are you Atlantean?" he asked, looking up at her suddenly, peeling away the lust that dulled his senses. For all he knew, she could be a Mata Hari, sent here to spy on them and find out about the Resistance. "Tell me the truth this time."

There was a long moment when he thought she wouldn't answer. But then: "Half," she said. "My mother was."

A rush of relief buzzed through Fence, and it took him a moment to realize why: that his manhandling and intimidation was justified. Maybe he wouldn't burn in hell after all.

But then again the way his thoughts were going . . .

"Now will you let me go?" she said again. Her shoulder moved beneath his hand, and he allowed it to drop away as she pushed against him. Tension emanated from her, and he regretted the discord.

Despite who she was and his darkening suspicions, he wanted her soft and pliant and relaxed. Like she'd been on the beach . . . all hot and moaning and sighing. Warm and wet—

A guy could do so much more with that. His eyes

moved back down to the bare torso only inches from his own. Just a sneak peek of the whole package and his knees were threatening to give out. His mouth was dry again.

"I haven't done anything wrong," she continued, but her voice was less strident. Almost breathy. And her fingers weren't pushing against his shoulder as firmly as before.

Why fight it?

"Well, let's see if we can change that, sugar." Fence allowed his knees to have their way, and as he grasped her by the hips, he sank down in front of her.

CHAPTER 10

Ana gasped when his lips brushed against her belly, just next to her navel. Her skin leapt with delicate tremors as Fence kissed her gently, so incredibly softly. His tongue slipped out, his lips full and warm as he tasted and nuzzled in sweet little circles over her torso.

She sagged back against the wall, needing the extra balance, and lost the loose grip on her knife. It thunked to the floor and she didn't even care . . .

He held her firmly at the hips as he nosed away the flap of her shirt, his mouth teasing over the soft rise of her stomach. The feathery tickling sensation sent heat welling inside her, shooting down to where she was growing full and warm and slick.

She held her breath when he came near the crystals, but he was gentle there, too, and then began to trail soft, light kisses all along the skin just above the rise of her jeans. She trembled at the delicate touch, her breathing rough—and her fingers . . . they fluttered a bit until settling on top of his impossibly wide shoulders. Hot and broad and sleek with muscle beneath the thin, tight shirt, he shifted beneath her touch.

When Fence came to the buttons at the fly of her jeans, he paused, then released her waist. A little jerk, a little pop, and one—no, two—buttons loosened.

Somewhere in the back of her mind, Ana knew she should protest, but she felt languid and loose, wrapped in the rush of pleasure. Her little knife was . . . somewhere, but nothing seemed to matter but the lush warmth spreading through her body, the rising *need*.

Fence rose to his feet, and the next thing she knew, he had her mouth under his, with lips so full and soft, coaxing and luring her into a world of pleasure. Demanding fingers eased down along the curve of her waist, beneath her shirt. They slid gently into the sagging jeans at her hips, then angled around to the top swell of her bottom as he pulled her sharply up against him. *All* against him.

And . . . *whoa*.

She hummed her delighted surprise from deep in her chest and felt his mouth smirk against hers, then suddenly felt the hard wall behind her as he pressed in even closer. She wrapped her arms around his neck, cupping the back of his smooth skull, leaning back into him.

She tensed nervously when he touched her right hip, his fingers now sliding deeper below the line of her jeans, knowing that her skin there was rough and puckered with scars . . . then she forgot all about it as he shifted his hips against her again, pressing urgently into her. The low rumble of his half-laughing moan sent a little spear of lust darting down deep inside her.

Then all at once she heard a voice, followed by a dull rolling sound, and then the voice was louder. More light spilled into the area, and Ana froze, the lust draining away as she realized the elevator door she'd been trying to get into had opened.

"—crazy batshit excuse, genius," a woman was saying. "I don't fucking need to be saving your ass every damn time I turn around, as fine as your ass might be." There was a rustling sound, perhaps even a bit of sloppy, sleek suction happening. "And it is a hellastically fine ass."

Fence had stilled, but despite Ana's instinct to push him away and put coherent thoughts back together— *get the hell out of here*—he made only a lazy move to step back. He glanced down at her, and she saw a glimmer of laughter in eyes that still smoked with pleasure.

"Right," replied a man in a voice just as precise and yet affectionate as the woman's was annoyed. "Except that you *live* to save my arse every chance you get. It's what keeps you going, luv."

The woman gave a snort, and apparently at that moment noticed them. "Who the hell are— Oh, fuck. Fence, can't you find another damned place to do that?"

By now Ana had pulled her shirt back into place and corralled her thoughts. She realized her partner, such as he was, had been doing her a favor by not moving right away—he'd blocked her from view.

"Well, you know me, Zoë," Fence said with that bass-deep chuckle that sent little shivers into the pit of Ana's belly. "When opportunity knocks, I'm always going to answer that motherfucking door."

Ana straightened up. *What the hell? Opportunity* knocked?

It was more like he bulldozed the darn door down. The last vestiges of pleasure now evaporated, she began to sidle away . . . but Fence's hand whipped out and caught her wrist.

He gave her a "not so fast" look, then turned his attention back to the man and woman, whose name appeared to be Zoë. She was a slender, athletic-looking woman whose body emanated energy and impatience. Her dark hair was short and spiked every which way about her exotic, mahogany face.

Her companion was a tall, well-built man with blond hair. He looked calm, unruffled, and neat—a clear contrast to the woman he had apparently been kissing a moment earlier. Nor did he look like the sort of guy who needed a woman to save his ass.

"I was looking for Elliott," Fence told them.

Zoë snorted. "Yeah, that's exactly what it looked like to me."

Fence flashed her a smile that infuriated Ana even more. "Well, yeah, like I said, opportunity and all that shit. We've got some things to tell him. And you as well." He tightened his fingers around Ana's wrist, and her heart began to thud harder.

She was in such deep murk now. He'd tricked and seduced her and now knew her secret, and he was going to tell everyone . . . and what were they going to do with her?

Ana's insides, so recently soft and fluttery with pleasure, now churned with nausea. She actually felt lightheaded, and a bead of sweat rolled down her spine. What a fool. A handsome face and broad shoulders and a way with children . . . and she gave right in. *I've got to get away from him. Out of here.*

"Dred's below," said the man, glancing curiously at Ana. "I was just examining the crystal—"

"And nearly lost his mind in the process," Zoë cut in, her voice sharp and furious. But beneath it Ana recognized the same bald fear that was in her father's voice when he lectured her about swimming alone too far away from home. "So I fucking made Quent take a damned break. Someone has to have more than an ass-crap brain—"

"It has to be done," the blond man, presumably Quent, said. Clear affection reflected in his tones, but also flat stubbornness. "It's the only chance we have—" He stopped, looking at Ana again. "Right."

"Right," Fence echoed, and the two men exchanged glances. They seemed uncertain about how to proceed.

"Oh for the *life* of me," Zoë burst out. "Put a fucking blindfold on her and take her down there before hell freezes over. She already knows where the fuck it is."

Ana tensed again. "I'm not going to be dragged around like some sort of prisoner," she informed Fence, and shot a look at Zoë. "Blindfolded like some sort of captive."

The terrible thought struck her. He wasn't going to keep her prisoner, was he? They didn't dare lock her up—but what if they sent her back to Atlantis?

Fence seemed to notice her distress, and he actually gave Ana a sympathetic glance. "We can't really let you see where we're going or how to get there. But you're not a prisoner," he told her.

"Great. Then I'll see you later," she said, pulling her hand away from him. She wished she had her knife, but it was over in the corner.

He grabbed her wrist again. "You're not a prisoner, but I'd like to ask you some questions."

"So now you'd 'like' to ask me questions? You're *requesting* me to answer some questions?" she said, glaring at him. "Well, you're just going to have to wait until opportunity 'knocks.' And let me tell you, this door is bolted pretty darn tight."

"Hot damn. I like this chick," Zoë said, watching with a smirk.

Fence chuckled too. "Hey, I saw her first," he warned. When Ana directed a furious glare at him, he merely smiled wider and let his eyes go a little warmer.

Her belly wavered, dang it.

"Zoë's got the right idea," Quent said. He looked at Ana. "My apologies, but we're going to need to speak with you. And in order to protect ourselves—and you— it would be best if you were blindfolded. The less you know, the less you can be forced to tell."

Well, when you put it that way. Ana's insides were twisting with apprehension. One thing was certain: whatever she was worried about happening with the sea, these people had other concerns on their collective mind. And they weren't taking any chances.

"Fine," she said flatly. Then she looked at Fence. "But this in no way can be construed as the door being answered."

"That's a damned shame," he said, his insouciant grin even wider, his eyes hot and steamy. "Because I love a woman in a blindfold."

Ana succumbed to the blindfolding partly because she didn't have much choice, when it came down to it— they weren't going to let her leave—and aside from that, Quent had made sense when he suggested it might protect her.

Both the Atlanteans—and by extension, the Elite— were entities she wanted to avoid. Come to think of it, she wanted to avoid everyone—both mortal and immortal, both land-walking and sea-living.

If everyone would just leave her *alone.* Better to be lonely than to be back in Atlantis.

Since she didn't have a choice, she could see that her

energies were best utilized by deciding how she would handle the upcoming interrogation, what she was going to say and what she wasn't—instead of trying to run away.

She also realized that this might give her some leverage: if she kept their secrets, maybe they'd keep hers.

The blindfold smelled like Fence, which was disturbing because she liked it all too well. He'd taken off that thin shirt and tied it around her eyes and the top of her head, then led her off.

They walked her around, presumably to mix her up on the direction, even though she knew that the elevator doors led somewhere . . .

And at last, after some walking, some stairs, some jerking, then an odd weightless feeling when she was standing, the blindfold was removed.

She found herself in a very brightly lit room that looked like something out of an old DVD. Sofas and chairs were gathered on one end, with a low table between them. The solid white walls were covered with a few old movie posters and a metal plate with the code WIXY 97 engraved on it. But taking up most of the very large, stark space were several rows of tables with what she supposed were computers on them. Screens. Keyboards. Other electronic devices she'd only seen in movies and couldn't identify.

The space had a constant low humming, rumbling sound, and beyond it she could see a door that led to another room.

A spike of fear leapt in her stomach as she looked around, searching for escape. She wasn't used to being confined in a space without windows to see or feel the outside world. She knew from descending the stairs that they were below the surface, and being underground was very unlike being on the bottom of the sea. Her breathing became rougher and more shallow. Even though the area was large, she felt the walls closing in on her, the ceiling heavy and low above her.

"Have a seat," Fence said, and then he must have seen the expression in her face, for he paused and gave her a good look. "Ana?" Concern colored his expression and words, mollifying her slightly.

"We're underground," she managed to say. Her skin felt clammy.

He nodded, moving closer to her, looking at her as if trying to read her thoughts. "Yes," he said. "No one's going to hurt you. We just need to know what's going on."

Ana drew in a deep breath, swallowing the words that would tell him that wasn't what she was worried about, and she used that thought as a distraction from her disturbing environment. By all accounts she should no longer be worried about them knowing her secret. And about being taken prisoner—for there was hardly any other way to look at her situation. No one knew she was here, and there was no way out unless they let her go.

Another zing of nerves shot through her, and she tightened her fingers in an intricate curl. *One step at a time. Fence hasn't done anything but kiss the heck out of you.*

But then . . . so had Darian . . . and more. And look how that turned out.

With that not so pleasant thought, she sat on one of the sofas as Quent and Zoë took their seats. A moment later Elliott, the doctor, came in through the other room's door.

Fence didn't beat around the bush. "Ana's part Atlantean," he said.

"Do you have crystals?" asked Quent. He didn't seem horrified by this news, but, rather, interested. As did Elliott and Zoë . . . all of them, in fact, seemed more fascinated than accusatory.

All except Fence, who, despite his sympathy a moment earlier, still wore a skeptical look.

Ana nodded in response to Quent.

"They help you breathe underwater?" asked Elliott. She nodded again.

"What's the gray stuff we found on the shore the first day you were here in Envy?" Fence asked.

"I don't know," she told them.

"You have some back home," Fence said, taking her by surprise. "In George's lab. Where did it come from? What is it?"

"I took some for Dad so he could try and figure out what it is. He hasn't been able to identify it, and I haven't either."

"Where is Atlantis?" asked Quent. He'd leaned forward, his eyes sparkling with fascination and determination.

Ana's heart was pounding now. Would they believe her if she told them she didn't know? "I left Atlantis when I was thirteen. I don't know where it is."

Zoë snorted. "Bullcrap. You must have some idea. You lived there, didn't you?"

Ana gave her a cool look. "It's a big ocean."

"What's it like? Is it really a city with a dome over it? At the bottom of the ocean?" Quent asked. "I can't believe it really exists."

She bit her lip. She hated the Atlanteans . . . but did

she dare divulge their secrets? Would she get caught up in the same wave of culpability if Fence and his friends found out exactly what her people had done? Would they blame her too?

"It's . . . yes, the original city has a dome over it," she said, deciding on a vague approach. "I don't remember that much about it . . . it's been a long time . . . I only went there once."

"The 'original' city. So . . . there's another one?" Quent's eyes had sharpened. "Is that the one that's in the Pacific Ocean now, the one that appeared after the Change?"

Ana swallowed. They knew more than she'd imagined . . . more than any land-livers did. How?

The others exchanged looks, and then by virtue of some silent agreement, Fence asked, "Why did you leave Atlantis?"

Here was where she didn't want to go. Ana kept her expression blank and reminded herself not to twist her fingers nervously. "My mother died, and so my father and I left. We didn't have any reason to stay," she said calmly. "My mother was the only connection."

"I want to show you something." Quent rose suddenly and walked over to a tall metal cabinet. The drawer screeched softly as he pulled it open, and then he extracted a cloth-wrapped object.

Ana felt something change in the room . . . a sort of vibration, subtle and deep.

Quent put the item on the low table in front of them and pulled the fabric away to reveal a large pale blue crystal. The stone looked like a piece that had been hacked out of some large gem. Bigger than her fist, it had jagged edges along the top and smooth, striated sides. A faint glow emanated from it.

"Where did you get that?" she gasped, staring in shock. It had to be from the Jarrid stone. The glow, the energy zapping from it, the color, all were the same. And now this one was glowing brighter too.

All at once she was aware of the growing heat beneath her shirt, emanating from her crystals. She glanced down, saw the faint glow through the fabric and realized what was happening. *No.*

Panic burst through her. *Shitshitshit.*

"Get it away," she cried, scrambling up from her seat. "Get it away from me!"

CHAPTER 11

The shock and terror on Ana's face was enough to have Fence lunging for the crystal. He scooped it up, whipping the fabric around it just as Quent got to his feet.

"What is it?" Fence asked Ana, shoving the bundle at Quent. "What's wrong?" He could see a glow from beneath her shirt, which still flapped enticingly—especially with her panicked movements.

"Just get it away," she repeated from between tight jaws. She was still backing as far from the crystal as she could, covering her own gems with her hands. She'd moved surprisingly quickly across the room, considering her lame leg.

"I'll be right back." Quent took the bundle, safely wrapped so its touch wouldn't drag him into the whirlwind of memories and power, and rushed it from the room.

Elliott had risen and gone to Ana's side as Fence stood, uncertain, as if blocking her from the crystal, but unable to do much else.

"Are you in pain?" Elliott asked, taking her arm gently.

With Quent out of the room, the glow subsided beneath Ana's shirt, and the stark panic eased from her face. She sat back down at Elliott's urging, eyeing the doorway through which the crystal had disappeared.

"No," she said. "Not pain. But it recognized me . . . my crystals. It must have . . . activated them. The crystals are all connected, and there are some that have the ability to call or to find others. If that's one of them—it made mine glow . . . my God, they're going to *find* me now." She bolted to her feet again as if looking for a way out. "I have to get out of here. And Dad—we have to get out of here." The urgency in her voice and movements made even Fence twitchy.

"Ana," he said, shifting into comforting mode with a gentle voice. This wasn't tears, but it was awfully close. And his suspicions about her had begun to wane in the face of her obvious terror. "The big crystal's gone now. Yours aren't glowing anymore. How about sitting down and telling us what that was all about so we can help?"

At first he didn't think she was going to talk—no surprise, for she'd been reticent all along. But Fence settled himself next to her and, to his pleasure, she curled her fingers around his hand when he rested it on top of hers.

"I've been hiding from them since Dad and I escaped. If they find me now because of that crystal, they'll take me back." Her look added: *And it'll be all your fault.*

He pulled out the important elements of her speech. "To Atlantis?"

"Yes."

"You don't want to go back to Atlantis," Quent confirmed as he strode back into the room.

"No," she replied stridently, her eyes fierce. Her hand slipped away from Fence's grip. "Never."

Fence recognized relief channeling through him. That was good. If she didn't want to go back, then she likely wasn't one of them.

He was down with it, definitely down with the idea that she might actually be on their side. His side.

Of course, he'd most rather have her on her *back*-side . . .

"So the crystal we have is connected to yours some-how?" he asked, collecting his wayward thoughts.

Ana nodded. "They're all connected by the same sort of energy. Some of it is more powerful than others, and that crystal you have—I just can't imagine how you could have gotten it. And I can't believe they haven't come after it. Found it. They must be . . ." She shook her head, worry warring with curiosity in her expression. "Who *are* you people?"

"That," Fence said, "is a very good question." He was willing to tell her now, but he needed agreement from the others.

"My father was one of the Elite," Quent said. "Parris Fielding. Do you know that name?"

Ana shook her head. "No. Should I?"

Fence shrugged and enjoyed the fact that his arm brushed against hers. He sidled a hair closer. "Maybe. He was one of the Inner Circle of the Elite, and from what we understand, they were in contact with Atlantis. Using the crystal Quent had."

"I was only thirteen when we left . . . I wasn't exactly privy to the inner workings of the Crown and Shield," she said.

"What's that?" asked Quent, once again leaning forward with interest. "Are they crystals?"

"They're people . . . the Crown is the male ruler, almost like a king. And the Shield is the female. They have a group of advisers that control everything. My mother's father was one of the Guild, as they're called. They make all the decisions, the laws . . . they're the ones who likely would have been in contact with . . . with the Elites."

"We haven't been able to determine how to use the crystal to contact Atlantis," said Quent.

"And genius here's almost killed himself trying to figure it out," Zoë said—speaking up, shockingly, only for the first time. "If you have any ideas, sister, we're all fucking ears."

"I'm pretty sure it's part of the Jarrid stone," Ana said. "That is—or was—a large crystal, about as big as this sofa cushion. I've seen what's left of it. Pieces were broken off and sent to far corners, placed deep in the sea in hopes that Atlantis would find a way to communicate with those above the water. Or with other Atlanteans, when and if they left the main city."

"Like a message in a bottle. Sort of," Fence said.

"How many pieces?" Quent asked.

"I'm not sure. Five maybe. You have to understand, this happened long ago—centuries ago. Maybe a thousand years. The rest of the stone is still in Atlantis. But how did your father get this piece?"

"I don't know. I'd guess he found it accidentally. Or maybe he discovered some sort of legend or map . . . he was very wealthy and had a lot of resources, and he liked to hunt for treasure. He belonged to a group called the Cult of Atlantis. People who believed Atlantis existed and wanted to find it. And, apparently, they did. And then they destroyed the world."

Ana was nodding. "Yes, I've heard the story of how

that happened." Her face was sober, and her eyes flickered toward Fence. For the first time, he saw an expression of revulsion twisting her face. "They talk about how it was a miracle, a great and wonderful event, The Rising."

"When the city rose up out of the sea?" Fence said, his own insides twisting.

"The Raised City. The one they were building and preparing for over centuries. That's where I lived most of the time for my first thirteen years."

"So it's *not* under the water? What did you need the crystals for, then? Can Atlanteans breathe out of the water?" The questions came quickly, Quent's interrogation echoing Fence's own thoughts and interest—and, based on the expressions on Elliott's and Zoë's faces, theirs as well.

"They can't live for long outside the water. Nor can they go far from the energy of flowing water, or the crystals will die . . . and then the Atlanteans will die. They became dependent upon the crystals over the centuries, and now they can't live without them. Even the Raised City is purposely flooded with water for that reason—streets, pools, everywhere. They live half in and half out of the water, as they're trying to evolve—I guess that's the word—into being able to live on the land again, without being restricted to the ocean." Ana turned to Quent. "How did you ever get the stone from your father?"

Quent's smile was humorless. "I stole it."

A thought, a bad thought, struck Fence. "Ana, are you telling us that they can track the location and presence of the crystal?"

She shrugged, looking at him as she brushed back a thick strand of hair. "I'm not certain . . . They didn't tell me much, even though . . ." Her voice trailed off. "But the reaction my crystals had to that big one could mean there's a way to sense its location. They're all tied together, all that energy. I'm afraid that my crystals activated or otherwise woke that one up, or that it woke mine up—because I felt its energy—and now because of that, they'll find us. If there are any other crystals from the energy source of the original Atlantis, they could be awake and alive, too, right now."

"You and George escaped? Were you a prisoner?" Fence asked.

"I didn't want to stay with them," she said.

"What about your mother? You told me she was an Atlantean."

"She died. And Dad and I left."

Fence had a feeling the story wasn't nearly that simple, but now wasn't the time, obviously, to dig deeper.

"Have you had any contact with Atlantis since you left?" Elliott asked.

Ana shook her head quickly. Too quickly, Fence thought. "No. I told you, I don't want to go back there. I don't want them to know where I am—why would I have contact with them? You obviously know what they did."

Logical. But not completely honest. "So you must have recognized the dead man who washed up on the shore. Is that why you were in this part of the building?"

She hesitated, then replied, "I didn't know him well, but, yes, I recognized him. I just . . . wanted to see him again," she said defensively. "To see if I could tell how he died."

"Looked to me like he was attacked," Fence said. "A shark or some other sea creature."

"Atlanteans don't just get attacked by sea creatures," she said, more than a note of derision in her voice. "I mean, they live with them, sort of. It would be very unusual. The ocean is just an extension of their world . . . like the forest and mountains is yours."

Abruptly, Ana shook her head and her face went cool. "I'm done talking. I think it's time you gave me some answers. Like, who the hell are you people? And what's this place?"

Fence's unashamedly lustful attraction for Ana went up a notch into admiration—not only because of the tone in her voice, but the way she settled back in her seat as if suddenly taking control. Ballsy woman, especially in the position she was in. He found he rather liked a woman who took charge, even if she was a bit higher in the maintenance area.

Smart. Brave. Ballsy. And she got his jokes.

The whole damn package . . . right here.

"I think we should tell her," he said, looking at Elliott.

The physician gave a slight nod of agreement, but then he asked, "What's your relationship with the Strangers?"

"Do you mean the Elite?" Ana said. "I don't have any relationship with them. I just want to stay out of everyone's way, all right? I'd be just as happy if I weren't even here, especially now that I think your damned crystal has given away my location after twelve years." Her voice was strained again. "I've got to get out of here."

"You don't know for certain," Fence began, but he exchange worried looks with Elliott and Quent. If the activation of the crystal had somehow identified their location to the bounty hunters, Elite or the Atlantean . . . they could be seriously fucked.

"I don't want to take the chance." Frustration sparked off her. "If I wasn't so worried about what's going on in the ocean, I wouldn't even *be* here."

Whoa, whoa, whoa. "What do you mean, what's going on in the ocean?" The room was suddenly vibrating with tension.

Ana settled back into her seat, passing a hand over her forehead and scooping back her hair again. "I don't know, but there's something wrong. Something's happening, something different. That's why I had the gray stuff at home—I'd never seen it before either. And I know the sea like you know—you know, the terrain. The land. I don't like it. It feels like something's going to happen. Something not good."

The room grew quiet. Fence exchanged a glance with Quent, who nodded in agreement at his unspoken question.

"When we were on our way here from Glenway," he told her, "and I went after that car, I overheard two bounty hunters talking. They said something about Envy being destroyed. That's what we've been doing: trying to figure out what's going to happen. We've got to stop whatever it is." He looked at Ana, and for the first time allowed the worry into his eyes. "I think you might be able to help us."

She looked wary. "What do you want me to do?"

"If there's a threat from the ocean, you'd be the one to recognize it."

She nodded, looking less nervous. "Of course. Believe me, I'd already planned to tell you—someone—if I discovered something. But I don't *know* anything. It's just that I feel something's wrong."

"Guess you'll have to get back in that big-ass ocean," Zoë suggested. "See what you can find."

"I'm not going back to Atlantis, if that's what you're suggesting. Even if I knew where to find it," she said flatly.

"Right. But what do you *think,* Ana? You know them," Quent said. "The most obvious threat would be an undersea army or navy of some sort, where we wouldn't see them coming until it was too late. Or—bloody hell, they did it once, they could do it again: a tsunami that destroys the city. And we wouldn't have a chance of stopping that, even if we had prior knowledge."

"We don't even know that the Atlanteans are the ones behind whatever is going to threaten Envy," Fence reminded him. "I heard the bounty hunters talking about some dudes knowing what was up—sounded like Elites to me. Hell, maybe we ought to go on a manhunt for some guys named Roofey and Kaddick, and find out what they know." He was half serious when he cracked his knuckles, as if preparing for a fight.

"Kaddick?" Ana's attention shot to him. "Freaking busted sword. Kaddick is the name of the Atlantean they found on the beach."

"That is not a good sign," Fence said. "And it can't be a coincidence."

Ana shook her head. "I'd say no to that."

She bit her lip and settled back in her seat again, looking more pensive than uncomfortable for the first time since her blindfold was removed. Her eyes darted randomly about the space, her face holding an expression that seemed to be a struggle, and everyone remained silent, as if sensing she needed time to think.

Then she looked at Fence. "Yes, of course I'll help, but I need some assurances from you first."

A woman who liked to bargain. He was cool with that. "Such as?"

"I need security—I can't be found or discovered here, because if word gets back, they'll come after me."

"Well, that's right up my alley." Fence grinned, launching into a warm, slow smile. "Personal security is my—"

Ana was smiling, too, but not at his joke. It was a cool, remote smile that reminded him of the Mona Lisa. "I don't mean that. I mean I need to know how to get into this place and out of it." She gestured to the room at large. "You have your secrets and I have mine . . . and it's only fair if I know yours too. That way no one's tempted to reveal them."

"Leverage," Quent said, his face expressionless.

Zoë was shaking her head in dismay. "I can't fucking help it, I really do like her."

"It's only fair. I trusted you, I told you things I had no business telling you—now you have to trust me. And," she added, looking back at Quent. "keep that damned crystal away from me. We have no idea what power it holds. It might already be too late."

Her crystal was *burning*.

Remy had been on her evening walk with Dantès, taking advantage of some time alone to think about when and how she was going to leave Yellow Mountain. The world was bathed in lengthening shadows, and a half moon had already risen in the west.

At first she hadn't noticed anything more than a twinge down by her belly. Then the twinge became a throb, and within the last ten minutes the throbbing had become deeper, stronger, and more acute.

"What's going on?" she said aloud, lifting up her shirt to take a look. Her crystal had never done anything like this except glow occasionally in twenty years.

What the hell?

Remy stared down at her navel, where the pale orange crystal was held in place by its gold and silver filigree setting. The slender, ornate wiring was pierced through her navel in four places to hold the thumbnail-sized gem in place—and the intricate design of the setting was meant to obscure the details of the translucent orange stone.

But now, through the curling, crisscrossing wires, she saw the stone *glowing*.

And it was burning her, searing into her skin.

Dantès crashed through the bushes, reappearing after an enthusiastic investigation of some noise or scent. He paused and looked up at her when she didn't greet him, still staring down at the gem and its growing heat. A sudden sizzle caught her by surprise and she hissed at the pain.

Her heart thudding, Remy tried to unfasten the prongs that curled in like tiny, delicate claws—but her fingers were clumsy with the complicated locks, and from her angle and distance she couldn't see them very well. It had been years since she'd had occasion to remove the stone, and even then she'd had a difficult time and needed help.

The fiery pain was growing stronger, and she was desperate to stop it. But the heat seared the tips of her fingers now, radiating along the wires and zinging into her skin. She couldn't contain a grunt of pain as she tried to pry the wires free.

Remy bumped into a tree, scraping her arm, and eased

to the ground. Maybe if she was sitting she could see better, find a way to fumble the thing loose. But the sky was growing darker, and in spite of the crystal's glow, it wasn't clear enough or bright enough to illuminate much.

The pain was becoming unbearable, and now she was frantic, ready to tear it from her skin, very nearly crying because of the burning sensation. She could hardly bear to touch it with her fingers, and started to scrabble for a stick. If she had to pry it off, she would do it. Anything to stop the pain.

All at once someone was there, crouching next to where she'd collapsed, gasping and holding her belly, fairly writhing on the ground, tears burning down her cheeks.

Dantès's damp nose was butting into her face as someone gently but firmly pulled her hands away from her abdomen.

"What the— Christ Almighty." It was Wyatt. "I think it's *smoking*."

"Get it off," she managed to gasp, uncaring in her agony that he was the one Dantès brought back for help. "Cut it, tear it . . . just *get it off*." Her voice rose in desperation.

"If you'd hold still," he muttered, firmly moving her fingers away again when they automatically returned to try and relieve the pain. "Christ." This last profanity came as he was fumbling with the wires himself, bending close to her stomach as she lay on the ground trying not to curl back up in the fetal position, trying to keep from moaning like an infant. "It's like Fort Knox here," he said tightly.

"Then *tear* it," she said in a low, desperate scream, her eyes closed. She could hardly breathe: her entire being was centered right at her belly, where the rising pain deepened and spread. She felt her flesh tightening and puckering, drying from the abuse. And smelled it as it burned.

His fingers moved against her bare belly with quick agility. They were cool, and managed to slide down between the set stone and her skin, giving a bit of relief. She wasn't certain how he managed it, but there was a sharp twist and some little yanks, and then she felt the wires sliding free and her tight skin release . . . and finally the scorching heat was gone.

When Remy opened her eyes, holding her belly, Wyatt was still crouched next to her on the ground. He was cupping the crystal in his hand, looking from its incessant orange glow to her and back again.

"We're going to need to get that burn taken care of," he said matter-of-factly. "But at least the skin isn't broken."

She looked down but couldn't see much more than the dark area around her navel, which could be due just as much to the shadows as to any sort of burn. It still throbbed, though, which wasn't a good sign. But there was no blood, which seemed to indicate that he hadn't needed to rip the thing out of her skin.

All at once it sunk in that he was holding the crystal. *Her* crystal. The one that Grandpa had told to her guard with her life.

And it was still glowing. What had happened to it?

It was almost as if it had been . . . switched on.

Trying not to look as if it mattered, she held out her hand. "Thanks."

She wished she could see Wyatt's expression better in the wavering light. Since he was looking down and they were surrounded by bushes and trees, all she had was the impression of dark brows and eyes in shadow, and the square line of his chin and jaw.

"What is it?" he asked, and dropped the crystal into her hand. It fell in a golden-orange arc.

Remy almost gasped at the heat that stung her. She'd assumed the burning had eased, and maybe it had . . . but not by much. Fortunately, the skin on her palm was thicker than that tender, ivory dermis on her belly.

But she had her stone back, and her relief at retrieving it so easily superseded the discomforting warmth. She shoved it in the pocket of her shorts and felt it radiate through the layers of fabric.

Dantès seemed to recognize her relief as well, and he butted his nose into her face, licking her emphatically, then turning to do the same to Wyatt.

The man actually laughed when the dog's enthusiasm nearly knocked him over where he crouched.

"Good boy," he murmured, rubbing Dantès's neck vigorously with both large hands. The dog's tongue was nearly on the ground, he was panting and smiling so happily, between the two people he loved the most. Remy could actually feel the heat of his breath when he turned to slop a dry kiss on her nose.

"She might not like it, but you did the right thing coming to get me." Wyatt was still talking to Dantès.

Remy stiffened. "Thank you for helping me," she said again. "I'm sorry if I seemed ungracious."

"Ungracious?" Wyatt snorted a laugh. "What a princess word. Not to mention a gross understatement. You don't have to kiss my feet, but at least think about what would have happened if Dantès hadn't come and found me."

A princess *word*?

"I thought I was going to have to tear it away," Remy admitted. "Thank you for getting it undone without having to resort to that."

Wyatt picked up something and whipped it into the night, sending Dantès racing off after it.

"What is that thing?" he asked again.

"A piece of jewelry," she replied. She would have gotten to her feet, but his hand moved like a sleek shadow and caught her wrist.

"Christ, Remy, do you think I'm an idiot?" His grip didn't waver, and in the dim light his eyes bored into hers.

So this was it. She'd either have to tell some of the truth or . . . or make up a good lie. A *really* good lie.

"Don't even think about lying," he said. "You owe me at least some sort of explanation."

"I don't owe you anything," she said coolly, latching onto that tangent. "Yes, you came and helped me, but I figured that was out of the goodness of your heart. You might be a dickhead," she continued, referring to the nickname she'd given him before she learned his real name, "but you're just not the kind of guy to stand around and watch a person in pain. Just like when you dragged me out from under Seattle's truck."

Silence stretched for a moment.

"You're really good at this," he said. "But unfortunately for you, I'm better. Now. Are you going to tell me why you are in possession of a crystal that glows, or am I going to have to assume that you're a threat that has to be contained?"

"Contained? That would make you no better than Seattle, turning me into a prisoner."

His fingers tightened into a painful vise. "Nice try," he said, and then they loosened a fraction. "But two seconds ago you just got done saying I wasn't that kind of guy."

"I guess I was wrong."

"Or maybe you could look at it from my perspective. After all, in the past few months you've shot at me. At close range, might I add. Thrown a snake in my face. And now you're evading my more than reasonable questions after I got you out of a very painful and difficult situation. Those seem to be the actions of someone with something to hide."

"First of all, I warned you not to move. Secondly, I didn't shoot *at* you. I shot at the wall above your head—exactly where I aimed. And thirdly, the snake was a harmless distraction so I could get away—"

"Thirdly is not a word. And I don't think the snake would have agreed with your assessment. And you threw it at me on the *stairs*. Not cool."

"I was there, remember?"

"How could I forget."

To her surprise, he released her wrist. "What's going on, Remy? Haven't you figured out by now that we don't mean you any harm? That we might be able to help you?"

"I don't have any reason to think that—"

"We know you're Remington Truth's granddaughter. And you're still here, safe, with us. We haven't turned you over to the Strangers or the zombies. Doesn't that tell you anything?"

"It tells me that you haven't figured out what to do with me yet," she managed. Her teeth were clenched, her heart pounding so hard she could hardly catch her breath . . . but she fought to seem calm.

"If it were up to me, I could think of a few things to do with you." His voice sounded . . . different.

Remy's heart stopped and her body flushed with sudden heat. And her mind shot to places it had no business going—hot, red, lush places. With Wyatt in them.

And then all of a sudden Dantès was back, crashing violently through the bushes, and she was stumbling away from her would-be captor as the dog barreled up to them.

That settled it. She had to get herself and her crystal out of here, away from Yellow Mountain, away from these people. And especially away from Wyatt.

As she rushed back to the house, leaving her traitorous dog with his new friend, Remy heard the familiar moaning wail of zombies in the distance.

Ruuu-uuthhh . . . ruuuuuuthhhh.

They were calling for her. Truth.

Remington Truth.

Ana could have told Fence and Quent about her communication with Darian, but even though they agreed to show her how to access the computer room, she still wasn't quite ready to divulge all of her secrets. She'd already told them she hadn't been in communication with Atlantis since leaving twelve years ago—but of course that wasn't exactly true.

She'd been with Darian.

Besides . . . she'd have to wait and see if her former lover responded to the signal she'd left in the mailbox. She was certain he intended to—for why else would he have made the overture in the first place—but he might not know anything that could help them anyway.

There might not be anything *to* know.

They could all be wrong about a threat to Envy.

Although Ana didn't really think so.

She insisted on leaving the subterranean chamber so she could visit her father, but her real motive was to get aboveground again, away from the piece of Jarrid crystal. Where she could breathe.

Although her own crystals no longer seemed to react to the fist-sized one's proximity, she didn't want to take any more chances than she needed to.

Nor was she about to tell Fence and his friends, quite yet, that she could probably help them learn to use the stone. She wouldn't take the chance of revealing her whereabouts to those in Atlantis who wanted her back.

She visited with her dad long enough to hear him complain that he didn't need to be kept in the infirmary, and what was the big deal, and where were his petri dishes . . . but then Flo came in and all at once he stopped complaining.

And he stopped listening to Ana, instead transferring his attention to the older woman.

Well, then.

Ana couldn't help a bemused smile, and she slipped out of the room . . . and nearly ran into Fence.

Her burst of pleasure at finding him suddenly, unexpectedly, was quickly submerged. *Opportunity knocked, huh?*

And, dang it, girl, you let him answer the door. Crap.

"Hey," Fence said, giving her that long, slow grin that turned her insides to mush. "Fancy meeting you here."

She kept her face blank, trying to remember to be annoyed with the man who, number one, made her give up her biggest secret and put herself in danger, and number two, practically turned her into a prisoner, and number three, called her an "opportunity."

And then there was the big jerkwad who'd gotten all snotty on the beach.

But somehow . . . the memory of him crouching next to Tanya and promising her an awesomely crazy mushy apology rose in her mind. And the love and intensity in his face when he pointed out all of the sights on their journey from Glenway, his smooth, warm narrative telling her he loved his world as much as she loved her sea.

"Meeting up with you here?" she said, forcing her voice to sound cool. "How strange is that?"

"Stranger than a green alien," he replied, deadpan. But his eyes smoldered and he drawled, "If I didn't know any better, I'd think you were following me around, just to try and get another of those knee-shaking kisses."

There was no doubt what was on his mind, and the realization had Ana's belly filling with delicious fluttering.

Nevertheless, she put on a surprised expression. "Huh. I never thought of that." And she smiled, wide but not quite nicely, and started to slip past him.

He lifted his arm to bar her way. "So, uh, I was wondering what you were planning to do now."

"Now?" she said, and glanced around to make certain no one was within hearing range. "Now . . . after I've been interrogated and imprisoned and forced to jeopardize my safety?"

He opened his mouth to respond, then must have thought better of it, because he slipped into a warm smile instead.

That pretty much infuriated her, thinking he could charm his way into her good graces—and possibly something else—with a mere smile and hot look. But what made her even more annoyed was knowing that it was *freaking working.*

What was it about him? He was so much more than a sexy smile and double entendres . . . why the heck did he have to hide behind them? Behind that superficial charm?

She forced herself to become silently indignant, and turned her expression into all innocence and wide eyes. "Actually . . . I was thinking about a swim," she said casually. "Want to join me?"

A hitch in his smile was the only sign of her direct hit, but then he smoothed it out. "Hmmm . . . skinny dipping," he said, his eyes now bold and warm. "I like it . . . but what say we do it without the dipping? Or maybe I should say, without the skinny . . . 'cause, ya know, there could be some dipping going on."

Somewhere beneath the fluttering heat that she couldn't seem to control, Ana realized that if any other guy said something like that to her, she'd be disgusted and annoyed and completely turned off.

But that was the thing about Fence, damn it. He *said* things like that, and he got the exact response he was obviously hoping for. Even though she wanted to snarl at him and then stalk away in disdain, he was like a magnet, keeping her there.

Right there. Tempting her.

And then all at once the thought struck her. He'd seen her crystals. He knew she was Atlantean.

She didn't have to hide it from him anymore. *Hot. Damn.*

Ana gave him a long, slow smile of her own. "Some dipping?" she said, watching his irises suddenly expand in those dark, hooded eyes. "Is that a promise?"

"Your wish is my command," he said, and flashed straight white teeth as he moved that big bulk of an arm out of her way. And . . . suddenly, she saw the veneer, the charming veneer, slip away to show *reality*. Some real emotion there, deep in his eyes. Intense . . . uncertain . . . warm.

The look made her belly quiver even more.

"Your place or mine?" he asked.

Ana was aware of her heart suddenly beating faster, of her belly being filled with the warm fluttering of anticipation. "Whichever one is closer."

"Yours," he said, and edged toward her.

There was no one around, so she didn't hesitate when he eased her against the wall and settled his mouth over hers. Lips, tongue, slick and warm, hungry and full of promise . . . and then he pulled back. "Got your knees shaking yet?" he murmured, brushing a lock of hair from her temple.

"Hardly a tremor," Ana said, trying not to sound as breathless as she felt. "I think you're going to have to do better than that."

His eyelids drooped even lower. "Oh, I will, sugar," he said with a thick drawl. "You can bet your sexy crystals on that."

Five minutes later he was well on his way to proving his boast.

They'd found their way to her room, made it through the door and closed it, and now he'd somehow, between more long, strong kisses, positioned them next to the bed. The mattress bumped against the back of Ana's legs, and she found herself grabbing his shoulders for balance.

It was then she realized this was the first time she'd gotten intimate with a man outside of the ocean. Normally, she had the water's buoyancy to help her remain upright on her bad leg . . . and to add its gentle surge and salty taste to the mix.

"So convenient," Fence was murmuring as he unfastened the row of buttons down the front of her shirt. "Easy access." He slipped warm, dry hands beneath her open shirt, covering her breasts with large palms. "And no bra," he added with a groan of appreciation.

Ana shivered as he found her hard, sensitive nipples with his thumbs. Heat swamped her as he circled over them, around and around with a feather light touch as he bent to kiss the soft skin at the side of her neck. Her knees were definitely weak, but that didn't stop her from pulling his shirt up and out of the low-slung jeans he wore and flattening her hands under the cotton, over his broad, warm chest.

Then he shifted away and with a faint smile stripped the shirt from his dark, massive shoulders. "That better?" he asked, looking at her, then down at her hands settled over his chest.

The breadth of his chest was impossibly wide, and being faced with such power and beauty made Ana's mouth go dry. When spread wide, the fingers of one hand hardly spanned the bulk of one pectoral.

"Ah . . . it needs some work," she replied, and bent closer to press a kiss onto the little rise of muscle and bone near the hollow of his throat. He tasted warm and fresh, a little salty, and smooth. His heart was pounding beneath her lips, and she couldn't help an extra little nibble. It was different . . . and erotic . . . tasting a man's skin that wasn't bathed in saltwater, cool and slick.

Fence chuckled, and she felt the deep, bass rumble in his chest. "I'll get right to it. But first . . ." His voice was so low as to be nearly inaudible. "I want to show you something that doesn't need a bit of work at all."

He had his hands on her shoulders, and Ana allowed

him to turn her to the right, so she was facing toward the other side of the room, then to slip off her unbuttoned shirt. As he tossed it to the floor, Fence came to stand behind her and said, "Look."

Ana looked up and found herself facing a mirror, just across from them. She was bare from the waist up of her suspiciously sagging jeans, which were somehow unbuttoned and showed a triangle of panty and a hint of hip bone. Her torso was nearly as long as Fence's, but much narrower and with different curves. Her crystals glinted dully in the low light, and her breasts looked like two dark-tipped teardrops.

"Now, isn't that just beautiful?" he murmured in her ear as his large hands came around from behind to curve under her breasts, holding them in two gentle handfuls.

As he stroked his thumbs over each nipple in turn, Ana found herself mesmerized by the erotic image reflected back at her, and the little prickles of arousal tingling down to her core. The light in the room was limited to a small table lamp she'd left on near the door, and it spilled a warm glow into the space that made her skin look like burnished gold. His dark hands, and the breadth of his shoulders and the bulk of his arms, burned like rich bronze around her, and her hair spilled in more golden-bronzy waves over his biceps.

She raised her arms and brought them up behind Fence's head, and her breasts lifted enticingly. She felt his cheek move and saw the smile flash in the mirror as he slid both hands along her midriff to settle over her hips.

"'S no lie . . . this is the sexiest thing I've ever seen," he said low in her ear as his fingers brushed the crystals on her right side.

His light fingertips brushed over her skin in small enticing circles over and over, down and wider, raising little, skittering bumps of pleasure. She could feel the heat of bare skin pressing along her shoulders and the rock-hard bulge from behind the fly of his jeans, and the deep, tingling response growing in her center. She felt damp and hot everywhere, and as he skated his hands up and down along the length of her torso, holding her breasts close and then releasing them to tease her nipples, she sagged back against him even more heavily. Her hands cupped the back of his skull, feeling the pleasure of warm, smooth skin, sliding forward to brush his jaw and temples.

He bent his face to her shoulder, still looking up at her as he sucked and nibbled gently on the slender ridge of tendon and skin. Using his tongue, he slicked along the curve, his lips moist and warm, so different from Darian's, and she couldn't control the delicious shivers radiating from his mouth.

When he went back down to the waist of her jeans and flipped a few more buttons open, she had a moment of panic and tried to turn in his arms, back to face him.

"We'll have none of that, sugar," he said firmly, keeping her in place. Facing the mirror.

His big fingers slid beneath the loosened band of her jeans, beneath her panties and down over each hip, and, as she watched, he shoved them down in a long, smooth movement.

Ana wanted to close her eyes, but she knew she needed to know what he saw when her mangled leg was revealed. She had to gauge his reaction, to notice when his eyes went there and stayed, unable to help themselves. It hadn't mattered with Darian, because in the water she moved with grace and speed . . . but here and now things were so different. She was crippled . . . and next to such a perfect body.

"Ahh," he murmured with great emotion in her ear as the jeans slid down and bunched at her knees. "Ana." He let out a long breath, warm against her cheek, and just held her there for a moment.

The full curve of her hips and the juncture of her thighs with its dark triangle of hair was now revealed, but Ana was looking at her left thigh where it joined her torso. Her soft swell of pleasure had ebbed, and all she could see was the texture of swirling scars, jagged marks, and the lumpy outline of damaged muscle that had never quite healed.

Horror washed through her at the sight of such unpleasant imperfection, but before she could react, Fence's dark hands moved all along the sweep of her hips, down over her thighs and back up again—all the while holding her in place.

"Now that's some crazy sweetness there, sugar," he said, and holding her gaze in the mirror, eased his hand between her legs. "Right here, baby. And I'm gonna sample it all."

Ana shivered as he slid his fingers down around her, slipping into the heat and damp there. A surge of pleasure surprised her, and she wanted to open wider and give him more access, but she was trapped at the knees by her jeans.

Fence's dark chuckle rumbled in her ear, and again that white smile flashed in the dim light. "Allow me," he said, and without moving his hands, lifted his foot and dragged her jeans down into a wad at her ankles.

Ana was able to kick them off now, at least from one foot, and he used that opportunity of her hopping on her good leg to cop a full-blown feel between her legs.

"Oh!" she gasped in surprise as he found her . . . oh, yes, he *found* her. And his fingers slid so easily into her hot, swollen core . . . she could feel the slickness, and every little movement, every little tease, was exaggerated by it. Ana stopped, trying to catch her breath as the little shudders caught her off guard.

"I promised you a bit of dipping," he said . . . but his voice was less steady than before, a little rougher and filled with breathiness. "Didn't I?"

He held her gaze, watching her in the mirror. She couldn't look away as he stroked and slipped in and around, his fingers sure and gentle and magical. He seemed to know just how to lure and coax, and Ana felt her body tightening, turning liquid with heat and pleasure, gathering up to explode. She watched his dark arms, one curved up to cover a breast and the other buried between her legs like some erotic bonds, holding her back up against him.

"Come on sugar . . . I want to feel you shiver and shake against me," he whispered. Her eyes met his, saw the heat burning there, and she felt the rasp of his breath against her hair, the unfurling in her belly suddenly, sharply, swelling to encompass her whole body.

And then she didn't think about anything more as he slipped into *just* the right place, and found the *very* spot and the rhythm . . . and then all at once she was gusting a long, happy moan, shivering and shaking and exploding against him.

He held her, murmuring into her ear, making the rippling pleasure last and last, teasing and slipping and coaxing, until she cried out in lovely, elated defeat.

When she opened her eyes, they were still facing the mirror. He was still behind her, his eyes still avid and hot, his mouth quirked in a tight, satisfied smile, one hand smoothing over her crystals again, the other brushing a thick lock of hair back over her shoulder.

"Now that," he murmured, "is some sweetness."

She would have turned in his arms, but again he held her firmly in place, chuckling in that low, sensual way of his. And then, the next thing she knew, he was tipping her gently, sideways, onto the bed.

As she collapsed backward in a tangle of her long hair, she flipped the second leg of her jeans free and worked herself fully onto the bed as he unbuttoned the fly of his own pants.

He watched her as he slid his hands down past the waistband of his jeans and briefs, and shoved them down with the same practiced motion he'd managed hers. His erection, full and more than ready, sprang free.

Whoa.

Her breath caught as he finished undressing, his flat, ridged belly and the curve of his rear gleaming with the rich bronze glow, all lean and muscled and *big*. Big and powerful and broad.

Everywhere.

Ana's heart was thudding with anticipation and delight as he caught her eyes again. His eyes crinkled at the corners as if he were trying to smile but couldn't quite manage it.

The next thing she knew, he was there, next to her, on the bed. His mouth went right to one of her breasts, and he swirled his tongue around her nipple in greedy, slick circles . . . then drew it deeply into his mouth in a long, pounding rhythm that sent matching pulses of pleasure down once again to her core.

Already feeling her body gathering up, ready once again, Ana reached down between them, skimming her fingers along the hard flat belly. His skin shivered just as hers had, and when she closed her fingers around his velvety, hard length, he gave a deep, heartfelt groan. He was heavy and hot and she could fairly feel him pulsing in her hand when she gave a little squeeze. His moan vibrated against her breast, and he lifted his face.

"How about some more of that dipping, sugar?" he suggested with a crooked, tense smile. "Either that, or you're gonna have a mess on your hands."

She smiled and would have given him a good, quick stroke if he hadn't pulled away. "What are you doing?" she asked when he half turned away, reaching for his pants.

He was doing something . . . *there* . . . and his hands were moving in short, sharp jerks . . . and then he turned back. "Now, where were we?"

"What—" she began to ask, but her words were swallowed by his mouth, covering hers in a hot, demanding kiss.

And then all thoughts and questions evaporated as he reached his hand between them. He gave her a quick, sleek stroke that had Ana catching her breath in pleasured shock . . . and then he guided himself just where she wanted him.

"So damned wet," he murmured into her ear as he settled between her legs, and . . .

"Ah," she sighed, lifting her hips awkwardly to meet him, balancing more heavily on her good side.

"Jesus, Ana, you're dripping for me," he said, his voice rough and awed in her ear. "Sweet, so sweet, and slick and wet," he said, and moved inside her . . . long and slow and *sweet*.

Oh God.

Ana closed her eyes, finding his shoulder and pressing her mouth against its powerful breadth as he moved . . . filling her so deeply, so thickly and rhythmically . . .

He held her close, gathering her up against him as he rocked, easy and slow. And then his breath came faster and harder, his chest hot and damp against hers, their rhythm increasing. Ana pulled away from his shoulder so she could breathe, and she felt that telltale rising of pleasure gathering up, ready to explode once again.

When it happened, she cried out, and then he released a long, pent-up breath . . . and seconds later gave a low groan and one last thrust.

And then he collapsed over her, dragging her on top of him as he flopped aside. His chest was heaving as if he'd been running. She closed her eyes and sagged against him, her mind filled not only with satisfaction . . . but also with erotic, sordid images of their bodies entwined.

She closed her eyes, a smile on her face, and hardly noticed the ache in her leg.

CHAPTER 12

About the time the last bit of satisfaction afterglow slipped away, Fence's eyes shot open.

Motherfucking idiot.

Suddenly filled with trepidation, imagining his mother with her death glare, standing next to Saint Peter, he moved gingerly away from Ana. She looked all gold and warm and basking, curled up next to him on top of the blankets. Her hair cascaded into a pile of silky bronze, onto the covers and over her shoulder.

Idiot.

"Hey," he said, easing her fully onto the bed. He couldn't help but glance at her long legs, noticing the scars and odd texture of her skin on one of them. She fucking limped when she walked. Her foot was turned awkwardly. Even the way her thigh joined her hip was not quite right.

He broke out in a cold sweat, remembering how he'd fit himself against her, relentless and determined, and pounded away.

Sure, he'd managed to remember the fucking condom—if you could call the thing he was wearing a condom—but he'd forgotten about Ana's handicap in his fog of lust.

And at the same time . . . Jesus, he was afraid to even ask her about it. She was awfully damn prickly about her leg.

Ana stirred as Fence peeled the condom from his now very limp dick and wadded it up to dispose of. As he slipped from the bed to find a trashcan, he heard a low laugh of surprise.

That was a good sign.

"What's so funny?" he asked carefully, walking back to join her. She didn't seem to be in pain. Or to have any residual injuries from his . . . enthusiasm.

You're a big guy, Bruno Paolo. You don't know your own strength, his mama had warned. More than once.

"Oddly enough," Ana said, stretching lazily and, thank God, removing his mother from the room, "this was the first time I've ever done that in a bed." She arched her back, twisting her torso like a sensual feline as she looked at him.

Of course, he noticed the way her breasts shifted and slid, taunting him with jutting nipples that just begged to be kissed . . . and the smooth curve of her belly and hips . . . and the soft shine from each of her crystals. Holy motherfucker, they were mad sexy, set delicately into her skin the way they were. He noticed, too, though, that she only used one leg and set of toes to help shift her body. The other one didn't move much at all, and when she finished her stretch, she ended up lying on her side with the injured leg on the bottom. Hidden.

Fence settled next to her. With space between them, so he could keep his head instead of reaching for her and—

Then her words sunk in, superseding his wayward thoughts.

"Really?" he said, wondering suddenly where and with whom she actually *had* had sex. And never in a bed? She certainly didn't seem inhibited, but until now he hadn't given it much thought because—as he'd told more than one bed partner—the only thing that mattered was here and now.

. . . Of course, that was usually when his partner wanted to know about *his* history. Which, he'd learned, wasn't a good thing to get into.

"Yeah," she said. "And it was also my first time out of water."

"Are you shitting me?" Did that mean this was her first dry hump? *Heh*.

"No," she said. "It's a lot warmer and drier outside the ocean."

Fence couldn't help it. "I don't know, sugar, it was pretty crazy wet where I was." Then before he got too caught up in that image again, he sobered, restraining his wayward thoughts. "Did I hurt you?"

To his unabashed delight, her attention drifted to his dick, which couldn't help but begin to stir under her regard. "Um . . . no," she said. "I could push a baby out there . . . I think I can handle *that*."

His cock twitched again, ready to take her up on it.

"I meant . . . your leg," he ventured. "I was a little rough, I think. I . . . uh . . . wasn't really thinking about it."

"Really? You were thinking about other things?" she asked, her eyes all wide and innocent in that way he'd come to learn was dangerous. "Counting sheep perhaps? Or the stripes on the wallpaper?"

He chuckled. "Well, I can't deny that I haven't done

that in the past . . . sometimes a guy has to, uh, hold things back for the lady. But," his voice dropped, "not in this case. Not with you. If I was countin' anything, sugar, I was countin' the number of times you groaned and moaned and cried out."

Even in the faulty light he could see a tinge of pink coloring her cheeks. "Was I loud? I didn't know . . . we . . . uh, underwater, we can't make much noise. We don't really talk."

He was fascinated in spite of himself. "Don't be embarrassed, sugar. It's a compliment to hear you making noise. Then a guy knows he's doing things your way."

She laid a hand over the center of his chest, right over the breastbone, and his heart begin to thunder. "I liked hearing you talk to me . . . saying those things," she said, looking not at him, but at her fingers.

"Is that so?" he asked, leaning into her hand, feeling the entire palm imprint itself on his skin. He ducked his head and found her lips, tasting them gently and slowly, savoring their fullness and warmth. "Well, I got lots more where that came from."

She smiled against his mouth. "I don't find that the least bit surprising."

He eased back, aware that things had already begun to awaken down south, but needing to take care of other business first. "Ana, you have to tell me straight—did I hurt your leg?"

"Not really," she said, and hot shame rushed through him.

Not really? Idiot, idiot, idiot.

She must have noticed his stricken expression, for she explained. "I mean, not any more than any other bump or getting my hair caught, or skin pinched, or

whatever. You know, the normal stuff that happens."
She smiled slyly. "Like when I bit you."

And the shame was gone. Just like that. "You bit
me?" He swore his heart stopped beating, then began
again with greater force. *Definitely a live one.*

"You didn't notice?" she said, still with that sly smile.
Her eyes danced with delight. "Right here." She traced
his shoulder, swirling her finger around in a little circle
over a place that might have been a bit more tender than
any other part of his body. Except the wood suddenly
raging between his legs.

Down boy.

First things first.

"Okay," he said, trying to keep focused. "So give me
a little guidance here. I want to make sure I don't hurt
you, so I need to know what your limitations are. Okay,
Ana?" He held his breath.

The sexy smile eased and a shadow flickered in her
eyes. "I know it's frightening to look at—"

"I don't think that at—"

"—but it really doesn't hurt that much," she finished.
"Most of the time."

He shifted up on one elbow and wished her bad leg
wasn't hidden by the bunched-up blankets so he could
show her he didn't care what it looked like. "How did
it happen?"

His dick sagged in disappointment at the change of
subject, and Ana's expression turned just as unenthu-
siastic.

"I'd rather—"

"Tell me," he pressed, to the dismay of his hormones.
Chill, easy rider.

"I'll tell you if you tell me your secret," she said at
last.

His body went cold. "I don't have any secrets," he said, wishing he'd have listened to his hormones instead. "What you see is what you get." Even his signature seductive chuckle didn't sound right to his ears. His shield was slipping.

"You certainly do," she replied. "I want to know how you came to be called Fence, and what your parents named you."

Relief poured through him, but he pretended to think on it. "Well, I suppose I could be convinced to give that up. As long as you make a lot of noise the next time."

"What makes you think there's going to be a next time?" she retorted. But that coy smile was back and she'd shifted just enough so her left nipple was hardly a breath away from his bicep. Pretty, rosy, and begging to be kissed.

He could have gone that route—she'd certainly opened the door, and he had this thing about opportunity—but something stopped him. He found he wanted to know more about her than just what made her cry out and groan and sigh.

"Tell me what happened, Ana. I really want to know."

She shifted, and the next thing he knew she'd flipped the edge of the coverlet and blankets up to cover her bare hips. "My father and I were escaping from the upper city of Atlantis and my leg got caught in one of the gates as it came down." She said it quickly and simply, as if explaining that the sky was blue.

He couldn't help a little laugh. "Well, now, sugar, that just creates a lot more questions than it answers. You know that, don't you?"

She nodded. "I suppose I should start at the beginning."

"That's where my mama always started her stories."

"Your mama sounds like a smart woman."

His eyes stung suddenly and his throat felt raw. "She was."

Ana looked at him searchingly. "I loved my mother too. She was an Atlantean, as you know, and she married my father against the wishes of her parents and the Atlantean Guild."

"The Atlantean Guild is . . . ?"

"The governing body of Atlantis and the Atlanteans. They didn't want the genetic pool or bloodline sullied by mere mortal blood. They feel they're much superior in many ways to those who live on land. But Mamya and Dad met once when he was fishing—he loved the ocean too—and his boat capsized. She saved him, dragged him onshore, and . . . What?"

"That sounds like a Disney movie. Did your mom have red hair and purple seashells over her—"

Ana laughed, and he felt the whole damn world shift . . . or something. Her eyes lit up, her face beamed, her beautiful mouth curved with mirth, her head tipped back so her hair tumbled down in a tawny-colored fall. *Jesus, Mary, and Joseph.*

"No, my mother wasn't Ariel," she said. "But I have to be honest, once Dad and I got away from Atlantis and settled on land, while I was recovering from my accident, I watched that DVD way too many times. It made me feel a little better, thinking of my parents loving each other enough to brave their respective worlds in order to be together."

"She got sick?"

"Yes. We knew she wasn't going to make it . . . her crystals were starting to flicker and fade. And when that happens . . ." Ana shrugged, but he could see the grief in her eyes. "Dad—he's really an amazing scientist—

tried to find a way to reanimate her crystals, to wake them up and get them working again."

"Yours don't glow all the time," Fence said suddenly. "Does that mean—" He stopped, aware that his whole body had just gone cold.

But Ana shook her head. "Mine, you know, mine are different . . . so they don't always glow like those of a pure Atlantean because of that. Anyway, my dad did a lot of experiments with other crystals, trying to figure out what the secret was to their energy . . . their life. But in the end he couldn't save her. Mamya's crystals died, and so did she."

"I'm sorry, sugar. I can't imagine what it was like, losing your mama at that age. It's terrible at any time, but at thirteen . . . just becoming a woman . . ." He felt grief swelling up inside him again. He'd been thirty when he lost his mother—and everyone else in his life. He loved his whole family, and Lenny too . . . but it was her loss that he felt the most.

"I really miss her. We were very close. And . . . Mamya was different from the others. She didn't really fit with them—maybe it was because she loved my dad, who wasn't an Atlantean. She didn't share the same prejudices that her people did, probably because she'd gotten to know a normal human. Or maybe that's why she was able to love my dad—because she didn't have the prejudice. Most Atlanteans have a sort of condescension toward land-livers—because they can't exist in the water the way the Atlanteans can. But in reality, it's the Atlanteans who are restricted, who are, in some ways, weaker than people like you. They're tethered to their watery world and can't leave the ocean for more than a few hours at a time. I think . . . I really think that the reason the Atlanteans hate land-livers is because they envy them their freedom. And I suspect there might even be a deep-rooted fear too. There aren't that many Atlanteans either. Only a few thousand. And I think they're afraid that if the humans find out about them, they'll destroy them."

"Just like the Atlanteans did to the land-livers?" Fence said grimly.

Ana's expression tightened. "It was beyond reprehensible what they did to the world. I remember hearing the stories when I was younger . . . but they were told as if it were a heroic thing, raising the new city up from the ocean. They didn't tell us about the mass destruction that happened here, or the hoards of people who were killed."

"Selective history," Fence murmured, thinking of the way the colonization of North America had been taught in schools, often glossing over the resulting genocide of Native Americans. "Happens all the time."

Ana continued, "But Mamya knew . . . and she and Dad made sure I understood the truth. That's why . . . that's one of the reasons Dad and I didn't want to stay after she died, and be a part of them. I'd like to forget that aspect of my history. But Mamya and Dad had to live in Atlantis because of her crystals and being tied to the water and its power—even though I think they would have rather not. Though she'd been raised to think and believe that land-livers were lesser beings, crude and simple compared to the Atlanteans, I know my mother realized otherwise."

"You said you had to escape. You had to break out of Atlantis?"

"Yes. Rather convenient how they changed their mind about Mamya and Dad's marriage once I came along. You see, I was the only living child of an Atlantean and a regular human—and possibly the only one ever . . . although I think there were two other biracial couples when I left. The Guild wanted to keep me there for obvious reasons—to keep their existence secret, but also to see how I grew up and lived. Dad implanted the crystals in me when I was just a baby."

"I couldn't help but notice that your decorations are a lot less gaudy and overdone than your friend who washed up on the beach. He had enough crystals to rival Elvis Presley." He wondered fleetingly if she even understood the reference.

"I'm only half Atlantean, and, as such, I was an experiment of sorts," she explained. "They implanted the oxygenating crystals in only one of my lungs, hoping that I could be fully functional on land in the mortal world as well as in the water. And . . . it worked."

"So . . . I don't know much about the legend of Atlantis, but I was always under the impression that the Atlanteans were just normal humans who had advanced technology, and whose city sank beneath the sea. Is that right?"

"Some of it. Their island city didn't sink, but much of it was destroyed by a massive earthquake that made it seem as if it had sunk. From the stories I've heard, it seems as though one day it was there, the next everything went crazy and then it disappeared. But before that, they'd already begun to build a city at the bottom of the ocean, so the survivors ended up there."

"How the hell did they breathe down there?" Fence couldn't quite control the dart of panic in his belly.

"They found the Jarrid stone—one of the largest of the deep-sea crystals. They realized if they held part of the stone or its crystals in their mouth, it enabled them

to breathe . . . like those things people used when they
. . . scoobered? Scoobied?" She frowned.

"Scuba diving," Fence interjected. "So the crystal
acted as a sort of regulator, allowing them to breathe.
That's amazing."

"The earliest Atlanteans were just as human as you
are, but once they found those energizing crystals and
began to utilize them—eventually experimenting with
ways of attaching them to the body, piercing them, and,
finally, implanting them—they began to change physi-
cally as well as mentally. But they realized too late that
the stones, though powerful, also made its user dependent upon them. They gave strength, power, and youth,
although not necessarily immortality—as well as the
ability to breathe underwater—but they also become
part of the body and weaken it when they try to remove
them."

A rush of horror erased any lingering sexual thoughts
he might have had. "Like an addiction? Do you mean
that you . . . also . . . are weakened? That you have to
stay near the water too?"

Ana shook her head and gave a half shrug from her
reclining position. "I'm perfectly able to live on land
without feeling weak, despite my crystals. That's why
they find me so fascinating. I could possibly be the
answer to the problem of the Atlanteans being tied to
the sea."

Fence thought of Marley then too, who, although
she wasn't an Atlantean, had a crystal implanted in
her body as well. It was true: when she was away from
flowing water for a great length of time, she became ill
and weak. But the crystal didn't allow her to breathe
underwater, and it gave her immortality. And Quent

had the one used for communicating with them. How many freaking kinds of crystals were there?

"And so you and your dad left Atlantis?" Fence asked, bringing the conversation back to Ana's personal story.

"Before she died, Mamya told Dad and me that we needed to leave. In fact, she tried to make us go before she passed on, but we sure as hell weren't going to do that. Dad wanted to take her with us, to see if anyone on land could help her, but she was too weak."

"Why did she want you to go?"

"She was afraid of what would happen to us once she was gone—what they'd do to me. Experimentation and who knows what else. And to Dad, because he'd been studying those crystals for years. She told us how to get out."

"There are gates?"

"Walls and gates, and the old city is of course underwater—although the Raised City is a place where we've—they've—been trying to adapt to for the last fifty years. Since the Above was destroyed."

Fence had a million more questions, but this was enough for now. "So your mother told you how to find a way out. A secret way, I'm guessing. And that's when you almost lost your leg?"

Ana nodded. "I wasn't quite fast enough—we only had a few seconds to get beneath the gate. Mamya told us how to time it, how to measure the beats of light in the crystal locks. Dad got smashed on the head as he was trying to help me when the iron bars came down. We were a bloody mess—it really is a miracle that we made it away safely. He did most of it, dragging me off, forcing me to swim, watching for sharks . . . and when we finally got somewhere safe, he conked out.

And when he woke up . . . he wasn't exactly the same. He'd lost some of his memory—mostly of our years in Atlantis. Although he's never forgotten Mamya."

"How did he breathe underwater? He doesn't have crystals, does he?"

"No. He wore one around his neck on a chain, like the early Atlanteans did until they learned how to implant them permanently. It helped him to breathe, but it also sapped some of his brainpower and memory. I think that might be part of the reason he doesn't remember much detail from Atlantis."

"Hell, the man seems pretty sharp to me," Fence said with a little laugh. "Growing bacteria for drugs and studying up on them. He asked Elliott if he could look at the crystals from Kaddick and study them a bit."

She smiled with affection. "Dad's brilliant in that way . . . but the rest of him has . . . shall we say gentled." And then, with a sudden slap of her hand onto the bed, Ana said, "Well, now that you know my secret— probably more than you ever wanted to know—it's time for you to pay up, big guy."

While Fence still hungered for more information, he also hungered for more of something else . . . and changing the subject was the first step in easing back into exactly where he wanted to be. So he had no problem following her lead and said, "Now what was it you wanted to know?"

"How you got your nickname. And what your mama called you."

"Brat," he said with a laugh.

She smiled back, and he felt that little tingle deep in his belly again. "I can see that."

"Yeah, all right then. My real name is Bruno, but I got the name Fence when I was about fourteen and a bunch of my buddies and I were . . . well, I'm not too proud of myself now, but we were causing some mischief—"

"What kind of mischief?"

Here he had to hesitate. Because, damn, the world wasn't the same back then as it was now, and how the hell was he going to explain they'd been teepeeing the houses and Saran-wrapping the cars of the opposing football team's coach and quarterback the night before the biggest game of the season? Too many parts of that scenario were dangerous to divulge. "We were—uh— digging around in some place we weren't meant to be, and we got caught, and so we took off running. We had to climb over a fence to get away and I got the ass of my jeans caught right on top of it. It was so bad I had to cut it loose, and I left half my pants—and my shorts—up there on the fence. And so I had to go home, bare-assed, and my buddies never let me forget that shit, 'bout how I got caught on a fence."

Ana was laughing again, and he thought he might have to tell the story one more time, just to see her face light up like that.

"What did you tell your mom and dad?"

His grin turned sheepish. "I didn't have to tell them. They already knew by the time I got home, because I'd left the evidence right there on the top of the fence." He skirted over the detail that his parents had learned of his mischief from a phone call—because then he'd have a whole lot of other explaining to do.

Although . . . hell, a woman who lived in the legendary city of Atlantis probably wouldn't be all that freaked out over a guy who was eighty but looked as if he were only thirty.

Maybe.

"Were Quent and Elliott in trouble too?" she asked.

It took Fence a moment to realize what she meant, and he was caught by surprise with another stinging rush of emotion. Though he hadn't even known Lenny, or any of the other guys from the cave back in 1995 when he earned his nickname, the surviving five of them had bonded deeply and in an unexpected way through their experience in Sedona and coming out of that time-warping cave.

"They weren't with me," he explained. "I didn't actually meet any of them until I was a lot older." Damn, why was he having to blink so hard?

He reached for Ana, more than happy to dismiss those thoughts.

But, with a smile, she gently resisted. "I have one more question, now that things are a bit less . . . intense."

Trepidation filled Fence and he tugged her closer again. "Enough with the questions, sugar. I didn't get a chance to taste all of you, and I swear I'm gonna turn into a shriveled-up piece of—"

Her hand closed around his dick, and he lost whatever cajoling words he had on tap.

"Funny, you don't feel too shriveled up," she said with a naughty grin. And then she slipped her closed fingers up and down along his length a few good times so his breathing went all out of sorts and his hands started their own wandering.

She stroked her finger over the top of the head, where the little bead of moisture had gathered, and the slip-sliding sensation had him curling his toes to keep from going over right there.

"Now," she said, sliding her hand to the base of his dick and loosening her grip. "My question. What were you doing just before we . . . um . . . got together. You turned away and I didn't see."

"A condom," he managed to say, still feeling the pressure of her fingers around him, even though she'd eased up. *And oh shit, thanks for the reminder.* He'd need another one.

Which he didn't have.

Motherfucking hell.

It wasn't as if he could go out to a drugstore and buy a box of Trojans either.

Birth control was frowned upon by the people in Envy and elsewhere. After so much of the human race had been destroyed, it was thought that attention should be given to repopulating the earth. Well, that was fine, Fence thought, but he wasn't just going to play Johnny fucking Appleseed, planting babies with his junk. He was even less interested in fathering a child with a woman he wasn't committed to.

"A condom?" Ana was frowning.

"To prevent pregnancy," he said. "A little cover that . . . uh . . . keeps me from spilling inside you."

"Really." She was looking down at the heavy length in her hand, and he had a moment of glee, hoping she was wondering how the hell he found anything that fit over *that*.

"No offense," he said, "but where I come from, a guy's careful about making babies unless he's ready to settle down and commit to the woman."

"Atlanteans have a difficult time getting pregnant," Ana said. "It's not impossible, but they think their fertility has been affected by the crystals because it doesn't happen as often as they might like. That's why Mamya and Dad only had me, which is about the average for Atlantean couples. But when they want to make certain to prevent pregnancy, they use a sponge to . . . um . . . block things. I'll get one," she added. "Tomorrow."

He started to respond with an okay but she'd moved her hand again, and this time she meant business. *Oooh.*

Fence closed his eyes when she bent to take him in her mouth and he realized he didn't need to worry about a condom this time.

CHAPTER 13

Ana opened her eyes to find sunlight streaming through the window. She stretched languorously, sliding along the warm body next to her.

Not only had last night been the first time she'd had sex in a bed, or even out of the water, but it was also the first time she'd ever slept—in the literal sense—with a man.

And awakened with him, warm and dry and cozy.

These land dwellers do it the right way.

She smiled to herself and reveled for the moment in the warmth, the comfort of blankets and softness. Everything beneath the sea was, of course, wet, but also cooler, and it had such a different *feel* to it. There was the slip-sliding all the time, the fine barrier of water and sometimes grit from the salt between bodies and mouths and elsewhere. Even the pressure of the water's weight.

Obviously, she'd had plenty of pleasurable moments in the ocean with Darian, but she could appreciate the difference being on land, and not being constantly buffeted or rocked by the rhythm of the water.

Darian.

The thought had Ana's insides squeezing up unpleasantly.

Back to reality.

She slid from the bed and Fence—or should she call him Bruno?—made a snuffling, snoring sound. Also something she wouldn't have heard in the ocean, and, in spite of her trepidation at what the day might hold, she grinned to herself.

She supposed he'd earned a good night's—morning's?—sleep after all of the activity. A deep shiver in her belly reminded her how she'd been the lucky recipient of those energies, and she smiled as she padded over to the bathroom.

It was odd, being able to talk with Fence—with anyone—about her heritage. She'd kept the secrets for so long, kept so many people—men in particular—at arm's length, even though she craved companionship and intimacy. Even Yvonne didn't know her secrets.

And now all at once she had found not only a group of people who seemed to understand her need for secrecy, who appeared to actually be on her side, but also a man who could turn her into a puddle of boneless desire with little more than a look. He was sweet and kind—a big teddy bear, in some ways, she thought, remembering him with the children. Hadn't he even been the "bear" they'd been tracking? She smiled, remembering his reverence for nature, for the world around them, helping her in the kitchen with such great ease that it seemed natural . . . and the way he talked about his mother. His eyes had gone moist when he mentioned her.

He made her laugh too, in spite of herself, with his huge yet charming ego. The ego that, she suspected,

was just a shield behind which to hide his soft heart . . .
and whatever else was bothering him about the water.

Ana realized with sharp clarity how much she liked
Bruno. How much she'd come to care for him in the
short time they'd known each other.

She just hoped she hadn't made a mistake, allowing
herself to begin to feel for him. Letting him in. Hoped
she hadn't placed her trust blindly, as with Darian.

Darian again.

It seemed, today, that all thoughts circled back
around to him.

But it was a fact, a reality. As delightful and amazing
as last night had been, this morning brought her to the
harsh eventuality of facing Darian again, and knowing
that her safety was now in jeopardy. She couldn't forget
that the crystal had ignited or activated hers, and that
somewhere, someone was probably out there looking
for her.

Trying to figure out how to find her in Envy right
now.

Ana shivered and swallowed hard. She would do this
on her terms, with Darian. She'd find him before he
found her. And she'd learn everything he could tell her
about what was going to happen to Envy.

By now Ana was in the adjoining bathroom and
finishing her morning ablutions. When she came back
out, her hair braided in a loose plait over one shoulder,
her face damp and fresh, she found Fence sitting up
in bed.

"Isn't that a pretty sight," he said.

His morning voice was even deeper than usual, not
quite as smooth, but definitely just as pleasing. It reminded her of something she'd had once, something
very rich and very rare, called chocolate. Darian had

given it to her when he was trying to woo her, and she'd shared the small, bittersweet dark block with her dad.

Ana paused in the doorway of the bathroom, aware of the picture she made—dressed in only a pair of panties, one of her few bras, and a black tank top— and deftly arranged her bad leg behind her good one. "Thank you," she said, her gaze lingering on his before she sauntered over to where she'd unpacked her small satchel.

"Except you have too many clothes on," he added. The grit was gone from his voice, and he'd pulled himself up on one elbow, the covers falling away from his torso.

Ana tossed him a smile. "I've got things to do. No more time to play." She pulled a crinkled peasant skirt from her bag and carefully stepped into it as he watched.

"Who said anything about playing?" he coaxed. "I've got some serious plans for you, sugar. Some real hard work. If you know what I mean."

He winked and she couldn't hold back a grin. The guy was ridiculous. But, heck, he made her laugh.

Ana had to go near the bed to get her shoes, and with a sly look, he lunged for her. Laughing, she dodged, but awkwardly. She stumbled on her twisted foot and before she could catch herself, fell smack onto the floor.

"Aw, Jesus." Fence was out of bed with grace and speed amazing for his size and gathered her up from where she'd landed in a heap of skirt-tangled legs. "Ana, I'm such a fucking idiot."

One of her knees had caught the brunt of her weight as she fell, along with her left elbow, but beyond those aches she wasn't injured, other than the shock of landing on those two points.

Yet she felt like a fool. Only moments ago she was standing in the doorway, pretending to be a seductress . . . and now here she was, an awkward, graceless, *clumsy* mess. Her cheeks burned and her eyes stung.

"I'm fine," she said, clenching her teeth to keep her voice from wavering. It was more annoyance and anger than pain or sadness. Despite her efforts to shake him off, Fence assisted her to her feet—which made her feel even more helpless and mortified.

"I'm *fine*," she said again, more firmly, when he insisted on looking at the elbow she was rubbing. "It's not as if I haven't done a few face plants in my life. Hasn't everyone?"

"I'm sorry," he said, looking so crestfallen that she nearly forgot her own bruised ego in favor of his. "I have to remember . . ."

His voice trailed off, and she had a feeling it was because of the dark look she knew was crossing her face. "You have to remember what?"

While she knew she was oversensitive, she also thought it was important to get the subject out into the open. If there was any chance of she and Fence becoming more than a one- or two-night "thing," he had to understand that she wasn't a glass figurine.

"I'm such a big, clumsy dude," he said, as if wading through deep, thick muck. "My mama always told me I don't know my own strength—"

"Don't be obtuse. This isn't about you, dammit, Fence. It's about me. I've been living with this"—she gestured to her leg—"for twelve years. I'm used to it, and I'm used to how it limits me and how it makes me look. You don't have to act like you stepped in a pile of horse poop every time I stumble or trip. Not only am I crippled, but I'm also more than a little clumsy."

"But Ana, I've got to be—"

"No. No you don't. You don't have to treat me any different from any other woman you've been with. Or will be with. Okay?"

"Will be with?" A furrow appeared between his brows.

Ana flapped a hand at him in dismissal. "Let's be realistic here, okay?" *Crap.* This wasn't the conversation she wanted or needed to have right now. Her knee still ached, her pride was banged up, and she felt like a mess.

"Well, yeah," he said. "Realistic is good."

"So, what I'm saying is—"

An impatient knock at the door stopped her. *Who can that be?*

Dad!

And at that thought, Ana hurried over as fast as she could.

She felt Fence's eyes following her awkward progress, but fortunately for him, he remained silent. And still. The knock came again, annoyance reverberating in its very tone, and Ana open the door to find Zoë standing there.

"Yes?" she said to her visitor.

Impatience vibrated off Zoë in waves. "Quent was looking at that stupid fucking crystal again and he found some weird-ass markings on the bottom of it. You need to get down there and look at them." And then she looked past Ana for the first time. "Well, there the hell you are, Fence. I guess opportunity just keeps showing up at the damn door, doesn't it?" Her eyes gleamed with delight.

Ana didn't bother to invite her in. Nor did she mind that Zoë seemed to be more than a bit interested in all of the parts of Fence that were exposed since he'd leapt, naked, out of bed to help her. Who wouldn't notice an amazing body like his? And he wasn't making too much of an effort to be modest either.

Zoë's understandable distraction had given Ana a moment to consider the request, such as it was. She did not want to get near that hunk of Jarrid stone again; there was still the slim chance that her own crystals' awakening had been too brief for any connection to be made back to Atlantis.

But at the same time she'd promised to help these people. It was also the least she could do after Elliott had taken care of Dad.

"Are you coming?" Zoë demanded, hands on her hips, eyes flashing with renewed annoyance.

In the end, Ana acquiesced. She figured Quent could draw the symbols or markings for her and she could attempt to interpret them, all the while keeping the crystal at a safe distance.

"I'll be over in a bit," Fence said, flashing Zoë a wide white smile, and Ana a less certain one.

When Ana and Zoë got to the subterranean chamber, there was a pretty redhead sitting at one of the computer tables, clicking away on the keys. She wore headphones, and her mouth moved as if she were either talking to herself or singing along with something on the headphones. Ana assumed it was Sage, who'd helped Theo and Lou Waxnicki put all these computers together on what they called a network. Whatever that was.

"Ana doesn't want that damned crystal near her, genius," Zoë announced to Quent as they entered the room. "At least someone's brain is engaged. She wants you to draw the symbols so she can look at 'em."

Moments later Quent produced a piece of paper and Ana took it from him. "It's the Atlantean alphabet," she said. "A bit like hieroglyphs, but more advanced. They also use the Roman alphabet, as you do."

He was peering over her shoulder. Sensing his acute interest, she began to point out the individual hieroglyphs and explain their meanings. "It appears to be instruction to the finder of this stone. There's a ship. Here's water, and this one—"

"Right. And I recognize that," Quent said, pointing at one of the symbols. "The labyrinth and swastika together are part of the symbol for the Cult of Atlantis, the group my father belonged to. They're the ones who have been in contact with your people."

"That's the sign Atlanteans use to denote themselves. And here . . . this I think is the direction or location where this piece of Jarrid stone was hidden, or otherwise left. And here . . ." She looked at him. "It's the instructions on how to use the stone for communication."

Ana saw the great leap of excitement in Quent's face. It was matched by the downward spiral of her own belly. "I have to warn you, though—there is a great chance, because many of these crystals are connected by intuitive energy, that if you activate it and try to contact them, they'll likely not only communicate with you, but also be able to identify your location. Exactly where you are."

The damage might already have been done.

"Are you saying that if he gets this damned thing to work, all those fucking Atlanteans are going to descend on us like a damned bunch of crystal-wearing zombies?" Zoë demanded. "Like, down here? No fucking way, genius."

Quent's head swiveled between her and Zoë, and Ana saw indecision in his face. "What do I have to do to activate it?" he asked, and Zoë leapt to her feet.

"Look, Quent, you don't want to risk every damn person's ass here—"

"I'm not quite that incompetent, luv," he said, with an edge to his voice. "I have to assess the risks, and—"

"What exactly do you have to fucking assess, genius? I can't be out there saving your damn ass every fucking day again. And everyone else's. I've got other—" Zoë snapped her teeth together audibly as her voice broke, and then silence reigned.

Except for the sounds of Zoë grinding her teeth together.

And the nonstop clicking of Sage's fingers on the keyboard. Ana noticed that the redhead seemed oblivious to the war going on around her. Probably just as well; it was clear that Quent and Zoë had a volatile relationship, and Sage was probably used to their fiery arguments.

"You think about things, assess the risks," Ana said as the couple glared at each other. "I'll be back in a little while; I have some things I need to check on."

"But—" Quent began.

"Don't," Zoë interrupted him. Now Ana recognized a glint of fear in the other woman's eyes, buried deep beneath her bravado.

Fence had told her that Zoë was several months pregnant, and that almost everyone except Quent knew about it. "There's gonna be some real fireworks when he finds out and tries to keep her sitting pretty at home like a good little woman," he'd said with a little chuckle. "That's gonna be some good shit."

Ana had been looking at the slender woman, wondering how far along she was, trying to see a sign of it . . . but she couldn't tell. Maybe beneath the loose cargo pants there was the beginning of a bump, but not a very big one. Ana had watched, in silent misery, all of the young women in Glenway through their various stages of pregnancy, and noticed how each one developed differently. Some women hardly showed at all for many months, or showed in different ways.

Gritting her teeth against the little nudge of grief, she decided to make her escape and leave Quent and Zoë to their own battle, and limped over to the staircase as quickly as she could.

After going back to the infirmary to check on her dad—who'd been moved from his hospital bed to a room similar to hers, unbeknownst to her, a room in close proximity to Flo's residence—Ana took a deep breath and left the big building.

It was time.

As she walked down the stone and dirt paved path that led to the shoreside gate in the wall, she heard her name and turned to see Fence ambling toward her.

Even from a distance she could see the brilliant flash of his smile. He was wearing a tight white shirt that showed every single detail of his pectorals and ridged belly, along with blue jeans that had been hacked off above the knee. And no shoes.

Her breath caught for a moment, and then her cheeks warmed at the memory of exactly how that massive body had felt, sliding along hers, all hot and damp and strong. *Whew.* She had to concentrate to get her breathing under control.

"Don't you have any clothes that fit you?" she asked as he approached.

"What?" he said, surprising her when he scooped

her close with one big arm and planted a good, long, thorough kiss on her lips. "Now what shit were you saying about my clothes?" he asked, his eyes dark and smoky.

"Um . . ." She'd forgotten already. Her lips were throbbing and her lower belly was already tingling as she recalled just exactly what could happen with a guy like this after a kiss like that. *Oh yeah.* "Every shirt I've ever seen you in looks like it belongs on someone more my size than yours."

His gazed dropped immediately to her breasts, then moved back up as his slow smile returned. "I don't know, Ana-sweet," he said. "I'm not sure this shirt could contain those lovely girls. But we could try and find out. Why don't you take yours off right now?"

Ana laughed. "Nice try, Bruno."

"Well, I already took my shirt off for you once, so fair's fair."

"Again . . . nice try." She patted his arm.

He kept his arm around her waist, and as she turned to continue her walk to the ocean, he tightened it. "Where are you off to now?"

"To the sea. I want to do some swimming." She smiled up at him, squinting a bit in the sunlight. "Wanna come with me?"

"Naw, that's all right," he said. "Don't want to ruin my 'do." His grin gleamed, but once again it didn't quite reach his eyes. "I've got something else on my mind, anyway."

Then he tugged her close, and holding her steady, turned her gently on her feet. The next thing she knew, she had the wall of a building scraping against her back and his mouth moving in on hers.

She lifted her face and met his full lips eagerly. Her

hands landed on the tight cotton of his shirt, and the heat from his belly and torso bled into her skin through two layers of clothing.

"I didn't get a chance to tell you," he said, shifting away slightly. His eyes found hers as he locked his arms around her waist. "Last night was mad amazing. You're so beautiful, and you taste so sweet," he added, sifting a bit of her hair through his thumb and forefinger. "And such a tease."

She smiled back up at him. "Talk about teases . . . that poor mirror will never be the same again."

"Well, she ain't seen nothing yet. That was just fore-play."

Ana couldn't help the little relieved flutter inside her chest. So it wasn't going to be just a one-night get-together.

She wasn't stupid; she knew he was . . . What did they use to call them? A player. Fence was a player. She'd seen how he worked the room the first night they met. And his easy manner, his jokes and generous mood, at-tracted the attention of a variety of women of all ages. Even the jaundiced eye of the adorably miffed Tanya had softened in the face of his warmth and attention.

And although she wasn't certain what if anything she wanted *this* to develop into, she knew she wanted more time to figure it out. To explore being with him.

She'd liked being in a relationship with Darian, liked having someone to talk to and be intimate with. And she'd certainly liked the possibility of having a family with someone she loved.

Although that was clearly rushing things, so she put the thought right out of her mind.

"Are you sure you want to run off?" he said now, still looking down at her.

"Run?" she joked. "Not me. I only limp. Unless I'm in the water," she added. "Besides, I'm hoping to see my dolphin friends again today."

His eyebrows rose. "You have dolphin friends?" He seemed interested in spite of himself. "That's cool."

"There's a female named Jag—she's got a hunk cut out of her dorsal fin, hence the name. And also Marco Polo, because I can tell he travels far but always comes back."

"How can you tell how far he goes?"

"The stuff that clings to him when he comes back— sometimes there are little insects or critters stuck in the fold of his fins. He likes it when I scratch him there."

"So they know you?" he asked. "They let you pet them?"

Ana nodded. "I've ridden on their backs before too. They swim all over the ocean, but they visit me regularly. Marco was here yesterday—he followed me from Glenway, I think, and I hope he's back today." She smiled. "They'd let you touch them if I were with you. I can call them closer—"

"Nah, that's okay, I'm good," Fence said, his expression settling a bit.

A sudden mischievous thought popped into her head. "You know," she said coyly, smoothing her palm over that indentation along his breastbone, "I've got an idea."

"What's that?" he asked, his hands planted over her bottom, his fingers slipping their way down beneath the band of her jeans.

"Well, last night was the first time I'd ever been with a man in bed, and you introduced me to it. Why don't I introduce you to sex in the sea?"

His arms stiffened and the teasing disappeared from

his face. "Nah, I don't think so, Ana. Too much salt. Might get in my eyes—or elsewhere." As if to punctuate that thought, he gave a little bump of his hips against her where they were pressed together and followed it with a strained chuckle.

"We don't have to be under the water," she said, remembering that she was *certain* he'd been breathing beneath the surface when she dragged him out yesterday. "We could just be—"

"No," he said. "Swimming's not my shit."

Ana's heart did a little thud. He'd never spoken to her—or to anyone in her hearing—in that tone of voice. *Okay then.*

She mustered up a smile. "Well, I'm going to walk down there and see if anything else washed up on shore. Want to come with me?"

He seemed to struggle, then gave her his own smile. And a weak one at that. "Sure."

But now things weren't quite as easy between them. It was the whole water thing, and she was completely confused by his reactions to it.

He *had* been breathing underwater, hadn't he? She was sure of it. Although she was completely mystified as to how he'd done so.

Maybe she was wrong. Maybe it had just been a fluke.

But then she had an idea. A way to figure out how to get him in the water.

"What are you grinning about, sugar?"

"Nothing," she said with a teasing glance. She drew in a long deep breath. "Mm. I love the smell of the sea. It's so . . . fresh and clean and salty. It's just beautiful."

Fence didn't respond, and by now they had walked through the gate and were making their way between the trees and bushes that grew on the expanse of land between the beach and the protective wall.

Ana's pulse accelerated as it always did when she got near her beloved Sea. Her skin felt as if it were coming alive, and her nostrils dragged in the beauty of the scent around her. She'd learned long ago that many non-Atlanteans found the smell of fish and algae unpleasant, but to her it was *home*. And it was the only place she felt fully whole.

But even as she experienced the familiar tug into the rushing, rolling waves, she felt Fence's demeanor change. He didn't speak, his pace seemed to slow, almost becoming reluctant, and his movements stiffened.

She was going to fix that. She grinned to herself again, and slipped out of her shoes, holding onto Fence for support when she had to stand on her bad foot.

"Doesn't look like anything washed up on shore overnight," Fence said, scanning the beach. From end to end, it stretched about a mile.

Ana noted their privacy with satisfaction. She could see they were far enough away from the wall of Envy that no one would see any of the details about to occur. "That's good," she said, and shimmied out of her skirt.

He was looking at her with interest, despite the tight corner of his mouth. "C'mere, sugar. How about a roll in the sand?" He reached for her, but without the force and speed from this morning—which allowed her to easily evade him.

"How about a roll in the waves?" she asked, backing away from him and into the water.

A surge rushed around Ana's ankles, and she smiled at the familiar, comforting feel of the Sea's embrace. Fence was watching her with a startled expression.

"What are you doing?" he asked. He grinned, but the smile seemed forced.

"Come on, Fence," she said, the water now up to her knees. She looked at him, caught his eye, and held his gaze with a smoky, hot one of her own.

Then she crossed her arms in front of her torso to grab the hem of her tank top, and brought it up and over, whipping the shirt free from her body. Spinning it around on her finger, she teased, "You wanted me to take off my shirt, didn't you?"

"Ana," he said. He'd moved toward her, but stopped at the point where the sand and dirt were darker from the reach of the oncoming waves. "Why don't you come on back here and let me help you with that." His *heh-heh-heh* sounded flat.

"Why don't you come on out here and help me?" With a sharp movement, she flung her tank top toward the shore. It landed on an in-bound wave, tumbling onto the sand near his feet.

She was past her waist and getting deeper, allowing the energy of the water to seep into her being through the crystals.

"Ana, what are you doing?"

"This," she announced, unfastening her bra. She slipped out of it quickly, her breasts bouncing free just on top of the waves. "Come on out here and give me a hand, why don't you?"

"Come on back here, Ana. Someone's going to see you," he said, taking one step toward the water and going no farther.

By now she was floating, treading water, and moving as easily as he did on land. "I know someone's going to see me. You are," she replied. "It's not that deep . . .

and it'll be fun. Come on, Fence. We can do a little slip-sliding around . . ."

She came back a little closer to the shore so she could stand once again. Her breasts were just out of the water, and she began to move enticingly, dancing in a way she couldn't on land, since the ocean held her upright.

She lifted her arms above her head, hands and fingers twining together, then grapevined down and over her torso like she'd seen exotic dancers do in DVDs. He watched avidly as she cupped her breasts, then slid her hands down below the water along the curve of her undulating hips.

"Come on into the water, Fence, darling," she coaxed. "Just think of what we can do—"

"I'm not coming in the water," he snapped suddenly. His face had become a hard, cold mask. "I'm not *fucking coming into the goddamn water.*"

Ana stopped, paralyzed in breast-deep waves. "Why? I've seen you in the water. What is the—"

"I told you," he said harshly, "I don't like to swim. Now *stop fucking playing games*, Ana, and come out of the damn ocean."

She felt as if a massive, icy wave had crashed over her on a hot sunny day. "Fence—"

"Come out of the motherfucking ocean."

Hot tears stung her eyes, but Ana couldn't make herself move.

Before she could speak, he turned abruptly and stalked away.

CHAPTER 14

Fence's hands were shaking. His insides were a fucked-up mess. He swallowed hard to keep from puking his guts right there on the damned beach.

He stalked away as quickly as he could without running, furious with himself, furious with her, furious with the motherfucking ocean for fucking existing.

Of all the women he had to fall in love with, why in the hell did it have to be a freaking mermaid who *loved* the ocean?

Hold up there, brother.

Fall in love with?

Uh . . . no. That was a bit of a stretch.

He'd only just met her a few weeks ago.

Fence paused, a surge of nausea getting the best of him, and gripped a sapling oak. Curling his other fingers tightly into a fist and concentrating, he managed to keep from vomiting his pussy-assed weakness all over the place. Jesus.

He was going to have to just stay the hell away from her now. He'd shown his ass, as his father would have said, and not in a good way. And it was just as well if he didn't have to be around such sweet temptation. Because this was never, ever going to happen. Even if he wanted it to.

But he didn't want it to. Not anymore.

This shit was too damn much work.

Ana's tears mingled with the saltwater so that she couldn't tell what was ocean and what was shock and anger.

I guess that was that.

She streaked through the sea as fast as she could. Trying to outrun her emotions. Trying to exhaust herself. Trying to understand what had happened to turn Fence into . . . someone *so* not him.

It was as if he were two different people: one on land, one by the water.

Just like I am.

That thought came out of nowhere, and Ana stopped as if she'd slammed into a wall.

But at least I'm not a complete whacko bitch in one of my personalities.

Except when you're jumping all over him about the way he treats your handicap.

She frowned and took off like a shot again, skimming through the water. Well, those weren't very palatable thoughts. She wanted to have a good mad-on at him, and her conscience was being too reasonable.

She'd swim it off.

And she was delighted, no, comforted, when the long slide of an elliptical shadow cruised above her. And then a second one followed, sleek and silent in the dark water.

Smiling, Ana shot up toward the surface where Jag

and Marco were ducking around, slip-sliding against each other.

Jag, the shyer of the two, looked at her coyly when she swam up between them, and then rolled away in the water, showing her smooth white belly. Ana patted her as she followed, until an insistent butting against her back indicated that Marco was waiting for his attention.

Ana played with them for a while, examining their smooth skin to make certain neither had any new injuries—a common occurrence when they swam through all of the man-made remains. She followed them as they chased after a school of herring for their dinner, playing hide and seek around a jumble of old cars.

She spent more time with them than she should have . . . but of course the reason for that was also her procrastination about checking the mailbox where she'd left the message for Darian.

But at last she couldn't put it off any longer, and watched her companions swim off.

Then, taking a circuitous route, she made her way back to where she'd seen Darian's sign. In preparation for this eventuality, even though she'd delayed it as long as she could, Ana had already retrieved her tank top from where it was caught at the delicate edge of waves onshore. Her bra was long gone, and that was a loss she felt deeply, for pretty blue ones were hard to come by.

She wasn't even at the mailbox yet but could tell he'd been there. Her insides flipped like a dolphin and she paused, peering around some massive metal object as if waiting to see what would pop out. Of course, nothing did—but it was the glow from inside the mailbox that told her he'd responded to her message.

Ana drew a deep breath and felt the rush of cool

water flooding her crystalled lung. Her palms would have been damp if she were on land.

She was about to approach the mailbox when something moved in her periphery. She spun, sending tiny bubbles into a twist, and came face-to-face with Darian.

His expression nearly disarmed her: it was a combination of his familiar chiseled features and a look of shock and delight.

Ana! he mouthed, and reached for her.

She surged backward, holding her hand up to keep him at a distance.

He stopped in confusion, the pleasure fading from his handsome face. *What's wrong?*

He used his hands to speak, for of course sound was lost in the water. Atlanteans relied on a complicated if stilted sign language, often punctuated by dolphinlike whistles and clicks.

I responded to your message but that does not mean I want to see you, she told him.

His dark hair floated around him in the water, and she could see the brilliance of his blue eyes. They were still as intense and bright as they'd been five years ago, and they matched his crystals perfectly in color. Darian's crystal pattern was also one of the most attractive ones she'd seen: they formed several small triangles around his muscular torso . . . which, of course, was bare above a pair of close-fitting trousers.

I have been looking for you for years, Ana, he said.

Why? I told you I wanted never to see you again.

If you never wanted to see me again, why did you respond to my message?

Good question. How exactly did she answer that? *Kaddick is dead.*

His eyes widened. *Dead? How do you know that?*

Did you kill him?

Darian shook his head emphatically. *No. What happened to him?*

She allowed the skepticism to show in her face. *I saw you yesterday. He was following you. And then he turns up dead on the beach. Looked like he was cut to ribbons.*

He was following me?

Even in the wavering light, Ana could see the cold shock on his face. Either he didn't know, or she was wrong. She knew Darian was the first Atlantean she'd seen yesterday . . . but she hadn't gotten as good a look at the second one. Maybe she was wrong.

Maybe there had been three Atlanteans swimming around near Envy. *I am not certain it was him. But I saw you. And someone was following you.*

His head whipped around as if to spy someone lurking behind him. *Someone was following me? When? Where?*

She explained where they'd been when she saw them. *Are you telling me you knew not it was Kaddick?*

Once again he shook his head with vehemence. *No. And now he is dead? I am a dead fish myself then.*

Why would someone kill him?

Darian shrugged, his hands remaining still this time. But the uneasiness still lurked in his expression, and she could have sworn he was watching behind her in case someone or something burst onto the scene.

The thing about being in the water, though, was that everything that moved made some sort of ripple. The sea was never still, but one could sense a difference in its pattern when a creature was swimming or walking. It was very difficult to sneak up on someone in the water.

Therefore, as long as she paid attention to the current, waiting and watching, she would hardly be taken by surprise.

You are doing what around here? You left a message for me? Ana asked.

I told you: I have been looking for you for years.

She allowed the skepticism to show not only in her face, but in her hand gestures that followed. *I don't believe you. That's drag. There is no reason for you to be looking for me at all, let alone for years.*

Despite what you think, I loved you, Ana. When you refused to come back to Atlantis with me, I was hurt and devastated.

Her hands slapped her signed response so violently that the sounds rippled through the water. *You mean when I refused to let you collect the reward for returning me to the Guild.*

If I had only wanted you for the reward, why spend a year loving you? he asked, reaching for her again. *I could have just taken you back at any time once we got together.*

Ana had dodged him, and slipped the knife from its sheath. She wasn't taking any chances again. *Not going back there. Ever. I will cut my crystals out first.*

Again he held up his hands to fend her off. *All right, Ana. All right. I was not completely honest with you.*

You? Not completely honest? How about not honest at all?

He grinned in chagrin, and for a moment he reminded her of Fence after he made a bad joke. Ana shoved away the resulting twinge of remorse and brandished her knife.

The truth is I really did love you. Yes, I was going to collect the reward—but that was only if you came back with me. If you did, I might take the money so I could build us a nice and private place to live. I was not trying to trick you.

Ana rolled her eyes. *More drag. I know you have not been looking for me for years, but you were obviously looking for me now. Why?*

I was looking for you . . . off and on, he confessed with a sharp click for emphasis. *Where have you been?*

She smiled, and the water seeped coolly into the inside of her mouth. *Do you really think I am going to tell you?*

Obviously near Envy.

I am just visiting. Sorry. I live far from here. You found me here anyway?

He twitched an arm lazily to keep himself from drifting away. *I recognized Jag swimming outsea from Envy a few months back and knew you must not be too far away. Thinking you would actually see my message was like believing you would find a fish egg in the coral.*

Ana was trying very hard to pull the truths from his stories and half-truths. And it was a challenge. So she figured she'd chased him around the coral long enough and went for what she needed to know. *Something is happening. What is going on? What was Kaddick planning?*

Darian's eyes bugged out almost comically. *You know this how?* Yet there was no humor in his face. It held serious concern.

I know the sea just as well as you do. I can probably sense change better because I'm not in it all the time. I know something is happening.

The Guild is going to wash out Envy. They're just waiting for the moon phase.

She had suspected as much, but hearing—or rather, seeing it—and recognizing that, for once, the compulsive liar in front of her was actually being forthcoming, turned her cold. *Which phase? What are they doing?*

They are using the Goleths. Lining them up on a flash-row to make a surge-wave.

So it had to be a full moon—when that celestial body was at her full strength, pulling and tugging at everything watery on the earth.

You must come back to Atlantis with me, Ana.

She noticed he'd eased closer to her again, and she swiped down with her knife. It cut through the water, causing swarms of bubbles and a surge of current between them. *Not going back there.*

But you could talk them out of it. You could save the city. If you came back, they would listen to you.

No, they would just be glad to have me back under their control so they can study me. And get me to breed. She looked at him sharply. *That is why you are here? To try and seduce me again?*

No, Ana. Really. I came to try and find you because I think you're the only one who could get them to stop.

You care about what happens to Envy?

He recoiled in surprise. *Are you serious? You think I'd want to see a city of hundreds washed away? Especially after what they did before?*

She nodded. All right, she did believe that. Darian might not be the most trustworthy man, but he did have a heart. *Why* are *they going to do it anyway?*

One of the Jarrid stones is missing, and they think a mortal has it in Envy. Aside from that, those sludges that call themselves Elites have lain the egg that Envy is getting too big, and too powerful. They think the land-livers will have ships and cars again soon, and that the people might find out about us. There was no hand or body sign for *car* in Atlantean, so Darian spelled it out with letters. *They are afraid the land-livers will begin to gather together and rise up.*

So they are just going to destroy a whole city.

He nodded, sober now. *Ana, please come back with me. You could talk to them.*

They would listen to me? I'm just a demiblood.

But you're the only demiblood. When she frowned and shook her head, Darian added, *Frithia's baby died a year after his crystals were implanted. And Swyllin hasn't been able to conceive. They need you.*

She shook her head and her hair followed, rippling outward in slow motion. *I'm not going to go back and subject myself to their tests and studies and control.*

If they don't find the Mother crystal in the next year or so, we're going to die out, Ana. It's been fifty years, and its residual reserve is nearly gone. If they can't find it, they need you to figure out how to stay alive.

Now she was frightened. And now she understood his motivations. She'd been right. It was all about him. *You think if I came back I—we—could stop the surge-wave on Envy?*

A light came into his eyes. *I am almost certain of it.*

They promised you what if you got me to come back?

He blanched slightly, but enough so she knew she'd hit the target. His shoulders moved as if he were taking a deep breath, and his crystals burned brighter. *Truth . . . Ana, I am a member of the Guild now. I have enough votes to get them to stop the surge if you come back with me and let them study you.*

Ana still held her knife and still watched Darian closely, but she'd also allowed herself to be carried a bit away by the current. The greater the distance between them, the safer she was. *I cannot leave without talking to Dad. He has been sick. I have to say goodbye.*

The naked hunger in his eyes flared then faded almost instantly—but it confirmed her suspicions. *You will go?*

Ana found it much easier to lie with her hands than her voice. *Yes. I will meet you later tonight, or tomorrow. Watch for my sign. I will do anything to save Envy.*

But only part of it was a lie.

And Darian had unwittingly told her exactly how to make it truth.

CHAPTER 15

"For sure, sugar, I'd be more than happy to take that off your hands," Fence drawled.

The hot piece of tail across from him giggled and pouted. Too bad he couldn't remember her name. "I think it might be too hard," she replied provocatively. "Even for a guy like you."

Not only did she possess a fine ass, she also had long blond hair that had been tucked up in a loose knot, with sexy little strands randomly falling down like she'd just been laid.

"Too hard? That phrase isn't even in my vocabulary," he said with a wink and his slide-into-a-hot-tub grin. "Neither is soft and floppy." His mama always claimed that smile could charm a rosary from the hands of a nun—and she'd know, because she had two sisters who were nuns.

Anyway, he could always find out the blonde's name later. He glanced over and cocked a hand at the waitress, signaling for another beer.

When Zoë made a disgusted sound next to him, Fence turned to her. "What? At least I'm not hiding a bun in my oven from the man I love to fight with so I can fuck him like a bunny afterward," he said in an undertone. "Who happens to be the bun's father."

He managed to resist the compulsive urge to turn the statement into a long spiel about hot dogs and buns and how the latter got into female ovens via wieners and franks, only because he knew Zoë wouldn't get the joke. They didn't really have hot dogs since the Apocalypse. Although, they *did* have sausages . . .

Zoë rolled her eyes. "What you just said is so full of ass-crap bullshit that I'm not even going waste my damn time responding." She glared at his beer as if daring it to jump into her hands and pour itself down her throat, then lifted her own glass of iced tea. "These are gonna be some long-ass nine months," she muttered.

"What did you say about nine months, luv?" Quent asked, suddenly appearing behind them.

Fence felt Zoë jolt in her seat next to him, and he hid a grin behind his beer mug. *Some big shit's gonna come down pretty damn soon.*

"I said I've had a great piece of ass in my hands for the last nine months," Zoë replied.

Fence cast her a sidewise look that said *Nice save,* but she didn't notice. He was pretty sure she was too busy swallowing her heart back into place.

"Has it been that long?" Quent said, pulling up a chair behind them. "I hadn't realized. I thought it was only six months. Hell, we could have had a baby by now."

Since Quent was right—it had been only six months since they'd arrived in Envy—Fence buried his face in his beer glass again, this time to hide an expression of "Fuckin'-a, Zoë's sunk," and realized he'd forgotten all about the hot piece of ass across from him. *Now what were we saying?*

It was a sad state when a guy like him got distracted by a foul-mouthed prego instead of a bed-headed blonde.

He never heard Zoë's response to Quent's possibly innocent comment, nor did he remember what he was trying to say to the bed-headed blonde, because the doorway he'd been watching obsessively was suddenly filled by a sun goddess.

She was scanning the room, and even from where he sat he could see that her hair was still wet from her hours-long swim.

Yeah, he knew exactly how long she'd been gone, because, damn him to a blazing hell, even though he knew better, even though he'd talked himself out of the hassle of this shit, he'd gone back to the beach after he got his pussy-assed self under control and waited until Ana strode back out of the water.

Three hours later.

Good God. He'd sat on a *beach* and waited for her for three hours . . . and then made sure she didn't even know it.

She hadn't seen him, for he'd been situated behind a ragged pile of grassed-over concrete. He was relieved to notice that she retrieved at least her tank top while he was off puking his guts, before she'd gone for her swim. But those three hours were much too long. More than once he'd walked down to the edge of the water and thought about going in.

"Thought" being the operative word.

He got as far as his ankles at one point, then gave it up when he broke out in a cold sweat and his sore stomach started churning again.

Good God. If anyone ever found out about this, he'd be done. Stick a fork in him. Cooked.

He then proceeded to talk himself out of the need to worry about Ana anyway, because she was half Atlantean. She was a fish. She was as comfortable and safe in the ocean as he was in the wilderness.

It was too fucking bad they couldn't be comfortable in the same damn place.

And aside from all that, for God's sake, what had possessed her to try and force him to go into the water? He'd told her he didn't want to swim. And then she pulled a stunt like that, trying to *trick* him into the ocean. Not cool.

But now as he looked across the room, even though he was still pissed his insides gave a long, slow shift—as if making a decision and then settling into it. He felt an unusual, uncomfortable hollowness in his middle and wasn't quite sure why it left him warm and jittery. Shame, perhaps. Guilt. Even annoyance.

No, definitely annoyance. She was out of line, trying to lure him.

But he did know that he'd rather be looking at—and consequently thinking about—Ana than the blond bed-head across from him. His sun goddess lived up to her name, with her golden-brown skin beneath a loose white tunic that bared her sleek, toned arms and showed a deep vee of cleavage. Her hair flowed in light and dark ripples over her shoulders.

Jesus. His pounding heart was pretty much out of control.

Ana had been looking around the room and when her attention came to the table where he sat with Zoë and Quent, she started to make her way toward them.

Fence was aware of a tightening in his chest as

she approached, looking not at him but at Quent. He watched how she moved with that little hitch, realizing that her gait was closer to a crab-walk than he'd realized. How easily he'd forgotten her imperfections, and how fixated she seemed to be on them.

No wonder she wanted to spend as much time in the ocean as she could.

But she needed to leave him the *fuck* out of it.

At the reminder of their confrontation, he felt even more miserable. Kind of empty. His hands were goddamn *shaking*.

I'm such a fool.

"Could I talk to you? Privately?"

Fence's heart skittered. Or leapt. Or did something acrobatic, and he turned to face Ana, suddenly ready to move in. Maybe even take a big bite of humble—

But she was leaning toward Quent, speaking to him . . . not to Fence. True, her hand was on the back of Fence's chair—awfully close—but her body was angled away from him. Pointedly angled away from him.

Great.

Not that it would stop him from following them. Since it was Quent she wanted to speak with, it had to do with the crystal. Maybe she'd found something in the water when she was on her three-fucking-hour swim.

Quent had already risen and was pulling Zoë's chair out so she could slip free, so Fence scraped his seat away from the table as well.

"Gotta run," he said briefly to the bed-headed blonde, who was looking at the four of them in mild confusion. He didn't even try to make a promise that he'd return. He wasn't thinking about that right now.

He wasn't thinking about anyone but Ana, damn it.

If Ana noticed or had a problem with him following them out of the pub uninvited, she didn't show it. However, other than a brief, impersonal glance, she didn't acknowledge him before leaving with Quent. That left Zoë and him to follow.

"So how the hell did you fuck *that* up so quickly?" Zoë asked, making no effort to keep her voice down.

"Did you say something about opportunity knocking you up?" he asked, just loud enough for her to get the message—but not enough for Quent to hear.

"Shut your trap," she hissed.

"Talk about fucking things up . . . what do you think is going to happen when he finds out you've been keeping that from him? Or does he know?"

A flash of misery crossed Zoë's exotic features, then morphed into stubbornness. "He doesn't know. I'm not even five damn months along."

"And you don't think he's noticed that your boobs are getting bigger?" Fence shot back.

"They are— How did you fucking know?" she glared at him.

Fence gave her a look. "I'm a guy, Zoë. We notice that sort of shit like we notice whether it's sunny or raining."

"Well, don't be sayin' ass-crap shit like that to him, okay? Or I'm going to have to hurt you." She stomped ahead of him, leaving Fence with his own thoughts.

And giving him a chance to watch Ana limp along from behind.

Normally, that was a natural thing for him to do— enjoy the rear view. And while she had a long, lean torso ending in a very nice ass, one he'd really enjoyed pressed up against him when he was showing her the mirror, her labored gait made him feel tight and nervous inside.

It wasn't that her long legs were imperfect, one of them marked with horrible scars and rippling, uneven skin that bulged in the wrong places like a lumpy pillow. No, he hardly noticed it—except when she tried to hide it, or got all tense when he touched her there.

What bothered him was that she couldn't move with the grace and ease that someone who looked like she did *should* be able to do. He wondered if there was anything Elliott could do to help her. Maybe he'd ask. He knew that Elliott had the ability to heal people in some circumstances . . . although there was a limit to what he could do.

Fence found himself slowing his normally speedy, fluid walk so he could remain far behind Ana and Quent.

A few minutes later, as he took a seat on one of the computer chairs in the underground computer rooms, he realized his whole body was tense and annoyed. He shook his head mentally and put away his issues to listen to what Ana had to say.

Though her fingers curled together in her lap and her face was a little pale, she spoke quickly and concisely. "I've learned some information about what's happening."

Fence was about to demand how and from whom, but Quent spoke first. "There is a threat, then."

Ana nodded. "Yes. You were right—it's to come from the sea. And it's going to be a great wave that will destroy Envy."

"We'll have to evacuate," said Quent calmly, smoothly, in that stiff British accent. "Everyone. Do you know when it's going to happen?"

"What about all of this?" Sage, who'd pulled off her earbuds for once, gestured to the room. "We can't leave this. And how in the world would we get it out of here? There's too much . . . so much. Everything we know, everything we've collected . . . it'll be gone. I mean, Vaughn could get the people out of Envy—if we have time. How much time do we have? Do you know?"

"It's tied to the moon phase," Ana replied. Fence noticed that her eyes seemed to scan the ceiling and walls every so often. Almost nervously, as if she were expecting them to cave in on her at any moment. "In this case, the full moon. Which means we have one or two days until it reaches its fullest point."

"One or two days? Bugger it. We need to be talking to Vaughn *right now* about getting everyone out of here," Quent said, looking at Zoë.

"There might be a way to stop it," Ana said. Her eyes seemed a little weary. Perhaps sad. "I think there *is* a way to stop it, it's just a matter of whether I can get to it in time."

"You know how they're going to do it?" Fence asked. "And you know how to get there?"

"If my information is correct, yes, I'm pretty certain I know that."

"And *who* is the source of your information?" he said. Not terribly nicely.

When her eyes shifted just a bit down and to the right, he had a bad feeling. "A friend," she replied smoothly. "An Atlantean—"

"You said you hadn't been in touch with anyone from Atlantis since you left," Fence said, taking no care to hide his disbelief. *Has she been feeding us lies all along?* Something unpleasant curdled in his belly. "And within a day of telling us who you are and what your people are like, you're now telling me you some-how got in contact with an old friend so quickly and easily? You expect me to—"

"Is your source trustworthy?" Quent interrupted. He gave Fence a quelling look.

"In this case, yes, I think he was telling me the truth. I can't think of a reason he would lie about something like this."

He.

"The Guild wants me to come back to Atlantis, and Darian is certain I could convince them to stop the wave. I—"

What the fuck kind of name is Darian? Fence couldn't control a derisive snort. "Yeah, right, and once you're back there they'll just do whatever the hell—"

"I'm not an idiot," she said, fixing him with a sharp look right out of his mama's playbook. "I'm not going to go back there, especially on such an uncertainty."

Fence relaxed a bit, which allowed Quent to inter-ject, "But you think there's another way to stop the wave? Tell us what you know."

"You already know how powerful the crystals can be. And as you might have realized by now, there are different ones with different properties. There's the Jarrid stone, which can be used for communication—I told you I think I've figured out how to use the one you have. But that would be dangerous, because once they realize where this piece of the Jarrid stone is, they'll be after it. Or they will definitely want to destroy it. So either way, *not* a good idea. And it could already be too late."

Quent nodded. "Right."

"There's also what they call the Mother crystal, which is the primary source of the energy for the

Atlanteans themselves—their body crystals. It's an orange crystal, about this big," she said, and showed them a circle with her thumb and forefinger about the size of cherry. "A part of it's been missing for a long time, and without it the energy reserve is dying out. If the Atlanteans don't get the missing piece back, their crystals will die and so will they. It's possible that the Mother crystal, wherever it is, was also activated when my crystals came into the same proximity as that of the Jarrid stone. Like I said, these crystals are all connected by energy and they can sort of recognize each other."

"So what the hell do they need you for? Didn't they put the crystals in you in the first place?" Fence demanded. He did not like the way this was sounding. "Does this mean your crystals are going to die out too?"

"Remember, I have normal human blood too. The Atlanteans have used their crystals and procreated among themselves for more than eight thousand years, and their blood's been changed—tainted, even—by the crystal energy. They have little gritty pieces of it in their organs and blood. The crystals that are in their lungs *grow* there from birth; unlike mine, which were implanted. As I told you before, that energy gives them strength and helps keep them youthful for longer, as well as help them to live underwater. But since I'm what they call a demiblood, my blood and body reacted differently to the crystals. They aren't a part of me."

"So they want to study you," Quent said. "Like a bloody lab rat."

Ana nodded soberly. "Now you understand why I didn't want that Jarrid crystal near me. If it helps them to find me, they'll take me back there."

"So, knowing that you're in danger of being forcibly taken back, you went out into the ocean for three hours today—and met up with an old Atlantean friend, who just happened to be hanging around?" Fence said.

She turned a frigid look at him. "What choice did I have? No one would go in the water with me."

Yeowch.

"Then you shouldn't have gone," he fired back.

"If I wouldn't have gone," she replied in that patient voice his mama had used just before he got his ass grounded, "I wouldn't know what they were planning."

"And when you're ready to actually *tell* us what the fuck they're planning," Zoë cut in, "we'd all be a lot fucking happier instead of going batshit crazy. And then maybe we could actually fucking *do* something to *fucking* stop it."

Ana cast the other woman a steady look. "As I was saying, there are different sorts of crystals with different sorts of energies. There's a collection of them, about the size of that chair there," she gestured to a computer chair, "called the Goleths. Their particular force draws energy—and in this case water, around them in a great circular motion. If they're lined up in a row—there are fewer than a dozen of them, from what I understand—the pull will be incredible. And it will cause the water to circle and surge around them, gathering up along the line, and then expel it in a great force."

"Creating a huge disturbance in the ocean," Quent finished.

"A tsunami," Sage added.

Ana nodded. "Yes."

"So how do you think you could stop them?" asked Fence. He didn't like the direction his mind was going, and so he put it on pause.

"If one of the stones is moved out of the alignment, it should disrupt the energy flow and cause the process to fizzle out and abort. I'd have to find the stones and move one of them."

"You said they're the size of this chair," Fence reminded her skeptically. "How in the hell are you going to move it, and what are you going to do with it once you do?"

Ana looked at him, her expression blank. "I don't know. But I guess I'll figure that out when I get there."

"Do you know where these big-ass stones are?" Zoë asked. "And how deep in the ass-crack of the ocean they are?"

"I don't think they'll be that difficult to find, now that I know what I'm looking for. In fact, I suspect—although I'm not happy about it—that they, too, might be connected to my crystals. I might be able to find them by using that connection somehow. And, yes, they'll be on the ocean floor, probably deeper than any of you can swim." She wasn't looking at Fence.

"We could rig something up to help move the stone," Quent said. "Zoë's brilliant at that sort of stuff." He flashed her a hot smile that made Fence glance at Ana, remembering the slant-eyed look she'd given him before he turned into an asshole.

But if she hadn't pushed him . . .

"We're going with you," Zoë said.

"And in the meantime, Vaughn can start to evacuate the city," Quent said. "I saw him this morning. He said there'd been a couple guys in the restaurant yesterday asking questions about me. Probably those gits you saw in the Humvee," he added to Fence. "But Simon sat down, chatted them up, and put out the word that I hadn't been seen here for a couple months. And then he made sure the bounty hunters left without talking to anyone else, and he's following them for a bit to make sure they don't come back."

Fence nodded. "Good for him. Wish I'd been around to see if I recognized them, but it doesn't really matter. They're deflected and redirected."

"Too bad we can't deflect and redirect the threat of a tsunami quite as easily," Sage said. Her eyes were scanning the room and she looked as if she were ready to cry. "I'll see what Theo and Lou want me to try and save." Then she sat down at the computer and began to type with rapid fingers.

"Simon, Elliott, and Jade will help you get as much equipment out of here as possible," Quent said. "Too bad Wyatt's not back from Yellow Mountain yet. Fence—"

"I've gotta come with you," he said without hesitation. "You can't go without a guide."

Quent nodded. "Probably right, but we could use the manpower here—"

"I'm going. You can't afford to get yourselves lost, or in some other mess. Besides, if we have to haul up a big fucking rock from the bottom of the ocean, you're gonna need some muscle."

He just wished to hell they were going to be traveling on land for most of the way.

Chapter 16

"Ana."

She paused at the top of the circular stairs, relieved to be out of that crushing space and back on the main floor again, and turned.

Fence was striding up with fast, smooth steps, skipping every other stair with his long legs. "Could I talk to you for a minute?"

"Yes," she said, keeping her voice and face emotionless. She moved out of the elevator and into the deserted corridor, giving him space to maneuver past her.

Despite the fact that her heart was pounding, and, when he walked by, the brief brush of his warm arm made hers tingle, she really didn't want to talk to him.

Try as she might, she could think of no reason for him to have gone so berserk earlier today. And so quickly. It was as if he were a coin, and flipped from one side to the other.

She did know, however, that it would be a lot easier to just keep her distance from the guy, especially since he seemed so . . . unstable.

Even though . . . jeez, he just looked so big and solid

and strong. Like a rock himself. With all these things going on in her life, she really would have liked to have someone hold her.

Someone she could talk to.

Ana blinked hard. She got so damned tired of holding it all inside.

"Do you have any idea where these stones might be?" Fence asked.

Ana had to admit to a stab of disappointment that he wasn't groveling at her feet, apologizing for being an ass, and instead was only worried about finding the stones.

And saving a city of hundreds of people.

Oh yeah.

Focus, Ana. This is not the time for a lovers' spat to murk up your thoughts.

She sighed and tried to answer his question. "I really don't . . . but I'm sure that once I get back in the ocean I'll be able to figure it out. I've sensed for some time that something's wrong, changing in the water, and I'm pretty certain this is what it is. The other aspect I didn't mention—because there are so many tangents and it's all so complicated—is that the stones will have to be situated on an energy center as well. So if I can find the closest one to Envy . . ."

"An energy center?" Fence frowned. "You mean, in the earth?"

"Yes, right. There are centers of energy all over the world, and they've used those in conjunction with the crystals in order to—"

"Cause the Change," Fence said, looking down at her, comprehension dawning in his dark eyes with those long, curling lashes. "They used them to cause the Change, didn't they?" That's what Theo and Lou had suspected.

She swallowed hard, thinking about the horror people must have experienced when the world fell apart around them. All of the terror. All of the loss of life. Mothers, children, families . . .

She looked at him and the same stark, horrified realization was reflected in his eyes. Ana nodded in acknowledgment. Yes, that was how they'd caused the Change.

This was the other reason she would never return to the Atlanteans. How could she be part of a group of people who'd caused such widespread genocide? The Nazis had nothing on the Atlanteans and the Elites—the latter of whom were even more guilty and despicable, for having killed off their own families and friends.

Ana shivered.

"When you say energy center . . . ?"

"The way I understand it," she said, "there are countless lines of energy that band the Earth. Whenever there's a place where several of them cross paths or connect, that's what's called an energy center. The more lines that intersect—some people call them ley lines, we call them flash rows—the stronger the energy center is."

"Whoa," he said. He seemed to be nodding to himself as if finally understanding something. "Yeah, I know all about fucking ley lines and their intersections, and what they can do. And so you're saying they—whoever 'they' is, the Elites, the Atlanteans, whoever—used crystals placed at these energy centers to what? Cause massive earthquakes and tsunamis throughout the world? Yeah, that's what did it. Once they all started, it was a chain reaction," he continued, half talking to himself. "Earthquakes, tidal waves, crazy storms, everything. Caused the whole damn Earth to change, with all those plates moving, crashing against each other—Jesus Christ."

When he looked at her again, gone was the cool-eyed, remote, postberserker Fence. And also missing was the flirtatious, charming, happy-go-lucky guy who'd lured her into his arms.

Instead, she saw the same bleakness she felt at the realization of what one race had done to another. Not to mention to countless other innocent creatures.

"I can't think of a goddamn bad enough name to call them," he said, his jaw tight. He blinked hard and smashed a massive hand over his bald head, causing his forehead to crease. *"My God."*

Ana nodded soberly. "I know. So, if my crystals can help lead me to the energy center that they must be using, it'll be a lot easier. But if I can't, it'll be a lot of hit or miss."

"The way the shoreline is . . . I wanted to talk to you about that. I know my way around pretty damn well, and if we look at a map, maybe we can figure out what makes sense for the direction the wave's gonna originate."

Ana nodded, but before she could speak, the elevator door opened again to reveal Sage. She looked as if someone had just lit a fire under her—or maybe it was just her brilliant red-gold hair. "I was just on the network with Lou and Theo. We think we've got it figured out!"

"What?" Fence asked, turning in obvious surprise. Then he glanced around the corridor as if to make sure no one was around and looked at Ana. "I know you don't like it down there, but we can't have this conversation here."

She drew in a deep breath, surprised he'd even noticed her discomfort. "It's fine. I'm fine." She joined them in the elevator, and once again the doors closed to whisk her down into the deep, dark earth.

Perhaps she was getting used to it, but this time the enclosed space didn't bother her quite as much. Or maybe it was because Sage had some interesting information to share, and Ana found herself absorbed by it.

"A few months ago, Simon and I found an old flash drive—a computer thing," Sage explained when Ana raised her brows in question, "that had belonged to Remington Truth."

"Remington Truth?" Ana leaned forward. "I know that name. But I'm not sure why."

"He was a member of the Cult of Atlantis," Fence said, "a core member, and something happened around the time of the Change. We're not certain what, but apparently he disappeared."

"He died?"

"Not then. But we know that the Strangers have been trying to find his ass for fifty years—and they've been sending their zombies out looking for him. We're not certain when he died, but we do know that his granddaughter is still alive. Her name is also Remington Truth, and she's a real piece of work."

"Do you know why they would be looking for him?" Sage asked Ana.

She frowned, trying to remember what she knew about Remington Truth. She wasn't even certain she'd known he was a man. It was just a phrase she'd heard, like a password or a motto. Always spoken with a sort of malicious reverence. "I didn't understand he was a person until you told me."

Now, knowing that Truth was a *man,* not a thing or phrase, she thought she might remember more than she realized. Then all at once . . . her breath caught. "*Wait.*

I remember now. I think . . . I think he disappeared around the same time as the Mother crystal went missing." Ana frowned, trying to extract the details from her groggy memory.

"What's that?" Sage asked. "The Mother crystal?"

"It's a very important crystal to the Atlanteans . . . the source of their energy. I mean . . . it's more like a *key* to their energy source, rather than the source. I don't know," Ana said, shaking her head, trying to remember, knowing she sounded vague—but she hadn't even been thirteen, and only heard snippets of conversation. "Whatever it is, they need it. They're desperate for it. I think there was a suspicion that Remington Truth destroyed the crystal somehow. All I know is it went missing at the same time he did."

"How in the world could Truth have gotten it if it was in Atlantis?" Sage asked.

Ana shook her head. "I have no idea. I'm just repeating bits and pieces that I heard . . . I could be totally wrong . . . You were starting to say something about Truth."

"Oh yes." Sage nodded and continued, "Simon and I found his flash drive, and on it was a list of numbers. Theo and Lou have been trying to figure out what they meant for the last few months, and only recently realized that the numbers were probably coordinates on the globe."

Ana shook her head. "I don't know what you mean by that."

"They're numbers used for plotting a specific location on the Earth," Fence explained. "But since the Change, not only has the geography been altered, but so have the axis points of the Earth. Things have shifted, and we're only just now beginning to understand how much and how to account for that change. I've been drawing maps up the ass and trying to use what I know of astronomy to figure out where the hell things are."

"Anyway," Sage continued, "based on what they found in Yellow Mountain, Theo and Lou have come to believe that this list of numbers are geographic points that are the locations the Strangers—or the Atlanteans, or both—used when they set the Change in motion."

Ana felt a sudden prickling burst of understanding, and she and Fence turned to look at each other. "The energy centers," she said.

"Where all those ley lines connect up—just like in Sedona," Fence said, glancing at Sage. "Strange shit happens."

The redhead was nodding. "When I gave Theo the update about everything you told us, Ana, he suggested that maybe one of the sets of coordinates—the geographic points—would be a logical location to place the Goleth stones."

"That makes sense," Fence said, already leaning over Sage's shoulder to look at something on the computer screen. "The one closest to us would be the most obvious. I'm going to have to look at these and transpose them onto one of my maps." He glanced over his shoulder at Ana. "It's going to take some time."

She stood. "The moon is at its greatest size tomorrow night. You'd better work fast."

And while they did that, she had other things to attend to.

"I've never seen them like this before," said Selena. "It's almost as if they've gone crazy. Like they're looking for something."

"Crazy zombies? Isn't that an oxymoron?" said Wyatt, looking down over the horde of gangas staggering toward them.

They were at the top of the wall surrounding the old estate in Yellow Mountain, where Selena, and now Theo, lived. Twenty feet of two-foot-thick brick separated them from the monsters. But the sight of the masses, toddling madly toward them with their glowing orange eyes and stinking, rotting flesh, made Wyatt more than a little uneasy. Selena was right: there was something different about the way these zombies were acting.

Wyatt had seen many disturbing sights in his lifetime—from the charred corpses of children and pets burned to death because their parents were too stupid to install smoke detectors, to the remains of marketplace shoppers after a suicide bomber in Iraq, to his first glimpse of an eerie post-Change city—but this one raised the hair at the back of his neck. Especially knowing, as he did now, that the zombies were nothing more than terrified, insane human souls trapped inside stretched and rotting bodies.

They were souls conscious of their skin and bones captivity, but unable to communicate or to control their desperate need for human flesh. And that made them bloodthirsty and dangerous . . . and yet pitiful, so desperately pitiful, at the same time.

Wyatt had been there. He'd been with Theo and Lou, and had seen the place where the Strangers turned men and women into zombies by injecting a tiny orange crystal into the skull of semiconscious humans. Thank God there was Selena, who had the special and strange ability to free the humanity trapped inside those terrible bodies.

Ruuu-uuuuth-ruuuthhhh-ruuu-uuuthhhh! the zombies moaned and cried, over and over, in a mournful desperate way.

"Are you sure you want to do this tonight, Selena?" Theo asked. His voice was tight, and he was watching her in the moonlight with serious eyes. It was a dangerous prospect, her need to mingle with the crazed beings and get close enough to help release them. "There are at least two dozen of 'em."

She nodded and climbed down from the platform that acted as a lookout post. "It's going to be fine," she told him, and Wyatt saw her reach over and touch Theo's arm, sliding her hand casually along its length.

A simple gesture, meant to comfort. An easy one, between two people familiar with each other, who loved each other. Who trusted, respected, *knew* each other.

He turned away and focused his attention on the zombies. "I'll keep watch to make sure they all make their way over to the holding area," he said, knowing that his voice sounded clipped and harsh.

Selena did her special something with the zombies in a unique space built by Theo and his brother Lou, along with the vociferously bad-tempered old man named Frank. Actually, Frank—who had to be at least ninety—had done most of the actual building, with Wyatt's help, while Theo and Lou used a cache of electronics and pinball machines to create a sort of funhouse experience that confused and hypnotized the zombies. That allowed Selena to do whatever it was that she did with the glowing pink crystal she wore around her neck.

Wyatt didn't know, they hadn't offered, and he hadn't asked for a detailed explanation. He'd come to believe that the less he knew about this hellhole of a Changed world, the better off he'd be.

Because if he knew everything that had happened, who'd caused it . . . if he allowed himself to even consider, to imagine what had been done to the world fifty years ago—to his friends, family, wife, and *children*—he'd go mad.

Right now he was holding onto simple existence by a very slender thread.

He looked back out at the mob of Frankensteinian monsters, noting that most of them had turned toward the north side of the wall, which was where Selena and Theo were waiting for them. The twin pinpoints of their glowing eyes marked their progress, along with the shadows cast by a nearly full moon. Small pairs of orange lights jerked and jolted as their owners tried—

Wyatt froze.

Orange crystals.

Something chilly rushed down his spine. Remy had a glowing orange crystal.

He was swept back to the incident last night, when he'd found her writhing on the ground, that glowing orange stone set in her sleek belly like a large and gaudy navel piercing.

Definitely not what he'd picture a woman like Remy wearing, despite her explanation that it was just a piece of jewelry.

He knew she was lying. Remy lied and prevaricated about everything. Of course she had something to hide—it was obvious since the moment he and the others found her in the small home where she had her pottery shop.

When she'd shot at him.

I wasn't shooting at *you.*

Bullshit.

He remembered her standing there with the gun in

her hand, those blue, blue eyes cool and determined. Settling on him as she warned them not to move, then pulling the trigger when he did. The memory of her taking that risk still made him cold with anger.

But his fury was offset by the remembrance of dragging her battered, bruised body from where she was chained beneath the bounty hunter's truck. She'd looked just as bad as some of the gang-raped women he'd seen in Iraq. Maybe worse.

His belly tightened with nausea at the thought of the evil men could inflict on others.

A soft, urgent bark caught his attention, and Wyatt's tension eased. He climbed down the ladder and found Dantès pacing uneasily, ears up at full attention. He wasn't panting with enthusiasm, as when it was time to play—he was silent, clearly worried, on alert.

"Do you sense it too, big boy?" Wyatt asked, crouching next to the big dog. "They're on a tear tonight, aren't they? It's like they're searching for something and finally think they've found it."

Dantès smelled like comfort and warmth, and Wyatt wasn't ashamed, there in the moonlight with that big furry body next to him, to squeeze his burning eyes tightly shut for a moment as he embraced the animal.

Not only had Dantès brought the light into his dark world simply by being loyal and unconditionally loving, but he reminded Wyatt of his own, long-gone companion Loki.

When he released the dog, Wyatt realized that he hadn't seen Remy since she ran back to the house last night, after he helped her remove that burning crystal.

He rose slowly, uneasiness settling over him. He tended to avoid her as much as possible, but everyone in the house generally ate together unless they were involved with something. She hadn't been at dinner, he knew that.

It wasn't as if he wanted to seek her out. He had no desire to do that—he knew he wasn't in any condition to be human toward anyone, let alone a woman who couldn't help but piss him off by her very presence. Especially one as damaged as she was. But something was up. He'd been in enough tense situations to know to listen to his instincts. And Dantès was acting oddly as well.

"Where's mama?" he said, forcing excitement he didn't feel into his voice. "Where is she? Let's go find her!"

Dantès had leapt to attention at the question and then gave a little whine that did nothing to ease Wyatt's concern. *Shit.*

"Come on, boy, let's go find her!" He gestured with his hand, and the dog took off for a few paces, then came circling back around with another little whine and a short, high-pitched bark. He danced in front of Wyatt, as if asking for assistance, confusion in his very stance.

And that was when he knew for certain: Remy was gone.

It was well into the evening when Ana heard the knock on her door.

She'd just returned from visiting her dad, who was relieved to see her, once he emerged from his absent-minded fog and realized how long it had been since he'd done so. She hadn't told him about her plans to help stop the tidal wave, knowing that Mayor Rogan would make sure everyone evacuated—and having seen Flo in action, Ana was confident that the nurse would make sure Dad left his experiments behind in exchange for saving his butt. According to Quent, he was currently examining Kaddick's crystals and comparing them to the one Elliott managed to obtain from one of the Strangers.

She'd come back to her room to change before going down to eat in the communal dining area, and was even planning another slide into the ocean to see if anything had changed.

She certainly had no intention of meeting up with Darian again. If he was waiting for a sign from her near their meeting place, he'd be otherwise occupied and out of her way.

But now someone was knocking on her door.

Ana opened it to find Fence standing there. He looked tired, especially around the eyes, and her annoyance and anger wavered.

"Uh . . . can I come in?" he asked when she didn't move from the threshold.

He leaned against the side of the door, his body taking up a good portion of the opening, all dark and beautiful. Ana had to force herself to remember what an ass he'd been, what a crazy, flipped-out jerk . . . but it was difficult, especially when she recognized the uneasiness in his demeanor. That reality behind the veneer of nonchalance.

She drummed up the memory of him standing there on the beach, eyes raging, face dark and angry.

I'm not fucking coming into the goddamn water.

"I don't think so," she managed to say now. "I don't think it's a good idea, Fence. We're . . . what do you want?"

He gave a little sigh and his full, luscious lips shifted

into a ghost of his normal smile. "I wanted to tell you what Sage and I figured out. We think we've found the location, based on the general area of each set of co-ordinates and the maps I've been able to plot. I mean, we found the coordinates that are the closest to Envy."

"When can we leave?" Ana asked, ignoring the way his muscled arm crossed the threshold as he leaned against the inside of the doorjamb.

"Tomorrow morning."

"Good," she replied, thinking of Darian waiting at their meeting place to meet up with her. She'd be gone before he realized it.

"Quent and Zoë are going to come with us. Vaughn got one of the fishermen's boats arranged for us to take, and Zoë's working on a sort of contraption that we can use to help you move the stone—as long as it isn't too deep."

Ana nodded. "Sounds like we're as ready as we can be, if the location is right. Thanks for bringing me up to date. What time are we leaving?"

He glanced down at his feet, then back up at her. "At sunrise."

"Okay. I'll be ready." She started to close the door, but his foot—and arm—blocked it.

"And, uh, I'm sorry I got so uptight today," he said in a rush. "It wasn't you—it was me."

"That's for sure," she replied tartly.

He looked at her, startled, and a little glimmer of humor showed in his eyes. "You sure don't mince words, do you, sugar?"

"I don't see any reason to float around it," she re-plied.

"Ana, would you mind some company?" He seemed to sense that sincerity was a better bet than that carefree smile, so he kept his face sober. "Tomorrow . . . well, I know tomorrow's going to be risky and tough, and I know you . . . well, hell, Ana, you saved my ass from drowning, you escaped from Atlantis, you even stonewalled Zoë downstairs, so I know you're a tough cookie . . . but I thought you might want to . . . might not want to be alone."

Her heart squeezed and she wavered inside. But common sense ruled.

"I don't think that's a good idea," she told him. "I find you very hard to resist—just like most women probably do—but at the same time, I don't see any reason to pursue this. You obviously hate the ocean, and for me . . . it's the best part of my life. I don't see how this thing between us can go anywhere."

His dark eyes were fixed on her, and she felt a tremor of attraction start deep in her belly and flutter up and out. *No.* She was not going to fall for that.

"Here's the thing, Ana-sweet," he said, dropping his voice to its deepest pitch—in the timbre that seemed to rumble deeply and deliciously inside her. "I'm going to be straight with you. I want to be with you tonight. Not anyone else. You keep mentioning other women—now and in the future—and the truth is, I don't want to be anywhere but here. With you."

Her heart was thudding, and she knew better, but her reservations were softening. She didn't want to be alone either. Tomorrow she was going to embark on a journey and task that could easily end unhappily—for her and for others.

The last time she'd undertaken something so risky had been her escape from Atlantis . . . and look how that'd left her.

Fence seemed to know she was wavering. He eased

farther in, grasping the door frame on either side with his hands, so that more of him was inside than out.

And before she could react, before she could gather her wits, he leaned in even more and covered her mouth with his.

Oh.

Soft and sensual . . . God, the man was a master at kissing. He took his time, convincing her with his mouth, with the slick, languorous swipe of his tongue, the gentle bussing all along her lips.

Ana closed her eyes when that smooth, delicious mouth eased over to her neck, taking its time to taste her cheek and jaw and even that delicate spot under her ear. Heat shimmered through her, weakening her knees, causing her heart to race and her lungs to forget to work.

He moved one of his hands from its place on the edge of the door, lifting her hair from her shoulder, sliding his palm around to cup her at the nape of the neck.

She was liquid and heat, and when he pulled away to look down at her, she saw the same heavy desire in his eyes.

"I want to spend the night with you, Ana," he said, skimming his hand down her spine. To his credit, he didn't push or pull her into him, or move into the room. He waited, his own breathing not quite steady, not quite silent and easy. "Just be with you. Not for any other reason than to be there for you . . . if you want."

Stepping back from him was one of the hardest things she'd ever done, but she managed it. Disappointment flared in his eyes, but he made no move to follow her.

"I think it's best if I get a good night's sleep," she managed to say, even though her insides were hot and fluttery and ready. *Besides, you were a jerk today.*

A flicker of his charming smile warmed his eyes and showed a brief flash of white teeth. "I can help with that," he promised, and reached out to gently caress her lips with a broad fingertip.

"I suspect that what you have in mind will keep me up all night," she countered. Her lips tingled from his touch, still full and moist from the kiss.

"Actually," he replied, his hand easing away, "I meant . . . I could give you a back rub. Very relaxing." He showed her his big hands, and she could already feel their smooth, long, easy strokes down her back.

Ana's heart lodged in her throat. "Yeah, right," she managed to say around the lump. "A back rub. That'll change about five minutes after I let you in."

"Only if you want it to," he said. "I swear on my mother's soul."

She remembered the grief in his eyes when he'd mentioned his mother earlier, and decided that was a pretty solid vow.

She also realized that if he wanted to be down in the pub, making eyes at that blond woman who looked as if she'd jump into his pants at a moment's notice, he could be.

But he was here. Trying to convince her that he wanted to be here. And only here.

She believed him. She wanted him here too.

"All right," she said, and stepped back.

CHAPTER 17

Fence awoke, as he always did, at the first rays of sunlight. This time, though, he had an armful of sun goddess to greet the day with him . . . and it was after a full night's sleep.

Not one damned nightmare, for the first time in . . . forever. *Whoa.*

As he looked down at Ana, her golden-brown hair tumbled all over her shoulders and the pillow, facing away as he spooned her from behind, and his heart gave that unfamiliar lurch he'd noticed last night in the pub.

She could be the One.

True to his word, hard as it had been—in more ways than one—once she admitted him to her room, he hadn't done so much as cop a feel or try to turn their doorway kisses into anything more than what they'd been.

Instead, they talked—both of them. And he even kept the off-color jokes and puns to a minimum, though she always seemed to find them funny. She laughed even when *he* knew they were terrible jokes.

He'd told her a little about his mama and dad, taking care not to mention anything that would reveal his true age—at least not yet. She had enough on her mind; he could see the strain in her eyes. But when they returned from this mission, if they did—and he was determined they would—he was going to tell her all about his experience with the ley lines in Sedona.

As he massaged her slender, tense shoulders, Fence had described some of his more harrowing experiences in the wilderness—some of which happened even before there were zombies.

And to his surprise, he wasn't even tempted to take it any further—even while rubbing her back, massaging her shoulders and neck, and trying to ignore the biggest damned hard-on he could ever remember having. He just enjoyed the intimacy of touching her, listening to her, talking to her.

Even now, when Ana shifted in her sleep, bumping against him in an enticing but innocent way, he merely closed his eyes and thought of cold showers.

Last night, as they talked, he'd run his hands over her long hair, feeling its silky waves, keeping his actions acutely platonic. He'd even slept in his shorts—and he couldn't remember the last time he actually slept in anything other than his bare skin when he wasn't on the trail.

She could be the One.

She might just be *the One.*

Terror washed over him. How could he fall for a woman whose life was the ocean, when he couldn't put his big toe in without pissing his pants?

What the hell kind of punishment was this?

Hell, he'd only known her for a few days.

But despite his misgivings, despite his abashment about the episode on the beach, something had compelled him to go to her last night after he finished working with Sage.

He could have gone back down to the pub, scouted out some willing companionship. He'd made friends with quite a few of the ladies—and there had been a new possibility in that bed-headed blonde.

Or he could have hung out with Vaughn and Elliott and tossed back a few with the broody Simon. "Drink tonight for tomorrow we may die," and all that.

Their task was going to be risky and difficult, possibly even deadly, if they reached the stones as he anticipated they would. He'd seen the tightness in Ana's face down in the computer room, and the worry remained in her eyes even when he joined her in her room. Not fear, but apprehension.

He didn't want her to be alone.

He didn't want to be alone.

And . . . it was Ana he'd wanted to be with, and he wasn't exactly sure why. He just knew he did—and not because he wanted a "We're going off to battle, so let's send ourselves off right, sugar" evening.

He just wanted to be with her. He recognized, too, a temptation to be honest with her. To tell her everything.

But the very thought made his belly tight and unsteady.

She stirred again, more insistently, and damn it all if she wasn't sliding that curve of her ass *right* where it could do the most damage.

Fence gritted his teeth as she bumped against him. He kept his hands from moving, even though one arm was around her waist from behind and he could slip fingers down between her legs—*don't think about that*—and the other could easily maneuver around to cup a breast.

Yet at the same time, he found that he couldn't release her and move away, which would have solved the problem.

Ana yawned, stretched, and managed to snuggle her tail right up against him even harder, and then as she moved and stretched, half turning toward him, her bare breast popped out from beneath the blankets—right in front of his face.

Right there.

He held his breath and looked down at a luscious, tempting breast, a bit larger than a navel orange, ivory-gray and tipped with a blue-gray-hued nipple in early dawn's light.

I'm so fucked.

Just then she opened her eyes and looked right up at him.

Even in the faulty light, he saw the mischief in her gaze. And then she shifted her ass once again, deliberately grinding backward into him, and he was suddenly flooded with uncontrollable need.

He bent forward and took that perky nipple between his lips, lightly at first, tasting her warm skin and gently tracing the tip of his tongue over the delicate rise. She gave a little sigh that shivered her breast against his mouth, and he opened wider, covering her, sucking and licking as he drew her nipple and its crinkling areola deeper into his mouth.

His arm, curved around her waist, was trapped by the bed, but he was able to move his hand down over her crystals to slide between her legs. The little bit of cotton panty was no match for his deft fingers, and he slipped beneath it.

She gave a little jolt when he found her, found the hot dampness at her core, and began to slide and coax and play. Ana was slick and full, and that made him surge even harder. And when she came, throbbing and undulating into his hand, her body shuddering against him, he nearly lost it himself.

Greedy and impatient now, he released her breast and used his other hand to work at the buttons of his shorts. When Ana reached around behind to help, he gave up and let her finish the work while he used his fingers to explore and coax her along again. The scent of her filled his nose as her warm, damp skin brushed against his, her hair tickling his face.

She freed him from the tight confines of his shorts and then turned away from him again, her breathing rising, her skin rushing even warmer against him.

He yanked away the panties from her ass and slid into her sleek heat, both of them groaning in tandem when he fit into place. *Oh, yes.*

With long, easy strokes, he shifted, keeping his hand and fingers in place as he moved from behind. Ana sighed and shivered in front of him, her soft moans erotic to his ears.

"Now this is what I call a *very* good morning," he murmured, easing all the way in with a sharp little thrust at the end. She gave a soft, gaspy moan, and he smiled into her hair. "Jeez, Ana, you're so freaking hot . . . but I've gotta make you cry a little louder than that, sugar. All this sweet honey down here's making me crazy." He moved his fingers around her swollen center to emphasize his words, feeling her skin dampen with heat.

"How about that, baby?" he whispered, hearing the unsteady rasp in his voice. "How about if I just take you all the way, right now?"

She was doing that short, sharp breathing that he'd come to learn portended her orgasm, and he shifted his rhythm and his fingering to take her there. "How about a little scream this time, love? When you slide right up against me? Hmm . . ." He chuckled deeply. "Oh, yes, I know you can do it just as good as a guy can . . . come on, sugar . . . let me take you, mm—mm." He bit off his words as she made it, giving a loud cry of release that nearly sent him over the edge.

Smiling big and happy against her hair, he held her as her shivers subsided against him. "All right, then, Ana-sweet," he said. "*Now* it's a good morning."

He had to close his eyes as he felt that familiar, sharp, hot rise, and knowing he was near the point of no return, he forced it off, until it built so hot and hard that he thought he'd lose his mind.

He barely had the wherewithal to pull free just as he came, and stifled her surprised cry with the convulsing, stroking of his fingers, finishing her off as he sagged into warm bliss.

The light was brighter when he opened his eyes again, although the sun had still barely begun her rise.

"Good morning," he said in her ear.

"It is," she replied, stretching sinuously against him.

"You trying to get something started again?" he asked hopefully, his fingers bumping over her crystals. *Mad sexy.*

She kind of turned in his arms, looking up with deep hazel eyes. "Much as I'd like to, we should probably get up."

She would have pulled completely out of his arms,

out of the bed, but he tightened his grip . . . all at once *sure*. And afraid.

Afraid, and yet compelled.

His mouth started moving before he thought it through. "I've gotta explain something. About the water."

She stopped moving, and he realized he'd come to another point of no return, this one much more ominous than the one earlier.

A shudder rippled deep inside him, but he kept going, like he had the football in his arms and three linemen had their hands on him, trying to bring him down on the last play of the game.

But he kept on, pushing the words out through a desert-dry mouth. "I . . . I can't go into the ocean. Or lakes or rivers."

How the hell am I going to explain this without sounding like a complete pussy?

He closed his eyes, glad she was facing away and couldn't see. *You can't. You are a pussy.*

Ana had stilled, and lay there silently, as if waiting for him. But he didn't know what to say.

I'm terrified of it.

I'm afraid of water.

I have a phobia.

"That's why I wigged out at you yesterday. I'm . . . I'm sorry. I'm really sorry. I was . . . out of line. I should never have spoken to you that way."

Ana hadn't moved, and Fence was aware of the horrible sound of his heart beating, thudding like a death knell in his ears.

He waited, and she remained silent, and the thudding in his ears became harder and faster and more menacing, and at last he said, "Ana?"

"I was waiting . . . to make sure you were finished," she said. Her voice was mild, not accusing. "I didn't want to interrupt. It was obvious you were having a difficult time saying it."

"That's it." His palms were damp against the sheets.

"Can I ask you a question . . . without you—um—wigging out?"

He squeezed his eyes closed. Hell, he deserved that. He nodded, realized she couldn't see him, then said, "Yeah." His throat was tight.

"I saw you in the water. Twice. I don't understand—what do you mean, you can't go into the water? Does it . . . hurt you? Or what?"

This was where it got dicey.

This was the real point of no return.

"I almost drowned when I was younger," he said in a rush. "Twice. And now I can't go in without . . . remembering that. I get really . . . uh . . ."

"Wigged out?" she suggested.

"That's one way to put it." He realized he was clutching the cotton sheet and made his fingers relax. "I can't think. I can't breathe. I go a little . . . it just . . . takes me back to those other times. I think I'm drowning again. It's my head, messing with me."

Now Ana moved at last, sliding away, making his heart leap up into his throat again. But when she turned to face him, his apprehension eased a bit. "Now I understand. Thank you for telling me."

He tried not to let out his breath in a great whoosh of relief. She didn't *look* disgusted or shocked or disbelieving.

He struggled desperately to find something to say that would ease his tension, make her laugh . . . but there was nothing even remotely funny about the situation. Even in his warped mind.

So he just watched her, and hoped he didn't look as pathetic as he felt.

She seemed to take this as an invitation to speak. "We were together in the ocean. I thought . . . you seemed to be breathing. In the water. That's why I couldn't understand . . ."

Fence's body went still. Even his thudding heart stopped cold. "That's impossible."

"But I saw you, I'm sure of it. You weren't drowning. And you weren't holding your breath."

He shook his head. Whatever it was, it sure as hell felt as if he were drowning. "I thought it was you, saving me. Your crystals, helping me to breathe."

"They don't work that way," she said. "You were breathing under water."

He shook his head again, but doubt crept into his mind. Simon could turn invisible. Quent could touch things and know their history. Elliott could read the inside of a body with his hands. Hell, he himself had just had sex with an Atlantean.

But the very thought of breathing underwater, of putting his face in and allowing the salty, cold sea to come in, was enough to turn him cold with terror.

"It's just not possible," he said. And even if it was, he sure as hell wasn't fixing to test it out again any time soon. "Whatever happened must have been some sort of miracle."

Ana looked at him with a long, steady glance. "I don't believe that. I know what I saw." She leaned closer and pressed a gentle kiss on his cheek, her eyelashes brushing his temple, then eased out of bed.

Time to leave.

Somewhere in the wilderness

Ian Marck looked down at the crumpled body with more than a hint of satisfaction.

Dead: neck neatly slit, eyes blank and staring at the dawning sky. Served the bastard right.

At least the son of a bitch hadn't been turned into a zombie. Nor had his flesh been torn away and devoured by one of those pitiful, abhorrent creatures. That was good, because it meant there were remains for him to search and acquire anything of value the man might have. Including his boots. Ian's were trashed.

All in all, he had no sympathy for the bastard. Roofey was dumb as the night was dark, and greedy on top of it. Not a good combination.

Especially since Roofey had a tongue that flapped without prudence or discretion. He'd been blabbing to anyone who'd listen that the Jarrid stone was missing from Mecca, and that Parris Fielding's son had it. It just so happened that he'd been one of the grateful recipients of that information as he sat in the corner of Madonna's, drinking—not sipping, not nursing, but definitely *drinking*—a healthy dose of whiskey.

Not only that, but he had actually met Quent Fielding some time ago and thought he knew just where to find him since he'd taken up with that bad-ass zombie hunter named Zoë.

Ian would have smiled if it hadn't hurt so much, even when it was a smile without humor. His body was still recovering from the beating and unexpected flight down the side of a deep ravine into a river, courtesy of that bastard named Seattle.

He knew he was lucky to be alive, and figured whatever he had left to do on this earth must not be done yet. Pity. Because he was fucking tired of living with an empty soul and a big hollow spot where his heart used to be.

But knowing that Quent had the valuable Jarrid stone gave him something to work toward. An opportunity. He was a bounty hunter, after all—the best and most feared. He was always looking for the next opportunity.

Finding and acquiring the Jarrid stone was only one of several distractions he could use to pass the time until someone actually did the job right and put him the hell out of his misery.

If Seattle hadn't already had his throat torn out by some wolf or dog, he would have hunted him down and done it himself. And maybe the bastard would have actually finished what Seattle started a month ago when he had his cronies beat the shit out of him and toss him into a river to die. All because of a woman.

Actually, two women. Ian sneered as he looked down at Roofey. As if he'd sully his hands or any other part of him with Lacey, a woman Seattle had wanted.

Now, Remington Truth . . . she was a different matter.

She was nearly worth getting the shit beat out of him. And she had a ferocious dog who'd tolerated if not liked him when they were together. He suspected Seattle had met his demise most fittingly at the jaws of that dog, which indicated that Remington Truth was likely still alive and kicking, out here somewhere.

He'd find her again, sooner rather than later. He'd take her to Envy with him.

And once he had her and the Jarrid stone, he'd be exactly where he needed to be.

Fence sat in the very center of the small sailboat's stern, shielding his eyes against the hot sun as he gazed out over the sparkling sea. The only reason he wasn't fighting rising panic was because there was land within sight, and because his seat was positioned down *inside* the sides of the boat.

That made him feel a little more grounded, a little safer—even though he was surrounded by a liquid death trap. But he remained in that seat, navigating and managing the sheets and lines, horribly aware of the fact that he wasn't wearing a life preserver.

The only thing that would save him if he went over or if the boat capsized was a rope strung with big Styrofoam pieces someone had scavenged. After all, Styrofoam was something that even Mother Nature couldn't beat down into dust.

He just hoped to hell they didn't do a *Titanic*.

The four of them had been traveling since midmorning, and the ragged coastline was in and out of distant view. He hadn't stopped praying for continued good weather, and so far it had been hot, sunny, and clear, with just enough wind to take the edge off the heat and keep them going at a good clip when they were actually sailing. But they paused every thirty minutes or so for Ana to take a dive and check for the Goleth stones, which made their progress slow and tedious. In fact, the boat was more of a vehicle to carry their equipment than a mode of speedy transportation.

More than occasionally, they encountered small islands that had probably once been mountains and now acted as oases to Fence in the middle of this vast watery desert.

"Once we find the stones, I'll dive down and see what they look like," Ana said. She was speaking to Quent and Zoë, who sat on the bow.

She'd settled in the center of the boat, on a small raised platform that might have been called a sundeck if it hadn't been a fishing boat. He had a perfect view of her golden body basking in the sun, wisps of her long, damp hair fluttering in the breeze. The sight helped to distract him from the liquid jaws of death that surrounded their craft and the conversation happening around him.

"If they aren't too deep—although I suspect they will be—you can join me," Ana added.

"Right, and Zoë's got the sling she made," Quent said. "If it's long enough, you can loop it around one of the stones and we can help move it out of place."

"It's three hundred fucking feet long," said Zoë. "And I've got extra cord if we need it. Damn straight it'll be long enough."

"Are you certain you know which stone to move? How many of them did you say there were?"

"I'm not sure," Ana replied. "No more than a dozen. And it shouldn't matter which crystal I pull out of alignment, the way I understand it—I talked to Dad about it a little too. He agrees with me that as long as the energy pattern is interrupted, that will be enough to stop the wave. Of course, then we have to figure out what to do with the stone so they don't just roll it back into place."

"We'll take it back to Envy," Quent said immediately. "We'll want to study it, and compare it to the other crystals we've collected."

Fence was acutely aware of the way Ana spoke only to Quent and Zoë, and not to him, when it came to these plans. In fact, once they'd gotten on the boat, Ana's attitude toward him had become . . . different.

She'd sidle up to him and slip her fingers into his hand, giving him a little squeeze as if to reassure him. Or if she had to pass him to scoot from the bow of the small boat to the stern, she'd pat him on the back or arm. Like he was a child on his way to the doctor or something. Not like she was his lover.

And his heightened sensitivity pointed out that she was very careful not to talk too much about the water, what she saw, what it was like.

Ana had been in the ocean more than she'd been out of the water, but every time she went in or came out, she insisted that Quent lean over to help her climb back aboard. She described what she saw to him and Zoë, while Fence sat back, listening like a bump on a log. She even used some odd clicking noises and splashes in the water to bring one of her dolphin friends over to the edge of the boat, and allowed Quent and a reluctantly fascinated Zoë to bend over and pet its nose.

Fence wasn't invited.

And yet he knew exactly what she was doing, and why. It was just as he'd feared: she was treating him like a child. Like less of a man.

As if he had a—

Jesus Christ.

As if he had a *handicap.*

Which, of course, he did. A fatal, debilitating handicap.

An unexpected blast of anger surged up, heating his face and chest, causing his fingers to tighten so that his knuckles turned nearly white over the tiller.

"What the bloody hell is that?"

Quent's exclamation drew Fence from his furious

misery. He looked up to see a sort of shimmery, wavering . . . *thing* stretching out over the sea.

"Oh my God," Ana breathed as she sat up.

"What in the fuck is it?" Zoë said at the same time.

"Stop the boat," Ana commanded, crawling awkwardly toward the bow. "Don't get near it."

Fence didn't bother to explain how impossible it was to stop a sailboat in its tracks. Instead, he reacted quickly and jerked the tiller so the vessel did a sharp turn—too damn sharp for his taste, bringing the water right up next to him—as he untied one of the lines and dropped the sail. When the water slopped over the edge onto his leg because of the boat's tilt, his heart lunged into his throat.

"What is it?" Quent repeated. He'd climbed as far forward as he could and was practically leaning out over the rail to get a better look.

Now that the craft was nearly still, Fence could take a better look.

The whatever it was stretched as far as the eye could see, along the horizon of water. They were in open sea right now, with the edge of land to the southwest and two miles behind them, but beyond there was nothing but water and sky.

Fence swallowed and focused on the odd, undulating sort of . . . curtain. It looked like a clear shower curtain, muted with water and light shining from behind it. Or like the heat that visibly shimmered up from asphalt during the summer. Whatever it was, it was transparent, except for the faint multicolored ripples that shone in the sun. Yet it was like a wall—for waves crashed up *against* it, but not through it.

He shivered when he thought about how they might have sailed right into it, if not for Quent's sharp eyes.

And, more likely than not, this was the reason sailors who left Envy, sailing north, never returned.

Fence couldn't control a deep, harsh shudder.

"Thank God we didn't come upon this at night," Ana said, as if reading his mind. "It would have been much harder to see. And we'd have been caught in it." Her voice was tense, and her face matched.

"What exactly is it?" Fence asked. As he watched, he could see that the ocean was much more turbulent on that side of the barrier, yet contained. It looked almost as if the water over there was stirred up by a storm . . . or an energy center.

"It's a barrier. A— Like an electric fence," Ana said. "It's to keep land-livers from getting too close to Atlantis, sort of confining them to this part of the sea. We can't cross it—in the boat, anyway."

"Let me guess. Crystal energy?"

Ana nodded, still staring at the transparent wall. "Crystals lined up along the bottom, sending their energy up and out like a . . . oh, like a . . ."

"Like a force field," Fence finished for her. "But I don't think this is the location I plotted—we're still too far south. You don't think this could be the energy center, do you?"

"There's only one way to find out," she said, already stripping off her tank top to reveal her bare torso. Her crystals glinted in the sun, and Fence's heart stopped.

Lord, You sure did amazing work when You made this woman.

Her torso was bronzed gold, flaring into the gentle curve of her hips, her tanned skin contrasting with the aquamarine crystal studs. She wore a serviceable bra that looked more like a banded cut-off tank top than those lacy things he used to look at in the Victoria's

Secret catalogs his sisters got—but on Ana anything was mad sexy. As he watched, she worked her hips out of loose, frayed jeans, revealing the ever present knife she had strapped to her upper thigh. Now she was dressed in nothing more than the bra and a pair of shorts that were so brief you could practically see her belly button. From below.

He was distracted only for a second before realizing what she had in mind. "Ana, what are you doing?"

"Are you sure it's safe?" Quent said, but Zoë had already taken matters into her own hands.

Before Ana could reply, the other woman fit one of her arrows into its bow and snapped it in a long arc over the water.

When the metal arrow went through the undulating curtain, there was a sizzle and a pop, and lightning or some sort of electrical current snapped, radiating from the center of penetration. The scent of smoke wafted through the air.

"Bloody hell," whispered Quent.

"You're not going down there," Fence said, grabbing Ana's arm and pulling her back from where she was perched to dive.

"Yes I am," she argued. "At the very least, I'm going to see what's below. Maybe the stones are there."

He shook his head. "How do you know there's not an electric current, or some other energy in the water, *right here*? Don't be stupid."

Her eyes flashed. "Let go of me. I know the ocean and I know the risks. And besides, look."

She pointed, and Fence noticed for the first time a dorsal fin protruding amid the waves.

"It's Marco. If he can swim there, so can I," she said, and with surprising strength and force, she yanked away.

Ana was in the water before he could react.

"Damn it," he said, lurching to the side where she'd gone over.

The sight of the rippling waves, dark and choppy, just beneath his face, made him queasy and damp-palmed, but he forced himself to look down into the dark water.

"You two men," Zoë said with disgust. "You never give us women the fucking benefit of having our own damned brains. Do you think we're stupid enough to *want* to get ourselves hurt or killed? But no, you have to try and think *for* us, and fucking tell us what to do, and what *not* to do, *all the damn time*!" And she burst into tears.

If Fence weren't so worried about Ana, he'd have stared at Zoë in shock. As it was, he was only mildly aware that the hard-as-nails, smart-assed-as-they-came zombie hunter was *crying*. For no apparent reason.

Still staring down into the depths of the dark water, Fence was vaguely aware of Quent's stunned reaction. He felt the boat shift alarmingly as the blonde man reached for his irate woman, pulling her into his arms even as she insisted that he "leave me the damn fuck alone! You've already done enough to stir things up!"

Ana, come on. Get your pretty ass back up here.

Fence searched the depths, unable to see anything but the glitter of sunlight on the dark blue waves.

I should be with her.

But the very thought had his stomach roiling. He squeezed his eyes closed, steadying his breathing at the thought of sliding into that cold, dark depth.

I saw you breathing under the water.

He shook his head to dislodge the thought.

Ana, where are you?

And then, suddenly, there she was, erupting from the

water right in front of him. Relief swarmed through him.

He looked down at her wet face, sparkling with droplets, freckles dancing lightly over her nose, her wide, lush mouth only inches away—and felt as if he'd been punched in the stomach.

It is *her. She's the One.*

"Ana," he said, bending over as far as he dared. The water was *right there,* so close he could feel its coolness. He drew in a deep, salt-scented breath.

She came close to the boat, her hair plastered back from her face, her hazel eyes clear, the lashes clumping together with drops of the sea, looking up at him as his head blocked the sun. "It's deep," she said. "Too deep."

"Too deep for what?"

"To swim beneath."

"What about the stones? Did you see them?" He wanted to reach out and touch her head, smooth his hand over her warm, wet hair just as she'd done to the dolphin earlier.

"I didn't see them, but I can feel their energy. They're nearby. They have to be. The water is wrong down there."

"Wrong? What do you mean?"

"The current is all wrong. It's messed up—that tells me the energy is being gathered. Look over there— you can see it already. I'm going to have to go on by myself."

"What the hell are you talking about?" Fence wanted to lunge for her, but he kept his grip on the rail. "You just said it's too deep to swim under."

"Not for me."

"No fucking way. You can't go by yourself, Ana. Don't be crazy."

She'd backed away from the boat, just out of reach of his hands. Now he could see the faint glow of her crystals just beneath the surface. "There's no other way. No one can swim deep enough to get past the barrier. I found a place to go under it, but it's too deep for any of—for Quent or Zoë. That's why it's here, you know. No human can get through it. But an Atlantean can."

"Ana, no. Get back in the boat now. We'll think of another way to do this." He didn't care that his voice had turned hard and commanding, that he sounded desperate and lost beneath the words. "Don't risk it."

She looked up at him, opened her mouth to say something, then closed it. Then opened it again. "I can do this. I have to at least try."

"But they're already evacuating Envy," Fence reminded her. "Vaughn said they'd be out of there by evening tonight."

Ana remained at a distance. "But think of everything else that will be destroyed. Everything that you've worked for—that all of you have built for the Resistance."

"Ana, no," he said.

She frowned, her brows drawing together as she eased even farther from the boat. "Bruno, you'd do the same thing if you were me. You wouldn't even hesitate."

"But—" His throat ached and his eyes were stinging. "Ana, you don't even know what's on the other side. What if there's a trap? Something you aren't expecting? What if there are Atlanteans there?"

"I'm one of them," she told him. There was a tinge of bitterness in her voice. "They won't hurt me."

"You said you'd never go back—" he began, but she interrupted.

"I've got to go. I don't know how far the stones are or how long it will take to—"

"Ana, please," he said. "Don't go. Don't go alone."

She looked right at him, as if about to say something. His heart stopped. His hands turned slick and damp.

Don't.

Don't say it.

His heart started thudding again, slamming hard enough to jolt him.

She didn't speak.

Instead, after holding his gaze for a long moment, she slid back under the waves.

Fence stared down into where she'd disappeared, vaguely aware that Quent and Zoë were still huddled together at the stern, arguing softly.

He felt the spray of the water, smelled the sea scent, and gripped the edge of the boat, blinking away the sting in his eyes.

He couldn't let her go alone.

He gripped the side of the boat more tightly.

But the thought of plunging off into the deep, dark, cold depths made him ill.

He closed his eyes, brought Ana's face into his mind.

You were breathing underwater.

He tore off his shirt with shaking fingers.

One . . . two . . .

His breath caught in a jerky sob.

. . . three.

He flipped himself over the rail.

CHAPTER 18

As he plunged into the dark water, Fence's mind went blank with terror. The sea cloaked him, surrounded him: cool, dark, close.

His lungs were full of the breath he'd taken before launching over, and already they began to burn as he struggled to keep from panicking, to keep from losing it and hyperventilating. He felt a sharp sting beneath his arms, one on each side, in his ribs.

He closed his eyes, floating there, praying for consciousness, for sanity as the sea embraced him.

It's cool. It's okay. You're okay.

He repeated this mantra over and over, but the ocean was heavy and he felt it in his nostrils, saturating his shorts and seeping into his warm skin. *I can't do this.*

His mind had gone black and blank, and he struck out blindly with arms and legs, trying to make it back to the surface.

Then something brushed against him and he opened his eyes with a start.

Ana.

She was there, right in front of him, her face close,

her eyes wide with question and concern. The soft blue glow from her crystals filtered in the water around them. Her hair wafted in gentle waves. She reached for his arm, and he grabbed her hand desperately, clinging to his last shred of sanity with her as a lifeline.

I can't do this. I can't do this.

He felt the panic rise and fill his lungs, and he knew he was going to have to flounder to the surface, find the fresh air and take in great, deep gulps of it.

She was lifting his arm away from his torso, pointing to his ribs. Where the stinging was.

He barely had the awareness to wonder if he'd cut himself. *Oh, God, blood will attract sharks.* His lungs burned and he let out some of the oxygen reserve, bubbles trailing violently from his nose.

I'm not going to drown, I'll die from a shark attack.

The desperation and panic won, and he pulled away from her to kick upward. His head broke the surface and he gasped for air. Already he was looking for the boat to grab onto. He *needed* something to grab onto, to pull himself out of this—

"Fence!" Ana burst up next to him. "Fence, Bruno— you did it."

But he was nearly sobbing in mortification and anger with himself. He looked, and the boat was out of reach. He'd have to swim several yards.

But at least his face was out of the water.

It wasn't far. He could do it. One stroke . . . the next stroke . . . don't think about—

"Did you see?" Ana's voice was urgent. "You have gills!"

At first her words didn't penetrate over the roar of desperation and panic in his heart and mind, but she said it again. "Bruno. You have *gills*."

By that time he'd reached the sailboat and grabbed onto it like a drowning man. Hell, he *was* a drowning man.

"What did you say?" Safely holding onto the edge of the boat, trying to forget that he was still in the ocean, he turned to look at Ana.

She'd come toward him, her eyes wild with excitement. "I was showing you! You have gills. You *can* breathe underwater."

"What are you talking about?" he said, but even as he did, he was lifting his arm to look at his torso. Which was still underwater, so he couldn't see anything.

Ana was there next to him now, and she took his free hand and slid it down beneath his arm and—

Holy Mother of God.

Sure enough, there was an opening that had not been there a few moments earlier. His skin had split open just like the gill on a fish, by God.

It was fucking freaky. Completely, madly freaky, sliding his fingers along the beveled edge of a slit, warm and moist, in his torso . . . like the time he broke an arm and saw the edge of the bone pushing against the skin from the inside.

It was his body . . . yet it wasn't.

"There's one on both sides," Ana said. She was right next to him now, her legs so close they brushed against his.

"I can't . . . it can't be," he whispered.

"What the hell is going on?" Zoë's face appeared in front of him. There were tear streaks on her cheeks, and her nose was tipped red, but from the way Quent hovered behind her, his hand curved around her middle, it was clear that whatever crisis they'd had was either resolved or put aside for now.

"Fence has gills," Ana said.

"Let me see," Zoë demanded, bending over farther.

Fence obliged, still numb and foggy-minded, by popping out of the water, using the bow of the boat as his pull-up bar.

"Hot damn, you've got some crazy-ass muscles going on there, Fence," Zoë breathed, and then, "I don't see any fu— Oh."

Quent was there, leaning over her shoulder, looking down at Fence's torso. "They're gone now. But they were there; I saw them for a second. Now there's just a little line. Like a scratch."

"They must come out when you're in the water," Ana said. "And close up when you come out. That's why you never noticed them."

Fence lowered himself back in and felt the now-familiar stinging on either side of his ribs. He'd had these gills all along?

"So does this mean I can breathe underwater?" he said faintly, still struggling to comprehend. And to figure out how, just *how* the *hell*, he was going to allow himself to take that first breath.

"I told you," Ana said. "I knew you were breathing underwater."

A particularly vehement wave nudged Fence, and he looked over just as Quent said, "Buggering hell! Look at that!"

His body went cold.

Just beyond the shimmery force field curtain were choppy, massive, gray waves. As if someone had stirred up a great big cauldron, or dropped a big stone in a bucket. The barrier contained them, for they splashed up against it as if crashing into a breaker, but the water was definitely getting rougher on this side as well.

"It's got to be the stones," Ana said. "They're gathering their water force. And when it's all stirred up and ready, a place will be opened in the barrier to let the tidal wave through." She looked up at the afternoon sky. "The moon's up already. It'll be at its fullest point and strongest pull in two . . . three . . . four hours," she counted. "I've got to go back down there and find those crystals."

"And we've got to get this boat to shore," Quent said, his face tight. "And far enough inland that whatever comes isn't going to get us."

Zoë had already moved away, and Fence saw her picking up the lines and trying to raise the sail.

"I've got to go," Ana said. She looked at Fence but didn't say anything else.

Another wave, with more violence, smashed against them, sending Ana surging into Fence. He reached down and felt his torso. It was underwater and, yes—it was a miracle—the gill was there again.

Open.

He didn't say anything. He couldn't. He just released the side of the boat and slid underwater.

Out of habit, he'd taken a deep breath of air and he propelled himself down as far as he could go, praying the whole way.

Ana's long, slender legs and the glow of her crystals appeared above him and began to sink in front of his face. She reached out, sliding her hand along his shoulder then down his arm until their fingers clasped. . . . and this time when she held his hand, he didn't feel like a kid going to the doctor.

He felt like a man with a partner.

He'd found his lifeline.

Fence held his breath, holding steady as long as he could. He managed to keep the panic at bay by testing his side to make sure the gills were still there, by counting, by praying, by looking into Ana's eyes.

When he could hold his breath no longer, he released it. And then he had to fight the urge to panic again. Even as he floated there, propelling his hands to keep him below the surface, he felt the water changing around him. Moving faster, harder, without its normal easy rhythm.

He was having a harder time remaining in one place, keeping from bumping into Ana.

Now his lungs were empty. Now he'd been holding his breath for a long time. Too long.

Now what?

He closed his eyes and forced himself to relax. Tried not to think about what he was doing. *Oh God.*

The burning in his lungs eased, and something cool rushed into them. Fence had another terrifying moment when he realized that cool rush was water, filling organs that were only supposed to be filled with oxygen.

But he felt no pain, no desperation, no panic.

He opened his eyes and found Ana there in front of him again, watching intently.

He breathed a few times, raggedly, carefully . . . and everything seemed to work.

There was no choking, no tightening in his chest, no panic messing with his mind—well, that wasn't true. It was still there, hovering, ready to slide into his consciousness if he had even a moment of uncertainty . . . but he managed to keep it at bay.

I'm breathing.

Under the fucking water.

When at last he smiled, Ana smiled back, and the next thing he knew, she had her arms and legs wrapped around him and was covering his mouth with hers.

The feel of her warm body sliding against his in the cool water was delicious and erotic, and he accepted the kiss from her without hesitation. Her tongue was hot in a world of cool darkness, and Fence realized just how pleasurable this could be. When her hands slid down along his torso, over his gills, he froze, heart pounding, and that panic threatened to turn his vision dark . . . but nothing happened.

She brushed over them, accidentally closing one for a second, and then slid her hands around behind to hold him close. *It's cool. I'm cool.* It was no more disconcerting than having one nostril plugged for a moment.

He smiled against her lips and kissed deeper, reveling in the sense of heat between their mouths while the rest of her felt cool.

Just as he was getting comfortable with the idea that he didn't have to even pull away from a kiss in order to breathe, Ana released him.

Her face had become serious and intense, and he looked in the direction she was pointing.

Even here beneath thirty or forty feet of water, the shimmering curtain glowed from a hundred yards away. It extended down into the depths so far that he couldn't see an end to it.

A rough surge of water reminded him that they were in a violent stew that was going to come to a boil if they didn't do something. And he also reminded himself not to think too hard about the fact that he was *underwater.* And going deeper.

And now that it seemed he no longer had air in his lungs but water instead, he wasn't floating back toward the surface. He was buoyant-neutral, hovering in place without having to work to keep himself down.

He drew in a deep breath—it felt so odd, with chill

rushing into him and not through his nose—and followed Ana as she took off down, down, *down*.

Down into the blackness.

Fence's heart hitched and his stomach hurt, but he went after her. He was breathing. The panic had subsided—mostly—but it was so dark. And silent.

At least in the depths of caves—which were just as dark, but not nearly as fucking wet—you could hear the drip or plop-plop of water . . . or the scrape of one's canvas-covered knees on rock, or the gentle *ding* of a metal helmet against the wall.

Here . . . it was a dead zone. There was nothing but silence.

The only thing Fence could see were Ana's crystals, and he was grateful for them as he followed their blue glow.

As he became more comfortable with this new and unbelievable development, he also became more aware of his surroundings. When they swam past a building, it took him a moment to realize that the structure extended several feet below and that he was near the roof.

It was surreal in a way the post-Change world had never appeared before. It was as if he were flying through a ruined city, several floors above streets and cars. But instead of having birds as his companions, there were schools of fish. Those orange ones from that Disney movie. He noticed a freaking *squid*, tentacles curling out of a dark space as if beckoning for some prey to enter his parlor. He passed destroyed houses, looking down into roofless rooms and past broken windows, and saw translucent shrimp as big as his hand with spiny blue eyes.

He had a start when he caught sight of a large shadow swimming above him, slowly and ponderously, and he nearly swallowed his heart when he realized it was a killer whale. They were big-ass creatures. He supposed that was why they called them "whales."

He recognized old, algae-encrusted, cracked signs as they swam over what had once been a large shopping center: one for Home Depot, with only the EPO still hanging on tenaciously. Another for REI—which gave him pause, because, wow . . . camping gear. Much of which would still be wrapped in indestructible plastic. It would be a treasure trove! If they had time, he'd stop and check it out.

But of course he didn't stop, and continued on over another store he vaguely recognized—it had the word "Bath" in the name—and then he saw half of a furry, bleached McDonald's M protruding from the wall of a building. And a jumble of cars from the long-ruined parking lot below.

Just as on land, the ruins were stamped with Mother Nature's decoration: fronds of green and brown stuttered in the increasingly rough water, algae and coral attached to brick walls and along the edges of doorways and car windows.

As they swam deeper and he could finally make out the uneven sea bottom, he saw other natural glows that illuminated the floor of the ocean. Starfish, seahorses, even a long, whiplike black snake slithered by. But still the curtain shimmered alongside them.

Once, he and Ana passed a small crystal, no bigger than his fist, set in the ground. It burned lavender and pink, and he realized it was a sort of fence post for the barrier—one of the crystals that connected its force field to the next. He wondered if by moving them out of the way, out of line, it would change the barrier.

He would have suggested it, but Ana led the way as

if she knew where she was going, swimming parallel to the electrical curtain. They were very close to the rise and fall of the ground, and Fence noticed that she seemed to be following a road. He recognized cars and other vehicles, streetlights, and even the yellow concrete bars that used to mark parking places, all littering the thoroughfare.

He also realized that the water was moving more violently, making it more difficult to swim in a straight line. The churning caused the sea grass and plants to shake and whip, and even a few doors that still hung onto their hinges shuddered and flapped.

At last Ana stopped and pointed. Fence swam up next to her and looked. The glow from her ever-present crystals illuminated the area enough for him to see a dip in the sea bottom. It was black as night, a great, deep vee.

But the barrier crossed over the top of it like a blanket covering a hole, and he knew she meant to swim through there to the other side.

There was no way to communicate in this deep, silent place other than wordlessly, and so he grabbed her arm and dragged her through the water, pulling her up against him.

Her arms went tightly around his neck, telling him that she was just as apprehensive. The fit of her body against his, the warmth plastered against him in this cold, blue world, was beyond comfort. It made him feel whole.

He bent his face to take her mouth, gentle at first, brushing her lips with his as they slid over a barrier of salt and cold damp. He kissed her, using his mouth and the caress of his hands to tell her what he'd just recently come to understand: there was no one else, there would be no one else, he had to be with her. And thank you.

The last bit of the kiss was all *thank you.*
Thank you for making me whole again.

When she pulled away, her face tinged by the blue of her crystal glow, her eyes were filled with emotion that matched what was billowing inside him, and he knew she understood.

And then she eased out of his arms, took his hand, and together they swam deep and far . . . into the black hole.

Ana was grateful for Fence's big strong hand in hers as she led them into the dark pit.

She couldn't believe she didn't have to do this alone. She had a partner, someone she trusted and relied upon. If her eyes weren't already wet from the sea, they'd be damp with happy, relieved tears.

The naked terror in his face when she first saw him underwater had been frightening, and that was when she truly understood the risk he'd taken, jumping in after her.

That was when she fully realized the kind of man he was. Not only how he felt about her, but that he would struggle to do what was right even when every fiber of his being tried to convince him otherwise.

Now, as the crystal barrier undulated up into the water just above her head, she paused, squeezed his hand, then darted down and forward.

When she felt them pass safely beneath the wavering curtain and the echoes of its energy, she drew in a deep breath of relief. The glow of her crystals fired higher at that moment, then returned to normal as she and Fence paused, now on the other side of the barrier.

Ana scanned the dark shapes that made up some

submerged cityscape, unsure where to go and how to find the stones.

Fence gave a little tug on her hand and gestured. She understood him to mean they should go back the way they came along the barrier, and she agreed.

Off they went, swimming quickly, no longer needing to hold hands.

As they zipped through the heavy, dark sea, Ana was aware of how readily Fence seemed to have adapted to his changed situation.

Her heart was filled to bursting despite the seriousness of their mission: How could she be any more fortunate to have found a man who could share in the secrets of the sea? And who wasn't an despicable Atlantean?

She'd been waiting for him without even realizing it.

She'd found her partner.

As they came along the barrier, Ana noticed a glow in the distance. It was an unnatural illumination, much too big to be fish or anemone, or even the Atlanteans themselves. Her heart began to race, and she gestured to Fence—but he'd already seen it, for he darted up next to her with strong, smooth strokes.

Using the cover of old buildings, they made their way down an old street toward the glow. As they came into closer proximity, the churning water became cloudier. There weren't any fishes or other sea creatures in this area, and even Ana began to feel apprehensive about the state of the water.

At last they could see the source of the glow. They'd swum higher in order to see over the tops of the waterscape—both natural and manmade—and Fence thrust his arm out to stop her from going any farther.

But water churned so strongly here that he had to grab onto something—the naked frame of a window—to keep from being dragged into the swirling mess, and he snagged her arm to keep her next to him.

Now they could see the whole picture.

Fence looked at her, and in the dim blue glow, she could see the stark intensity on his face. In his eyes shone concern and determination, and not a little of *holy shit*.

She felt the same way, for looking out at the glow that illuminated even this stirred-up water made her stomach hurt. There were seven Goleth stones, and she'd been right about their size. They were about four feet high and three feet in diameter and looked like moonstones, with a soft gray light burning inside each of them.

She and Fence hovered there, holding hands again, staring in horrified fascination. The stones were lined up in two rows of three, with the seventh one set apart from them at one end. As they watched, the water rushed down in the channel between the rows and gathered up, spewing forth beyond the single one at the head like a horizontal waterfall.

Dirt, debris, plants, everything was kicked up and churned in the vortex of water, turning the world murky. They were far enough away, and off to the side of the water funnel, so that the tug wasn't pulling them into the vortex . . . but Ana sensed it was only a matter of time and proximity.

It was as if they were watching a cyclone begin, a long, horizontal one gathering up its force and spewing it forth. It was like being in the midst of a thunderstorm, but completely silent and darker.

Fence was staring at it, and Ana wondered fleetingly if he was becoming panicked again. She wouldn't blame him; she'd been in many sea storms before, but this was different and it frightened her.

How the hell were they going to get close enough to move one of those stones out of alignment?

That was when she remembered, with a start, that they'd left Zoë's sling behind in their hurry to get below, and now she looked at Fence, gesturing: *What now?*

He didn't seem to understand, so she took his hand and spelled out *forgot sling* on it with her finger.

He shook his head, smiled that devastating white smile, and flexed his massive biceps.

Oh. Yes. Ana smiled back and felt a surge of heat flush through her, followed by relief.

She wasn't alone.

He gave her hand a squeeze and then raised his eyebrows as if to ask: *Ready?*

She nodded, and allowed him to guide her out of the shadow of the building that had shielded them. As soon as they did, the buffeting water caught them. It took her by surprise, but Fence held her, and she realized he was grasping a dark shape anchored in the ground.

His grasp was the only thing that kept them from being drawn into the vortex of water and debris. And so they progressed, bit by bit, Fence's strong hand tight around hers while his other held onto some stable object until he released it. Then they surged to the next as if being washed down a river, and he reached out and snagged something else to hold onto.

The speed and power of the churning water whipped Ana's hair and stung her skin and face with the sharp bite of debris. Her crystals glowed brightly as they fought to breathe in murky water, and she felt Fence look down at her more than once, as if to gauge her safety.

The Goleth stones were only yards away now, their

glow casting a grayish fog in the stirred-up water, but the force was so strong Fence nearly missed the last two anchors. He pulled Ana through a window into a dark building for a moment of relative calm. The water storm raged beyond, stirring the water in and through the old structure, but its walls acted as somewhat of a shield, slowing the vortex's force as it channeled through. Now they could catch their breath, and she looked up when he turned her to face him.

In the faint blue glow that cut through the dark room, she saw question in his eyes, and before he even lifted her hand to spell it out, she knew what he was going to say. She began to shake her head violently, then stopped.

There was no sense in making things more difficult. She knew the closer she got, the more powerful the water would churn. She knew she wasn't strong enough to fight it—heck, she'd nearly been swept away already. *Not as strong as you. Will follow but stay back to keep watch*, she spelled before he could grab her hand.

He moved closer, his body warm in the chill, and brushed her tangled hair away from where it floated into her face. In the glow of her crystals, she could see the warmth and emotion in his eyes.

Brave, and then *smart,* he lettered on her chest with his finger, then tapped her there as if to say "you." Tapped again, more firmly. Then he spelled, very slowly, as if for emphasis: *L-O-V-E . . . Y-O-U.*

A rush of heat and pleasure surprised her, and she nodded, blinking at warm tears that mingled with the cold saltwater. Smiled. *Will stand watch. Be safe*, she sketched on his broad chest, then showed him the way to make a sound that would echo through the water: slapping her palm onto the end of a fist. The noise wouldn't be as loud in the hurricane of water, but it was the only way they could communicate.

Just then a sudden gust from beyond sent a sudden forceful rush of water into the room. Old furnishings and pieces of rock and metal swirled around them with less force but no less malignancy than beyond those walls. Yet it was eerie because the violence was silent.

Fence shielded her from the embattled room's contents, and when the silent roar of water eased, pulled her with him into another space. Here, the walls were intact, and since it was an interior room, there were no windows.

Go to Q and Z if I don't make it, he spelled onto her shoulder.

She nodded. *Will wait in other room. To watch.*

What do with stone? he asked.

Ana spread her hands and looked up at him, shaking her head. *Bring back?*

He shrugged and nodded, then mimed breaking it with a hammer and raised his brows in question.

Ana nodded with a smile. That could work. Then they could bring just a piece back for Quent. He helped her into the next room, where she could see the glowing crystals from an old window. The waves swirled and surged, but she was able to find a sheltered beam near the window to hold onto.

Go now, she sketched on his right pectoral. *Moon growing.*

Fence held her by the shoulders, gave her a sweet kiss on the forehead, and then he was gone.

CHAPTER 19

Fence swam out of the abandoned building and into the raging, buffeting water. He knew if he didn't have the soft moonlike glow of the crystals he sought, he'd be lost.

But at least he knew he didn't have to worry about holding onto Ana. And if anything went wrong, she'd be able to get away and get back to warn the others they'd failed.

Now he just had to concentrate on getting to one of the crystals.

Easier said than done.

He clung to the frame of a glassless, open car door as the rush of water tried to suck him into its rhythm. Once he let go, he'd be gone.

His heart raced and the water pummeled him, reminding him how powerless he was against the force of the sea.

Underwater. Deep, dark, close.

And now, in the midst of a below-water windstorm. Nearly as frightening as the time he'd been caught in an avalanche in the Tetons.

But not as terrified as his spill during white water rafting, when he was caught on the tree branch and nearly drowned.

Fence closed his eyes, blanking those memories before they could pull him back into a world of blind panic, and drew in a long breath. He felt the twinges of grit prickling against the insides of his gills, then the cool rush of water flowing inside him.

How can this be? he thought for the hundredth time since discovering his own personal Change, once again touching his gills. How did this happen to *me*? It was a miracle.

How did I find Ana?

Another miracle.

After a moment he opened his eyes, back to the task at hand. If they had Zoë's sling, he could attempt to use it like a rappelling line and hook one of the stones. From what he understood, once a crystal was moved from its position, the madness would stop.

But until then getting close was an impossibility.

He considered the possibility that someone or something was watching and waiting, protecting the crystals—but rejected it after a bit of contemplation. The water was too messy and stirred up here for anyone to be lurking about. They'd get washed away, just as he was threatened to be.

And even if they were, what could they see? Little but foggy, murky water, and since he wasn't constantly surrounded by a glow of crystals, he could move unnoticed.

However, he was aware that there could be an Indiana Jones trap set: the moment one of the stones was moved, something could be set into motion.

But that was a chance he would have to take. It wasn't

like he was being greedy, trying to steal a gold icon. He was fucking trying to save a city. He figured he was due a damned break.

As he contemplated his next move, Fence watched the dirty, murky water rushing around him, funneling into the back of the rows of crystals and then blasting forcefully down the channel between them.

After a bit of observation, he squinted in the dimness and eased himself into a low crouch, his hands curling around the edge of a concrete slab protruding from the sea floor . . . and the violent pushing and pulling eased up.

Now he was tugged and buffeted instead of being tossed and flipped, and he knew that had to be the plan.

Stay near the ground.

If he could army crawl to the nearest crystal, he'd be below the strongest part of the energized current.

Careful to use stable handholds jutting from the uneven ground, Fence began to inch his way toward the crystals. It was like climbing a mountain, except he was on his belly on the sea floor. If the current managed to get under him, he'd be yanked free and tossed into the maelstrom.

Fighting to keep his legs and feet from their natural urge to float up was the most difficult part, and he felt the tension in his abs and glutes as he kept his body pushed down.

That was fine by him—he hadn't had a good workout in a while and was starting to feel a little flabby.

Of course, there were parts of him that had been in a near-constant state of *un*flabbiness ever since he'd gotten close to Ana.

Realizing that if he was making bad jokes to himself again, he must be getting comfortable in this new world, he smiled.

Inch by inch, he crawled, dragging himself, fighting the current, aware, too, of the edge of panic that never fully left him. It was always waiting there to rush in and overtake his consciousness.

At last he was close enough to one of the middle crystals to feel its energy emanating through the water. And when he lifted his hand to pull himself to the next handhold, he saw that his fingers were slippery with something thick and slick.

A brief glance told him he'd found the sparkling gray glop. That solved one mystery.

Now, faced by the crystal that rose above his supine figure, he concluded that to have any chance of moving it, he'd have to launch himself to the big stone and latch onto it, arms wide in a desperate embrace.

If he let go of his anchor and missed . . .

Not possible.

He wouldn't even consider it. He closed his eyes. Focusing, he visualized the movement of the water, of himself, thought about the trajectory, the position, the angle . . . and opened his eyes.

One . . . two . . .

. . . three.

He released his grip just as he used his feet to push off toward the crystal.

For a moment he was weightless in the churning water, and then its full force slammed into him. A corner of red-hot hysteria eased into his mind, but he would not allow it, and pushed it away as the moonstone crystal spun closer.

His foot hit something and he pushed hard, toward the stone, and a sudden blast of waves slammed him into the rock.

But Fence was ready; his arms were wide and he grasped the stone, trying to find purchase for his scrabbling feet as his fingers struggled to meet on the opposite side of the crystal. The strength of the gale was beyond belief, trying to suck him in, and he felt his arms slipping as the pull nagged and beat at him. But at last his fingers met and clasped, and he held the rough crystal in a passionate embrace while using his feet to leverage it out of place.

His arms around the stone, he felt the vibration of energy buzzing through him, realized that his bare skin was being burned, and at the same time that the stone was slimy with a thin, sticky gray overcoat. He tasted heat and something dark and gritty. As he drew in a steadying breath, trying to center himself in the midst of this silent, violent storm, heat instead of cool rushed into his lungs, filling them.

It took him an instant to realize his gills were trapped against the crystal as he desperately clutched the stone in his arms. The energy was scorching him, sealing them closed, cutting off his breath . . . and then he lost his tenuous grip on sanity.

Everything turned black and swirling red, and the sea came crushing down on him. Stifling, terrifying, heavy, dark . . . He couldn't breathe, he couldn't think— his feet moved wildly, his arms stiff and desperate as he held onto the stone: his only anchor.

His mind went blank and his face banged and then scraped against the crystal and he gasped for a desperate breath, dragged in heat that was *wrong*, blindly kicking and fighting . . .

I'm in the water—I can't breathe—I can't breathe.

He struggled for a minute, battling the fear, knowing that somewhere he had sanity. Somewhere in his head he found his center again, and he took in another breath—a heavier, more difficult one, but a breath nevertheless. *Easy.* The stillness he'd grasped in his mind wavered, threatened to dissolve.

Focus. He breathed, focused, tried to grasp sanity again, but it eluded him, and he continued to tumble into mad panic.

Then suddenly there were hands on him, gentle, as if pulling him back to reality. He was able to open his eyes, and there was Ana, her face slack with concern, her hands pulling at his death grip.

And that was when he realized he'd moved the stone, and everything around him had changed.

The sea was calm, the moonbeam glow gone, and he was covered with sparkling gray glop.

Oh, and he was still breathing.

Ana saw the war of emotions on Fence's face: shock, surprise, and finally annoyance. The latter, she assumed, was due to the fact that she was there with him, and not back in the building where he'd left her.

She had watched his large, shadowy figure inch along the sea floor toward the crystals, and then after what seemed forever, launch itself at one of the stones. Then the flow of water had eased, but Fence didn't move. She'd darted out after him, watching sharply for any sign of threat.

But the sea was calm and almost back to her normal self, and she was with Fence now, and they had the stone. His chest was moving roughly, as if he'd just completed some great effort—which, of course, he had.

Something heroic.

She smiled up at him and patted him on the arm, then gestured to the crystal. He'd moved it out of alignment, scraping and tugging it along the bottom of sea so it was just beyond the others. Instead of looking like a soft glowing pearl, it seemed dead and devoid of energy, and appeared just like any other boulder. The other crystals were dead too.

The crisis was over.

But their work wasn't done. The rock could just as easily be put back, and then the threat would start all over again.

At that thought, Ana glanced around again, suddenly nervous. Surely the Atlanteans wouldn't have left this place completely unguarded. Although they couldn't get close during the sea storm, they likely had some sort of monitor—a guard or watch, even if it were just observing the energy of the sea. By now the surface would have settled back into its normal rhythm.

She grabbed Fence's arm and forced him to look at her. *Hurry* she spelled onto his hand.

He nodded, his expression matching hers. Then he gestured to his side, lifting his arm to reveal his gills.

Ana looked and saw for the first time that his chest, inner arms, and the sides of his torso were covered in a thin, sparkling gray sheen—similar to the gray stuff they'd found on the beach. It had crusted over one gill, the edge of the slender lip of skin darker than the rest of him, and it stuck together in places, as if it had been seared shut and was trying to work itself loose. The other side was hampered in the same way, and now she understood why he seemed to be struggling to breathe.

Ana gently helped to spread the skin so the gill worked fully again, and inside the flaps of skin on both sides she saw a faint, healthy pink color.

Better?

He smiled, relief in his eyes, and nodded. Then he looked down at the stone and once again mimed taking a hammer and smashing it.

She nodded, and through gestures and spelling agreed to move the crystal farther away from its original position before going to look for something that might be heavy enough to break it. If it was out of place and hidden, no one would find it.

But as Ana moved closer to the Goleth stone, closer than she'd been, it began to glow ever so faintly from deep in its core. She felt her own crystals reacting as well, growing warmer and brighter, and quickly pushed herself away in a surge of water. The large stone stopped glowing, turning dead and gray again.

Better stay back, Fence spelled quickly.

Nodding, suddenly nervous again, Ana watched as he used a long metal pole he found on the sea floor to leverage under the crystal and shift it out of place. Little by little he rolled it along until it careened down a small incline and crashed against an old car in a cloud of sea dust. He moved a large piece of metal in front of the stone to hide it—probably not necessary, since now it looked like every other gray-blue boulder, but it was best to take all precautions until they could come back and destroy it.

Then Fence grinned at her and held out his hand. She let his large fingers close over hers, but instead of leading her off, he pulled her up against him.

His sleek, warm body pressed against hers, and Ana was struck by the difference in sliding against a land-person and an Atlantean in the water. Darian had always felt neutral to the touch—the same temperature as the water. But Fence's heat bled into her, from his muscular arms to his belly and chest, to his mouth and that strong, hot tongue.

The next thing she knew, his legs were fluttering against hers and they were rising, sifting slowly up through yard after yard of ocean. The buildings and seascape fell away, the water lightened, and then they abruptly emerged from the water into evening light. The sun had half set in a glorious array of red and gold. The full moon was showing strong and fat in a darkening sky, its magnified pull no longer a threat to them.

"Wow," she said, smoothing her hand over his face to wipe a bit of gray glop away. It sparkled all over the front of him like tiny stars in a thin layer of glue, and now it clung to her as well. "And I'm not talking about the sunset," she added.

"The hero always gets to kiss the beautiful woman after he saves the world," Fence told her with a cheeky grin, moving his legs lazily to keep their heads out of the water now that they were both breathing air. "I guess I'd better step up." And he proceeded to do so once more.

Suddenly, beyond the shimmering barrier behind him, she saw a streak of light go into the sky and then explode into a small starlike puff. "What was that?" she said, grabbing his arm. They were still on the far side of the barrier, the side the Atlanteans considered theirs, but the shot had been on the Envy side.

At the whistling sound of the streak, Fence had spun in the water, but now she felt his muscles relax. "That's Quent and Zoë," he said. "They can see that the water has calmed and are sending a signal back to Envy that all is well, that we've stopped the tidal wave."

"Is that what you call a flare gun?"

"That's one definition for it." He grinned and eased her closer. With his other hand, he pulled a lock of hair away from where it clung to her cheek and then paddled gently to keep them afloat. "There are flare guns . . . and then there are guns with *flare*," he said, linking his arm around her, just above the curve of her butt, and pulling her up against him. "Like the one I have right . . . here."

Ana laughed as she felt the very hot and hard *something* filling the space between them, and a little shiver of desire caught her by surprise.

Her breasts were pressed against his bare chest, only the thin fabric of her bra separating them. Their legs bumped and slid sinuously beneath the surface. She smiled and shifted against him. "I'm guessing you haven't experimented in the water," she said with a naughty grin. "At least for a very long time."

"It has been a long while," he replied, allowing them to sink a bit lower into the ocean. "But I think," he said, lifting his mouth out just enough to speak, "it's time I changed that."

As his warm body plastered against her torso, his chest moved and filled against hers . . . and they began to descend slowly back into the depths.

The boat rocked on gentle waves as Quent put the flare gun down. "Right, then. Now they know the danger has passed," he said. He sounded remote and almost cool—even for him, with his formal, precise tones. "Vaughn can call off the evacuation. Sage will be relieved."

Silent, Zoë watched him, feeling a heavy stone in her belly that had nothing to do with the scrap of life growing within.

Well, maybe the hell it did. Dammit. She groped for something to say, and for once came up empty.

That heavy stone in her belly had been expanding, erecting a solid wall between her and Quent for some time now.

In the distance several miles behind them, a shoreline rose against the evening sky with dark and jagged shapes. Behind it were the faint lights of Envy, creating a soft orange glow in the lowering light. The boat, which Quent had pulled halfway onto land when the sea got frighteningly rough, rocked rhythmically, and the only sound was the soft lick of waves against it.

"So now that that's done with," he said, looking out at something in the darkness, "perhaps you and I ought to attend to the other matter while we wait for them to come back."

"What other matter?" she asked, suddenly feeling light-headed. That stone in her belly felt ass-crap heavy now, sickeningly heavy. And all at once she felt her lips moving and words coming out before she realized it. "I've got something to tell—"

"Too bloody late, Zoë," Quent said, talking over her from between clenched teeth. "Did you really think that I didn't know?"

The fact that he was still staring out into the dark night sent a chill wave over Zoë. Her heart began to beat harder, her palms growing damp. This was way fucking worse than the first time she'd come face-to-face with a zombie.

"That I couldn't bloody *tell*?" he continued, still talking to . . . the damn ocean or some night bug or something. Not to her. He wasn't even looking at her. "That I hadn't noticed the changes in your body? Did you think I was stupid?"

Now the nausea that she'd never experienced early in the pregnancy came rushing into her. Zoë's insides churned like the ocean had done, and for a moment she had to fight to keep from horking right there. *Fuck.*

"Am I the only one you didn't tell?" Quent continued in that flat, emotionless voice. "Zoë." On that, his voice cracked softly and he at last turned to look at her.

"Quent," she said, swallowing hard, unable to dredge up even a hint of her normal bravado. But this wasn't the time for bravado, was it? "I . . . *wanted* to tell you—"

"No, luv, I don't think you did. In fact, I think you were bloody, buggering *scared* to tell me. So instead, you told everyone else—"

"No! I didn't fucking tell everyone else. Only Elliott, because he's a doctor, and Lou, because he was leaving—but it just slipped out with him . . . and . . . and I don't know how everyone else found out." To her shock and mortification, another bout of tears swelled in her eyes. Goddammit, she'd been crying more than a fucking fountain lately.

"Presumably, you've been taking care of yourself, at least in some ways, if you've talked to Elliott," Quent said. He still sounded cold. "At least I can be grateful for that."

Zoë couldn't handle it anymore. Her fingers were shaking and her insides were a maelstrom of emotion. "Quent, I'm sorry. I know I should have told you, I knew it all along, but I . . . I was afraid . . . I knew you wouldn't let me . . ."

For a moment the only sound above the lashing of

waves was Quent's breathing. It sounded rough and agitated. Then he spoke, and his words were soft . . . emotionless and dead. "You were afraid *I* would make you be more careful. That *I* would restrict your hunting expeditions. *Make* you stay in, and safe. So that nothing would happen to the baby. Or to its mother. Apparently," he said, his voice getting louder and more clipped, "*you* aren't concerned about the safety and health of the child. You might not even *care* if something—"

"*No!*" Zoë blazed, horror-stricken at the thought. "No! That's not true, Quent, it's not true! I—I admit, I was scared when I first realized it . . . having a baby is the most crazy-ass thing that could happen—in a good way—but I was scared. And I wasn't sure that I could . . . do it. Be . . ." She swallowed hard and blinked back tears. Her hands were still shaking, her heart pounding as misery and guilt weighed her down.

Had she done it? Had she ruined everything?

Did he really think that she'd want something to happen?

"Quent . . . I . . ."

"I've known for two months, Zoë. Have I done anything to make you feel restricted or smothered or controlled? Have I done anything to keep you from doing what you *wanted*? No. I haven't. I've looked the other way, kept an eye on you, gritted my teeth, bloody *waited* for you to *tell* me . . . but you didn't. But . . . you're getting further along now, and it's even more important that you . . . take care. Because I don't want anything to happen to my baby. Our baby."

Zoë looked over through a film of tears. He was looking in her direction, but not at her. Down, off to the side, out into the darkness where a tree hovered over them. His chest rose and fell in agitation, his hands tightly fisted in his lap.

She knew, suddenly, that if she didn't swallow her pride, her fear, and make a definitive move, they might never get beyond this. He might never forgive her.

"Quent," she said, launching herself toward him without a hint of the reserve she still often harbored. As the boat rocked with her sudden movement, Zoë knelt on the floor, taking his hands in hers, looking up at him, trying to get him to look at her. "I've been fighting the damned guilt for weeks. I know I should have told you, but I was beyond afraid. And scared. Really scared. I don't know if I can be a good mother—look at how I fucked this all up. But I know that you're going to be an amazing parent. Good enough for both of us."

His fingers loosened slightly, and she was able to curl hers more tightly around them. "Will you forgive me?" she asked . . . and couldn't ever remember saying those words to him, or to anyone else.

"I love you, Zoë," he said at last. "I'm hurt, but that doesn't mean I don't love you. I still love you more than anyone I've ever known . . . and I couldn't be happier that we're going to have a baby. But understand this: I don't want anything to happen to either of you. And you're going to have to take that into account from now on . . . that you're not just living for yourself anymore."

"I know. I *have* been careful," she said, and tried to tone down the hint of annoyance in her voice. She had been. "I haven't gone out zombie hunting for weeks."

"I've noticed," he said. "Which is why I haven't said anything before now."

"So you knew all along," she said, feeling a flutter of relief begin to unfurl.

"Right," he said. "I was just waiting for you to tell me."

"Quent," she said, lifting his hands wrapped in hers, so she could kiss them. "You're going to be a father."

"Thank you." In the dim light, she saw his lips move in a faint smile. It wasn't all that she wanted, but it was enough. For now.

Fence kept Ana close to him as they sank back down beneath the depths, twined together, but in the back of his mind was the knowledge that no matter how delicious the feel of her body against his, they had business to attend to first.

And he didn't want any distractions when he stripped her long, golden body and buried his face between her legs in the bottom of the ocean.

The literal version of muff-diving.

He snickered to himself, and Ana noticed, pulling her face away with a questioning look. There was no way to explain now, of course—although he would later, because he had a feeling she'd appreciate the sentiment—so he just slid his fingers down the front of her jean shorts and found a hot, slick patch of Ana, right in the midst of this cold, dark sea.

She shivered against him, and her eyes sank closed as he held her around the waist with one hand and eased his two fingers in and around, over and over, watching in aroused fascination as her crystals surged brighter and softer, brighter and softer, with each of her breaths. And when she came, a little jolt and then the great throbbing shudders, the crystals blazed bright as candles.

Hot damn, there was nothing like getting his freak

on in sleek, sexy water with a crazy hot woman. It was a damn shame he'd wasted so much of his life *not* doing this.

Of course . . . there was no one he could be doing this with besides Ana.

No one he *wanted* to be doing this with.

Then Fence grinned. He wondered if she'd get it if he asked, *What's long and hard and filled with seamen?*

He snorted a chuckle in the water, which sent a strange array of bubbles shooting in all directions, causing her to look at him again with that raised eyebrow expression.

He shrugged and managed to look innocent, but when she looked up at him in that bluish glow and he saw the understanding affection in her eyes, he got all shivery and warm. And it didn't have anything to do with the submarine raging between them.

Careful of the mast there, sugar.

Heh.

When their feet brushed the top of a Dumpster wedged into the ground, Fence withdrew his hand from her shorts. He noticed that some of the gray glop that had clung to his body from the Goleth stone had rubbed off on her, and she sparkled in several places on her arms, legs, and especially breasts.

It made her look like a sea goddess now, silvery-glittery in the cool hues of the ocean, her hair even cast with bluish-gray as it wafted around her like a great fan. What a lucky man he was: he had a sun goddess *and* a mermaid.

But . . . time to get back to business. They needed to find something to destroy that crystal with, and he had an idea where to look.

Leading the way, he swam back along the shimmery

barrier to the safe passage they'd used. He didn't deny that he felt a little more relaxed now that they were on the "safe" or Envy side of it, and considered the fact that they might even have time for a bit more slap and tickle.

Or, in this case, motion in the ocean.

Heh. He really did crack himself up.

It didn't take long to find their way back to the old shopping center he remembered swimming over, and Fence headed right for REI.

As were many things he'd done since emerging from the Ballbusting Bitch, this was an utterly surreal experience. But swimming down into the old store from a hole in its caved-roof, and finding themselves inside the place, had to rank up there as one of the most bizarre things he'd done.

It brought a whole new meaning to the concept of diving for treasure, and he found it amazing how some of the shelves still held their wares even after half a century.

Of course, many of the aisles were no longer distinct, and inventory was scattered on the ground, rusted away, or had otherwise been destroyed by decades of saltwater and sea creatures . . . but as he'd had cause to note many times before, even Mother Nature had to admit defeat in the face of man's evil concoction: plastic.

The glow of Ana's crystals was barely enough light for them to find their way through the collapsed store, and that also gave him an idea.

He could sense her curiosity and interest as they swam and he led the way up and down as many aisles as he could. He hoped the section he needed wasn't under the caved-in roof.

But then there they were: rows of flashlights, encased in clamshell plastic. Even the paper inserts were intact, which wasn't surprising, given how impossible the things were to open.

He pulled Ana along, needing her light to see what he was looking for . . . then suddenly

Ah. Yes!

He plucked up the package containing not only a waterproof flashlight, but one that used manually generated power—through a hand crank.

Ana watched in fascination as he struggled to get the package open, then offered him her knife. Moments later he had the light in his hand and was cranking the handle rapidly.

When he turned it on and a bright glow filled the area, Ana's eyes went wide with surprise and delight. He grinned and showed her how to work the crank, how to turn it on and off . . . and then grabbed a second one.

Moments later they were cruising along with two bright lights, scanning through the remains of the store for something heavy like a sledgehammer. Fish scattered in the wake of the unusual illumination, and glowing eyes watched them from dark aisles. The contents of the store seemed even more eerie in full light: greenish and worn, every detail of the texture of sea growth more evident.

He paused at the section with the self-inflating air mattresses, pleasantly distracted by the thought of using one for a round of slip-the-sub . . . but practicality prevailed and he swam reluctantly past, privately promising himself that they'd return as soon as possible.

When they'd surveyed as much of the store as they could and didn't find what he was looking for, Fence had to admit defeat and decided that they could make a stop at Home Depot.

Another very odd thought.

They swam out of REI and he started toward the remnants of Home Depot . . . but then Ana stopped up short and grabbed for him. Fence saw it too: a faint bluish glow just beyond the jut of some block of sea stone.

He flipped off his light and reached for Ana's as well, his instincts going sharp.

Their lights went dim and the world returned to a darker one, tinged with Ana's pale blue glow, as they hovered for a minute. Waiting.

When the figure came into view, Ana froze and reached for Fence's arm. Her fingers curled tightly over him as a man approached.

Her heart was pounding, for she recognized him.

Darian.

It was impossible to hide, for he'd already spotted them—either due to the flashlights or the natural illumination from Ana's crystals, and he was swimming toward them.

Fence tried to hold her back, but Ana shook her head and quickly spelled *Darian, contact,* on his palm. She felt his hesitance and the tension riding up along his arm, but there was no other opportunity for communication.

Found the stones, Ana signed to Darian as he approached.

Expected you would. But not so quickly. Surprised me.

She frowned, watching him closely. His expression was difficult to read, and she saw his eyes shift to Fence, then back to her . . . and then behind them.

She whipped around to look, but saw nothing in the darkness.

Yet something in Darian's demeanor tripped concern deep inside her, and she eased her knife from its sheath, holding it out of sight. Fence must have felt her movement and comprehended, for he eased a bit closer, as if to help hide the blade. She could feel his tension and realized he would have no idea what they were talking about through their sign language.

Think that I would really go back to Atlantis? she signed to Darian.

Yes. Hoped you would. Better than this.

Again she didn't understand what he was getting at, but he did nothing . . . just hovered there, looking at her.

Needed to lure you away, he told her. *Looked for you for years.*

Something lodged in the pit of her stomach, and that was when she realized that he'd never been honest with her. Even when he professed to love her, he'd never been honest.

Fence seemed to recognize the change in her, and drifted even closer. She could feel his muscles gathering up, ready, and she shot him a warning glance she hoped he could interpret in the faulty light.

I stopped the tidal wave, she told Darian.

He didn't look pleased. *Knew you would try. You were not supposed to get here in time. Too quick. Should not have waited for you when you said you would meet me.*

And that was when the other piece fell into place. A violent shiver caught her by surprise. He'd told her about the Goleths in order to trick her into trying to stop them.

In order to trick her into coming far enough away from safety—from land—so he could . . . what?

Convince her to go back to Atlantis?

Until that moment, she still believed he didn't truly mean her any harm. That he truly wanted her help to save their race. But now she saw the truth in his eyes.

This whole thing, she gestured in the direction of the Goleths, *to get me here?*

He shrugged, and she saw his gaze flicker to the right. Fence spun to look, the surge of water thrusting her away. Still holding her knife, she looked in the other direction.

Nothing. She turned back to Darian as Fence continued to hover, surveying the area around them. He might not exactly comprehend the conversation, but he obviously understood the basics.

The Atlanteans would have destroyed a whole city just to get me back? Ana signed with hands that had suddenly turned cold and stiff.

Do anything to survive.

A chill zipped down her spine, and she and Fence looked up at the same time.

Something dark whipped through the water, a big, heavy net weighted with stones.

It settled over her, but Fence dodged quick enough so it missed him. His face was a dark, furious mask as he turned to face the two large men who'd emerged from behind a dark wedge of cracked wall. Their crystals glowed so dimly, Ana realized they'd somehow hidden them beneath cloth or wrappings as they waited for their chance to attack.

All through these observations, she was slashing violently at the net with her knife, thankful she'd been prepared.

Yet she couldn't fully extricate herself before Darian was there, wrapping the net more tightly around her, twisting it around so that even with her knife she couldn't cut through it fast enough.

The net bound her so closely she couldn't raise the knife or bring it down, and with a sharp movement Darian grabbed her wrist and twisted.

She cried out, her screams eerily silent in the depths, and dropped the weapon as he wrapped the last trailing piece of net around her. Then tucking her under his arm like a rolled up carpet, he launched himself off into the dark water, taking her away from Fence.

CHAPTER 20

They had Ana.

Fence saw the man—Darian—swim off with the bundle that was Ana.

He darted after them, his insides going cold and sharp, but he found his way blocked by the two large figures who'd dropped the net. Crystals glowed brightly at their midsections, and for the first time he saw that one of them held a long, slender black thing studded with three tiny lights, curling in the water.

Instead of trying to dodge them, Fence propelled himself straight on, smashing into them with every bit of force he had, noting in the back of his mind that obviously neither had played football.

As the one with the whip spun away, the other flailed back in a ribbon of bubbles, then darted around and grabbed Fence's leg. He ducked, somersaulting down and back toward his assailant as he gave a powerful, snapping kick. Water, he found, made him a lot more acrobatic than on land.

He twisted, banked right then left, and shot away just as that slender black thing snaked through the water. Fence dodged its tiny glowing crystals but felt the snap of something like a shock as it flashed past him. He crashed into something hard and metallic as he dodged, and felt rust and grit crumbling against his skin. The whip came again, and, infuriated, Fence darted straight toward the other assailant again. As he connected with his target, something burned over his shoulder—hot and sharp in the cold sea. He felt the shock zap through his body as he slammed his opponent into the corner of an old building.

Fence's muscles shivered, now slow and clumsy from the shock, but he was fast enough to spin around and use the man as a shield while the whip snaked silently through the sea again. Blood clouded the water, dissipating in a dark cloud as Fence gripped the man's arm to swing him around one more time. But his muscles were slower and less graceful, and they faltered, leaving him floundering awkwardly against a wall.

Something surged up toward him. He ducked, trying to turn, but was propelled forward with great force—shoved violently into the side of a big old truck by a pair of feet. The metal door handle smashed into his temple in a flurry of bubbles and more dark blood.

Pain blasted through his head, and his world darkened and shifted as he tried to recover, gasping for breath, disoriented. But the assault came from the other side now as both of his attackers slammed against him once more.

He tried to pivot, but something held him there, four hands, pounding into him, smashing his head into the rusted edge of the vehicle, feet kicking and pummeling, the sharp sting down his back, over and over. Trapped against the metal, unable to turn, he tried to kick up behind him, tried to twist around, but they were too strong and had the advantage as his head spun, nausea gathering in the back of his throat, his muscles shocked and weakened.

Then all at once Fence realized he was *at the bottom of the ocean.*

Heavy. Dark. Cold.

He fought back, tried to keep the thoughts at bay, but his murky mind was twisted and the panic edged closer.

No. Stop.

Something stung him again, right over the top of his right gill, and he dodged, fighting hysteria.

Not there, not there, not there . . .

The darkness threatened to pull him in, and he became slower and sluggish as madness teased at the corner of his mind, pain driving him into paralysis.

When strong arms came around him from behind, covering his gills and tightening around his torso, Fence knew this was it.

Someone else smashed his forehead into something hard and the darkness wavered, strong and beckoning as pain reverberated through him again.

His gills were closed, the arms of his assailant still tight, choking and smothering him, and Fence felt his lungs tighten, restricting, trying to move. Trying to breathe.

At the bottom of the ocean. Underwater. Underwater.

Panic rose, red and black flashed in his vision, battling him as he fought blindly, his movements desperate and futile.

Not here, not here, can't breathe, can't breathe . . . help . . . help me.

Then all at once he remembered: Ana.

They had Ana.

They were taking Ana.

He was going to save her.

The thought settled over him, almost peacefully . . . and then everything else was gone. Cold fury replaced the hot, red hysteria. The pain faded into determination. His brain began to function, and he realized he was still taking some air in through his stifled gills.

He made himself go limp, sagging against the truck even as the arms tightened around his torso. Tighter. *Tighter.*

He fought to remain still and soft, to keep his breathing shallow and unnoticeable . . . and then as the vise tightened further, he had to hold his breath. Wait. Wait. *Ana. I'm coming. I'll be there.*

The moment his attacker loosened his grip, Fence swung into action. He spun around, taking his assailant by surprise, and slammed him into the truck door once, twice, then heaved his limp body up and through the jagged-glassed window.

Blood streamed into the water like dark smoke, and he turned just in time to see the black cord snapping toward him once more. Fence dodged, still clumsy, but managed to avoid all but the very tip of the whip . . . and then he launched himself toward his assailant. This time he butted the man in the gut with his head, and, furious and coldly desperate, didn't ease up before pummeling him with his fists in a swirl of bubbles.

One good smash to the gut and he was able to snatch the whip from the man's hand, and as he looked up, Fence realized all at once that they were close . . . very close . . . to the shimmery barrier.

He didn't hesitate, but threw the whip to the side. As his attacker dodged for it, Fence grabbed him and flung him at the barrier.

On land the man would have flown through the air in a great, smooth arc . . . but here in the water, he sort of tumbled and floundered . . . and tried to stop himself by kicking out, swiping his hands through the water.

But he was too late. It took only the tip of his foot to break through the wavering curtain, and as Fence watched, the man jolted, convulsed once, and then dropped limply to the sea floor.

Motherfucker.

If he'd had any thoughts about trying to chance his way through that barrier, they were now gone.

Just as quickly as that reality sunk in, his focus went back to Ana, and the direction they'd taken her. On the other side of the barrier.

Fence darted off back toward the small dark valley he and Ana had slipped through before. They had to be bringing her back to Atlantis, and he'd find a way to catch up to them. The only illumination now that the crystalled men were gone was a faint glow from the shimmering wall. As he shot along, staying close to the ground so he wouldn't miss the passage, he noticed little smudges of the sparkling gray glop in the dim light, as if someone had reached out and touched objects at eye level as they went along.

Ana. She'd left a trail for him. *Smart.* A little bit of his tension eased.

But when Fence found the little dip in the ground, it was filled with the shimmering curtain.

He stopped short, staring in disbelief at the tiny gray glop at its edge.

It was closed. They'd blocked him. He couldn't get through.

Ana slid her fingers over her belly again, and when she pulled them away, they were slick with the gray glop. She reached out and unobtrusively touched the side of an algae-covered car as Darian pulled her along.

After the netting had caught on more than one object, and made her a heavy burden, he'd extricated her from it once they were past the wavering barrier. He'd also done something to change the force field to block the passageway. Ana noted that he didn't seem to have any concern for his companions, the ones Fence was battling—leaving them trapped on the Envy side as well.

Yet another indication of Darian's true loyalties.

Now, he towed her through the water as she did everything in her power to slow them down: dragging her feet, widening her legs and body, making her shape anything but hydrodynamic.

All at once Darian came up short, stopping in the middle of an open space. The remnants of twenty-first century civilization echoed around them in tilted, dark, and ruined eruptions. Still gripping her arm with bruising fingers, he scanned the area and she felt his tension.

Let me go. It was hard to sign with one hand, but she managed. And then she swiped her fingers on her abdomen and left another mark as she prayed, *Please let Fence be safe. Please let him catch up before we get too far.*

Because she knew that he'd follow them if he could get away from the two Atlantean guards Darian had left behind. He'd find a way to get through that barrier.

Her captor ignored her plea; he seemed to be looking for something. As they waited, a long, sleek grouper slid by. Then came a bottom-feeder, its tail barely disturbing the water.

Finally, she saw the faint bluish-green glow as two figures emerged from the shadows. They eased toward her, eagerness in the very movements of their fluttering fingers and sliding legs.

As they came closer, their accompanying glow revealed their bodies and faces. A man and a woman, both with long dark hair streaming in the water behind them.

Ana's heart stuttered and then pounded in a faster rhythm. What were the Crown and Shield of the Guild doing here? Venturing far from the safety of their protected city?

Anastancie, spelled one of them in Atlantean, then continued in sign. *Daughter of our world. It has been very long.*

What do you want? she signed back. Darian had released her, obviously believing she had no chance of escape with the three of them present.

We are in need of your assistance, answered the Crown. She didn't even know his name; he'd always been referred to as the high master lord, or Crown. Her maternal grandfather had been—and as far as she knew, still was—his closest confidant and advisor. *I do hope you will help us, for without you we cease to exist.*

I help you? You tried to destroy Envy, she replied with sharp motions.

Darian shifted beside her and his stance was one of obeisance. *The plan worked, my lord. The threat to the world she now favors drew her out of hiding.*

The Shield fixed him with her eyes, and Ana saw a flare in the glow of her crystals. *But it worked not. She stopped the threat.*

Darian stilled next to Ana. His hands flailed as he tried to respond, making nonsensical gestures.

Nevertheless, you failed in your task, said the Shield sternly. A dull click emphasized her displeasure.

But she is here. I have brought her to you.

And for that reason alone you are still, at this moment, living. But Envy is still intact. And it appears it shall remain so. Therefore, you shall not be compensated as promised.

Darian looked alarmed and seemed desperate to make his case. *I took care of Kaddick. He was talking too much to the Elites, telling them many secrets. He's dead now.*

Ana tried to follow their conversation even as she searched for a route of escape. The water's natural pull allowed her to drift slightly away.

Do not fret, my dear, the Crown was signing to his companion. *We have Anastancie now, and that is what we really need. This slug is worth no bother.*

Ana took the chance, when their attention was focused on each other, to dart away. But she made it only a few strokes before strong hands grabbed her, pulling her back by the hair. She reached blindly for her knife, then remembered it was long gone. Then she struggled, kicking and twisting, grabbing for sea rocks or pieces of man-made debris, and tried to beat him off . . .

Gasping for breath, her crystals glowing brightly with the effort, Ana looked up into the cold dark eyes of the Crown. He wound her hair around his wrist, pulling so tightly hot tears filled her eyes.

I think not, Anastancie, signed the Shield, appearing in front of her. *Return to that world? Never.*

And then Ana saw the blade in the Shield's hand. It was already covered with blood, blood from someone else, dissipating into the sea.

Chapter 21

Wyatt still couldn't believe that Remington Truth had left her dog behind when she took off.

What in the hell had possessed her to do such a damned foolish thing? And why would she take a risk, on her own, out beyond the safe walls of the estate?

He looked over at Dantès, who seemed to be just as confused as he was. The dog whined and licked his hand briefly, as if to say, "Where is she?"

It had to do with that damn orange crystal, he was sure of it. But to leave Dantès behind? He couldn't believe she'd ever do that.

Even when he found the note on her bed: *Take care of Dantès for me. I don't want anything to happen to him.*

Well what about her? Didn't she care about her own safety?

What the hell was she up to?

If she hadn't left a note, Wyatt would have wondered if she'd somehow been kidnapped or taken away against her will when she went outside the walls during the day. But obviously she'd planned for and executed her own disappearance.

And that was why, against all logic, the morning after realizing she'd disappeared, he went beyond the safe walls himself. He led a horse by the reins as Dantès roamed ahead, sniffed and scanned the area in great big sweeping S shapes, then bounded back to his current master as if to touch base.

So far the German shepherd mix hadn't picked up his mistress's scent, which added to the concern in his intelligent, amber eyes, but his determination was evident.

Three hours later searching the perimeter of the walls, and more than a mile in circumference, Dantès finally found her trail.

But no sooner had he sounded the alarm than he took off and was gone. For good, leaving Wyatt standing there with a wry smile on his face. He'd have to follow as well as he could, but it would take a lot longer on only two legs.

At least Remy wouldn't be alone.

And he hoped to hell she showed a bit more appreciation if he found her and brought her back to safety than she did the last few times he'd saved her butt.

I didn't mean to sound ungracious.

Hell, she'd been the epitome of ungracious since he'd first laid eyes on her. Ungracious and haughty. Like a damned princess.

The stab of grief caught Wyatt by surprise, and he rubbed his stinging eyes with a brisk thumb and forefinger. His precocious little Abby had been fond of princess words, and in fact that was how the phrase was coined.

Oh *God*, he missed her.

Wyatt rubbed his eyes harder, as if to blot out the memory even as he tried to pull up an image of her in his mind. His cell phone, which had a variety of pictures on it and had been his most prized possession since coming out of the cave, was back in Envy. He kept it safely in his room so he could protect it and keep it charged as needed.

He couldn't breathe for a moment, remembering Abby's sparkling eyes and curly dark hair. He grieved for her and for David, his towheaded mischief-maker who never had more than a brief moment of bad temper.

He'd lost them . . . lost all of them—and a year after coming out of that damned cave, could still hardly comprehend that they were gone.

He hadn't been there for them. To protect them and save *them* as he'd done for so many others.

No matter what, he should have been there. He should have been there to save his family.

And that was why, whether she liked it or not, Remington Truth was going to have to deal with him.

Because he knew she was important, and he was going to find her and protect her if it was the last thing he did.

Fence swam up and down along the shimmering barrier, desperation making his strokes sharp and jerky. *Ana.*

He had to find a way to get through that curtain. There had to be a way.

But he darted back and forth, like a trapped fish himself, with no sign of another safe passage, and realized he didn't have any more time to waste.

There had to be another way.

Could he move one of the anchor crystals? He'd seen one earlier, when he was with Ana.

Unable to see much in the dim light, even with the shimmery curtain, Fence darted back to where he'd left the hand-cranked flashlights and snatched one up.

Once he had the light, it took him only a moment to locate the nearest one of the fist-sized lavender stones settled on the ground. He recognized the way the energy emanated from it, fanning out in a slender but extensive array of undulating energy.

He didn't dare get too close, so in the end he decided to try the billiard route. He found a pole and a relatively circular stone, lined it up like a cue ball on the flattest part of the uneven ground, and took a shot.

He missed the first one, drew in a deep breath that brought a wave of cool inside his hot, panicked body, and focused. Lined it up.

Shot.

Click.

Although the sound was lost in the depths of the water, he imagined the satisfying noise the makeshift cue ball must have made when it slammed into the crystal.

To his satisfaction, the glowing stone was knocked out of place and rolled several feet . . . taking its shimmery wall with it.

Fence stared at the new development in growing frustration and felt the edge of panic threatening once again. This time, however, the panic wasn't for him.

It was for Ana.

Ana.

He drew in another deep breath and thought some more. He knew how to remain calm in emergencies, and this was the height of emergency.

Think, Bruno Paolo, fucking think.

If he could disrupt the force field in some way, he could get through.

For some reason, the image of a bird sitting on a wire popped into his mind, and he thought about . . . energy takes the path of least resistance. What would disrupt the flow of electricity?

He wasn't certain that the force field was made of electricity, but with nothing else to go on he forced himself to think clearly and logically. *Rubber . . . glass . . . Rubber.*

That was it. He took off back to REI, surging through the ocean like a fierce submarine. Due to the fact that he'd already surveyed the remains of the store, he knew exactly where to find the self-inflating *rubber* rafts.

He had a bad moment when he could only find one . . . but then spied a second plastic-wrapped dingy yellow package and snagged it, hoping and praying this would work.

If not, he was fresh out of ideas.

Fence returned to where the safe passageway had been because he had to follow Ana's trail. It took only a few moments for him to inflate one of the rafts by pulling its cord, but immediately it began to float toward the surface. He had to waste precious moments locating a heavy piece of metal to lash to it, but once he accomplished that, his plan moved along readily.

A few moments later he had two rafts, each lashed together on one end. Then he bent them at the ties to make a sort of inverted vee, weighted down and ready to shove into place in the center of the force field.

One, two . . . three.

He maneuvered the shield into place, suddenly worrying that the rafts weren't wide enough to cut through the force field . . . but they seemed to be.

When he saw that the shimmering curtain was disrupted by the bright yellow vee, he had a surge of real hope. But did he dare try it?

He was just about to dart through, taking his chance, when he felt something move behind him.

Spinning in a cyclone of bubbles, he saw a large, sleek fish cruising toward him. Perfect.

Fence waited impatiently for the creature to come closer, then chased it through the vee and watched in relief as it traversed the passage without hesitation.

He followed, shining his light around in search of the trail Ana'd left, his heart leaping every time he saw a new spot of gray sparkle. She'd done an amazing job of leaving a trail of bread crumbs for him.

He was looking so hard for the gray sparkles that he almost missed it, but a cloud of something dark and inky wavering in the water caught his attention as his light shone past. He swung the flashlight back and saw with a horrified start that it was red ink . . . blood?

His insides plummeted and cold fear rushed through him as he dove toward it.

It was the man, Darian. He was dead, his neck slit, crystals sliced from his abdomen, his skin white and ghostly in the darkness. His eyes stared at nothing.

Fence's heart raced. Ana wouldn't have done that . . .

Then he turned, desperation rising inside him again, and caught the flash of something else pale and white. His insides plummeted as he darted closer to see.

It was Ana, pale and limp, lying on the ocean floor. A large boulder rested on her arm to ensure that she'd have no chance of making it to the surface. *My God, those fucking bastards.*

And blood . . . it rose in little red spirals from the four neat, empty places in her rib cage.

Her crystals were *gone*.

Fence turned to ice for an instant, then shot into action. *Ana*.

Her crystals were gone. She was bleeding.

And, oh God, she can't breathe down here without them.

He shoved the boulder away and gathered her up, terrified when she didn't move, when she hung limply in his arms as he propelled himself back through the makeshift tunnel in the shimmery barrier, then shot up like a rocket: up, up, ten, twenty, thirty, forty, fifty feet . . .

Until he burst free into the clean air.

"Ana," he gasped, choking and out of breath as he waited for his lungs to catch up with the change from gill to nose. *"Ana!"* He shifted her sharply in his arms, getting her face out of the water, terror shuttling through him.

They were so far from shore—it would take forever to get her there. She needed CPR . . . he had to get her to land . . .

Even as he realized it was too late, that she had to have been down there too long, he was kicking with powerful thrusts, orienting himself toward the land he knew was south and west.

He paused and bent over her there in the water, his legs fanning back and forth, breathing a deep gust of air into her mouth, wondering if this was how to give CPR to an Atlantean—if it would even help.

As he blew the breath into her mouth, blood spurted from the holes where her crystals had been. He froze, his body going numb.

He was literally blowing air—and blood—into and through her.

Oh God.

Shaking with terror, Fence stared down at her, his feet working madly to keep them both afloat. *Elliott! I fucking need Elliott!*

He closed his eyes and hovered for a moment, pressing his powerful hands against her wounds while horribly aware of the blood oozing from her side, slick and warm on his skin, drifting into the sea.

And then something warm and rubbery bumped his leg. Fence whirled in the water and saw the silhouette of a dorsal fin less than a foot away.

For an instant he was sure it was a shark, attracted by her blood . . . but even in his blinding fear for her, he realized a bloodthirsty shark wouldn't have wasted any time attacking.

Was it possible it was one of the dolphins she'd petted? What were their names?

The bump came against him again, and though Fence couldn't see many details despite the full moon, he reached for the animal.

Then something else bumped him from behind and he felt the second dolphin nosing against him. Stunned, he wasn't certain what to do, flanked as he was by the animals. But they seemed to want something.

When they made no attempt to move and instead seemed to be along for the swim, Fence did something he'd never imagined doing. He grabbed the jagged dorsal fin of one and lifted Ana on top of the animal, using his arm to hold her in place, then curved his other arm around the other, letting his legs sag into the ocean.

The dolphins shifted, moving close together and holding him in place so he could use himself to cover the wounds as well as he could, pressing her body hard against him in the front and positioning his hand over the four spots on the back of her torso to try and stanch them.

And then he gave her CPR.

Breathe . . . pump, *spurt* . . . breathe . . . pump, *spurt* . . . breathe . . .

Was he doing her any good? Frustration and fear trammeled through him, and his eyes stung from something other than saltwater.

Then all at once she stiffened, jerked, and began to cough. More blood, and now water, oozed from her wounds, and Fence didn't have time for relief as he flipped her over so she could spit up the water lodged in her lungs.

She coughed, shuddering violently and expelling more blood. Then he felt her body shift into a ragged rhythm of breathing.

"Ana," he said, and then *Thank God* in his head. She was shivering now, bleeding harder, and he knew that though she was breathing—at least from one lung—he had to get her to land. Find something to wrap her up, to stop the bleeding.

Desperate to try anything, he shifted her position on the smaller dolphin, the one with the ragged fin, so she was lying on top of it with her hands positioned around the fin, and he climbed onto the other dolphin. Holding Ana in place, he gripped around the neck—if a dolphin had a neck—of the one he was on and then climbed onto the other creature.

Neither of the dolphins seemed to object; in fact they seemed to communicate with each other, using hollow clicks, and started swimming off in tandem. They were in perfect synchronization, neither moving ahead of the other, staying exactly together, nose-to-nose, dorsal fin to dorsal fin, streaking through the water.

The wonder of the moment was tempered by cold fear, however, as he held Ana in place, trying to read through the press of his fingers against her whether she was still breathing, whether she was getting warmer or shivering or reacting in any other way. The full moon revealed the dark trails of blood trickling down over his hand, onto the dolphin and into the water.

It seemed too much time had passed when dark land at last loomed ahead of them and Fence stumbled off his ride and gathered up Ana, slogging to the shore.

"Ana," he said, gently shaking her as he leaned over her on a debris-strewn beach.

She moaned, coughed, and began to shiver violently, though it wasn't cold at all. Blood covered her torso and clung to her hair as he huddled her close, curling around her in a seated position and settling her on his lap.

"Turns out," she said in a wavery, rough voice, "it wasn't me they wanted." She coughed, more blood gushed out, and he stroked her back, horror turning him cold and empty. "It was my crystals."

She shifted, and he felt her move as if to touch her torso. "They're gone," she whispered, her chest moving raggedly as she pulled away a blood-streaked hand. "They're all gone."

He felt her weakening, growing limp and chill, and he shook her. "Ana! Ana! Don't leave me!"

Hearing a soft splash, he looked up, tensing, ready for yet another blow to his world: zombies or some wild animal of prey.

"How the hell did you get back here so fast?" Zoë demanded, stepping out of the ocean next to him. "We could hardly keep up."

For the first time, Fence looked around and realized he was back on Envy's shore.

"I need Elliott," was all he said.

CHAPTER 22

Ana opened her eyes.

She was in a dim room. A line of white light around a curtained window indicated that it was day. Her body hurt, her head felt light. She sensed that she wasn't alone, but whoever was with her neither spoke or moved. In fact, she thought she heard the soft sound of a snore.

That was fine. She needed a moment . . . She remained quiet, trying to sift through the vague images of what had brought her here. The last thing she remembered was—

All at once it came back in a rush of memory. The pressure of hands, holding her down . . . violent tugs, slicing pain, the heaviness in her chest as the sea weighted her, smothered her.

Her crystals were gone. *Gone.*

She closed her eyes. *No.*

Her hand moved slowly beneath the covers to her torso, her fingers brushing cold against her abdomen. She felt along her rib cage, over warm skin: the little ridges of her ribs, the give of elastic skin between them. It was smooth and soft.

Unmarked . . . where her crystals had been.

As if they'd never been there.

A terrible chill rushed through her as the realization set in.

No.

Had she dreamt it? Dreamt those years of life under the sea?

She must have made some sort of sound—a gasp, a choked sob—for he erupted from the shadows.

"Ana."

It was Fence, suddenly next to her, jolting the bed as he sat.

She was glad it was dark so he couldn't see the tears streaking her face, and she squeezed her eyes to blink the rest back.

"How are you feeling?" he asked, reaching to open the curtains next to her.

Rays of warm light filtered into the room and she could see his face: beautiful and haggard in its concern. Something glittered on his chin and cheeks— little unshaven hairs.

"They took my crystals," she said. Her voice was rough and scratchy. It burned when she tried to swallow.

"I know," he said, and his hand settled over her forehead. "Ana, I'm so sorry. I'm so—"

"They took my crystals . . . and left me to die."

His full lips tightened into a flat line. "The bastards put a boulder on top of you, Ana. To hold you down at the bottom. To make sure you died."

"Atlanteans. Every one of them . . ." She swallowed, trying to catch her breath, keep her voice steady. "They're evil."

He covered her hand with his. "Not all of them." He tightened his fingers.

She shook her head against the pillow, squeezing her eyes closed as another tear leaked out. They were all evil. Her family, her people.

Not one had ever done anything good.

It saddened and frightened her to know she carried that in her.

"Ana," Fence said, as if to pull her from her morbid thoughts.

"How could I have survived?" she asked suddenly, as dullness settled over her. Her life had changed irrevocably. "Without my crystals, trapped at the bottom of the ocean?"

Fence brushed the tear away with his thumb. "I don't know how long you were there before I found you. Elliott thinks you managed to continue to breathe water for some time, even though your crystals were taken. He saw remnants—little specks of crystal—in your lungs. He thinks they must have settled in there over time, flaking off from the bigger studs you wore. They must have enabled you to ingest just enough oxygen to keep you breathing until I found you."

Ana closed her eyes, a little wing of hope fluttering inside. "Does that mean I can still . . ."

She felt him shake his head, his fingers closing over hers once again. "I'm sorry, Ana. You weren't breathing when I found you. Whatever those little flecks were able to do, it was temporary."

Her wave of hope evaporated and the black despair returned.

"Why aren't there any scars? Why aren't there any marks?" she said, abruptly sitting up. Terrified. Had she lost days, weeks, *years*? "How long have I been asleep?"

"Only since yesterday."

"Since yesterday?" Her voice rose. "What happened to the scars? The holes, and where they cut me?"

She felt the hysteria rising in her voice, in her breathing, in her mind, and could do nothing to keep it at bay. Tears spilled from her eyes and she felt as if she were going to start screaming . . . and not be able to stop.

There'd never been a time that she felt so dark and empty. Even after her leg was damaged, she hadn't felt this depth of despair. For even then she still had the sea.

Now she didn't even have that.

She couldn't ever swim deep and long and low, she couldn't explore ruins, scavenge for treasure. She couldn't play hide and seek with the dolphins or watch the graceful bounce of shrimp as they scavenged for parasitic food.

She could never be free and elegant and graceful again.

Now all she had was an earthbound body hampered by a limp and a hitch. Bitterness welled in her heart.

"Ana." Fence's deep voice had a note of command to it, and it penetrated her consciousness as she started to spiral into confusion and pain. "Open your eyes."

When she did, not even realizing she'd closed them, she found him there, filling her vision. His gaze was soft and concerned, and overflowing with some intense emotion.

"What?" she said, trying to bat away the gentle little flutter in her belly. Fence was *here*.

But she didn't *want* to feel happy or warm or cared for.

She wanted to be angry.

And to feel violated.

And to know that her life was wrong now.

"I love you, Ana."

She shook her head, angry tears spilling forth. She wasn't *Ana* anymore.

"Look at me," he said firmly. "Please."

She wiped her tears away. "I'm never going to be the same."

He nodded. "I know, Ana. I know. But you're still the woman I love. Every part of you."

"It's not fair!" She felt as if she'd lost a limb.

Hell, she'd lost *half her life*. Half her body.

"No, by God, it's not fucking fair." His face looked murderous—darker and more frightening than she'd ever seen it. "But you're alive, and safe. And I've never been more grateful for anything in my life. You almost died . . . and I don't know what I would have done if you had. I love you."

"But how can I not have any scars?"

He tilted his head just a bit and his gaze held hers as he replied, "Elliott healed you."

Her heart stopped and her breathing caught, and before she could think, really understand what he meant, her fingers slipped down along her left side, toward her awkward hip . . . over the mottled and striated scars of her leg.

And then her hand sagged.

Nothing there had changed. She was still crippled and mangled. That leg still only felt half of what the other did.

And her foot was still curled up into a vee.

"You were bleeding to death when we got back here, hemorrhaging from the holes in your lung," Fence continued. "Elliott healed you. He saved your life. That's why you have no scars."

It took a minute for the words and their meaning to

penetrate. But they didn't make sense. "How could he have healed me so quickly? How can I not have scars?"

There was silence for a moment as he hesitated. Then . . .

"For the same reason that I have gills," he told her. His eyes were fastened on her, and even through her despair she recognized apprehension and hesitation.

He drew in a deep breath, and she realized she was holding hers. He was about to tell her something . . . big.

"We were trapped inside a cave during the Change, and the best we can guess is that an energy center— what do you call it, a flash row?—was inside the cave. And when the Change happened, with all the energy being conducted, we were altered as well. There's no other explanation."

She stared at him, once again trying to comprehend his words . . . but it was almost as if he were speaking in a foreign tongue. Ana grasped one piece of information. "The Change. But that was . . . almost fifty-one years ago."

His face tightened then, even as he copped a smile. It wavered a bit. "Yeah, so the truth is . . . you've been getting your freak on with a much older man."

She blinked, staring at him, her mind racing. "You sure don't look eighty years old."

"True, that. There aren't too many eighty-year-olds who have guns like this." Flexing his biceps beneath a tight T-shirt, he flashed that special smile. But it didn't quite reach his eyes, and she realized he was afraid.

She dragged her gaze away from those smooth muscles and another thought struck her. "So you haven't aged in fifty years? Are you . . . um . . . are you immortal?"

Fence shook his head, a bit of sadness in his eyes. "No. I know that for certain, because one of us—my best friend—died shortly after we came out of the caves. And I figure I'm fixing to start showing some gray and wrinkles any time now." He laughed uneasily. "I mean, I'm not going to turn into an old man tomorrow . . . but it seems like my body was frozen in time for a while. And now it's starting to age again as normal."

And then he lapsed into silence.

Ana realized she'd been holding her breath, and now she let it out easily. "Well, it was no wonder you knew exactly where to go in that big store," she said. "And what to look for."

"Does it freak you out?" he asked.

"Knowing that you're older than my father? No, wait . . . that you're older than my grandfather?" she replied, injecting a bit of levity into her tone. But then it evaporated as she continued, "I don't care about that. You are who you are. And I love you."

His eyes widened and she realized it was the first time she'd actually said the words to him, even though she'd been thinking them for longer than she cared to admit.

"Ana—" he began, but she interrupted.

"But doesn't it bother you that I'm half Atlantean? That my race killed your family and friends?"

He was looking at her soberly. "But that wasn't you, Ana. That was long before your time, and you've already demonstrated how far you'd go to keep something like that from happening again. You are who *you* are."

Yes. But she wasn't sure who she was anymore.

At that moment, she noticed for the first time that

there were marks—cuts, scrapes, even burns—on Fence's arms and neck, peeking from beneath his shirt. "Why didn't Elliott heal you too?" Glad for a distraction, she reached over to tug the sleeve's hem away from one big bicep to see ugly scrapes and bruises beneath.

"What? These little things?" he scoffed. "That's nothing compared to what I got when I played football, or when I was first learning to mountain climb." Then he took her hand, curling his fingers with hers. "Ana, I love you. All of you . . . the way you were, and the way you are now. It doesn't change how I feel about you."

She felt tears threaten. If only she could find a way to love her damaged self.

CHAPTER 23

Ana sat on the beach, staring out into the rushing, foamy waves.

They surged up around her ankles, soaking her seat and sprinkling salty water over her face.

It had been three days since she woke without her crystals, but it was the first time she'd ventured down here to the sea. She'd had to wait for a time when Fence wasn't around because this was something she needed to do on her own.

A farewell she had to make by herself.

The salty tear trickling down her cheek was the result of grief, not the overzealous sea, and for a moment she couldn't hold back the sobs. They caught her by surprise, fierce and deep, and she let them come.

She'd had to say goodbye to so many things in her life: her mother, the full use of her leg, the man she thought she'd loved . . . and now the best part of herself.

The part that made her feel whole.

At first she didn't even want to attempt to go in; it would just remind her too much of what she'd miss. But Ana still loved the sea, and she couldn't keep herself from taking off her shirt and struggling out of her cargo pants.

Dressed only in panties and a tank top, no longer having to worry that someone would see her crystals, she waded out into the sea.

The rush of pleasure and familiarity struck her with such great force that she thought it would knock her to her knees . . . but she kept herself upright.

And then, all at once, she dove into the water.

The Sea embraced her as She always had, cool and comforting . . . but right away Ana sensed the difference. She felt the heaviness in her lungs after only a few minutes: burning, constriction. The instinctive need to *breathe*.

She hadn't even gone far from shore when she realized she had to go back.

For a moment she considered dragging in a long, deep breath and letting the Sea have her . . . but the image of Fence's face rose in her mind and she popped to the surface.

The slog back to the beach was tedious and seemed to take forever, and she collapsed onto the gritty ground. Her hands shook and more tears threatened, but she blinked them back bravely.

This was the beginning of a new life. With a partner who loved her . . . and who understood her and how her life had irrevocably altered—for he'd lived through something similar.

She no longer needed to fear the Atlanteans finding her and bringing her back. She didn't have what they wanted any longer.

Ironic, wasn't it: when she first met Fence, he couldn't bear to go into the water. And now that they'd found each other, everything had changed.

Something moved in the water, and she saw Fence emerge: tall and broad and dark, glistening with the sea. He looked so delicious, so welcome, that she wanted nothing more than to throw herself at him and feast. Just the sight of that massive chest, so chiseled and firm, made her feel light-headed . . . not to mention the way it eased into lean hips and long, strong legs.

And he *loved* her.

Yes, this does make up for it. A little.

Well, a lot.

"Hey," he said, seeming surprised to see her there.

"I went in the water," she told him, wondering what he'd been doing.

Fence nodded and sat behind her on the beach, pulling her back into the warmth and protection of his damp body. "I would have gone with you."

"I know . . . but I needed to do it myself. It wasn't so good," she said.

"It'll get easier," he replied, rubbing his cheek against hers. "I've been thinking . . . you know, we're lucky to have you."

"I knew that," she said, a little wavery smile starting on her lips.

He laughed softly. "What I mean is, aside from the fact that you are the craziest, madliest sexy woman I have ever known—*and* you are smart and brave *and* you are determined *and* . . . you manage to stay upright even after I lay my very best kisses on you."

Ana couldn't help but laugh. "True. Very true. And don't forget, I laugh at all your jokes."

Fence gave that deep chuckle near her ear and sent a shiver of excitement down into her middle. "Very true. But aside from that, you have so much knowledge and information you can share with us—verbally and through your drawings. Even, and maybe, especially now. Now that it feels like . . . well, almost like it's going to be an all-out struggle between us and the Atlanteans. I get the feeling they're not just going to stay back in their Raised City."

She nodded. "You're probably right . . . although they do have my crystals now, and that's what they really wanted. Maybe they'll just leave us alone for a while."

"Maybe. But I intend to spend a lot of my time out there, watching for signs of a problem," he said soberly.

Ana submerged a pang of envy and grief that he'd be doing it without her.

She rested her head back against Fence and it settled onto his shoulder. His jaw was right there, and she turned to press a kiss to it, noting that it was rough with stubble. "I'm going to be all right. I got through this before," she said, gesturing to her leg. "And I didn't even have you."

Fence squeezed her tightly. "We're together now. I'll be here with you, just as you were with me."

She nodded, then turned her attention to other matters. "What did you find, out there?"

For a moment his arms tensed and she was afraid he was going to prevaricate—keep stuff from her, now that she couldn't experience it for herself. But he relaxed then and said, "The barrier is gone."

"Gone?" She sat up and turned to face him, her knee bumping his awkwardly. "That doesn't make sense."

"I went to destroy the crystal—and was successful," he added, then pulled a shard from his shorts pocket. "Brought this back for Quent. But it's in little smithereens all over the bottom of the ocean now, down in a few holes and hidden inside some cars. They'll never find the pieces. And the barrier was gone."

Ana was nodding, looking out at the sea, her mind working. They had her crystals, they didn't need anything else from her. If her guesses had been correct, part of the purpose of the Goleth stones was to lure her out of hiding. But also, the barrier had been closer to Envy than it needed to be, so the stones could be set up in a protected area in order to cause the tidal wave. "If I had to guess, I'd say maybe they just moved it. Out farther to sea."

"That's possible. I'll be checking further." His voice was determined and sober.

A sudden spike of fear lodged in her chest. *"No!"* She grabbed his arm. "No. You can't go after them, you can't go to Atlantis."

His mouth tightened mutinously. "They have to pay for what they did, Ana."

They should. They had taken the best part of her away. But she was filled with terror at the very thought of Fence going back there, to Atlantis. To a place where they'd know at first sight that he didn't belong there.

They were Atlanteans. They'd kill without thought.

"No, Bruno, please. They have what they want . . . they're no longer a threat to me."

She had that, at least. It wasn't enough, but she had that. And she didn't, *couldn't,* lose him too.

She shook her head. "You'd never even get close to them. They're protected. Darian—"

"He's dead."

Dead.

A little shift inside her middle told her that despite what Darian had done, she still had some feelings for her first love. It just confirmed that she wasn't as cold-blooded as the rest of her people.

But that little flicker was nothing compared to what

she felt for the man next to her . . . and the very thought of him trying to fight his way into Atlantis to the Crown and Shield made her whole world fall apart. She could not lose him too. "How?"

"I figure they killed him right around the time they hurt you—slit his throat."

Ana remembered the blood dripping from the Shield's blade as she approached her. Darian's blood.

Terror filled her. "Fence—Bruno—promise me, please, promise me you won't try it. Please."

He was watching her with soulful eyes, but this time a little warmth came into them. Hesitant, but present nevertheless. "I'll promise you that if you promise to stay here with me and make some fat, chunky babies."

What she'd wanted for longer than she could remember. Ana started to smile, then it faded as reality set in. They'd be Atlantean too. They'd have that streak in them, that part of her she hated . . . and yet had loved.

"What is it?" His face had tightened with concern.

"I don't . . . Bruno, I'm part Atlantean."

"So what? You're afraid our baby would grow up to be an evil murdering creature?" He looked and sounded so affronted she almost laughed.

And that was a relief: to feel something warm and light stirring inside her. And when he put it that way, she realized how ridiculous she sounded. After all, she was part Atlantean. And if her father had felt the same way . . . well, heck. Her father had loved her mother. And so had she.

All Atlanteans couldn't be evil.

"You're right," she said, that warmth stirring more strongly inside her. "I guess if you can forgive me for what my family did to yours, then I should be able to do the same."

"So you'll stay here with me?" He looked down.

Ana nodded and realized there was no other place she wanted to be.

Even . . .

She looked out over the ocean, the Sea's beautiful rolling, glistening waves brilliant and beckoning. And then she looked up at Fence.

No, she realized, there was *no* other place she wanted to be.

"I guess so," she said. Then, drawing in a deep, shaky breath, she joked, "Though I was really looking forward to introducing you to underwater sex. Guess we'll have to stick with dry humping, huh?"

He did that deep chuckle that never failed to make her insides tingle. "Well, sugar, you know it ain't all that dry where I've been . . . especially going down on you. It's like you've got your own sweet honey, just waiting for me to lick it all up." His voice dropped deep and low.

She shivered again, just hearing those words, and smiled a real smile now. "Don't let me stop you."

"Oh, you won't, Ana-sweet. You won't." And he reached for her.

Epilogue

Remy heard a rustling in the bushes and, heart thumping in warning, looked up. Dantès went on high alert, his ears upright and tail still.

She'd been on her own for a week, missing Dantès, when yesterday, all of a sudden, he showed up. She'd half expected Wyatt to be right behind him, but the man never materialized. Of course, she'd purposely picked up her pace and made Dantès stay with her so he wouldn't go back and *lead* the guy to her.

The rustling stopped and she peered into the deep undergrowth, noticing that Dantès seemed to be alert but not apprehensive, which was a good sign. She should find shelter for the night soon.

She'd lost her gun when Seattle took her, but managed to steal it back out of his truck after Wyatt and Elliott found her. Now, she hefted it in her hand, aware that she had only five bullets.

Each one would have to count.

The crystal had stopped burning and glowing, although it was still warm to the touch and seemed brighter than before the burning incident. Whatever happened to it had been temporary, but Remy didn't know whether something had permanently altered it.

What she did know was that she had to go back to Envy. There was someone there who might be able to help her. An Atlantean named Ana, who, according to Theo, had become friends with Quent and Elliott and a guy named Fence.

If anyone knew what to do with the crystal, Remy suspected, it would be her. And if she had to get tough about it . . . well, she had her ways.

Grandpa had entrusted her with this crystal, and she would do whatever it took to find out why.

Just as she was about to put the gun down, a shadow emerged from the undergrowth.

Dantès gave a short bark of recognition, but Remy silently commanded him to stay, and he did—despite the fact that he quivered.

She aimed her gun as the silhouette came into full view, and her hand jerked in shock as she recognized him.

"What the hell are you doing here?" she demanded, aware that her heart was pounding uncontrollably. "How the hell did you find me?"

He just smiled his tight, humorless smile and sat down as if he belonged there.

"Are you certain?" Fence asked, trying to keep the excitement from his voice. Ana was on the other side of the door, and he didn't want to get her hopes up unless . . .

George glanced at Elliott and they both nodded. "I was the one who did it before," Ana's father told him. "There's no reason it can't be done again. It just took me some time to prepare, and I didn't want to mention it until I was certain it would work."

"And if something goes wrong, I'll be here," Elliott said. "Actually doing the surgery. There's no risk."

No risk . . . but the biggest fucking gift ever.

"How did you manage it?" Fence asked, looking from one to the other. His heart was growing lighter by the moment.

"Ana's original crystals came from the Atlanteans, just like these," George said, showing Fence the small box containing eight conelike gems in it. At the base, each was no bigger than a pea, and hardly as long as the width of his pinkie. "I was the one who adapted the original ones before Ana was even born, so they could be implanted in a demiblood. I even wore several myself for a few months to test them out." He smiled crookedly. "I had nine months to work on it, you know."

"But he never let the other Atlanteans know that he'd worn them," Elliott said. "And that also explains the alteration I noticed in his lungs, when I scanned him. The remnants of the crystals there."

"But since I'm a pure blood land-person," George explained, "the crystals eventually stopped working for me, and they drew too much of my oxygenated blood. So this implantation wouldn't work unless the recipient was of Atlantean blood," he cautioned. "There are some crystal elements inherent in their genetics now, after so many thousands of years, that makes it . . . well, anyway, you don't need all the details. These are Kaddick's crystals. It took me some time, but I've prepared them for Ana just the way I did originally, by slightly altering their chemical makeup. This will ensure they'll be accepted by her body."

"And you'll be able to implant them in her again?

And she'll be . . . the way she was?" Fence was exuberant . . . not because he cared whether Ana could breathe underwater again, but because he knew how much she missed it. Because he'd seen her grief, and could only begin to understand the loss she was experiencing.

And . . . there was the whole aspect of underwater sex, too, of course. Motion in the ocean. Navel maneuvers. Slip the sub.

The mental jokes came fast and thick, and it was all he could do to keep from laughing out loud.

"Yes, indeed," George said. "Ana will be the way she was before."

Elated, Fence knocked on the door to their room and opened it to find Ana looking at one of his underwater maps.

"This is good," she said, glancing up. "But you're missing— Dad? Elliott? What's wrong?" She stood, her expression growing apprehensive as she looked at the three of them.

Fence came over to her, swooped Ana up in his arms and murmured, "Now about that underwater sex you were hoping for? Well, sugar, we've got it covered."

SINK YOUR TEETH INTO DELECTABLE VAMPIRE ROMANCE FROM *USA TODAY* BESTSELLING AUTHOR

LYNSAY SANDS

BORN TO BITE

978-0-06-147432-3

Legend has it that Armand Argeneau is a killer in the bedroom. But with all three of his late wives meeting unfortunate ends, it's up to Eshe d'Aureus to find out if this sexy immortal is a lover or a murderer. As an enforcer, it's her job to bring rogue vampires to justice, even if the rogue in question makes her blood race red hot.

HUNGRY FOR YOU

978-0-06-189457-2

As one of the most ancient in the Argeneau clan, Cale Valens has given up on finding a life mate. His friends and family, however, have not. In fact, they believe they've finally found his perfect match. Getting them together, however, requires one little white lie . . .

THE RELUCTANT VAMPIRE

978-0-06-189459-6

Rogue hunter Drina Argenis has been many things in her years as an immortal, but bodyguard/babysitter to a teenage vampire is something new. There's an incentive, however: the other vampsitter, Harper Stoyan, may be Drina's life mate.

LYS5 0312

At Avon Books, we know your passion for romance—once you finish one of our novels, you find yourself wanting more.

May we tempt you with . . .

- **Excerpts** from our upcoming releases.

- Entertaining **extras**, including authors' personal photo albums and book lists.

- Behind-the-scenes **scoop** on your favorite characters and series.

- **Sweepstakes** for the chance to win free books, romantic getaways, and other fun prizes.

- Writing **tips** from our authors and editors.

- **Blog** with our authors and find out why they love to write romance.

- **Exclusive content** that's not contained within the pages of our novels.

Join us at
www.avonbooks.com

AVON *An Imprint of* HarperCollins*Publishers*
www.avonromance.com